CLUES OF THE CARIBBEES

BEING CERTAIN CRIMINAL INVESTIGATIONS OF HENRY POGGIOLI, PH.D.

T. S. Stribling

DOVER PUBLICATIONS, INC.
NEW YORK

Published in Canada by General Publishing Company, Ltd., 30 Lesmill Road, Don Mills, Toronto, Ontario.
Published in the United Kingdom by Constable and Company, Ltd., 10 Orange Street, London WC2H 7EG.

This Dover edition, first published in 1977, is an unabridged republication of the work originally published by Doubleday, Doran & Company, Inc., Garden City, New York, in 1929.

International Standard Book Number: 0-486-23486-X
Library of Congress Catalog Card Number: 76-56999

Manufactured in the United States of America
Dover Publications, Inc.
180 Varick Street
New York, N.Y. 10014

CONTENTS

The Refugees

*In which the Spanish temperament has a
curious effect upon a glass of wine.*

THE REFUGEES

HERR KAREL HEINSIUS, police inspector of Curaçao, Dutch West Indies, sat glancing first at the passenger list of the incoming Dutch steamer *Vollendam* and then through his window at the storm signal flying from the customhouse staff. And the inspector saw a sardonic fitness in the fact that the barometer should fall on precisely the forenoon when the noted—not to use the vile but more exact term "notorious"—Cesar Pompalone, deposed dictator of Venezuela, landed in the harbor of Willemstad.

Half an hour after the "Magnificent" Pompalone came ashore one of Heinsius's men telephoned that the ex-dictator had lodged in the Hotel Saragossa in Otrabanda, and Heinsius instructed his informant to remain at the hotel until the refugee president shipped north.

Inspector Heinsius hoped, but did not expect, that this incident would end his relations with the Magnificent Pompalone. It was the inspector's duty to see that the ex-dictator did ship north. Deposed presidents flying out of Venezuela are a fairly ordinary phenomenon in the West Indies; and there is an informal international agreement among the powers that own these islands that once a dictator leaves Venezuela he must not be allowed to return. All the rest of the world is open to the fugitive's business or pleasure, but not Venezuela. His native land he must never see again.

The reason for this harsh and apparently unjust mandate is simple. All those powers that own West Indian

islands also possess large commercial interests in Venezuela. The flight of a dictator means the end of a revolu-
tion and more stable business conditions, but the return
of an ex-dictator marks the beginning of a new revolt and
a new series of financial disturbances. Therefore, by this
informal agreement, the road of dictators out of Venezuela
is devoted exclusively to one-way traffic.

Not until the following day did the Magnificent Pompalone obtrude himself again on Herr Heinsius's attention.
The inspector was eating breakfast, which occurs in
Curaçao from twelve to one o'clock, when the telephone
called the inspector to come at once to the Hotel Saragossa in Otrabanda.

The officer immediately imagined a clash between his
agent and the Venezuelan. He hurried into his motor and
then down the white street between the gayly painted Dutch
houses of Willemstad. As he drove he pondered what he
would do with the Magnificent Pompalone: put him in the
cuartel there in Willemstad, ship him north, willy-nilly, to
New York, where the American secret service would keep
him safely away from Venezuela, transport him to London? Back of this pondering he knew that he would ship
his man on the first steamer out, no matter where it sailed.
Still, of course, the fellow had certain selective rights.

A few minutes later the inspector was motoring across
the long pontoon bridge that connects Otrabanda on one
side of the sea canal to Willemstad on the other. At a pier
a hundred yards away lay the *Vollendam*, disgorging her
hold of Dutch products to be reshipped to South and
Central American ports. On the rising wind came the smell
of shipping and the tang of the sea. Inspector Heinsius
thought ruefully that his two storms were rising together.

The Hotel Saragossa in Otrabanda is a large hostelry,

brightly painted in reds and greens. This building, and
indeed the whole Dutch city, gives the impression of having
been constructed out of big, gay toy blocks for overgrown
children.

Around the entrance of the hotel was a rabble of dirty
enough Negroes who had been attracted to the place by
that nose for the exciting and the uncanny which the West
Indian Negro possesses to a degree.

As the motor drove up the hotel physician, Dr. van
Maasdyk, appeared on the piazza and made a gesture of
relief at seeing the inspector. Heinsius jumped out and
ran up the steps, speculating what trouble his man had
had with the Venezuelan. The sight of such a crowd suggested a fight.

"Has anything happened to Barneveldt?" he asked the
physician quickly.

"Not to Barneveldt, to Señor Grillet, the proprietor."

Heinsius was surprised.

"What's the matter with Grillet?"

"He is dead," said Van Maasdyk, with excited brevity.
"Has been dead for an hour at least. We found him a few
minutes ago."

"There was no fight, no disturbances?" queried the inspector, trying to orient his ideas to this new phase of
things.

"Nothing of the sort. He was found in his study. I gave
the body a cursory examination and was about to pronounce
it heart failure, but——" He hesitated.

"But what, Herr Doctor?"

"Well, there was a peculiar twist to our old friend's
death—but you will see. We left the body sitting at the
table exactly as we found it. I thought——"

The two men were now entering the lobby of the Hotel

Saragossa, where a number of guests of half a dozen different nationalities were assembled. The doctor and the officer were too close to the group to continue their remarks.

Barneveldt, the inspector's man, had corraled the entire hotel in the lobby, and the guests were talking in a low babel about the proprietor's sudden death. An American was saying in an aggrieved tone:

"It's a shame we can't go in and look at the body. I paid my three bucks a day here, and they told me it included everything."

From the upper story came the sound of a woman's weeping. Somebody in the crowd whispered:

"There's the inspector now."

A glance over the lobby showed Heinsius the squarely built form and aggressive olive face of a man who·he knew instantly must be the Magnificent Pompalone.

Renewed suspicion, entirely unfounded now, floated through the inspector's head, that if any foul play had been dealt to Señor ·Grillet somehow this Venezuelan was at the bottom of it. He wondered for an instant what possible connection there could be between the flying president of Venezuela and a simple tavern keeper in Curaçao. The next moment he said above the subdued excitement of the guests, first in English, then in Spanish:

"Gentlemen, señores, may I request that none of you leave the hotel until I finish my investigations. Her Majesty's government will appreciate this courtesy."

He bowed to the lobby in general; a number of citizens bowed in return. The American grumbled *sotto voce:*

"Courtesy! If we try to go out we'll get pinched."

On the second floor the inspector and the doctor were met by Hortensia Grillet, daughter of the deceased man,

a tall, olive-tinted girl who showed clearly her Latin extraction, although she wore the usual apron and cap of
the Dutch. As a last Dutch touch, the girl had a dustrag
in her hand.

"Which room, Hortensia?" asked Van Maasdyk, for the
doors·opening into the upper hallway were confusing.

Hortensia, still sobbing, pointed to a door and then
turned away in a renewed burst of grief. The physician
murmured some word of consolation to the girl and the
two men entered the study.

Instead of any ghastly effect such as Herr Heinsius had
anticipated, the proprietor of the Saragossa Hotel might
have been asleep in his study with his head leaning over on
his arms on his greenheart table, save that he sat too still.
Around the walls of the room ranged bookcases of the
same cool-colored hardwood. On the floor were rare Peruvian llama-wool blankets used as rugs.

The inspector stood looking about the library from the
doorway.

"You mentioned something unusual, Herr Doctor, something that aroused your suspicions."

Dr. van Maasdyk moved silently across the Peruvian
rugs and touched a yellowed photograph which lay at the
hand of the dead man.

"It's this. I'd like you to look at it."

Herr Heinsius came over and regarded it attentively.
It was the picture of a young and extremely pretty Latin-
American woman, and the photographer's signature bore
the address of Caracas. Written in a fine old hand in faded
letters was the name: "Ana Sixto y Carrera, 1902."

A resemblance between the woman in the picture and the
girl he had seen weeping in the hall caused the inspector
to remark:

"That must have been Grillet's wife, Hortensia's mother."

"Undoubtedly," agreed the doctor. "Now, look here! This is why I telephoned you."

He turned the picture over and showed on its back in the same faded letters: "Account of 12 *de agosto*, 1906." And immediately beneath this in fresh blue ink was the entry: "Account settled 5 *de enero*, 1925."

Beside the photograph, where it had dropped from Señor Grillet's fingers, lay a fountain pen making a little blue spot on the blotter where its point touched.

The two men stood looking at each other thoughtfully in the presence of the dead man. This entry, the last he had ever made in life, held its faint suggestion of mystery and bygone drama.

"If it hadn't been for that," explained the doctor, "I should have attributed his death to heart failure without hesitation."

Heinsius nodded.

"There is nothing about the appearance of the body that suggests an unnatural death?"

"Nothing at all. His end evidently came as peacefully as sleep. But the photograph suggests that he realized his end had come."

"Nineteen hundred and six—that was only a year or two before Señor Grillet came to Curaçao and bought this hotel, was it not?"

Van Maasdyk smoothed his whiskers.

"He came here, I believe, about nineteen hundred and five or six. Hortensia, I remember, was about three years old, for I attended her during an attack of fever."

"Sixto y Carrera," repeated the inspector. "That must have been this woman's name after her marriage with some

man by the name of Sixto; then Grillet's removal from
Caracas to this island—— Let me talk to Hortensia, Doctor."

The two men reëntered the hallway and found the girl
still sobbing, and wiping her eyes with the back of her
wrist to avoid getting the dustcloth in her face.

"Fräulein," began the inspector, "have you any memory of your early life—where you were and what you did
as a child?"

"I have always lived here, Herr Inspector."

"Do you remember your mother?"

"She died when I was born, Herr Inspector. This—this
leaves me all alone." And the girl began sobbing afresh.

The two men glanced at each other, and the inspector
changed the direction of his queries.

"Have you been in this upper story all morning, Hortensia?"

"Coming and going, mynheer."

"Was your father up here too?"

"He came and went as usual, mynheer."

"Did he seem in good health?"

"He was never any other way, Herr Heinsius; in fact,
he seemed more lively than usual this morning. I mean
more in a rush, more excited——"

The girl burst out weeping again as she talked of her
father.

"There, there, Hortensia. I remember when my own
father died——"

"Oh, Herr Inspector!" sobbed Hortensia. "You had
nothing on your heart. Just an hour before my poor father
died, I—I quarreled with him! Oh, if I had only known,
Herr Heinsius! I can't endure it! I can never tell him how
sorry I am!"

"Poor child, I am sure it amounted to nothing."

"But—but it was the first time he ever spoke sharply to me in all my life! He was carrying breakfast to the room of Señor Pompalone and Señor Afanador."

"What did you quarrel about, my poor Hortensia?"

"The wine. He had been down in the cellar after some very fine wine. He said they were going to have a rare breakfast together."

The inspector's attention veered a little from his sympathy to the story the girl was telling.

"They? Who, Hortensia? Señor Pompalone and Señor Afanador?"

"They and my father. He meant to eat with them; they were countrymen of his. And he was coming up the stairs with three bottles of rare old wine, and I took them, meaning to rub the cobwebs from them, when my father cried out, 'Caramba, Hortensia, you are as stupid as the Dutch! Don't you realize that cobwebs grace a wine bottle as pearls did the neck of your beautiful mother?' But I said, 'Father, it is so dirty!' And he said, 'Attend to your rooms, and let me alone!' "

Inspector Heinsius was now engrossed in the girl's narrative.

"So your father went on and ate with his guests?"

"Yes, mynheer, he always showed honor to any of his own countrymen."

"I see. Will you please show us the room these men occupied, Hortensia?"

The girl was a little unwilling.

"I haven't cleaned away the breakfast things yet, Herr Heinsius."

"That's all right. I've seen breakfast things before; just show us the room."

A little farther down the hall the girl opened a door and displayed an unmade room, with the leavings of a breakfast on a little center table. Evidently it had been, as Hortensia suggested, a rather finer breakfast than usual. On the plates were the remains of a sea-turtle steak, broiled flying fish, a salad of alligator pears, three bottles of wine, some grafted mangoes from Trinidad, and the inevitable wineglasses, coffee cups, and tiny liqueur glasses of Curaçao.

The inspector glanced around and saw the salver on which the things had been brought. He picked it up and began rearranging the dishes on it.

"May I ask you to open that window screen a moment, Herr Doctor?" he requested.

"*Caramba*, you're not going to dump all this out the window!" cried the medico.

"I'll set it out of the way a moment while we look around."

The doctor swung open the screen and the inspector placed the tray on the window sill inside the bars. Then he went to the door again and called the girl. When she appeared with her red eyes he asked in a lowered tone:

"Hortensia, when your father brought in this breakfast did he and his guests eat immediately?"

"Yes, mynheer," gasped the girl, about to weep again.

The inspector frowned thoughtfully.

'You are sure your father remained in this room from the very moment he brought in the tray till the meal was eaten?"

The girl evidently tried to remember, then said doubtfully, "I—I think he did." Then she exclaimed, "Oh, look, the screen's open; the room will get full of flies!"

"Yes, I opened it. And your father was not called out?"

"Yes, he was," recalled Hortensia, still looking at the open screen. "Our Negro boy, Zubio, came up and wanted a special wine for one of the Americans downstairs; Father had to go down and get it for him."

"So your father left this tray in this room and went back to get wine for the American; then he came back up and had his breakfast?"

"Yes, mynheer."

"Very well; thank you, Hortensia."

Heinsius turned back to the window, followed by the physician. Here the officer stood looking over the tray of leavings. A butterfly was unfurling its tube into the liqueur glass while a swarm of flies were already at the fish and fruit. A bumblebee buzzed away at the men's approach. In one wineglass and on the neck of one bottle lay half a dozen dead house flies, two or three bees, and one of those curiously marked "89" butterflies which are found in the West Indies.

The inspector studied these dead insects and nodded; then he said to Van Maasdyk with a certain professional pride in his voice:

"You see, Doctor, this is a rude but fairly effective test for poison. No doubt Cesar Pompalone dropped something in his host's bottle when he left the room for a moment."

Dr. van Maasdyk stared at the inspector.

"But, Herr Heinsius—Pompalone, the ex-dictator of Venezuela—what could he have against a poor tavern keeper in Curaçao?"

The inspector lifted his hands.

"I should hazard that Hortensia's mother was not Señor Grillet's wife. The photograph suggests it—the name on the photograph was Sixto. But that's a mere guess; the trial jury will have to search out the motive if they want any.

I don't. I'll go down and arrest the two men. You can bring this wineglass and bottle as evidence."

Van Maasdyk moved in the tray, closed the screen, picked up the glass and bottle, and followed the inspector downstairs.

"We'll have to keep this from Hortensia as long as we can, Heinsius," he cautioned; "at least until after the shock of her father's death."

A little later the two men came down the stairs into the lobby under the inquiring glances of the guests of the hotel. The murmuring conversation which had been going on ceased, and the group in the lobby tried to read the officer's conclusion in his face. So pronounced was this scrutiny that the inspector, who was by nature a courteous man, lifted his hand to the group, then descended into their midst and walked over to the powerful and picturesque figure of the Magnificent Pompalone, who stood somewhat withdrawn from the other patrons of the establishment. He spoke in an undertone:

"Pardon me, Señor Pompalone, but may I ask you to come with me for a moment to my office in Leidenstraat. I would like to ask you some questions."

The refugee president looked intently at the officer.

"Couldn't you ask your questions here, Herr Inspector?" he inquired in English.

"I might. Didn't Señor Grillet take breakfast with you in your room about two hours ago?"

"He did."

"I have the wine left in his bottle and glass. I have evidence that suggests it has been poisoned. Until we can prove that the wine is harmless, or that you personally did not tamper with it, I will have to hold you under arrest pending the investigation of the death of Señor Grillet."

The ex-dictator straightened and stared in cold astonishment, first at the inspector and then around the lobby, until his eyes rested on his traveling companion, Señor Afanador.

"Herr Inspector," he asked, "do you consider it possible that I, a fugitive from my own country, would be so mad as to further complicate my already harassed flight by committing a murder in the first safe port I reached?"

The crowd gathered around officer and prisoner at this remarkable charge and declaration.

"But, Señor Pompalone, I found poisoned wine left on your breakfast table, where Grillet had eaten."

"Then I ask would I have been so childish as to keep the remains of the poison in my room? I am not a child. Besides, what motive would I have to murder the first man who took me in?"

"I can't go into your motive here, Señor Pompalone."

"Cá! Then you have discovered a motive!"

"I suspect one. It has something to do with a woman, with a Señora Sixto." The inspector peered at the ex-dictator sharply.

"A Señor Sixto?" repeated the Venezuelan with an uninformed expression.

He stood ruminating on the name, "Sixto—Sixto," which apparently yielded him nothing at all. Again he glanced at his companion, Afanador. Then he said:

"You must realize, Herr Inspector, I am here in Curaçao on an important mission. I must frame my defense as quickly as possible. May I have a sample of the poisoned wine?"

Van Maasdyk instantly poured a little into the glass and offered it to the dictator.

"Now will someone bring me a piece of shell?—conch, oyster, any sort of shell."

Heinsius motioned to his man Barneveldt, who left the lobby and in a few moments returned with a piece of abalone. The dictator dipped the shell into the wine several times, watching the reaction closely. Presently the pearly tint of the nacre turned a cream color, which later strengthened into a yellow.

"Señores," he said, looking at the yellowed shell, "this is a test I have made at frequent intervals during my presidency of Venezuela. In fact, as president of my country I formed the habit of feeding to a cat or dog a little of all the food I meant to eat, and then awaiting results. This poison I could not test in that manner because it can be so timed that it will have no effect from one to twenty-four hours, and then it will act instantly and fatally. This is a poison obtained from the Orinocan Indians, and is called *Las Ojas de la Culebra.*"

"Are you admitting your guilt?" asked the inspector.

"Not at all, Herr Inspector—establishing my innocence. I have had so many attempts made on my life I feel this was also directed at me and went astray."

"Who do you think it was, Señor Pompalone?" inquired the inspector.

"I have a theory which I prefer not to state openly, but I would like to make a request of this group of *caballeros.*"

He turned toward the lobby.

"Certainly, anything you please."

"Gentlemen," said the ex-dictator, lifting his voice a trifle, "as you see, I am about to be placed under arrest here in Curaçao, and will not be free to construct my own defense. Now, when travelers are dispersed, which will be within a day or two, my defense will be impossible to make, for naturally someone in this hotel used this poison. So, if it is to be done at all it must be done at once. Now I ask, if there is any criminologist, secret-service man, or a trained investigator in any line in this hotel, would he oblige a fellow traveler by aiding him in freeing himself? I would greatly appreciate it and would reward him well."

"Why don't you hire a lawyer here in the city?" suggested the inspector.

"Because I don't want a man who can quibble over evidence. I want an investigator who can produce absolute evidence."

The group of travelers stared at this strange request. Presently one of the Americans said:

"I'll have a shot at it, Mr. Pompalone. I'm a great reader of detective stories. I think I know the methods by which——"

The ex-dictator glanced at the fellow.

"What is your profession?"

"I am a commercial traveler. I sell soap."

"You sell soap in the West Indies?"

"That's my occupation," repeated the salesman a little curtly.

"Then I am afraid you lack the reasoning faculty if you are trying to sell soap in the West Indies. Is there anyone else?"

There was a cavalier humor about this which gained the sympathy of the crowd. Another man, a smallish dark-eyed gentleman of a certain academic appearance, spoke up from the group.

"If you are really innocent, Señor Pompalone," he stated crisply, "I can demonstrate that scientifically in about thirty minutes, but if you are not really innocent I would do you more harm than good."

"That's splendid, splendid, if you can make good your word. Are you a criminologist, señor?"

"No, I am an instructor in psychology. My name is Poggioli."

"Are you from an Italian university?"

"No, I am an American of Italian parentage. I teach in the Ohio State University. I am taking my sabbatical year. To get back to my proof of your innocence, I can demonstrate it very simply."

"How do you do it?"

"By giving you scopothalamin and simply asking you the question, 'Did you poison Señor Grillet?' If you did you will say so; if you did not you will say you did not. The drug deadens all sense of caution."

The inspector spoke up.

"We don't know any such drug as that in our criminal practice here in Curaçao."

"I am aware of that," said Poggioli with the slight acerbity of a college instructor toward a forward undergraduate. "I am simply explaining a method of finding out the truth almost instantly. I do not know of any court in any country which uses it now."

"Mr. Poggioli," inquired the inspector courteously, "would you expect me to turn a prisoner loose on evidence no court on earth would accept?"

"Wouldn't you prefer to loose an innocent man, even in an unconventional manner, than to see him go to jail for life, or perhaps to the gallows?"

Here the Magnificent Pompalone smilingly interrupted the colloquy.

"Gentlemen, allow me a word. It is true I did not poison Señor Grillet, nor do I know anything at all about him. However, I have innumerable other things in my mind which I would not expose for my fortune or my life. So, if my freedom depended upon my taking this new drug and telling all I know, I would go very cheerfully to the gallows instead."

The psychologist hesitated a moment and then with a little bow said:

"I suppose, then, you don't care for my assistance?"

"On the contrary, I will be glad indeed to enlist you in my behalf, but work on the facts, not on my sense of caution. Also, I would like Inspector Heinsius to place me in my room here in the hotel under guard, and allow this gentleman, Mr. Poggioli, the privilege of consulting with me at any time he sees fit."

Heinsius considered a moment and then agreed. He called his man, Barneveldt, then motioned to the dictator's traveling companion, Señor Afanador, and these three men, together with the American psychologist, went up the stairs to the dictator's suite of rooms. As they went up the American in the lobby growled out:

"Hybrid American! He won't be no good—highbrow, hasn't got any practical sense."

On the second floor Señor Afanador and the Magnificent Pompalone went into their separate apartments, and the dictator nodded for the inspector and the psychologist to follow him. When the door was closed the ex-president turned suddenly from suave self-possession to flushed and swollen anger.

"Señores," he whipped out with that effect of hissing common to excited Latin Americans, "I know the man who committed this outrage." He shook a finger toward Señor Afanador's room. "That traitor! That serpent! That crawling *Pizanista!*"

"But, señor," interrupted the psychologist, "what grounds have you for your charges?"

"Isn't Grillet dead? I had nothing to do with it, so Afanador must have done it!"

"But if he is a traitor and a *Pizanista*, what motive had he in killing Señor Grillet and not you, Señor Pompalone?"

"*Cá*, there's the subtlety of it, Señor Poggioli!" exclaimed the dictator tensely. "I am worth more to the *Pizanista* alive in prison than dead. As long as I live there will be no other leader of my cause, but once I am dead"— the Magnificent Pompalone made a gesture—"some other patriot will spring up!"

He stood staring at the two men with black eyes protruding in rage.

"All I ask of you, Señor Poggioli, is to prove to Herr Inspector that this vile and perfidious wretch, Afanador, my secretary, sold out to my enemies and tried to betray me!"

"But, Señor Pompalone——"

"Señor Poggioli, this is not a debatable question! That is the solution! Now you prove it!"

"But I was going to say," persisted the psychologist, "this doesn't take into account the photograph of the Señora Sixto which Herr Heinsius mentioned, and the strange entry which Señor Grillet made on the back of the picture as he was dying."

The ex-president frowned, snapped his fingers.

"I have it. He timed the poison. He knew when Señor Grillet would expire. So he slipped into the señor's room, found a picture—any picture of a woman—made this entry to give it an appearance of mystery, to involve me in an imaginary intrigue. To show that he chose completely at

random, he didn't even select a woman anyone knew—a
Señora Sixto. Who is Señora Sixto? Nobody knows. Why,
his plot is puerile! It's elementary!"

Inspector Heinsius stood with a skeptical look on his
broad Dutch face.

"It seems to me, Señor President, it is not simple at all.
It's rather too far-fetched to be true. I can't imagine a
man working out such minutiæ to his crime."

"Herr Heinsius," interposed Poggioli, "I ask you not
to discard my client's theory merely because it is foreign
to your Northern temperament. What sounds far-fetched
to a Hollander may be a most natural procedure to a Latin.
Not that I agree with Señor Pompalone, but I recognize
his hypothesis as tenable."

The inspector gave a faint shrug.

"I see you are a man of learning, Herr Professor, but I
have had twenty-four years of experience as an inspector,
and I have found that when a woman comes into a murder
she is a real woman, and not just a picture."

"This may be the one exception. Now I suggest that we
go to Señor Afanador and hear his version of the tragedy."

The Magnificent made a movement forward.

"No, let him alone, señores. He will prejudice you
against me!"

"But we must hear what he says, Señor President," explained the inspector.

"Then be prepared for the most outrageous fabrica-
tions," warned the dictator. "He will stick at nothing! I
don't doubt he will swear to you that he saw me place the
poison in the bottle with my own hands!"

"That will be difficult proof to offset," observed the inspector.

"*Dios in cielo*, it will be!" sibilated the dictator, making a furious gesture. "To be laid by the heels by such a scurvy liar; a cur; a worm, a foul maggot of a spy! *Cá!*"

He broke into a rasping laugh and made a great sardonic gesture toward the door.

"Go! Go listen to him as if he were a man!"

The two Northerners went out of the room, moved in spite of themselves by the Venezuelan's melodramatics. In the hallway they passed Barneveldt on guard, and a moment later entered the apartment of Señor Afanador.

At first glance Poggioli received a little shock, for the room appeared empty. But the next moment he was reassured, and somewhat disgusted, to see the secretary pressed as closely as possible against the door communicating between his own and the dictator's room. Afanador had his ear to the crack of the door. His face was colorless, and his black eyes rolled as he listened intently to his chief.

When he saw the psychologist and the inspector, instead of exhibiting shame, he drew a breath of relief and came toward them panting, as if after some great exertion.

"Señores," he said in a whisper, getting out a handkerchief and dabbing his brow, "I know that His Excellency, the president of Venezuela, suspects me in this matter, does he not?"

Heinsius nodded briefly, moved by a distaste for the man.

"He does, Señor Afanador."

The secretary stretched out a hand that trembled.

"*Ole!* señores, I——" He glanced with widened eyes at the door communicating between his own room and Señor Pompalone's. "Is that lock strong?" he whispered.

"Certainly," tossed out the inspector. "It's an old Dutch lock. It would hold an ox. Nobody can get through it without a key."

Afanador breathed a little more easily.

"That's good, that's very good!" He smiled wryly. "Señores, you do not require a guard to keep me in this room."

The inspector's contempt for a coward got the better of his voice.

"Señor Afanador," he sneered, "I suppose you are prepared to say that you saw Señor Pompalone drop the poison in the wine bottle?"

"*Caramba!*" cried the secretary, coming out of his ague of fear in his surprise and denial. "I am prepared to say nothing of the sort! His Excellency, the president, is as innocent of that murder as a saint in heaven! It is as shocking and mysterious to him as it is to me."

The psychologist stared at this direct denial of what he had expected to hear. Then he observed that the secretary made this statement in a loud tone. He went immediately to the fellow and asked under his breath:

"Is that your real opinion, Señor Afanador?"

"*Sí, sí*, señor," nodded the fellow earnestly, now speaking in an undertone himself. "I know His Excellency, the president, had nothing whatever to do with the poisoning."

Heinsius stared in puzzled contempt.

"Then why are you shivering and shaking and asking about that lock, if you are going to stand by your employer like a man?"

The fellow's face, which had resumed a little color, went sickly again.

"Because His Excellency suspects me, señores," he whispered. "Do you know, up until now he has had nine private secretaries? They are——" He waggled a finger and pulled down his lips dolefully. "One after the other they fell under his suspicion; some for one reason, some for another. No doubt many of them were innocent, as I am, but"—he shrugged miserably and spread his hands—"His Excellency cannot risk anything. He is so much more valuable than we. Perhaps we are innocent, well—we die for our country. We are patriots! I have heard His Excellency explain it many times. We are all patriots—I am the tenth patriot."

Señor Afanador moistened his dry mouth with his tongue.

The psychologist was moved to an equivocal sympathy and disgust. There was more than a hint in this of the old Incan caste which caused those Indians to lay down their lives in unquestioning self-sacrifice for their rulers. He recalled that much of the Venezuelan blood is of Indian origin.

Herr Heinsius muttered a contemptuous oath under his breath.

"Help us clear the matter up, Afanador," suggested Poggioli. "If you can show another murderer, he will no longer suspect you. What is your idea about the poisoning of the wine?"

"Do you know who did it?" questioned the inspector bluntly.

"I don't know who did it, but I know when it was done."

Heinsius gave a snort.

"That isn't a very difficult problem. It was done when Señor Grillet went to his cellar, naturally."

"Ye-es," admitted the secretary, a little taken aback. "But I can be even more exact than that. It was done when His Excellency and I walked with Señor Grillet down the hallway to the head of the staircase."

"Did all three of you leave the room together?" inquired the inspector in astonishment.

"*Ciertamente*, señor!" ejaculated Afanador. "We had paid for our rooms. In a way we were the hosts of Señor Grillet, and you do not imagine we would allow a guest to walk out of our room unaccompanied! We are Venezuelan *caballeros*, señores, always. We went with him. When we returned I observed that someone had entered during our absence and had moved the wine bottles."

"How long did you stay out of your room?"

"For ten or fifteen minutes, señores. Neither of us had seen Curaçao before, and we stood at the window looking out on the canal and the houses."

"And who do you think came in and tampered with your wine?" interrupted Heinsius, a little more credulous of the story.

Afanador spread his hands.

"Señores, this may sound impossible to you, but I believe some spy, one of the *Pizanistas*, followed us here from La Guayra, slipped into our room at that unfortunate moment when His Excellency and I were out, and poisoned our wine."

Heinsius shrugged in the awkward manner of a Dutchman in Curaçao.

"Moonshine, Poggioli; every tale they concoct fizzles into moonshine at last. I don't see that we need to go any further with this investigation. Pompalone poisoned Grillet over an old affair with a woman, and that ends it."

"Just a moment, Inspector—— Señor Afanador, have you any theory why this supposed spy did not poison all three of the bottles, and be sure of killing Pompalone?"

"That would have cast suspicion on some fourth person, and he himself might have got apprehended. No, the logical thing was to kill one man; the other two would certainly be arrested and held prisoners, while the actual poisoner would be free of any suspicion at all."

The inspector laughed.

"Señor Afanador, you have concocted the flimsiest story of all—a third mysterious Venezuelan unseen, unknown, floating into your room and poisoning your wine in a fifteen-minute interval. That would make good fiction, but poor testimony before a court of law."

The secretary flushed, lifted his right hand.

"Señores, calling on Him Who reads my heart, I swear to you somebody tampered with our bottles while His Excellency and I were out. There is no doubt about that. They were moved. I know they were moved!"

"Well, anyway," returned the inspector ironically, "I don't suspect you of the crime, Señor Afanador, and I don't believe the court will, either. You can rest easy on that point."

The psychologist had just an opposite thought in his mind.

"But, señores!" cried the secretary, "I would give my life a thousand times for His Excellency. He alone can save my poor country, my poor Venezuela!"

The inspector turned on his heel in disgust and walked out of the room. When Poggioli followed and closed the door Heinsius reiterated:

"There is no use pursuing their investigations. Their suspicions chase around and around, like a puppy after its tail."

The psychologist stood stroking his jaw and looking at Barneveldt.

"I think someone did enter their room during their absence, Herr Heinsius," he said.

The inspector stared.

"Surely Afanador hasn't converted you to the theory of the imaginary spy!"

"No, but still I think somebody did."

"Who could it have been?"

"Well, everybody was downstairs at breakfast except these two men and the girl Hortensia."

The inspector, who was staring down the stairway, stopped and stared at his companion with the color draining from his sunburned face.

"*Gott im Himmel*, Herr Professor! What are you saying? Not that my poor crushed little Hortensia murdered her own father!"

The American lifted a hand.

"Don't let your feelings enter into this problem, Herr Heinsius. I know she is your friend; that you feel almost like a father to her. But she herself told you that she had quarreled with her father about the wine bottles."

"*Ach*, yes, but it was only a little quarrel. She only wanted to wipe the cobwebs off the bottles, Herr Poggioli."

"That is true, but she is an only child and probably a spoiled one. And then she is of Venezuelan blood, fiery and rash. Perhaps she committed this mad act in a moment of fury. Now look at her; her grief is uncontrollable."

"Why, that's scandalous, outrageous, an infernal explanation; that innocent child, that bereaved daughter. She is as innocent as a saint in paradise!"

"I certainly hope so," returned Poggioli warmly. "But in solving a problem, Herr Heinsius, it is our duty to pursue every line of evidence. You don't object to my talking for a moment with the Señorita Hortensia, do you?"

"No, no, not at all. I will go after her. I am sure you will find her—as you have found all the other witnesses—

quite innocent." And with a faintly ironic bow Inspector Heinsius set out up the hallway to find the Señorita Hortensia Grillet. Poggioli entered his client's room to await the return of the Dutchman with the girl.

The psychologist found the ex-dictator standing by the barred window of his room in a bellicose attitude, with his shoulders thrown back and his head down, staring at the shipping along the canal as if it were the enemy's works which he meant presently to charge.

As the American entered Pompalone turned and said: "I suppose Señor Afanador testified against me in every detail?"

"No," returned the psychologist, "quite the contrary." And he told what Afanador really had said, and how he had expressed a desire to give his life for Pompalone's freedom.

The Magnificent Pompalone broke into the account with a gesture.

"Don't you see the subtlety of this viper?" he cried. "He has concocted a perfectly unbelievable tale to cast a darker suspicion on me. A second *Pizanista* on my trail! Excuse me, Señor Poggioli. One is quite enough for me, and he is that scurvy cur, Afanador!"

"But, Señor Pompalone, is it a fact that you and Señor Afanador accompanied Señor Grillet to the head of the steps this morning and remained at the window for several minutes before returning to your rooms?"

"Certainly, that is the truth," snapped the dictator. But Afanador simply seized that fact to hang a long cock-and-bull story on it. No, nobody entered our room in our absence. Who was there in the second story to do it? It's his treachery!"

The psychologist saw it was impossible to discuss the

secretary's theory, and he turned impatiently to the door, wondering what was detaining Herr Heinsius and the Señorita Hortensia. He stepped outside again and saw the inspector standing at some distance down the hallway with a pleased expression on his broad brown face.

"What are you waiting on?" called Poggioli impatiently.

The inspector winked silently in reply.

The psychologist's patience was of academic brevity. He advanced sharply on the officer.

"What is it? What's the matter?"

"Nothing at all," returned the Dutchman in the best of spirits. "I've thought of a little plan to trick this scoundrelly Venezuelan."

"You have? How have you done it?"

The Dutchman studied the psychologist a moment.

"You won't warn your client? You won't give me away?"

"No!" snapped the American. "If he is guilty, I am as keen to see him hanged as you are!"

"So—I told Hortensia to put on her mother's clothes."

"What was that for?"

"You know how much like the photograph Hortensia is. Perhaps when Pompalone sees the girl he will be shocked into a restoration of his memory."

The psychologist was moved with the first touch of admiration he had felt for the Dutchman.

"By George, Heinsius!" he whispered warmly. "Capital! Splendid! I'll give you an 'A' on that!"

"Thanks! Thanks!" whispered the inspector, gratified.

Both men now stood looking eagerly up the hall for Hortensia.

Three minutes later a door opened and Hortensia Grillet came out. At the sight of her a little thrill moved even the pulse of the psychologist. The girl wore a black dress with a band of mourning purple at her bosom. Her dust cap was gone and her dark hair was piled high after the stately fashion of a Venezuelan señorita. About her neck hung a string of matched pearls.

The two men stared at the transformation. Almost as an afterthought in the wake of her loveliness, Poggioli recalled what he had meant to ask the girl.

"Señorita," he began a little awkwardly, "I have a question to ask you. This morning when your father went to his wine cellar did you see Señor Pompalone and Señor Afanador come from their room and stand looking out of the hall window at the canal?"

"*Sí*, señor." The girl nodded faintly, questioning the American with large eyes.

"And may I ask, señorita, if you or any other person entered their breakfast room while they were out?"

"I did, señor," breathed Hortensia.

"And what did you do in there, señorita?" queried the psychologist, studying her face intently.

"Señor, I—I—one of the wine bottles was so cobwebby, señor, I could not endure to see it set before Venezuelan *caballeros*. So I slipped in and wiped it clean. But I am sorry now, señor, I disobeyed my poor father's last wish."

She was about to cry again.

"Well, don't feel so badly about it, Hortensia—that was all you did, cleaned a bottle?"

"*Sí*, señor."

The psychologist stood nodding gently.

"That shows Afanador was right in this respect, Herr Heinsius. Someone did enter their room in their absence."

"I hope I did nothing wrong," exclaimed the girl in alarm.

"Nothing at all," assured Heinsius. "Just a little question between me and Herr Professor. Now I want you to come with me and repeat what you have just told me to Señor Pompalone."

"That is a very simple thing, señores," agreed the girl in a low tone. "I will tell it to anyone."

The three passed the sentry, Barneveldt, and went into the dictator's room.

The Magnificent Pompalone had flung himself down on a sofa. As the group entered he looked up, saw Hortensia, and sprang to his feet with the swiftest change of expression.

"Maria in heaven!" he exclaimed in amazement. "Is this the exquisite Ana Carrera again? Has my good angel so blessed me?"

The girl was bewildered at his words and his emotion.

"Señor Pompalone, Ana Carrera was my mother."

"Your mother!"

"Sí, señor."

"Is it possible! Why, señorita, you are her very flesh and spirit; the same look, the same soft music of her speech——"

The girl flushed a trifle.

"My mother died when I was born, señor."

"*Pobrecita!*"

The Magnificent Pompalone crossed himself, then went to her and, with the utmost gentleness, lifted and pressed her small work-hardened fingers to his lips.

"Poor little dove, left all alone in the world."

Hortensia caught a breath that lifted her bosom and her pearls.

"*Sí*, señor, my mother and father are both gone now."

The dictator touched the jewels with delicate fingers.

"*Ole!* señorita, these were Ana's pearls. I remember how

long I was collecting them from Margharita Island. The divers——"

"Oh, señor, did you gather these pearls for my mother?"

"And I could swear they were about her neck this moment!"

"Am I indeed like her?"

"As two orchids from one stem!"

"Was she as tall as I?"

"To my shoulder, both of you."

"And her hair so black?"

"It was like a silken summer night with jeweled combs for constellations."

The girl stretched her hands toward the dictator.

"*Mia madrecita!* My poor little mother!"

She began to weep once more.

Neither the inspector nor the psychologist was so hardened as to break into the girl's eager questioning about her lost mother. The two Northern men stepped quietly out of the room and left Hortensia and her informant to their causerie.

Outside, Inspector Heinsius drew a long breath.

"So-o!" he breathed, without any triumph in his voice. "It was as I expected. He forgot himself, gave himself completely away over a woman. Herr Professor, these Latins are incomprehensible beings—so subtle, so simple, so complex, yet so easily entangled; so like fiends out of hell and yet so lovable." He sighed, and then added quite irrelevantly: "*Ach,* I'm glad I didn't marry one, anyway."

Then he said that his work was over, that he would go back to his office, send men back to arrest the dictator and throw him in jail.

The psychologist was depressed over the interview upstairs. He asked the inspector to keep the dictator under guard in the hotel that afternoon and give him time to think over the whole problem.

"Come back and take dinner with me here this evening," he suggested, "and I will tell you the result of my analysis."

The Dutchman shrugged, awkwardly but finally.

"There can be but one result, Herr Professor."

"I am afraid so," agreed the American. "And yet Señor Pompalone wears every aspect of innocence."

"Except of course that he has practically confessed his crime," grunted the inspector, and shrugged.

Mr. Poggioli accompanied his friend to the door of the hostelry and watched him shoulder his way through the half gale that was sweeping along the street. The wind, driving in from the sea, felt moist, and the sunshine that struggled through the vaporous air might have been English sunlight instead of the usual diamond brilliance of Curaçao.

As the psychologist turned back into the lobby a group of the guests watched him, and the American salesman called baldly:

"Poggioli, what did you find out—did the greaser kill him?"

"I don't know," returned the psychologist heavily, and hurried upstairs.

The salesman winked at the silent group.

"Highbrow, no practical sense. Now if I had that case——"

In the upper story the American asked Barneveldt where Señorita Grillet had gone.

"To her room, mynheer," answered the guard.

The psychologist was vaguely disappointed. He had an inclination to question Hortensia a little further. He hardly knew along what line. Her father, her mother, perhaps. But he would not disturb her in her room.

He moved on, his mood tuned to the gray tragedy, thinking over its conflicting details. His steps carried him into the private library where Señor Grillet's body was by now laid out for burial.

The psychologist walked over to the greenheart table, picked up and looked at the photograph with its two enigmatic annotations on its back. He read them silently, "Account of 12 *de agosto*, 1906. Account settled 5 *de enero*, 1925."

Poggioli wondered if the dead man, lying under the white sheet on the cane settee, had stolen Pompalone's wife or betrothed on that August day in 1906.

After all its permutations, the riddle had come back to the inspector's simple solution—"When there is a woman in a murder case," the Dutchman had said, "my twenty-four years' experience tells me she is a real one and not a photograph."

And so it had proved.

But there was a snarl somewhere in the burden of proof. It did not seem to Poggioli that the Magnificent Pompalone was a man who would murder by strategy. He could not imagine the dictator slipping poison into a wine bottle. Afanador would have done that.

He began reviewing the dictator's case against his secretary. This, also, was too nebulous, too fantastic.

The psychologist's mind went over other details of the tragedy—the accidental, the irrelevant details: the murdered man's anger with his daughter for wanting to clean the bottles, her disobedience in slipping into the room and dusting them after his injunction, the girl's eagerness to hear about her mother, of whom, evidently, her father never spoke. Naturally, he would not.

And still, the Magnificent Pompalone seemed to hold no bitterness against Ana Sixto y Carrera. This, too, seemed not quite in keeping with his temperament. In fact, the only suggestion of the dictator's innocence was psychological. What would a jury of hard-headed Curaçaoan Dutch make of a defense founded on psychology?

The wind was piping now an eerie threnody about the eaves of the big hotel. The dead man, done to death by some mysterious assailant, lay on the long wicker couch with the sheet drawn to his chin. On the table, beside the photograph of the woman, lay the contents of the dead man's pockets: a small penknife, a few pieces of Netherland money, a ring of keys—noncommittal relics beside the faded photograph.

Then it occurred to Poggioli that this woman had not come to Curaçao with the tavern keeper. According to Van Maasdyk, Herr Heinsius had said, Señor Grillet arrived in Curaçao accompanied only by his baby girl, Hortensia. The psychologist could not piece together these details of the tragedy. As he sat listening to the wind and the far-off resurgence of the sea he had a feeling as if he were working with some jigsaw puzzle. A number of pieces seemed to fit, but he felt they were wrongly placed, yet he almost dared not undo the few articulating sections for fear he would never make even an approach to a pattern again.

In an effort to relieve his mind of these incongruities, he opened one of the bookcases and selected two or three volumes. They were all old-fashioned romances of revenge, *The Corsican Brothers*, *Vendetta*, *The Count Balderschino*. Apparently the whole library was of this tenor.

It struck the investigator that Señor Grillet had been fearing this very fate, and that explained the mystery of the last notation on the portrait. He had expiated his abduction of Pompalone's wife or mistress. His account had been settled with his life. Now he lay in the darkening library, the sheet drawn up to his chin, with a rising storm wailing his requiem.

After all, the Magnificent Pompalone had done this man to death. It was somehow out of character, but Pompalone was even more Latin than the American-Italian who was trying to understand his crime; and an individual of one race is always more or less out of character to a man of another.

From the lower story there floated the three notes of the dinner gong, repeated over and over. Even if the storm brewed and men were murdered, travelers had to eat. The psychologist got up and went below.

In the lobby the American found Herr Heinsius awaiting him. The two men went together to the dining room, which already was full. They took a small table in the corner of the room. The Negro, Zubio, brought them water and the menu card. The inspector looked over the good Dutch dishes with pleased eyes.

"Suppose we do not discuss our problem until after we eat, Herr Professor," suggested Heinsius, with a Dutchman's respect for a good meal.

"We don't have to," said the psychologist. "I have come to a decision."

The inspector glanced up keenly.

"You have?"

"Yes, I agree with you."

"*Ach*," exclaimed the inspector, with a falling of the

face. "I am sorry to hear it, Herr Professor; I had hoped somehow you would fasten the murder somewhere else than on Herr Pompalone, but, of course, the facts remain facts."

Zubio approached with the soup.

"Let us think no more about it until after we have dined."

He began swathing himself with a huge napkin while his mild eyes shone at the clear green turtle soup.

Over the big dining room the other guests were eating in accordance with their national manners. An Englishman was diligently using his knife and fork, holding one in each hand without ever laying down either implement. It gave him a certain rushed appearance. A German pinched each piece of bread on a plate before he selected his roll. An Italian made a. sucking sound as he inhaled the spaghetti from his plate. All were mutually bad-mannered, each to the other. The American soap salesman drummed his knife on the table and called to Zubio:

"Here, nigger, come here, you!"

As Zubio approached, the soap seller began in an offended tone:

"Do you call this stuff wine?" He tapped his bottle.

Zubio bobbed.

"Yas, suh, dat—dat's whut I calls it, *senyo*."

"Well, I call it ditch water! Have you got anything a man can drink?"

"*Sí, senyo.*"

"*Something old and prime?*"

"*Sí, sí, senyo.*"

The American flipped out a coin.

"Go bring me some of the oldest and best you've got in this joint."

"Yah, yessuh, *si, oui, m'sieu*," he bobbed in polyglot, moved by the money.

Zubio hurried away, and presently Poggioli heard him calling in his thick, blurred tones in the lobby:

"Señorita! Oh, señorita, come down! *Un Americano* wants the best wine, the oldest wine——"

Poggioli cursed the salesman for disturbing the grief-stricken girl over a glass of wine.

There was more long-distance conversation which the psychologist could not understand. After a while the señorita came into the dining room and approached the salesman.

"Señor," she said in a low tone, "nobody but Father knew much about the wine. He always attended to it himself. I don't know which is the best or the worst."

"Bring me the oldest," ordered the American roundly, "and here is a five for yourself."

But the girl hurried away, leaving him holding the bill in his fingers. She said to Zubio:

"I think you will find the key to the wine cellar among Father's things on the library table upstairs."

Then she hurried from the room.

Poggioli condemned the salesman again, looking across the tables at him; then with a swerve in his thoughts he began pondering on what the girl had just said: her father always had kept the key to the wine cellar. For some reason he recalled once more that Señor Grillet had quarreled with his daughter that morning over cleaning the dusty bottles. Both of these little points were odd—Grillet's anger at the girl for offering to polish a bottle, and the fact that she had slipped in and cleaned it anyway.

It seemed to Poggioli that these pieces of the grim jigsaw puzzle suddenly fitted together perfectly. There was something exciting about it. It cast a vague light over the whole tragic occurrence. He tried to think out a fuller connection.

A cat, which probably haunted the dining room, rubbed against his ankle and disturbed the delicate skein of his thoughts. He tried to kick the animal under his chair. A moment later Zubio entered with a single, very cobwebby bottle of amber liquid borne aloft on a silver tray. The black carried it to the drummer's table and began opening it with elaborate ceremony.

As he was pouring the liquid into the American's glass a sudden impulse seized the psychologist. He swooped down, picked up the cat at his feet, and the next moment sprang up and strode toward the salesman's table.

"Just a moment," he called in a low, urgent tone. "Wait, put that glass down, sir! Let me test it before you drink it!"

The soap salesman stared at Poggioli in amazement and irritation.

"Where the hell do you come in?"

"I don't know exactly. I have an idea, an impression. Give me a spoonful of that wine. I believe it's dangerous!"

The American stared with glass uplifted, but he did not drink. He got his spoon and dipped into the liquid. The psychologist produced the cat with a certain effect of legerdemain.

"Pour some down its throat. I'll hold its mouth open!"

Came a chorus of ejaculations and grunts from the other tables. Inspector Heinsius hurried to Poggioli's side. The cat mewed and scratched, but the wine was poured into its mouth. After a moment of watching the psychologist commanded:

"Another spoonful."

"Aw, you're kiddin' me," cried the salesman, growing red in the face.

"You try it, Inspector," directed Poggioli briefly.

The inspector reached for the spoon. As he tried to pour more wine in the cat's mouth he ejaculated:

"*Ach!* The creature's dead!"

The soap salesman turned cotton-colored.

"Dead! How come it's dead? What killed it?"

Excited comments set up throughout the room. Came a movement of guests toward the table. Inspector Heinsius was amazed.

"Herr Professor, how did you know? Why did you suspect?"

"Come out of the crowd," directed the psychologist. "We can't talk here."

The inspector ordered Zubio to retain the poisoned wine as evidence, and the two men went into the lobby; but the lobby was instantly filled from the dining room. The inspector and the psychologist passed on out the door into the night together. A gale laden with spume whipped them as they entered the canal side.

"Come to my office on the Leidenstraat!" shouted the inspector above the wind. "We can talk there."

In the dim street light the psychologist wagged a nervous negative finger.

"Let's stay out awhile. I'm jumpy. I've been indoors too much to-day."

"Let's turn up this street where it's quieter."

The two turned down a side street, and went holding each other's arms in the occasional gusts that swept the narrow thoroughfare. After they had walked some distance the inspector came back to the point they had been discussing.

"Why did you suspect that bottle of wine was poisoned? It came straight from the cellar."

"The thing that set me off," said Poggioli, lifting his voice, "was the fact that the bottle was cobwebby and dusty, exactly like the one Señor Grillet had served to the men upstairs. Added to that was a complex of associated ideas touching Grillet's quarrel with his daughter. As a matter of fact, Herr Heinsius, what we call our reason is never the fatally sure, mathematical progression we fancy it is. If you will examine reason in the making you will find it a very cloudy process, a kind of blind jumping among hypotheses. When it finally hits the right one, it then proceeds to build a logical bridge from its point of departure to its goal, and it imagines it has crossed on that bridge, but it has not. The bridge was flung out afterward."

The inspector laughed briefly.

"That's all right how you did it, Herr Professor. I am neither an undergraduate nor a fellow in psychology. Why should Grillet poison himself? Why should Zubio infallibly have brought up another poisoned bottle out of a cellar of good wine? Why——"

"Here, take a question at a time," cried the psychologist. "The Negro brought up a poisoned bottle because he picked out the oldest one in the cellar, according to the order of the soap salesman."

"Why should the oldest be poisoned?"

"Because Señor Grillet brought a case of poisoned wine with him from Venezuela when he came to Curaçao some twenty years ago."

"You don't mean," cried the inspector, "you thought of all these things when you leaped up and ran to the American!"

"No. I received what the vulgar call a 'hunch.' Now when we analyze 'hunches' we find they are composed of an instinctive correlation of facts which have not yet reached the surface of consciousness——"

"That's all right about hunches, but why did Grillet bring poisoned wine with him from Caracas twenty years ago?"

"Because the Magnificent Pompalone had stolen his wife. You see we approached the problem with a reversed theory. We worked on the idea that Pompalone had a grievance against Señor Sixto, *alias* Grillet, and murdered him for it. In reality, Sixto had a grievance against Pompalone.

"If we had paused to consider feminine nature we might have known that a man like Grillet could never have alienated the wife of a man like Pompalone. On the contrary, what could be more natural than the dictator of Venezuela seizing on the wife of some humble fellow and possessing her. These dictators have a high-handed way with them."

The inspector nodded in the darkness.

"That hangs together all right, Herr Professor, and then what happened?"

"Then Grillet, or Sixto, took his infant daughter, Hortensia, and a case of poisoned wine and emigrated from Venezuela to Curaçao, and here set up the finest hostelry in the city."

"Perhaps he had been a tavern keeper in Caracas?"

"I doubt it. I feel sure Señor Sixto studied out his complete revenge on the Magnificent Pompalone twenty years ago. He reasoned Pompalone would be deposed eventually; that he would fly for sanctuary to Curaçao, which is the nearest free port to Venezuela. He knew the Magnificent would lodge in the finest hostelry in the city. Therefore, to accomplish his revenge, he must possess that finest hotel, together with his case of poisoned wine."

The inspector nodded, impressed by the psychologist's extraordinary analysis. "Sixto accomplished his purpose," he said. "His meals were a delight, and his rooms as sweet as the sea air itself. Even his daughter, a native Venezuelan, was cleanlier than we Dutch."

"That was all built up, waiting for one man to enter his door and die. That·man was the Magnificent Pompalone. And here is the irony of it, Herr Inspector, the satire that sometimes makes me believe in the old pagan gods who laughed at the antics of mankind. The very carefulness with which Señor Sixto trained his daughter led to his own death."

Heinsius listened interrogatively.

"When Hortensia, who could endure nothing dirty or dusty, cleaned the cobwebs off the wine bottle in the breakfast room, she killed her own father."

"How did she do that?" cried the officer in amazement.

"When Señor Sixto carried the breakfast with.the poisoned wine to his guests, naturally he was tremendously excited. The vengeance of twenty years was about to be consummated. He meant to hand the Magnificent Pompalone the oldest, dustiest, and cobwebbiest bottle on the platter with a pretty speech such as all Venezuelans know how to make, and poison him.

"When he met Hortensia on the upper floor she wanted to clean the poisoned bottle. That was his mark, the cob-webs. It unstrung him. He reprimanded her severely and told her to go about her work. Then he was called.down to the wine cellar, for naturally he never allowed anyone to enter that dangerous place except himself. His guests accompanied him to the stairs. Hortensia, annoyed by the dust, as he had trained her to be, saw her opportunity to slip in and clean the worst of the bottles, the poisoned one. When Sixto returned with the excitement of murder upon him, he did not observe the change. He gave his enemy the dustiest bottle, and drank his own bane. Herr Heinsius, if it were in our power to exchange our earthiness for the high divan of the gods, if we could look down on this tragedy—this romantic, revengeful man, after twenty years of waiting and hating and planning, then sitting before his enemy and drinking his own poison, all through mere excess of training his child—Herr Heinsius, I think we, too, would have been moved, as were the Olympian gods, to enormous laughter."

The inspector was somehow dismayed at his companion's phantasy. He said uneasily: "But naturally we don't believe in the old pagan gods any more."

"Oh, no, certainly not," agreed the psychologist. "But they really do explain life more accurately than our modern theology, don't you think? Sometimes it seems to me that men have a reverse theory of the gods, just as you and I had of the murder. Suppose men assumed that the gods were inimical or satiric toward them instead of friendly, how many of the perplexities of life that would explain!"

"Well—I'm a good churchman myself," said Heinsius.

"Oh, so am I," agreed the American.

The two walked on with a feeling of spiritual disjunction at this little quirk in their conversation. Poggioli regretted he had mentioned his whimsy.

The two had walked out past the houses now onto a little pleasure beach, which was quite deserted in the gale. A string of pale electric lights along the water's edge showed the curves of the incoming waves which marched in endless procession from the dark Caribbean. Spindrift blew in past the lights in torn veils, and its last mist beat grate-fully on the faces of the two companions. Poggioli con-tinued musing over the ironic death of the hotel keeper and the odd triumph of Pompalone. There was a moral planlessness, an anarchy about it. The line of a poem re-curred to his mind: "Perpetual strife amid confused alarms." That was life—perpetual strife.

Here the inspector touched the scientist's arm and pointed out to sea.

"There's a brave soul out there," he called above the surf.

Poggioli looked and saw a red-and-green signal burning in the darkness.

"Fishermen?" queried Poggioli in a friendly tone.

"Natives in a jack boat, I suppose. They brave any sea."

The inspector had begun a description of jack boats—solid logs with the bottom hewn out—when he was inter-rupted by two figures silhouetted against the row of watery beach lights. A large man and a slight one were hurrying toward the surf.

The psychologist and the inspector watched them curiously, when at a certain resolute bearing of the larger man the inspector gasped suddenly:

"*Mein Gott!* That's the Magnificent Pompalone!" And he dashed down the strand after the dictator.

Poggioli set out after him, running.

"Let him go, Herr Inspector!" shouted the American. "He hasn't committed any crime in this country!"

"*Gott im Himmel*, but he mustn't go back! That's worse than a crime! It's against business!"

The police inspector jerked out a pistol as he ran and shouted against the blast:

"Stop! Halt! I'll shoot!"

But at that moment the two figures dashed across the last shining foot of sand and plunged headlong into the curve of an incoming wave.

The inspector fired four shots into the surf, then with an oath turned his fire on the signal lights at sea. But perhaps the tossed sailors never knew that a man on shore was firing at them. After some fifteen minutes the signal lights blinked out.

As the two men turned back to the hotel the psychologist said frankly:

"Heinsius, I'm glad he's gone. He was a very devil, no doubt, but there was something likable, something rather splendid about the fellow."

"You mean he was Pompalone the Magnificent——"

At this moment a figure dashed out of the side street, shouting—a huge, mouthy Negroid shout as if the fiends were after him:

"Herr Inspectuh! Senyo Inspectuh! Mistuh Inspectuh!"

Both men stared in the new direction and saw the white-eyed figure of Zubio appear against the night.

"He's coming to tell us they're gone!" said the Dutchman.

Zubio made for the two.

"Herr Inspectuh!" he gasped. "Come to the hotel, *pronto!* Quick!"

"I know they are gone, Zubio."

"Gone! Gone! No! Poor Senyo Afanador, someone has struck a dagger to his heart!"

Heinsius swayed in the gale.

"What! Afanador murdered! *Mein Gott!* I saw him that moment. Where was Barneveldt?"

"Sitting by the door where you put him, Herr Inspec-tuh. Somebody opened the doors on the inside between all the rooms; somebody with a key; and now Señorita Hortensia is gone, run away, mad, perhaps."

Simultaneously the two men whirled and stared out into the black, incoming surf. They could see nothing at all.

On the following day, immediately after the funeral of Señores Grillet and Afanador, the Hotel Saragossa was closed and the windows and doors boarded up.

The Governor of
Cap Haitien

*In which the professor uncomfortably
beards a witch doctor.*

THE GOVERNOR OF CAP HAITIEN

T HE trig gentleman with that slightly foreign flavor so characteristic of Americans nowadays sat in the steamer chair next but one to that of Mr. Henry Poggioli, and called across the chronically seasick woman who separated them to wager, he said, dollars to doughnuts that the American marines would be recalled over there within six months. With the "over there" he indicated by a motion of his cigarette the landfall of Haiti, which lay like an opalescent mist on their starboard.

Mr. Poggioli, who was interested perhaps too strictly in the racial psychology of the West Indian Islands, and not sufficiently in their politics, presently admitted his ignorance of the fact that the American marines had been withdrawn.

At this the trig gentleman glanced at the psychologist, then silently but obviously made a revaluation of Mr. Poggioli's acquaintance. If Poggioli did not know that the American troops had been withdrawn from Haiti, then he must be nothing but a tourist—a perambulant checkbook, a pair of leveled binoculars, a clicking kodak, a human insect bewildering itself in the changing kaleidoscope of geography. The trig gentleman evidently had thought Mr. Poggioli another traveling American business man engaged in the sane enterprise of selling goods here in the West Indies; but a tourist . . .

He replaced his cigarette between his lips with the discernible intention of ending the conversation.

"Well, they have," he stated, no longer in the tone of equal to equal, but of the informed to the uninformed. "I'm stopping off to close my company's insurance offices in Cap Haitien and Port-au-Prince; cancel all outstanding policies and repay unearned premiums. That's what the insurance folks think about the future of the Black Republic, and the insurance boys are pretty wise fowls, brother—they weren't hatched day before yesterday."

The seasick woman gasped a desire for ice. The trig gentleman flagged the steward with cold, unsympathetic efficiency.

Mr. Poggioli said absently that he didn't doubt it. Then the insurance man's evil predictions for the future of the Haitian government brought to the psychologist's mind the odd cablegram which he had received in Curaçao and which really had started him toward Haiti. He continued thinking of it a moment, could not quite reword it, and presently fumbled in his pocket and drew it out. It read:

PROFESSOR HENRY POGGIOLI, PSYC. D. CURAÇAO, D. W. I.

If you are a corresponding member of the American Society for Psychological Research, report at once to Aristide Boisrond, governor of the Department of Cap Haitien, Cap Haitien, Haiti. Fees no object.

DR. VAUQUIÈRE,
Minister Department of Health.

It struck Mr. Poggioli now, as it had struck him when he had first received it, as the most uncommunicative communication he had ever received. The thing suggested questions and answered none. Presently he asked the trig gentleman:

"Are you at all acquainted with the government officials in Cap Haitien?"

"Unpleasantly. Why?"

"I wondered what you would think of that?" He handed the cablegram over the sick lady, who never relayed anything.

The insurance man took it, and as he read his face changed.

"I thought you were a tourist!" he blurted out.

"I saw you did."

"You must pardon me, Mr. Poggioli," apologized the trig gentleman.

"No offense," assured the psychologist. "In fact, if the truth were told, I have occasionally toured myself. To India once and once to Nova Zembla. I don't uphold the practice, but I regard it with charity."

"Sure, sure," stammered the insurance man, quite discomfited.

"Naturally would." He scrambled out of his *impasse* by returning to the cablegram. "I see you are a—a psychologist." He pronounced the syllables slowly. "That's a—er— a man who—m—m—weighs the soul, isn't it? I saw a notice of it once in a Sunday supplement. Picture of one coming out of a dead woman's mouth. They weigh about an ounce, don't they?"

"Something like that," agreed Poggioli, not caring to split milligrams over so simple a matter.

The insurance man nodded solemnly.

"By George, science is a wonderful thing. No telling what we'll find out in the next ten years!"

Having offered this original observation in an impressed tone, he was moved to become more closely acquainted with a genuine man of science. He leaned across the sick woman and offered a spontaneous hand.

"My name's Osterwasski, Mr. Poggioli," he said warmly.

"I'm an American, too, full-blooded, I suppose, as both my parents landed in New York months before I was born. I am always glad to meet a fellow American anywhere. In the blood, I suppose. But you ought to know, you're a psychologist."

Mr. Poggioli supposed it must be in the blood, and then once more directed Mr. Osterwasski's attention to the point under discussion.

"Just what do you know about this Governor Boisrond or Vauquière?"

Osterwasski hesitated as became a discreet business man.

"I know something about Boisrond—well, about both of them."

"What is it?"

The trig gentleman cleared his throat.

"This is confidential," he said in an undertone across the sick woman, "but they are—well, they're the cat's ankles, all right."

"You mean——"

"I mean you couldn't find two worse crooks in a corkscrew factory."

Poggioli stared his amazement.

"But what in the world would a pair of rogues want with a corresponding member of the American Society for Psychological Research?"

"Are you that?"

"Yes."

The insurance man hesitated, became aware of the sick woman, got out of his chair, and nodded for Poggioli to follow. Standing by the railing, Mr. Osterwasski tossed over his cigarette stub and said in the grave tone with which one good American warns his fellow countryman in a foreign land:

"If I was you, Poggioli, I wouldn't step off this ship."

"Why?"

He nodded at the distant island.

"That place ain't safe. Hell's li'ble to break loose over there any minute."

Poggioli nodded, waiting for something more specific.

"Besides, Boisrond won't pay you anything. I've got a suit against him right now, or rather he has against my company, trying to collect fake insurance loss."

"Doesn't make much difference about his paying me," dismissed Poggioli seriously, "but danger. I'm not out hunting trouble."

"Well, unless you want to cash in your life-insurance policy, I'd pass that island up if I was you."

"You're going to land, aren't you, Mr. Osterwasski?"

"Oh, well, that's different. I'm out for business; you're just out for science."

"I've heard of men doing some fairly adventurous things even for science, Mr. Osterwasski."

The insurance man lifted his brows, drew his head into his shoulders slightly, and spread his hands.

"Very well. I was just telling you as one American to another. You know your business. Of course it's up to you."

It was clear that while he was not exactly offended, Mr. Poggioli's decision had not been pleasing to him. He said he had some packing to do before he went ashore and, with a motion of his finger to his deck cap, turned and went to his cabin.

Poggioli watched him go, a little amused, a little thoughtful at his warning. Osterwasski's attitude of "one good American to another" struck Poggioli as droll. Yet after all, Osterwasski was an American. Just as authentic an

American from the top of his head to the soles of his feet as any descendant of the *Mayflower* pilgrims.

He was American through elimination. He was no more a Russian Jew, simply because his parents were Russian Jews, than he was Chinese. He had the factory mark of New York's East Side and the trade-mark of lower Broadway, about the twenties, and probably owned an apartment on Riverside Drive. He could have been evolved nowhere else in the world. As he said, he was an American.

Here Mr. Poggioli's thoughts veered back to the queer message in his pocket, to the rather deterring information he had just received from his fellow American, and to the gloomy mountains of Haiti solidifying out of the opal mists ahead of the liner.

Some three hours later, amid the usual fanfare of bumboats, lighters, passenger dories, and amphibious Negro boys diving about the ship for tourists' pennies, the liner dropped anchor in Manzanilla Bay. A little later Poggioli was rowed ashore and stepped into the black world to which he had been so oddly summoned.

On a wide plank wharf amid a furnace of sunshine and the stench of raw hides and baled tobacco, Poggioli was at once beset by a rabble of black beggars and porters who swarmed about him and the other passengers, beseeching nickles and almost fighting for the privilege of carrying handbags to the customhouse.

Two stalwart blacks were pulling at the psychologist's traveling case and cursing each other in an impossible French to let go, quite as if the white man were an inanimate object without any power of choice within himself.

In the midst of this uproar two black horses hitched to a stanhope came rattling up the board wharf. The

driver caught sight of the American's distress and called
out in crisp French:

"Is that you, Mr. Poggioli?"

When the psychologist gasped out an affirmative, the
driver, a yellow man, swung about his courageous blacks
and fairly charged into the rabble. Came a general scut-
tling away. One of the horses bowled over a hunchback
mendicant, while the rest of the crowd fled like a flock of
disturbed and angry blackbirds. There was something ruth-
less and effective in the maneuver. Carriage and horses came
to a halt beside the American. The yellow man leaned out
ceremoniously.

"Allow me to introduce myself. I am Dr. Vauquière.
Sorry you were annoyed by these tatterdemalions, Professor Poggioli. The hand of our government is quite lax.
One must admit it although the recent change in policing
would explain that. Have you presented your bags at
customs yet?"

"No," said Poggioli. "I'll run over and do it."

"Don't walk!" implored Dr. Vauquière in a shocked
tone. "Here, I'll drive you there, m'sieu."

The customs building was not more than fifty yards distant, but apparently this distance was unwalkable in Haiti.
Poggioli stepped into the stanhope; the blacks clattered
across the boards and drew up at the big stone customhouse which the Americans had built during their occupation of the island. At the door of this building stood an
easy-going black man in uniform. Vauquière motioned
to him.

"LeClerc!" he called. "Run out here and pass Dr. Poggioli's bags, will you? He's a guest of the governor's."

The black man called LeClerc nodded and advanced
with a sort of dignified alacrity through the sunshine, as

another door opened and a tall, lank white man with a long, sun-blistered nose and a hard lipless mouth stood framed in the doorway.

"LeClerc!" he bellowed in English. "Go through that fellow's bags according to regerlations! Tell him to come in here and sign a declaration in my office!"

The black inspector's manner changed.

"Yes, yes, Mr. Clay!" Then he approached Poggioli. "I'll have to request you, m'sieu——"

"Mr. Clay," called Vauquière, in explanation, "this is Dr. Poggioli, a house guest of Governor Boisrond."

"Don't make a bit o' difference to me if he is house guest to God!" barked Mr. Clay, apparently at the end of his patience. "He's got to go through customs right!" And he turned back into his office.

In the meantime Poggioli was out of the stanhope, hurrying to make his declaration. As he entered he saw a number of other passengers with their valises open on a long counter. Two or three black inspectors were poking among the bags. Mr. Clay stood behind the counter waiting for Poggioli with a scowl on his long, sun-bitten face.

"These damned niggers don't know what regerlations mean," he growled, presumably to the psychologist, as he opened his bag.

Mr. Clay glanced inside, saw the usual traveler's assortment, and continued his monologue.

"Run a guv'ment! Good God, better be pullin' the bell cord over a mule's back in the cotton rows!" He turned over shirts, pajamas, and toilet articles and kept up a running disparagement of the population of Haiti. "Got to keep 'em in their places. Ridiculous, the airs they give themselves. Governor Boisrond, Dr. Vauquière, M'sieu Armand—make a man sick!"

After a while he returned Poggioli's bag disapprovingly and said:

"Of course, you know your own business, mister, but are you goin' to be a house guest of this Governor Boisrond?"

"I am," nodded the psychologist, studying the lank, hard-faced man.

"Come from the States, don't you?"

"Yes."

"Yankee, ain't you?"

"Yes."

"Thought so. Well, by God, you Yankees comin' down here in Haiti mixin' and minglin' with these coons makes it mighty hard on us folks who's down here tryin' 'to put the fear of God in their hearts."

Mr. Clay looked strained, as if he really did find this an exhausting task.

"The fear of God?" repeated Poggioli curiously.

"Yes," irritably, "tryin' to keep 'em in their places!"

"What place is that?" asked Poggioli, beginning to be amused.

The chief customs officer stared at him.

"Hell, you don't believe a nigger is the equal of a white man, do you?"

Poggioli gave this a moment's thought and then inquired:

"Do you believe the leopard is the equal of the polar bear, or the dodo the equal of the wallaby, Mr. Clay?"

Mr. Clay snorted in irritation.

"That shows you're a Yankee all right—answerin' one question by askin' another'n. I'll say good-day and be damned to you."

Evidently the sun had peeled something besides Mr. Clay's nose.

Poggioli took his traveling bag and returned through the heat to the stanhope where Dr. Vauquière sat waiting patiently. The yellow man seemed not so much to endure the downpour of sunshine as somehow to avoid it. His shirt and collar were not wilted; he was not even perspiring.

"Sorry I annoyed you with that little scene," he apologized equably in French.

"Who is this man Clay?" asked Poggioli, still amused at the conversation he had had.

"The American collector of customs here in Cap Haitien."

"I thought the Americans had withdrawn."

"Their troops, not their customs officials," explained Vauquière dryly. "This Mr. Clay comes from Georgia, which, I understand from him, is the richest, most progressive, most aristocratic commonwealth in America. Clay got his appointment through some political service for a Georgia congressman, and was sent down here because he was supposed to be very good at keeping our republic in its place." Vauquière looked at the psychologist with a certain droll expression on his face, then touched his horses and clattered away toward the central *place* of Cap Haitien.

The streets of Cap Haitien swarmed with black and brown pedestrians who made way for the stanhope with startled cries. In this somnolent coast town of Haiti vehicles seldom moved faster than the lumbering two-wheeled carts drawn by donkeys. The whole population walked in the center of the street, the women and girls balancing on their heads packages wrapped in palm leaves or held in tin containers. These shining tin cans, borne on the heads of women, dotted the crowd in every direction. Dr. Vauquière finally mentioned them, saying they were shipped to Haiti by the oil companies, filled with kerosene or lubricating oils.

"Our lower classes buy them for a pittance," he went on, "and use them for every purpose, from cooking utensils and drinking cups to wash pots and hamper baskets. They have almost displaced the old calabashes and woven reed baskets our people used to make."

There was a note of regret in Vauquière's voice as he mentioned this change. The stanhope entered the *place* or central plaza of the town. Here in the noonday heat loitered literally thousands of black marketeers—gossiping, laughing, chaffering over tiny piles of bananas, nuts, guavas; for the women venders sold their wares not by weight or measure but by piles which were large or small as their fancy dictated.

"These tin cans," continued Dr. Vauquière, "have robbed the *place* of half its picturesqueness. The lines of a calabash made a graceful curve on the poised heads of our women, and the red and yellow patterning of the baskets was a pleasure to the eye."

Poggioli nodded.

"That would help. These cans give the market a back-alley effect, and," he added in a reflective strain, "it might have a direct influence on the art development of the people. For example, would the Grecian world ever have developed Phidias if the Greek women had carried water from the public cisterns in Standard Oil containers?"

Vauquière looked at Poggioli intently.

"You are jesting?" he queried gravely.

"M—yes, but what I have said probably has some truth in it."

"Quite enough," agreed Vauquière with a certain bitter

tinge in his tones, "but I daresay you're the first white man who ever hit upon that point of view."

"It just occurred to me, the oil tins——"

"Precisely. And these oil containers typify in a small way what is happening to our people in a large way all over the island, Mr. Poggioli."

"What's that?" asked the scientist curiously.

"Our native racial development here in Haiti is on the verge of being completely wiped out and replaced by routine American civilization. That civilization, m'sieu, is like these tin cans—handy, efficient, and delivered at our doors."

"And costs little," added the scientist.

"No, these tins are very expensive, m'sieu. They have cost us our folk art in basketry and pottery. That's a strange and a tragic thing, m'sieu, a whole art motif of a people destroyed by tin cans."

"It is an unhappy result," admitted the psychologist, as the horses were forced down to a walk through the market place.

"The whole world loses by it, m'sieu. Only the folk who originate a motif in art can develop it in all its implications. To-day modern sculptors go to old African carving for a new *point d'appui*, but what they evolve is not what Africa would have evolved. That is utterly lost."

There was a certain intensity about the yellow man's conversation that was novel to Poggioli.

"That is probably true," he admitted. "But it's all in the laps of the gods. Individuals can do nothing in the major trend of racial developments."

"That is where I disagree," said Vauquière with greater briskness. "In fact, it is precisely why you are here in Haiti to-day."

"I?" cried Poggioli, suspecting a jest.

Vauquière nodded.

"Just at this moment, m'sieu, we Haitians have a chance to pick up our lives and go on with them. The American marines have been withdrawn. We have our own officials and constabulary. If our Negro civilization is ever to stand erect, m'sieu, now is the hour."

Vauquière enunciated this with the earnestness of a zealot.

"But how can I forward such ends?" asked the scientist.

"By educating our people, M'sieu Poggioli. The marines took over our government because of our lawlessness. Our hills are full of insurrectionary bands called *cacos*. The marines dispersed them, but now since they have been withdrawn the *cacos* have broken out again in the mountains."

The white man nodded attentively.

"But mark this, these insurrectionary leaders base their authority on the superstition of the Negroes. They are workers of magic, voodoo doctors."

"Yes——"

"Now, that is where you come in. We want you to demonstrate to these ordinary Haitian Negroes, these black folk here"—Vauquière waved a hand out into the crowded market place—"that voodooism is baseless, that their *caco* leaders are quacks, and that they would best cling to the organized government, and not follow every Papa Loi who takes to the brush."

Poggioli looked at the swarm of black folk around the stanhope.

"I can't imagine one man having much effect on such an old folk belief as voodooism."

"The problem is not so wide as that. It is individual. The name of the *caco* leader is Jean LaFronde. If you could explain the rather sinister effects he produces, that would break his hold on his followers and ease our native government over this crisis."

"Has he really created a governmental crisis?"

"Yes, he is trying to make himself such a nuisance that the authorities at Port-au-Prince will have to recognize him and give him a governmental berth. That is the beaten path to political preferment in this island, m'sieu—insurrection."

There was something grotesque in the idea of a Haitian Negro's reaching a civil-service post because he qualified as a voodoo practitioner. Also that he, Henry Poggioli, had been summoned to Haiti for no better purpose than to expose this black charlatan's tricks. For this purpose Governor Boisrond had cabled for a "corresponding member of the American Society for Psychical Research." Poggioli hardly knew whether to be amused or offended, whether to withdraw or to go on into the details of this extraordinary commission.

Dr. Vauquière was watching the white man's face.

"M'sieu," he said, "I attempted to enlist your sympathies for my people. I had hoped that a great scientist like you would not be merely amused at this danger which threatens my people. It is usual to smile, m'sieu, but unusual to help."

There was a gentleness to the rebuke that touched Poggioli. He stopped his faint smiling and half apologized by saying there was an incongruousness about the situation, then brought his thoughts back to the actual problem in hand. He visualized a black miracle worker being held somewhere in custody until he, Poggioli, a Fellow of the American Society for Psychological Research, could get to him and explain his mystifications.

However, he maintained a sober face. He wondered what phase of savage occultism the *caco* leader would affect— fire-walking, sword-swallowing, apoplectic spasms, prophesying. The difficulty was that Poggioli himself did not completely understand these abnormalities. He did not quite see how he could make it clear and simple to the rabble of Negroes in the *place*.

"Are we going straight to the prison, Dr. Vauquière?" he inquired out of these thoughts.

The physician looked around in surprise.

"Did you want to examine his victims, m'sieu?"

"His victims? Whose victims?"

"Jean LaFronde's. You sounded as if you knew that he cuts off the ears of men sent to him and sends them back mutilated as an advertisement of his power."

Poggioli stared at his companion.

"Why, no, I didn't know that!"

"You spoke of wanting to see the prisoners."

"I thought you had LaFronde himself in prison."

"If we had him in prison, m'sieu, we wouldn't need a psychologist to help break his power."

"How do you hope for me to see him and analyze what he does?" cried the psychologist.

"You may be able to arrange a visit to his camp in the mountains. You would go there, of course, in the rôle of a purely scientific investigator. I am sure LaFronde has heard of your tour through the West Indies. I fancy he would feel flattered to have you visit him."

"M—— But didn't you say that the men you have sent—ah——"

Poggioli broke off, not quite caring to express the uncertainty in his thoughts.

Vauquière interrupted and answered them.

"Oh, they were black fellows," he answered lightly, "sent out as the commonest sort of spies. LaFronde cut off their ears and sent them back. Naturally, he would not treat a scientific man with such discourtesy. Besides that, you are an American. LaFronde wouldn't want the marines back any more than we do."

Mr. Poggioli's amusement had vanished completely by now, and he sat frowning thoughtfully over this phase of his undertaking.

"By the way," he asked suddenly, "did you say these returned spies were in prison?"

The physician replied in the affirmative.

"But aren't they Governor Boisrond's own men returnèd to him? Why is he keeping them in prison?"

"Well," hesitated Vauquière, "that's the governor's idea. Public policy, I believe. But he will probably explain that to you himself. That is his mansion up there."

By this time the stanhope had threaded the crowded *place* and was approaching a long stone fence which delimited a jungle-grown hillside from the hot, flat market place. This hill rose sheerly behind its stone barricade, clad with lush shades of green of the jungle trees, and through the openings in the foliage an observer in the *place* below could catch glimpses of a column, the turn of a cornice, a window, or a stretch of the eaves, all of which hinted of a mansion of great magnificence on the summit.

Vauquière drove up to a great double gate guarded by two Negroes in the faded uniforms of American marines. These black men with rifles stood at attention as the stanhope approached, and saluted the occupants with a sharp military gesture as the vehicle whisked inside.

A shell road wound up this acclivity through the jungle, and the moment Poggioli passed out of the sunlight into the greenish gloom he felt as if painful little weights had been lifted from the back of his eyeballs. An earthy hothouse smell surrounded him, composed of the fragrances of flowers and the decaying odor of rank vegetation. The road itself ascended by easy turns and finally brought the stanhope to a terrace on the height where stood the mansion itself. A deep piazza surrounded the building on all four sides, and on the western sweep of the piazza sat three or four persons of color grouped around a great massive black man.

As Dr. Vauquière got out, a servant in livery hurried from some door beneath the piazza and took the horses. Poggioli followed his host up a wide flight of stone steps to be presented to the governor of Cap Haitien.

After the rather heavy magnificence of these surroundings the psychologist was quite taken aback at the governor himself. Boisrond was a massive black man with the heavy, rolling, almost alarming features one sometimes sees in thoroughly Negroid faces. Where Dr. Vauquière was trimly and gracefully vulpine, not to use the word in its bad sense at all, Boisrond was ursine. He was dressed in a great black broadcloth suit which he wore loutishly. When he acknowledged his introduction to Poggioli he did not use the meticulous French of Vauquière, but spoke a slovenly articulated Gallic, dropping now and then a word of the corrupt Creole used by the black plantation laborers on the island.

After recovering somewhat from his surprise at such a governor and an accompanying vague wonder as to how he had ever attained his seat, Poggioli turned his attention to the other persons on the veranda. One was the wife of Dr. Vauquière, a very pretty woman, an octoroon or thereabouts. There was a tall, well-tailored, chocolate-colored youth called Armand. Another woman was a Mrs. Napoleon LeClerc, a rather full-bodied, deep-breasted yellow woman with fine eyes. At a little distance from this group, in a spot of sunlight on the piazza, lay a disreputable old hound, intent, apparently, on baking its brains in the heat while it watched the massive governor with sleepy, faithful eyes.

There was still another person who might or might not have belonged to the party on the porch. Now and then she came out on the piazza for a few moments at a time; a fat old black woman hopelessly gowned in purple silk. She would come out, touch one of the potted plants or slightly move one of the empty chairs, then pass into the house again, only to reappear a few minutes later through some door or French window, repeat her trivial adjustments and vanish again. The manner in which Mrs. Vauquière and Mrs. LeClerc followed these in-and-out movements and once in a while smiled at the old creature suggested to Poggioli that this was Madame Boisrond, the governor's wife.

Madame Vauquière was the only discursive and lively person in the group. She began a feminine chatter as soon as she was introduced to Poggioli. She trusted that their beautiful Haiti had made a good impression on the psychologist. She said she never looked at the mountains out of her bedroom window of a morning but what she recalled her husband's remark in Paris. At that time she was on the stage acting opposite her husband, and Dr. Vauquière had said to her:

"Madeleine, we are going to Haiti."

"Why, Pierre?"

"Because the theater is too prosaic for me. My temperament requires a more theatrical *milieu*."

Here Mrs. Vauquière laughed deliciously at her husband's ancient *mot* and Armand laughed with her, the soft oily laugh of his race.

Vauquière spoke up, justifying his remark:

"The scenery here does give one a drop-curtain effect, M'sieu Poggioli. It really is rather more dramatic than a theater. Just step here and look."

He moved quickly to a certain position on the piazza and pointed toward some blue peaks visible in the southeast.

"Do you see that wide reddish scar on the crest of that central mountain, m'sieu? That is the most extraordinary piece of architecture on the Western Hemisphere. It is"— he paused and dropped his voice dramatically—"it is La Ferrière."

Poggioli looked at the distant red blur. As a matter of fact, he had never heard of La Ferrière. He was meditating whether he should ask a question and reveal his ignorance when Governor Boisrond broke into the conversation with an ill-bred brusqueness.

"We'd better stop staring at La Ferrière and tell M'sieu Poggioli what we want him for. No doubt he is in a hurry. Most *les blancs* are."

The small talk fell into an awkward silence; then the physician said smoothly:

"I was just about to suggest it."

He glanced about the group and added in that faint

intonation which dismisses unnecessary persons from a business conference:

"Perhaps we could have a pleasanter breeze at the other end of the piazza, Governor?"

At this the women arose hastily, declaring they must get their embroidery and magazines. Vauquière begged them with polite insincerity not to disturb themselves, but the governor simply frowned at them in a forbidding silence until the porch was cleared. Then he turned to Poggioli and reduced his voice to a husky rumble.

"M'sieu, you see in me a man tied up in spider-webs. I can't get at this Jean LaFronde. *Parbleu,* if I could only reach him with a handful of men, I'd——" He clenched a huge black fist in the thin air.

The psychologist nodded sympathetically.

"But I catch no more than that." He opened his empty, light-colored palm. "Move against him where I will, he reads my mind and is not there. It is chasing a jack-o'-lantern, m'sieu. He reads my mind. He knows where I will strike before I touch my sword. It is impossible to hew him down!"

The governor flung down his rough hands hopelessly.

The psychologist nodded again.

"I see. A clever tactician."

And he wondered where a psychologist would enter a purely military problem.

Vauquière sensed his slight disconnection.

"What Governor Boisrond means, m'sieu, is that this Jean LaFronde actually reads his mind, that he is in telepathic communication with him."

Poggioli stared at the executive.

"You don't mean he reads your thoughts?"

"Certainly I mean it," rumbled the black man in an

undertone. "If he could not read my mind I would catch him at once with my *rurales* and shoot him on sight." The rolling face contracted in a frown. "I know the mountains as well as Jean LaFronde does. I can fling a squad of men through the brush as fast as he can. I was a *caco* myself once, M'sieu Poggioli, before I forced M'sieu le Président to recognize me and appoint me governor of this department."

At this casual admission Poggioli suddenly understood this big, crude bear of a Negro who had pawed his way up from the meanest social depths to his present station.

Vauquière glossed over this somewhat awkward admission by saying: "Those were the days before the American occupation, M'sieu Poggioli, when the purest patriots of our island were forced to take to the brush to put down tyranny."

"That's right," nodded Boisrond grimly. "And if I don't keep this *caco*, Jean LaFronde down, he'll get my post."

"Why do you believe he can literally read your mind?" asked Poggioli curiously.

"*Parbleu*, m'sieu. He does it. I can't catch him. When I send spies to his camp he reads their minds at once, cuts off their ears, and sends them back to my *rurales* as warnings."

"I would not conclude from that that he had telepathic powers."

"Undoubtedly he is a voodoo, m'sieu."

"It is more likely that he has spies in your camp who keep him informed as to who will visit him."

The old dictator frowned.

"I am not a baby, m'sieu. Naturally I had thought of that. So I have secretly selected a trusted soldier and sent him to Jean LaFronde's camp as a deserter. No living soul knew of it except me and the soldier. Within a day he came to me with his ears off. And he would walk about the barracks—talking, talking, saying, 'Jean LaFronde is indeed a Papa Loi. He reads the heart. No living man can deceive Jean LaFronde. There's never been a bullet molded that can touch his skin.' "

Here the old *caco* drummed on his broadcloth knee.

"*Diable!* All my men believe it! There stands the fool with his ears off to prove it, and my own *rurales* go off in droves to join this Jean LaFronde against me!"

"I see," said Poggioli with more interest. "And these deserters from your army who go to him—does he cut their ears off, too, and send them back?"

"No, no, m'sieu!" bellowed the massive Negro with a bob of his woolly head. "If the man is really a deserter Jean LaFronde reads his heart like an open book and puts him into the *caco* ranks, but if he is a spy, *snip!* Off go his ears, and back he comes to me!"

"But why does he send them back?"

Here Armand interposed to say tensely:

"Because, m'sieu, it is the most successful method of advertising himself you can conceive of. Our *rurales* desert to him in shoals. The plantation Negroes hear of it and hurry to his camp. Every new mutilation creates a furor."

"Where are some of these mutilated men?" queried the psychologist.

"They are all in La Ferrière now," rumbled the governor in an annoyed growl. "When they come back I have to put them in La Ferrière."

"Is that a prison?" asked Poggioli, taken aback at the grimness of the situation.

"It's—La Ferrière," hesitated Armand. "Of course it

was not built for a prison, still——" He paused significantly.

"You see," interpolated Vauquière smoothly, "there was nothing to do except place these mutilated men in confinement. They would talk. A wonder had happened to them. They went about with a continual unconscious proselyting."

"My heavens!" cried Poggioli. "What a profound injustice! The very soldiers who were faithful and loyal, who suffered mutilation in your service, then to be cast into prison for their fidelity!"

"M'sieu," rumbled the governor dryly, "the reason I cabled for you was not to exclaim over half a dozen odd *rurales* in prison, but to keep the others out."

After a little pause Poggioli asked:

"Well, what do you want me to do about it?"

"*Diable*, m'sieu, I want you to give me and my men a *wanga*, charm, against this fellow. He has a strong *wanga* against us. Now you are a great Papa Loi. Make a stronger charm than this Jean LaFronde possesses, so we can read his mind and he cannot read ours. Then I'll catch him and —burn him like a dried stalk!"

Poggioli arose.

"You are ridiculous, Governor Boisrond," he said sharply. "I'm not a voodoo doctor, going around making amulets. I——"

Vauquière held up a placating hand just as Boisrond was about to belch out some furious retort.

"Wait, wait, m'sieu, just a word——"

"But this governor"—Poggiolo said the word with disgust—"seems to consider me a voodoo doctor."

"May I explain?"

"There is nothing to explain. If he imagines———"

"Won't you allow me, m'sieu, to show you that Governor Boisrond is paralleling in his world of thought, as best he can, the universe as you know it?"

A certain scholarly tang to this sentence caused the collegian to subside somewhat.

"Go ahead. I'm willing to hear what you can say."

"Then let me suggest, M'sieu Poggioli, that when an unschooled man speaks of voodooism or witchcraft he means exactly what the psychologist means when he speaks of phenomena. Both men are talking of the same thing. Everybody knows strange effects can be produced. A savage wants relief and he asks for a charm. An American wants relief and he asks to be psychoanalyzed. You two gentlemen have grown angry over your terminology, which is the basis of nine tenths of the philosophical and religious disputes in this world. All Governor Boisrond is asking you to do is to prevent Jean LaFronde from getting any further knowledge of his intentions."

Poggioli was forced to agree to this analysis. He regretted his curtness of speech. He said he supposed it was an outcrop of his mental attitude as a college professor, which ran to much dignity and little patience.

Dr. Vauquière was smiling over this *amende honorable* when Boisrond interrupted to ask bluntly:

"But what are you going to do about this *caco?*"

"First," said Poggioli good-temperedly, "I would like to see these mutilated men and have a talk with them. I want to analyze their statements and mental attitudes."

The ponderous executive got himself out of his chair.

"They're in La Ferrière. Let's go and see them now."

There was a directness about the big black man's actions which somehow reinstated him in Poggioli's esteem. If his vocabularly was rambling and somewhat insulting, his movements at least were pointed with the logic of the occasion. He was evidently about to set out at once for La Ferrière. It occurred to Poggioli that it was now high noon—the sunshine was like a Russian bath—also that he had not had his lunch. By way of indicating his feeling, he looked at the distant scar on the peak and asked suggestively:

"How far is it to La Ferrière, Governor Boisrond?"

"Twenty-two miles," rumbled the governor.

"How are we going to get there?" asked Poggioli, a little dismayed.

"In carriages. It will require about two hours."

Poggioli drew out his watch and looked at it significantly.

"Perhaps we'd better have lunch here and start a little later," suggested Dr. Vauquière.

"Are you hungry, M'sieu Poggioli?" asked the black man in a manner which suggested that he ate when he was hungry, regardless of the hours.

"I must confess I have an appetite."

"That's easy enough." He turned toward the hallway and boomed impatiently:

"Gateau! Gateau! What's keeping you, Gateau?"

Just as Boisrond was drawing in his breath for a really thunderous bellow the fat old black woman in purple silk appeared in the doorway.

"Gateau," said the governor, "have the servants make a meal at once."

"*Oui, oui*," bobbed the old crone in even more deplorable creole than her husband used.

"And, Gateau," ordered the governor roundly, "have it served in La Ferrière!" He made a gesture toward the dis-

tant mountain to make perfectly clear what he meant, then
rumbled:

"Now, let's be off!"

There was a stir among the men as they made ready
to go. Armand rushed into the house after his sun helmet
and linen ulster, without which, apparently, he could not
travel. When he came striding out on the porch with these
articles the governor growled briefly at him:

"You go on down the road to the gate with Vauquière.
I'll walk down the path with M'sieu Poggiolo."

Vauquière bowed his agreeableness, and he and Armand
started out, the short and tall figures of two carefully
dressed Negroes passing through the sunlight around the
curve of the shell road, and so out of sight.

Governor Boisrond watched them go, then set off at a
shambling gait with Poggioli about a half step behind him.
Twice the American made a little skip step to be even with
his host, but he was at once dropped a little to the rear
again by the ungainly black man. After a little distance
Boisrond deserted the road for a path that wound round
the hill through the jungle. Here there was not width for
walking abreast, and the psychologist followed on the
giant's long, noiseless steps. Presently the governor asked
over his shoulder in a low rumble:

"What do you think of this Jean LaFronde?"

"I'll have to gather more data to draw a conclusion,
Governor Boisrond."

Another silence as the executive lowered and twisted
himself about to avoid limbs and vines.

"Do you think Jean LaFronde pays my spies to have
their ears cut off?" he queried out of a clear sky.

Such an abrupt *volte-face* from his former superstitious
remarks about the *caco* leader surprised Poggioli.

"It is improbable that every one of your men would yield in the same way. Human nature usually has more variety than that."

"Then you think he really is a Papa Loi and can read men's minds?"

"I'll have to obtain more data."

The two moved on for some distance in silence. Presently the black man halted under a banyan, lifted his arms, and caught hold high up on two tertiary trunks. His broadcloth coat and white collar were twisted askew by the muscles in his massive shoulders and long powerful arms. Indeed he looked like nothing so much as some somber and grotesquely attired gorilla. He stood supporting the greater part of his weight on his arms and watching the American with his deep-set eyes. Evidently he was about to catechize the scientist. He stood so a few seconds and then asked in a muted rumble:

"What do you think of Mr. Clay?"

The question was so far away from the range of Poggioli's thoughts that he simply stood staring in the green twilight and repeated inanely:

"Mr. Clay?"

Boisrond nodded. "The customs collector," he explained guardedly.

"Why—I—saw him. He was impolite, dogmatic, rather extreme in his racial prejudices. Why do you ask me about Mr. Clay?"

"What do you think of Armand?"

"He is the usual adjunct to a wealthy man's household. Nobody knows what those people do but they seem to prosper in their profession, whatever it is."

Boisrond's bossed face and great lips formed into a molding of mirth.

"That is Armand. I like to see him about. Once I almost gave him a hundred *gourdes*, but somehow I didn't. He seems to have money. I don't know how he gets it. That's a point you should remember."

Poggioli began to see that this conversation was partially for his own instruction. He nodded and said nothing.

"Dr. Vauquière?"

"I think he is the smoothest courtier I ever saw," said the white man.

"He was an actor once in Paris."

"So I gathered."

"It was his profession," ruminated the giant, "to appear to feel what he did not. That is a point you should not overlook."

Poggioli began to study the dusky ogre with a perception of some unfathomed subtlety behind his sloping skull.

"What do you think of Madame LeClerc?"

"I barely saw her before she went into the house."

"She is the wife of Napoleon LaClerc, an assistant inspector of customs under Mr. Clay."

The American nodded understandingly. "I see you don't put complete faith in the theory that Jean LaFronde's information was acquired solely by mind-reading?"

"When a man sends for a doctor, m'sieu, he tells him his aches and gripes."

"I hope," said Poggioli, "that your suspicions do not include me, Governor Boisrond."

"M'sieu, you flared up at me a moment ago for asking you a silly thing. You are the first man except one who has been openly angry at me since the day I ordered former Governor Milleteau shot."

Poggioli nodded.

"And this other man who was openly angry with you, who was he?"

"Mr. Clay. The first time I went into his office he looked at me, leaped up, cursed, and almost frothed at the mouth. I could not understand English. Armand was with me. 'Armand,' I asked, 'what is he saying?' 'He is requesting you to take off your hat,' said Armand."

At such an episode Poggioli burst into loud, surprised laughter, but at that very moment was startled into silence by a faint rustling among the leaves just outside their covert. This slight noise caught at the psychologist's nerves with a painful start. The governor's whisperings and vague blanket suspicions of everybody had keyed the scientist up, unknown to himself. A moment later, however, their suspense was relieved by the governor's hound nosing into the little space where the two men stood.

The dog apparently plunged the black man into deep thought. He stood for several moments studying the animal, then broke off to say briskly:

"Well, on to La Ferrière to see what Jean LaFronde does to the prisoners!"

He swung himself about with his arms and the next minute was striding down the difficult path with such swiftness that several times Poggioli was forced to ask him to slacken his pace.

At the gate of the governor's grounds the men arranged themselves in a waiting carriage with that instinctive selection which places congenial persons together. Poggioli and Dr. Vauquière occupied the rear seat; Armand and

Governor Boisrond, the front. Armand drove a pair of gray English coach horses at a round pace over the hard-surfaced road.

As soon as the party was clear of the squalid reaches of Cap Haitien, the queer three-ply civilization of the country set in. At intervals along the road were moldered ruins of that old French life which, during the Napoleonic era, had made Haiti one of the richest of France's possessions and Cap Haitien the Paris of the American hemisphere.

Out in the sugar fields lay the outlines of those vanished manors, and beside them, often upon their crumbled foundations, stood the miserable *yagua* huts of the Negroes who had overthrown that opulent French world. In final contrast to these survivals was the beautiful hard-finished road which the Americans had built and which they now, in turn, deserted to the black population.

It was a queer ensemble of history, of colliding human desires and ambitions, and as the psychologist drove through the sun-baked acres, it filled his thoughts with a certain dim questioning which seemed, somehow, to involve this very rôle which he personally was just beginning to play.

In the midst of this silent catechism which his surroundings propounded, Armand swung aside his grays to allow the passage of a rather dilapidated American automobile which came clacking down the road. Poggioli came out of his musing to see the long angular form of Mr. Clay at the wheel, and by his side sat the Jewish insurance agent, Mr. Osterwasski.

Poggioli recognized his fellow passenger with that odd sense of pleasure a man feels in meeting on land a person he has known on shipboard. The psychologist brightened up, waved a gay hand at Osterwasski, and went so far as to nod affably at Clay. The two men, however, merely glanced at the carriage with the briefest of nods and rattled on down the road.

The psychologist was surprised at this slight, especially from Osterwasski, who had seemed one of those punctilious, coldly agreeable men who would carefully avoid making either an enemy or a friend.

Vauquière smiled dryly and explained their grievance.

"The *cacos* have raided the Minot plantations a little farther on, and the owner is wanting a settlement with the insurance company for his losses. These men have been out to take testimony in the case, and Gravelotte Minot, that is the man the *cacos* robbed, was not at home."

Poggioli stared at his companion.

"Why should he cut me?"

Vauquière spread his hands.

"A general social *malaise*, m'sieu. They are soured on the world."

"But the cause of their offense is absurd—a man not being at home!"

"*Cá*, to tell you the truth, m'sieu, this Gravelotte Minot will not be at home and they know it. He has doubtless followed the *cacos* and joined them. They will not get his testimony and certainly will have to pay the insurance."

The scientist was still more amazed.

"You don't mean he joined the *cacos* after they robbed him?"

The governor turned in his seat and bent his big gargoyle face on his guest.

"That is exactly what they do, m'sieu. Every Negro who is robbed immediately joins the *cacos*. How to stop that is part of your problem. It is the work of the devil!"

A little later the carriage passed the Minot estate, as

the West Indians call their farms. The Minot hut stood at some distance from the road in a field of ill-tended sugar cane. The travelers could just see the thatched roof of the hut above the waving green cane, and still higher than this, stuck up on a pole as a guard against the spells of the voodoo, hung the long white skull of a horse.

Under the palms at the edge of the boulevard stood a ragged Negro woman, where, no doubt, she had been summoned by the white men for interrogation. She had not gone back to her hut, but had remained under the shade of the palms with the listlessness of her kind.

"Do she and her husband own this plantation?" queried Poggioli curiously.

"*Sacrebleu,* man, no," rumbled the governor. "It's my plantation! They're my tenants, the shiftless idlers! Ho, Isabel!" shouted the giant as he went past. "Go back and get to work! Do something!"

The woman turned with sullen, unwilling movements and slowly retreated with her rags and pigtails bobbing in protest. And, indeed, what profitable task Isabel could do when she reached her hut, Poggioli could not imagine.

As the carriage bowled on, remnants of an old stone fence lay beneath the organ cactus which now served the purpose of a hedge for the governor's estate. The stone ruin implied again the thriftiness of the murdered French colony. This and the organ cactus hard beside the wide American road suggested once more to the scientist the same vague problem on which the discourtesy of Clay and Osterwasski appeared to hang.

He rode ahead, somewhat disturbed and quite unable to clarify this feeling of being somehow implicated in this incongruous blending of past and present, when Dr. Vauquière said:

"You must not judge our race's ability by this poor scum, M'sieu Poggioli. That would be as unfair as estimating one of your American cities by its slums. Look up yonder at the mountain top. You will have to admit that into the text of this scenery, *mon ami*, before you can get at the truth of this situation."

The psychologist was surprised at how closely the yellow man had shot at his reverie. He followed Dr. Vauquière's gesture and saw that the red gash which he had seen from the governor's piazza had now expanded into a vast reddish precipice.

Poggioli was still unaware of what La Ferrière might be, and now he stared at this prodigious cliff in the mountain's massif, quite at sea as to what possible connection this salient feature of a gigantic landscape could have on the perplexity in his heart. He continued staring at its enormous surface, still so distant that the swift trot of the horses had no perceptible effect in adding to its details. However, there was something about it which suggested that it might be something else than merely a prodigious mountain face. Finally his growing curiosity made him ask:

"Dr. Vauquière, what is La Ferrière?"

At the question, the governor and the two colored men looked at their guest in the blankest amazement. After a pause Vauquière said with a certain expression:

"Don't you see, m'sieu, it is a precipice rather higher, I should say, than your Woolworth Building."

"That's what it seems," admitted Poggioli doubtfully.

At this Armand broke into his courteous, oiled laughter.

"Certainly, that's just what it seems, and no doubt it is what it is. Everything in Haiti, M'sieu Poggioli, is exactly what it seems. That's a characteristic of our country."

Governor Boisrond burst into rough laughter at Armand's friendly satire, but after a moment became sober enough once more.

The white man gazed at the monstrous expanse, and by this time the carriage had gained on it sufficiently to show the lines and gloomy modeling of a cyclopean masonry.

The effect of seeing the mountain resolve itself into some sort of enormous castle or citadel was one of the most amazing experiences Poggioli had ever known. Considered as a mountain, it dominated the landscape, but as a work of man it dwindled all the hot, wide-flung country about to a scene in Lilliput.

The governor's party behind the big English coach horses were reduced to the folk out of a fairy story, whisking along in a walnut shell behind a team of mice. The very jungle trees at the foot of this vast architecture were shrunk to a green moss. As the carriage went still nearer, La Ferrière's bulk obscured the southern sky, and even then its distance was stingy of detail. Innumerable eyelets became visible in the lower part of its upward sweep. Vauquière pointed them out.

"Those dots, m'sieu—you can make out some of the lowest ones—are the embrasures of cannon."

Poggioli looked his stupefaction.

"That is why I asked you to reserve your opinion. All that was thought out and built by the same people who live to-day in these little *yagua* huts, M'sieu Poggioli—the Haitian Negroes."

Poggioli stared in silence as the carriage began winding upward toward the hugest piece of masonry on the Western Hemisphere.

A little farther on the governor's party was forced to leave the carriage and mount a narrow, rugged path on foot. By the time they had ascended to the heights of the fortification all were blown and lagging except possibly the executive himself, who still walked with the same shambling strength which he had exhibited at the beginning of the climb.

Once on the heights, Poggioli's heart was quickened by the far horizon of a mountain view. Almost under his feet lay Cap Haitien beside a bay of transparent blue. Far to the south along the gleaming sinuosities of the coast line he could make out a blur which was Port-au-Prince. To the west arose the blue peaks of Santo Domingo.

This royal aerie was hewn along vast lines. Poggioli might have been standing in the midst of a fortified plain. Rows of huge ancient cannon, each with its pyramid of rusty cannon balls beside it, extended in a long curve around the parapet until they diminished in perspective to children's toys. The walls through which these ancient dogs once bayed were twenty-five feet thick and were built of solid hewn stones. How such monoliths were elevated to this dizzy height stunned the imagination. The panorama and the cyclopean work seemed to excite Dr. Vauquière.

"This was built by Henri Christophe, a slave who made himself an emperor! Think of it! What a gesture!"

Poggioli approached the vertiginous brink. The thought of men straining at these enormous stones, truing their edges over empty space, dizzied him.

"What a toll of lives this must have taken!" he ejaculated.

"Thousands," agreed Vanquière readily. "If we can believe the legends about Christophe, hundreds of men were executed in forcing the labor."

"What an abominable tyranny!"

Vauquière flared up out of his customary suavity.

"A tyranny that leaves a work like this, m'sieu, is not abominable. It at least erects something that will stand against the current of time. A tyranny is admirable because, in the hands of a great autocrat, it can focus the whole force of a people on some great work like La Ferrière or the pyramids. But a democracy—that is, force scattered among a multitude of insignificant purposes—accomplishes little or nothing."

"It accomplishes freedom," retorted Poggioli.

"And what is democratic freedom except a vicious system of government by which the natural leaders of mankind are forced to spend three fourths of their power persuading men to follow them instead of commandeering a people and devoting their whole energy to some magnificent undertaking? The colored races form natural despotisms, m'sieu, and it is significant that the mightiest works in the world have been lifted by dark hands—the Taj, the Alhambra, the Sphinx, the Temples of Elephanta, and La Ferrière."

Just as Vauquière reached this rather surprising conclusion the two men were interrupted by the rumble of Governor Boisrond's voice calling in brusque creole:

"M'sieu Poggioli, if you want to talk to the prisoners, come and talk to them!"

The American looked around and saw the huge black man apparently sunk to his knees in the stone pavement of the fort. The two men went forward quickly and found the executive on a great stairway that led down into the lower stories of the citadel. This flight of stairs was of the same herculean proportions as the rest of the building. On descending it, the governor and his party entered a huge chamber with its gloom relieved only by the light which this stairway admitted from the side. They descended still another flight of stairs and still another, until they had gone down five stories of this stupendous fortress. The walls of every story were pierced for cannon, and the huge rusting guns still peered out into the abyss. The great fort was exactly as Emperor Christophe had left it more than a century before.

On the dank bottom floor of this fortress Poggioli walked through the alternate lights and shadows admitted through the embrasures, and presently was startled to see a man lying chained to the breech of one of the cannon. At the approach of the party this man got to his feet. At the next cannon beyond another figure arose, and so on with a rattling of their chains until seven Negroes stood lined up along the embrasures. They lifted their hands stiffly to their kinky heads in salute to the governor. The smell of closely confined men filled the clammy air.

The ponderous governor waved an ursine paw at the dismal line-up.

"There you are, m'sieu," he said in an echoing tone. "That first man's name is Clocher. Ask him what you like and I'll have him answer."

Then Poggioli saw that Clocher's ears were missing. This repulsive detail was repeated in each one of the seven men. The plight of these unfortunates, whose only offense was their fidelity to the governor and the natural garrulousness of simple men, moved the psychologist to a keen pity. He began questioning Clocher, at the same time wondering how he might set the wretch at liberty. When did he go to Jean LaFronde's camp? Who appointed him as spy? Did anyone besides Governor Boisrond know he was going? Did he go alone?

To all these questions Clocher mumbled his answer and nodded his kinky head this way and that after the fashion of illiterate Negroes.

It appeared that four other *rurales* had gone to the *caco* camp with Clocher. These four had been genuine deserters. They had slipped out of Cap Haitien for the *caco* camp at about two o'clock in the morning.

"What time did you arrive?" went on the psychologist.

"It took us till sun-up," mumbled Clocher, casting an uneasy eye at the governor.

"How did you find the way?"

Here Vauquière interposed to say that LaFronde had *cacos* posted along the route to direct deserters to his camp.

"He is doing a wholesale business!" ejaculated Poggioli.

"He wants to be governor," growled Boisrond. "Unless you can stop him, m'sieu, I might as well fly from Cap Haitien while I am alive."

The scientist turned to Clocher again.

"What happened to you at the camp?"

"We heard them singing and dancing and the guard went to see if we could come in."

"You were admitted?"

"*Oui*, m'sieu."

"Did you see Jean LaFronde?"

"*Oui.*"

"What sort of fellow was he?"

"A tall, dark man, m'sieu, with a knife stuck through his arm."

Poggioli hesitated at this unexpected detail.

"A knife through his arm?"

"Through his wrist, m'sieu. He ıs a Papa Loi."

Poggioli turned to his companions.

"There is a clue to the whole performance, gentlemen. A cheap street-fair trick like that."

Clocher repeated earnestly the conviction which had got him chained down in the bowels of La Ferrière.

"It really was through his wrist, m'sieu. I saw it with my own eyes. The point came out three or four inches on the back of his wrist."

The psychologist nodded.

"That's all right, Clocher. Then what did he do to you?"

"We walked up to him through a long line of dancing *cacos*. The guards took away our knives and rifles. When we came to him he took a drop of our blood, put it on his tongue and swallowed it. That gave him power over us."

"Why so?" asked Poggioli.

"M'sieu, he was a Papa Loi. He had swallowed a drop of our blood!"

"Yes, yes, then what happened?"

"He said, 'Are you a true *caco* at heart?' and all of us said, '*Oui, oui,* Papa Loi!' He said, 'When these drops of blood reach my heart I will know what is in your heart. If you are not honest *cacos* go away now and never let me see your faces again.'"

Clocher's eyes widened at this uncanny reminiscence.

"But you didn't go away?"

"No, m'sieu, I was a spy."

"What about the others?"

"They stayed, too. They were true *cacos* at heart."

"But he didn't cut off the ears of these other men?"

"Oh, no. When their blood reached his heart he knew they were true *cacos*, and he knew that I was a spy."

Here the simplicity of Clocher's belief somehow annoyed Poggioli.

"Clocher," he cried, "don't you know that's all foolishness? When all those drops of blood went down his throat together what makes you think he could tell one from the other?"

Clocher stared at the psychologist, clearly surprised at such skepticism; then he turned his head in silence and pointed at his missing ear.

Poggioli recovered from his impatience and smiled. It occurred to him that pragmatism had seduced abler minds than Clocher's.

"Let me see," he began again. "LaFronde said he would know when your drop of blood reached his heart. There was a time element in it. He didn't know immediately that you were a spy."

"No, m'sieu."

"How long did it take him to find that out?"

"When that drop of blood reached——"

"That's all right about the drop of blood. You may, forget that. When did he come up to you and say, 'Clocher, you're a spy, I'm going to cut off your ears'?"

"He—he never did say that to me, m'sieu."

"Well, when did he cut off your ears?"

"He—he never did cut off my ears."

"They're gone!"

"*O-Oui*, they're gone. He—jest wished 'em off. He's a Papa Loi."

"Clocher!" snapped Poggioli with a professor's impatience, "tell me what happened after this blood ceremony!"

"Tell him," rumbled Boisrond, taking a step toward the prisoner.

Clocher began rattling:

"Me and a guard went to a *yagua*, a—a little house. He left me by myself. I sat down. I was in the *yagua*——"

"Well, we know that. You've said it a dozen times!"

"Then my ears fell off, m'sieu, and I went home," finished the Negro, in evident mystification himself.

"Perhaps a beating would assist his memory!" rumbled Governor Boisrond angrily.

Dr. Vauquière gave a shrug. "There's no getting any sense out of these Negroes."

Poggioli proceeded on another line of attack.

"Your ears came off and you went home at once? What time was it when you left the *caco* camp?"

"The sun was straight up."

"About twelve o'clock?"

"*Oui*, m'sieu."

"How did you get away from the camp?"

"A *caco* blindfolded me and led me around and around in the jungle. When he took the cloth off my eyes I was on the road to Cap Haitien."

"Now, look here, Clocher," cornered the psychologist, "you reached this camp at sunrise. You left it at noon. Then you must have stayed there for six hours. What did you do in that time?"

"M'sieu, I did not stay six hours! I went away at once!"

"But you were forced to, arriving at dawn and leaving at twelve. Now what did you do?"

Clocher seemed amazed. He scratched his bullet-shaped head, leaned over and looked at his feet. He had never before observed that gap in his recollections. Suddenly he had the solution.

"M'sieu!" he cried in relief, "Jean LaFronde cast a *wanga* on the sun and made it jump from the horizon to the top of the world all in a minute. I saw him do it. Jean LaFronde is a Papa Loi."

The psychologist gave up his attempt with Clocher and

turned to the other Negroes, but they had taken warning from their comrade. Their testimony coincided precisely with his except they left no gaps of time unexplained. Each one of them had seen Jean LaFronde point at the sun, and had seen the sun leap suddenly to midheaven. However, it became clear that each of the earless men had remained in Jean LaFronde's camp four or five hours, although what they did during this interval Poggioli could not determine.

Governor Boisrond naturally observed this hiatus in their stories, and he motioned Poggioli aside.

"My spies are lying," he said in a heavy undertone. "I think we would best beat them after all."

"No," said Poggioli, "that would do no good. They are genuinely confused."

"But why do they say the sun jumped and their ears came off?"

"They are rationalizing."

"What's that?"

"They don't know what happened, and their minds automatically try to bridge in the gap. What they are striving for is a logic to carry on their thoughts. Logic is supposed to be a test of truth, Governor, but it is the mother of a million falsities. The human mind cannot accept a gap in its reflections, so it invents fillers, and that is the basis of religion and metaphysics."

"I believe a beating would help," persisted the governor.

"For heaven's sake, don't make martyrs out of these men!" cried the psychologist. "Somehow or other, torture sets a rationalist firmer in his faith." The scientist stood staring out through an embrasure onto a diminished landscape a thousand feet below him. "Here, I have thought of a way. I believe I can change these poor devils into good patriotic *rurales* whom you can set at liberty and who will automatically become advocates of the regular government."

"How's that?" rumbled the giant skeptically.

"Let's go back to the men a moment."

The two men returned to the fettered Negroes and Poggioli braced his thoughts for a genuine forensic effort. He cleared his throat.

"Men," he began to the seven Negroes, "who do you think would make the best governor—a Papa Loi, who could read your hearts, or just an ordinary man like one of us?"

The seven stared at Poggioli, and then looked around at each other at this remarkable question. Finally one of the Negroes in a low tone answered truthfully:

"M'sieu, a Papa Loi, of course."

"But look here," argued the American, "think how unpleasant it would be to have a governor who could read your hearts. Look at this Jean LaFronde who cut off your ears for telling him one lie. Now suppose you had a governor who knew every sinful thought in your hearts, who instantly detected every theft, every perjury, every drunkenness, every assault. Don't you know that everybody would land in jail or on the gallows? Do you suppose there is a man in Cap Haitien who hasn't done enough at some time in his life to be hanged? Why, gentlemen, a Papa Loi would be the most dangerous governor you could have. What you need and what Cap Haitien needs is just an ordinary man like Governor Boisrond, if you hope to stay out of prison."

The seven chained Negroes stared at this remarkable viewpoint of supernatural governors with widened eyes.

"*Oui, oui,* dat's right, m'sieu!"

"Instead of talking about how Jean LaFronde read your hearts, you men should have pointed out what a dangerous governor LaFronde would make."

"*Oui,* that's a fact," agreed Clocher. "He cut off our ears just because we told him one lie."

"What would he have done if his wife and daughters had been there?"

Armand suddenly shouted with laughter at this extraordinary twist Poggioli had given to the qualifications for a governor.

The psychologist came back to Boisrond, smiling.

"If you could get these fellows to proselyting for you instead of against you. You see their missing ears are just as good an argument for you as for LaFronde. I don't see why you couldn't order the wretches released and let them spread that point of view."

The men were walking back toward the great staircase again.

"I had never thought of that argument," rumbled the governor. "I hope we can find some way of spreading it over Cap Haitien, but these men"—he nodded back at the prisoners chained to the moldering cannon—"these men saw Jean LaFronde point at the sun and make it jump."

On the drive back from the Brobdingnagian fortress the governor growled:

"What do you think of this Jean LaFronde now, m'sieu?"

"A charlatan, no doubt."

"Did he read the prisoners' minds?"

"The Negroes mix what they saw and what they imagined so badly. It leaves a man balanced between two or three hypotheses, Governor."

"What are they?" asked the giant, turning in his seat to look back at his guest, while both Vauquière and Armand gave the American closer attention.

"He may have a system of espionage by which he is able to keep pretty close tab on deserters and know which are spies and which are genuine deserters."

Both Armand and the governor nodded.

"Then, he may be an actual mind-reader. There are such persons. Thus, in a way, he would qualify as a voodoo doctor, but there would be nothing supernatural about it. However, that point would be difficult to explain to the *hoi polloi* here in the islands."

"That's exactly what it would be," laughed Armand.

"Then, that gap in the memories of the prisoners suggests a possibility of the use of drugs of some sort, but I don't quite see how a *caco* in the Haitian brush would get hold of a pharmacopœia."

The three black men considered this.

"As I said before," rumbled the governor, "this La-Fronde is a man of education, M'sieu Poggioli. I wouldn't wonder if he had accomplices in Port-au-Prince itself."

"Well, that's one phase. Then he may be a simple sleight-of-hand artist, as the knife sticking through his wrist suggests. By scaring the recruits he may be a skillful enough reader of character to determine his friends from his enemies."

"That's a good many different sorts of explanation," grumbled Boisrond.

"Certainly, it is like a chemical analysis. One tests everything."

"When you see this Jean LaFronde for yourself," rumbled the governor, "you will be able to explain his tricks and stop his influence."

Poggioli fell silent. He enjoyed the analytical part of the problem, but this notion of going out into the brush to interview an outlaw was something different. Armand began whistling a lively waltz under his breath. There was a certain hint of raillery in his music.

The psychologist was really curious about this *caco* chief and his wonders, real or pretended; on the other hand, he had no desire at all to jeopardize his own safety, just as Armand's whistling suggested. Poggioli felt very strongly that the world should be made safe for science. In other words, Poggioli had the conservative temperament of the brunette type. As the horses bowled along he decided positively that he would not go to the *caco* camp, and began thinking what excuse he could make. He decided he would enter the plea that he did not have time, that he was sailing for Barbados on the *Talleyrand* at the end of the week.

As he decided on this, the grays clattered into the dusty *place* of Cap Haitien amid the usual excitement of Negroes getting out of the way. The governor directed Armand to drive by the market, a great open shed filled with stalls and presenting a kaleidoscope of tropical wares: fruits, caged birds, palm-fiber hats, and the rainbow fish of the Caribbean. Flies buzzed everywhere. The smell of tropical flowers and decaying vegetables was in the air.

The governor stopped the carriage in front of an old crone who squatted on the pavement beside some piles of arica nuts, potatoes, and charcoal, which formed her stock in trade.

"Auntie," called the governor, "when you go back into the mountains send word to Jean LaFronde that M'sieu

Poggioli, the great American voodoo inspector, will come and inspect his camp."

The old woman, whose face looked like dark wrinkled crape, stared in amazement at this remarkable message. Her mouth dropped open.

"A voodoo inspector, *mon gouverneur!*"

"Certainly, you know the Americans inspect everything. Tell Jean LaFronde to have his men on the lookout and see that he gets safely to his camp."

"Maria in heaven!" gasped the old negress. "Inspect a Papa Loi! These Americans are utterly mad!"

By this time the conversation had collected quite a gallery. Somebody called out:

"Is m'sieu not afraid?"

"Not of the devil himself, m'sieu," laughed Armand. "These Americans would inspect the grids of hell."

The withered old vender crossed herself.

Poggioli turned to Vauquière.

"Is it possible for the governor to send a message to Jean LaFronde by the first vender he sees?"

The physician made a gesture.

"Cap Haitien is like a spider's web, m'sieu. Touch a thread and it all quivers."

Poggioli said to no one in particular and with an air of sudden remembrance:

"By the way, I won't be able to go on this junket. My ship sails to-morrow."

A Negro's voice from the press called: "What ship, m'sieu?"

"The *Talleyrand.*"

Two or three voices called out in unison: "Do not worry, M'sieu Voodoo Inspector. The *Talleyrand* is three days late. The wharfinger got it over the radio."

Poggioli looked around over the crowd and repeated earnestly: "I don't want to miss that ship."

While they were at the market place Armand and Vauquière got out to follow to the executive mansion on foot. As Poggioli drove back with Governor Boisrond he hatched up more objections to the proposed trip to the *caco* camp.

"By the way, Governor, I can't possibly get to this Jean LaFronde's camp without a guide."

"He will have men posted to watch out for you."

"But he won't allow a psychologist in his camp coming with the avowed purpose of exposing his tricks."

"If he does not, every Negro on the island will say at once he is no true Papa Loi. He would not dare refuse you admittance."

The carriage rolled on a bit.

"I don't suppose he would try to cut my ears off to show his power?"

"Ill-treat an American? He would be afraid the marines would return and that would end all his plans."

Just then the psychologist's reluctance struck out a perfectly new objection.

"Look here, Governor," he exclaimed with quite a show of frank willingness to go, "there is no use in my making the trip after all. The mystery to be solved is how Jean LaFronde can pick out spies. If I go to the camp alone there will be no new arrival of either spy or deserters for me to observe."

Boisrond nodded.

"I had thought of that, m'sieu. I shall select two men to go with you, a genuine spy and a genuine deserter. You can see what happens to both."

"You have two such men?" asked Poggioli with a dampened feeling.

"I have the spy, m'sieu. A deserter can be picked up along the road."

"Who is he? I hate for another man to have his ears lopped off."

"This man won't," stated the black giant positively. "I think all my other men were frightened by the knife in Jean LaFronde's wrist. The man I will send is afraid of nothing."

"Who is he?" repeated the American curiously.

The governor scrutinized his companion.

"You will give no sign, m'sieu, no hint?"

The scientist spread his hands.

"I will have to know anyway to see if he picks the right man."

"That's true." Came a pause, then the huge black man said simply, "I am going myself, m'sieu."

The white man stared at the Negro.

"Not you!"

Boisrond nodded.

"If he gets you in his power don't you know he will kill you?"

"He will not know I am the governor. Merely a clumsy black deserter flying from Governor Boisrond's camp."

"But even if he finds out you are a spy and cuts off your ears, don't you know your prestige would be utterly gone? Not one of your *rurales* would remain with you!"

"No, but if he fails to detect the governor, m'sieu, that will be the end of Jean LaFronde. He wagers as much as I do."

Poggioli was genuinely disturbed, and used all the arguments he could summon against such a venture, but he could not budge the huge black man.

It struck Poggioli as he studied the great gargoyle face

that this was the very stuff out of which were woven the epics of any primitive people. From such material were cut the sagas, Beowolf, the Germanic legends, except that this man was black.

As the carriage passed into the grounds of the mansion, the governor rumbled:

"Be ready to go with me at two o'clock in the morning, m'sieu. We will pick up some deserter already on the road."

A little later they drew up at the mansion. Servants came out to take the horses. As they climbed the steps Boisrond roared for a man to come show M'sieu Poggioli to his rooms.

The two men separated in the extremely high hall of the mansion, and Poggioli followed a servant up to the second story to a suite of chambers which had been set apart for his use. His bags were already in his dressing room. His sitting room had large windows giving a view of Manzanilla Bay, where the sinking sun had paved the waters with a shimmering brass. From a western course of windows he could see the mountain peaks wrapped in copper and purple; and in the midst of this a patch of carmine marked the distant fortress of La Ferrière.

The scientist set about dressing for dinner, thinking of the fortress, the vanished tyrant Christophe, and Vauquière's odd defense of tyrants and tyranny. That was an odd position, as if the human race were created for the especial purpose of leaving behind it monuments. His thoughts drifted to his engagement with Governor Boisrond. At two o'clock he and Governor Boisrond would set out for the camp of Jean LaFronde. A mixture of anxiety and curiosity arose in Poggioli as to the outcome of such a quixotic adventure. What really was Governor Boisrond trying to do? Cast discredit on Jean LaFronde? Poggioli had a feeling that behind any such vague purpose as that the man had some clear-cut, definite object. The black giant's direct, logical actions suggested this. But what this purpose might be, Poggioli could not guess. He was still thinking about it when the dinner gong sounded through the building. Poggioli finished his toilet and went down.

At the dinner table Armand was bubbling over with news of the market place. He said everybody was discussing which would make the better governor, a Papa Loi or an ordinary man. It seemed the servants who had started to La Ferrière with the lunch failed to reach the fortress in time for the governor's party, so they had given the food to the Negro prisoners.

While they ate, these seven men debated the question Poggioli had left with them—the relative merits of a Papa Loi and an ordinary man for governor. The servants in turn had seized on the question, and when they had returned to Cap Haitien they had offered it to the wisdom of the market place. The result was that everybody was vociferously debating the political expediency of Papa Loi and non Papa Loi governors.

"See what you have done, M'sieu Poggioli," cried Armand with tears of laughter in his black eyes. "You've introduced a new note into Haitian politics. This will become a national issue. Miracle workers will run for the presidency on Papa Loi tickets."

"How did the sentiment go?" inquired Boisrond, taking the question with perfect seriousness.

"An even split," laughed Armand, wiping his eyes. "I never saw a single debater without an opponent."

Vauquière was philosophically amused at the question. "I say the Papa Lois will win. The human idea of a final judgment day with a deity as an arbiter is nothing more than a magnified Papa Loi, a judge who can read the human heart."

"But everybody dreads the judgment day," laughed Armand.

"You are wrong," persisted the physician. "Every human being thinks a really omniscient judge would pardon him because deep in his heart every person feels all his acts are justified, even to the most wicked and foolish. That is the real root of religion, messieurs—humanity's longing for an omnipotent being who understands and pardons all."

Poggioli scarcely followed this odd discussion, but pursued his way through the many courses of the dinner preoccupied with the thoughts of his own and Governor Boisrond's coming adventure. Now and then he glanced at the governor, who sat at the head of the table swathed in a great napkin in the French style. Each time he wished for the governor's success, and more and more feared a tragic outcome.

Poggioli finished his meal, and soon after excused himself and retired to his suite of rooms. He switched on the light in his big cool chamber and began to lay out his clothes for his early-morning expedition. Then he began to fill a bag with certain psychological instruments he thought he might use. It was barely possible that he might make some genuine advance in the theory of primitive occultism. Here his natural scientific enthusiasm caught him up and he fancied himself making all sorts of laboratory experiments upon both the *caco* leader and his victims. He would read the result of his study before the psychological association. He had quite a moment there alone in his room.

When he had finished his bag the scientist's enthusiasm moved him to walk downstairs and out on the terrace, where he sought the sedative of a cigarette and the star-strewn sky.

He chose a beat on the edge of the terrace between the dark outline of a Bougainvillea on one end and the lacelike film of a frangipanni on the other and began a slow, peripatetic musing back and forth.

His nerves were still jumpy with the idea of some new brilliant theory on primitive psychology. If he could determine some quantitative relation between, say, heartbeats and insensibility to pain, his discovery might go down in the history of psychology as Poggioli's Theorem.

And then he would become immortal.

Along with Galileo, Helmholtz, Freud.

Poggioli moved up and down the terrace with the stars in his eyes.

Once, as he was turning away from the Bougainvillea, he heard a faint rustling in its inky shadows. It did not disturb his musings. He made two more circuits when he heard it again more strongly. He was just leaving the heavy bush. This time it caused him to glance over his shoulder. He saw an indistinct figure reach out of the foliage. In the darkness it seemed to be running from him, but the very next breath he saw it was some man charging him. Poggioli tried to fling himself into a position of defense. As his assailant closed with him he glimpsed the glint of steel in the starlight. He grabbed at the knife hand, caught the wrist, the next instant staggered backward under the rush. He struggled to hold off the steel and shouted for help at the top of his lungs.

The miscreant tried to jerk the knife loose, but Poggioli clung on desperately. He jammed his hand into the fellow's throat, but the assassin clenched down his chin while he slowly bent Poggioli's arm backward. The psychologist leaped back, whirled the fellow around, struck with all his might. He yelled and lunged backward again. At that moment his foot went over the edge of the terrace.

Through some mental twist Poggioli received a hideous impression that he was falling from the enormous battlement of La Ferrière. As he fell he shrieked his despair. The next moment he struck the soft grass a few feet below him. His assailant was somehow flung completely over his head, out into the very edge of the jungle.

Poggioli kicked desperately to straighten up and receive another attack when lights came swarming across the terrace. Voices shouted in Creole:

"Who is it? What's the matter?"

The psychologist scrambled upright and saw Governor Boisrond and Armand and half a dozen guards with rifles. He began panting out that he had been attacked; his assailant must have darted off in the jungle.

"What direction?" roared the governor.

Poggioli pointed.

"Lie down!" rumbled the governor, making a smashing gesture at Poggioli; then, "Make ready, men! Take aim! Fire!"

Came a terrific crash of old-fashioned American Krags right over Poggioli's head. The six guards had discharged their rifles in the direction Poggioli had indicated. The American realized what was about to happen in time to throw himself flat on his stomach. Even then the crash of the rifles sent pains through his ears.

"Charge down there; arrest anybody you find!" roared Boisrond, and the palace guards dashed off into the thick growth with their lights.

The American stood watching them with shaken nerves, until their lanterns got farther and farther away and were, at last, mere dim reflections among the trees.

"I don't suppose they hit anybody or will find anybody," grumbled Boisrond as they disappeared, "but that was the only thing to do."

A few moments later Vauquière came running out of the mansion, asking the cause of the uproar.

The governor explained with his customary precision.

"What effrontery! Right here in the governor's grounds! Who do you suppose did it?"

Poggioli had no idea. He recalled now a perfume of sandalwood about his assailant.

"It may not have been meant for you at all, M'sieu Poggioli, or it may have been LaFronde's answer to your proposed visit to his camp, or it may have been pique at your philosophy about the undesirability of a Papa Loi for governor——"

He broke off, pondering.

"It wasn't Jean LaFronde at all," rumbled Boisrond.

"Why do you say that?" asked Vauquière in surprise.

"He hasn't had time to get our message and return instructions. It's somebody in Cap Haitien."

"His spies, perhaps?"

"They wouldn't have ventured such an attack on their own responsibility."

"You may be right," agreed Vauquière without confidence.

A slight sound behind the three men caused them to turn; Poggioli and Vauquière with a start, Boisrond deliberately. Then they saw the governor's disreputable hound sniffling at his master's legs and wagging a dim tail at the happy reunion.

The hound seemed to give some obscure cue of action, for the men turned and started briskly down the shell road to see if the *battue* of the soldiers had scared up any game. They walked by the light of the governor's lantern, and were perhaps halfway down when they heard shouts and a shot from the direction of the gate; then a loud altercation.

They hurried on, when at the turn in the road there was a flashing of lighted lanterns; then just inside the gate they made out three men, confronted by eight or nine guards with rifles.

"Look!" cried Vauquière. "They've got them after all!"

Poggioli went forward, trying to see who it was, when he heard one of the guards cry:

"Yes, you is been in here, too, white man, 'cause you try to kill the voodoo inspector!"

To this a furious nasal voice rapped out in English: "If you niggers contradict me one more time I'll wipe you off the face of the earth! Where is this damned Poggioli? I want to see him!"

Another of the three bayed men repeated in a composed businesslike voice: "Yes, we want to talk to him."

"Talk to him!" shouted the guard. "You mean you want to kill him."

Poggioli and his companions entered the circle of lanterns and, to their amazement, made out the tall, angular form of Mr. Clay, the trig figure of Mr. Osterwasski, and a black man whom Poggioli did not recognize.

Boisrond growled to Poggioli: "See what they say."

The American stepped forward toward the trio.

"What do you want with me?" he asked, still amazed.

One of the guards answered.

"Want to stick a knife in you, m'sieu."

Clay turned and pointed a long forefinger at the guard. "Nigger, interrupt me again and I'll blow you to Kingdom Come, so help me God!"

Poggioli advanced on these men who had attacked him a moment before.

"Want to see me?"

"Yes, sir," snapped the collector of customs with stiff formality.

"Which one of you fellows tried to knife me up on the terrace not three minutes ago?" inquired the psychologist, peering at the three.

"None of us," rapped Clay. "We entered the gate a moment ago. It was unguarded. A moment later these niggers came runnin' down through the brush, and one of them fired a shot at us."

"But you did come here hunting me?"

"We came here to see you, sir, to interview you, to reason with you!"

Mr. Clay delivered this in such a stiff formal tone that Poggioli was half convinced of the fellow's sincerity.

"Well," said Poggioli at length, "here I am. What do you want to say?"

Clay motioned with his head.

"Let's get away from this damn black riffraff."

"No," said the psychologist. "Somebody tried to stick a knife in me and the guards seem to have rounded up you fellows. Whatever you want to say you can say right here."

The customs officer cleared his throat, stared angrily at Poggioli, and finally asked: "You're a white man, ain't you?"

"Certainly," said Poggioli, surprised.

"Then what you mixin' up with this Boisrond gang for? God knows, us white folks here in Cap Haitien has plenty of trouble without you comin' buttin' in!"

This was said so accusingly and with such long-standing irritation that Poggioli was convinced of his sincerity.

"Mr. Clay," said Poggioli, a little more amicably, "I was entirely unaware that you were mixed up in any way with this trouble. Governor Boisrond certainly is in difficulties. He sent for me and——"

"Didn't know we were in trouble!" cried the collector. "Suppose you had investments in this island, and suddenly the natives should take over the government, the *cacos* break loose and rob your plantations, the niggers quit work and take to the brush, and everything go to the devil. Wouldn't you call that trouble?"

"That's exactly what I came here for," interrupted the psychologist, "to help clear out the *cacos*."

"Clear out the *cacos*! What are you talking about, Mr. Poggioli?" ejaculated Osterwasski.

"That is precisely my mission," repeated the psychologist.

"Ma-an," drawled Clay, "is it possible that you are such a damn' stupid idiot that Boisrond has pulled the wool over your eyes like that?"

"I'm in Governor Boisrond's employ," repeated Poggioli sharply.

The group stood regarding each other at this *impasse*, then Clay once more nodded for Poggioli to follow him, and he and Osterwasski withdrew a few steps. This time Poggioli, with certain misgivings, followed.

"Well, what do you want?" he asked in a somewhat lower tone when they halted.

"Don't you know that Governor Boisrond is the *caco* chief of this island?" asked Clay, *sotto voce*.

"Certainly not!" cried Poggioli.

"Well, he is!"

"Boisrond a *caco?*"

"He was a *caco* before he got to be governor," snapped Clay.

"Yes, I knew that," admitted Poggioli.

"Once a thief always a thief. Ain't that right, Mr. Osterwasski?"

The insurance agent nodded gravely.

"But, gentlemen, what reason, what proof——"

"You tell him, Osterwasski," nodded Clay. "Tell him how this damn' *caco* governor insures his own plantations, then robs 'em hisself and collects the insurance off your comp'ny."

Osterwasski nodded.

"That's correct, Mr. Poggioli," he stated with the cool precision of a business man. "We are now defending two or three insurance suits on just those grounds. When you met us this morning in Mr. Clay's automobile we were returning from a search for a witness, a colored man named Minot, but Boisrond had spirited him away. He can't be found."

"Now those are the facts, Mr. Poggioli," put in Clay, "and we've come to ask you as a white man to pull loose from a damn' thievin' clique like this and leave 'em."

Poggioli could not doubt the sincerity of these men in their present contention. He attempted to put forward his own opinion.

"Gentlemen, I am positive you are wrong about Governor Boisrond. He brought me to this island himself to help rid his department of the *caco* chief, Jean LaFronde."

At this the two men stared at one another and each burst into characteristic laughter, Clay's loud and sardonic, Osterwasski's silent and skeptical.

"Then why did he bring me here?" demanded the scientist with a certain pungency.

"Why, to make a figgerhead of you," returned Clay readily, "to pretend he was after the *cacos*. Now, for instance"—here Clay stepped closer and tapped Poggioli on the chest—"suppose he was after the *cacos*. What account would a city-bred Yankee like you be to him? You wouldn't be worth two whoops in hell. Even you ort to know that." Here Clay ceased his tapping and nodded comfortably. "That's why he picked on you, Mr. Poggioli. Because you're a zero. You don't mean anything."

Such frankness astonished and annoyed the psychologist who, being a college instructor, was not accustomed to such an attitude.

"You are mistaken about that," he replied stiffly. "I am here for a very definite purpose."

"What's that?" asked Clay indifferently.

"To expose the falsity of Jean LaFronde's claims to voodooism and help swing public sentiment away from him."

"Help swing what?"

"Public sentiment."

"Public hell. They ain't no public in this island. Nothin' but a black riffraff. And how in the hell are you goin' to swing them?"

"By demonstrating the falsity of Jean LaFronde's claims."

"Yes, I imagine these black bucks would understand your demonstration. I imagine it would have a lot of effect."

Here Poggioli felt that perhaps his own case was a little weak. He concluded with:

"Well, at any rate, that's why Governor Boisrond hired me. My personal objective is to study folk psychology. I will at least accomplish that much."

Here Mr. Osterwasski had a sudden idea, for he said: "Look here, Mr. Clay, don't you see through this? They're going to use Mr. Poggioli to prove there is such a person as Jean LaFronde. I'll venture they are going to take him to LaFronde's camp. That would about cinch their insurance case."

Clay nodded in sudden enlightenment.

"That's about what Boisrond's up to. Pretty damn smart nigger!"

The fact that Osterwasski had hit upon this much truth carried a certain weight with Poggioli. He struck off on a new line.

"Who attacked me awhile ago? You men?"

"Certainly not," from Osterwasski. "You might have life insurance in my own company, for all I know."

"Then it must have been one of LaFronde's agents. That shows there is such a man as LaFronde and that he is opposed to Governor Boisrond."

Clay snorted.

"More circumstantial evidence they are manufacturing. But all right, Mr. Poggioli, suppose there is a LaFronde, which there ain't. And suppose you could help him out, which you couldn't, still I ask you as one white man to another to drop this thing."

"On what grounds, now?" queried Poggioli. "I thought you were against all *cacos*."

"I'm against *cacoism* when the governor is his own *caco*.

But if there is really another *caco* somewhere out in the brush, I say for God's sake let him alone. Let him keep raisin' hell until he brings back the American control and we get a decent government again. Or if he doesn't do that, maybe we'll get a political reshuffle from Port-au-Prince. Then I'm going to recommend a man of my own, a dependable nigger who knows his place and will do what we say."

"Who's that?" asked Poggioli curiously.

"LeClerc here, my assistant collector of customs." Clay nodded at the brown man who had stood a listener to all this conversation. "He's a good nigger, knows his place. Make him governor and the people with property here in Cap Haitien won't have any more trouble. We'll run things. *Cacoism* won't last long."

Poggioli nodded, enlightened.

"I see what you mean."

"Sure you do. So quit this black bear right now and tell him you're through."

The psychologist stood pondering Mr. Clay's stratagem. He reached for his case and thoughtfully lighted a cigarette.

"Mr. Clay," he asked, "when you say 'property holders' you really mean, of course, the white population in Cap Haitien."

"Nachelly."

"How many are there in the department?"

Clay thought.

"We-el, about twenty-four—twenty-six, countin' you and Osterwasski here."

"Two dozen?"

"Yes, sir."

"And how many Negroes?"

"Oh, God knows. Fifty or a hundred thousand, more maybe."

"Had it ever struck you, Mr. Clay, that fifty or a hundred thousand persons ought to be allowed to run their own country in their own way and not be forced to arrange their political life for the convenience of two dozen foreigners?"

Came a blank silence as both Osterwasski and Clay stared at this novel point of view; then Clay burst out with pent-up indignation.

"Allowed to run their own government! Of all damn fool notions! Don't you know we Americans will give 'em a better government than they've got? Don't you know we'll keep down *cacoism* and insurrections? Don't you know we'll make their property safe, same as our own, and their lives, too? Why, we'll give 'em roads, schools, churches, hospitals, things they'll never in the world git for themselves, and yet you stand up and say, 'Leave 'em alone!' That's the damnedest fool talk out of a white man I ever heard! Come on, Osterwasski, I told you this feller was no good the minute I saw him ridin' with Dr. Vauquière."

With this final and complete damnation, Mr. Clay turned on his heel and marched away through the night. His two companions followed him without another word to Poggioli.

The governor's guards, although they clearly suspected Clay of attempted murder, made no effort to stop him.

The psychologist turned about and slowly rejoined Governor Boisrond. The huge man probably had caught the drift of the conversation, for the voices of the men had been lifted several times in anger and surprise. But all he said to Poggioli was:

"Be ready to start at two."

"I'll be ready," said the psychologist. Then, not seeing Vauquière, he asked where he was.

"He went back to the house. He wanted a little rest. He has a good deal of professional work this time of year. A lot of *paludisme* in the country."

Once again in his suite in the governor's mansion, Poggioli went to bed and attempted to sleep, but the sharp and contradictory incidents of the afternoon danced in his thoughts like the units of a puzzle demanding to be pieced into a coherent whole.

The psychologist tried to drive the problem from his mind and sleep until his two-o'clock engagement, but in the very midst of his effort he would wonder:

Could Governor Boisrond possibly be Jean LaFronde? Was he, Poggioli, being duped to be made a witness in a vicious lawsuit?

He tried to sleep again, but other angles of the riddle stole into his mind. Who had attacked him on the terrace? Could it have been LeClerc, the assistant collector? Had the attack been a bona fide attempt upon his life? or was that, too, as Clay had suggested, another bit of manufactured evidence?

Poggioli lay thinking, trying to resense the fight, but could capture nothing more definite than a blur of strain and action, then his horrifying fall over the terrace.

Through the tricky mental associations of approaching sleep Poggioli seized on his illusion on the terrace that he was falling from the battlements of La Ferrière and he speculated upon it with a sort of absorbed emptiness. La Ferrière, its battlements, its terrific height, its somber African architecture, Vauquière's defense of tyrants and tyranny. Somehow these purely extraneous details seemed to hold the solution of the riddle which filled his thoughts. A little later he was completely asleep.

Some time after that Poggioli was shocked out of a troubled slumber by a touch on his shoulder. As he started up in confusion, he saw his lights were on and a Negro servant stood in his room.

"The governor told me to wake you at two, m'sieu," said the servant in blurred French.

Poggioli rubbed his eyes, blinked.

"Is he waiting for me below?"

"There is a carriage below, m'sieu."

"That's the governor."

Poggioli tumbled out of bed and got into hunting trousers, high boots, and a rough tweed coat. He picked up his bag of instruments and went clumping downstairs. When he reached the piazza he saw a barouche awaiting him on the driveway. The side lights of the vehicle were burning and showed a man on the driver's seat. Poggioli went out and, as he stepped into the vehicle, he wished the governor good morning. Then he saw the dark interior of the barouche was empty. He paused on the step to ask the driver:

"Is the governor to meet us here?"

"I don't know, m'sieu. I was ordered to pick up a man here and take him eleven kilometers on the Ouanaminthe road."

"So you don't think the governor is coming?"

"I don't know, m'sieu."

Poggioli got inside a little uncertainly and drew the blanket over his legs, for the night was cold. The driver touched his horses and the barouche moved off.

The horses went at a ringing trot, and soon passed out

of the grounds into the market place. Here were great
two-wheeled carts already standing by the stalls, while
their owners shivered around bonfires awaiting the coming of the stall keepers to buy their produce. There was
something solid and matter-of-fact about these early
market carts that relieved a certain air of unreality which
hung over Poggioli's adventure. The barouche whisked on
out of the *place*, past an ancient cathedral which towered
against the stars; a relic of the days when Cap Haitien
was the Paris of the Western world. A little later they
were spinning through the squalid purlieus of the town
and then along the new American road among the slovenly
estates. After about three quarters of an hour's traveling
the barouche stopped and the driver called down:

"This is the place, m'sieu."

Poggioli stuck out his head and saw a dim empty countryside and a dark background of the mountains beyond.
Everything was quiet except for the breathing of the
horses.

"There is no one here, driver," said Poggioli.

"No, m'sieu," said the driver.

"There must have been some mistake. The governor was
to have joined me. It's chilly and uncomfortable." He
shivered and added, "We've evidently missed connections."

"*Oui*, m'sieu."

Poggioli sat a little while longer.

"I think the best thing I can do now is to drive back
home with you."

The driver hesitated, then said apologetically: "M'sieu,
I am very sorry, but the governor ordered me to bring a
man here."

Poggioli looked at the fellow.

"Well, you have."

"But he did not order me to take a man back."

The psychologist considered this with rising resentment. "You mean you won't take me back?"

The driver said in a humble tone: "M'sieu, if I take you back the governor will have me punished for disobeying him. If I refuse to take you back, the governor will have me punished severely for discourtesy to one of his guests."

Poggioli remained in the carriage for perhaps a minute longer. It struck him that this lonely ride might possibly be a part of some prearranged plan. The driver sat silent on his high seat; the horses pranced restlessly in the cold. At last Poggioli took his bag and clambered out into the road. He stretched his numb legs and walked stiffly up and down.

"Well," he said at length, "I don't know what to do. I don't want to get you into trouble. I can get back somehow if I don't go on. You may go."

The driver tipped his cap very courteously, turned the horses about, and vanished in the night at a swift trot in the direction of Cap Haitien.

When he was left entirely by himself in the obscure highway, the feeling that this was some prearranged plan disappeared entirely. Poggioli then knew that Governor Boisrond simply had overslept and he had launched forth alone on this wild-goose chase. Then he reflected that he had come alone in the night for the express purpose of meeting a band of outlaws. The hazards of such an enterprise presented themselves to him for the first time in their true guise. He listened intently, but all he could hear was the shrill, faraway challenge of a game cock and, over toward the mountains, the hooting of an owl.

Poggioli began a nervous speculation on exactly how

the outlaws would find him when he heard the sound of padded feet coming up the road. He became motionless and opened his mouth to hear more perfectly. Then he saw two dim figures with rifles approaching him through the darkness. As they came he heard them mumbling in an undertone. They were almost on him when one of the figures paused and grunted:

"White man aroun' here."

His companion replied: "How you know?"

"Smell lak something dead."

"Maybe it is something dead."

"*Non*, m'sieu, white man."

Here the two blacks came to a standstill, looking and peering intently. Presently one grunted:

"There he is, by the cabbage palm."

With a little feeling of surprise, Poggioli noted that he really was over in the edge of the road hard by a bole of a palm tree. He was unaware of when he got there. He was momentarily amused at his own subconscious maneuvers. He called out briskly enough:

"Can you boys tell me the way to Jean LaFronde's camp?"

At this came a frightened gasping.

"Me! Us! *Non, non*, m'sieu! We good *soldats!* Rural guards! Don't want to meet no *cacos*, m'sieu."

"I want to go to the *caco* camp," repeated Poggioli, considerably heartened by the fact that these men were not going there.

"Ain't you white man, m'sieu?"

"Yes."

"I thought *les blancs* hated *cacos*."

"I had heard this Jean LaFronde was a Papa Loi,"

returned the psychologist in a matter-of-fact tone. "I wanted to investigate him."

At this the two soldiers fell into great consternation. "Fuh Gawd's sake! Investigate a Papa Loi!"

And the other one gasped: "White man, is you dat voodoo inspector we's heard about in Cap Haitien?"

Poggioli admitted his identity.

"Good Gawd, niggah, no wondah I smell dis man. He wucks wid de debbil."

Whatever errand moved the two Negroes through the night, they possessed the large leisure of all Haitians. Now they stood staring at the man who followed the fantastic trade of inspecting the emanations from hell. At last one of them said:

"We ain't gwine to de *cacos, buckra,* but we is gwine kinder in de direction of de *caco* camp. You come along wid us if you feels our comp'ny would be more welcome to you dan for to ramble along by youse'f as you now is."

A certain touch of self-consciousness about this winding sentence told Poggioli that he was receiving a formal invitation to become one of the party. He replied, a little ungratefully perhaps:

"I might as well. I'll freeze standing here."

So he started on with them, his shoes *tap-tapping* on the hard road, and the naked feet of the Negroes padding in unison with them. As he closed in with them he saw that they too had shoes, brogans which are regularly furnished the *rurales,* but these brogans were swung over their elbows by the laces. This perhaps was for comfort, and also to reserve their footwear for dress occasions.

The two soldiers moved along silently with an occasional side glance at the highly questionable white man. One of the Negroes was short and stocky, the other large. At last the short man mumbled:

"I know why you come out at night, *buckra*."

"Why?"

Another silence, then:

"Ain't you de white man who said to de niggahs over in La Ferrière dat an ordinary man would make a bettah guv'nah dan a Papa Loi?"

"I believe I said something like that," admitted Poggioli, beginning to be amused.

"Uh-huh, dat's why you come out at night."

"What do you mean?" queried the psychologist, puzzled.

"Some of the ign'ant niggahs was surprised to hear you talkin' against youse'f like dat."

Poggioli became attentive to catch the idea back of this disconnection.

"Talking against myself? I don't understand."

The short one chuckled.

"You don't! Well, you bein' a Papa Loi inspector, we know who sent you out."

"Who?"

"De gin'ral of a army sends out officers to inspect his army, m'sieu. De president sends out men to collect taxes fuh de president. De daddy sends word to his young chillun by his old chillun. . . ."

And here the stocky one fell into a highly significant silence.

A possibility of what the Negro was driving at came over Poggioli in a mixture of amazement and amusement.

"You mean you think the devil must have sent out a voodoo inspector?"

The stocky one adhered strictly to innuendo.

"If I was to lebel dis rifle at you an' pull de triggan,

eider the gun wouldn't fire or de bullet wouldn't come out
or it would switch aroun' an' go spank into my own heart."

"Don't try it," said Poggioli seriously.

"I sho' won't."

And to reduce the liability he turned the muzzle of his
rifle across his shoulder so that it pointed away from Poggioli into the ear of his companion.

"Of co'se," continued the short Negro meditatively, "we
all knowed why you said a ordin'ry man would be a bettah
guv'nah dan a Papa Loi."

"Why?"

"To test us."

"Test you?"

" 'Vide de sheep frum de goats."

By a sudden intuition Poggioli realized that this was a
characteristic movement of the Haitian mind: to interpret
an argument for a normal governor as a device of the devil
seeking to pick out the faithful among his followers.

"Dat's why you come out to inspect Papa Loi at night,"
concluded the stocky soldier, reverting to the beginning of
his argument, a point which Professor Poggioli of the
Ohio State University had forgotten.

Within the distance, say, of two miles, Poggioli and his
companions caught up with a number of rural guards, and
a little later still others overtook them, so that at last a
group of six or eight men marched on through the night
toward some destination, nobody said where. However,
there was a negative certainty about the matter. They said
they were not *cacos* and were not going to the *caco* camp.

At a certain point the whole band deserted the highroad
and took to a footpath through the mountains, and still no
particular member of the expedition seemed to be a guide.
It gave Poggioli the impression that nobody was leading

and everybody following. Still, they managed to guide themselves without hesitation.

The path they now followed was a mere crack in a dense brake of giant grass and wild coffee trees. They walked single file, and the way was so inkily black they were forced to reach out and touch each other to stay together. As Poggioli stumbled along the lowest slope of the mountain it occurred to him rather belatedly that he was in the midst of a string of liars, and that this was an escort sent out to conduct him to the *caco* camp.

From the turnings and twistings of the line Poggioli deduced that he was being led intentionally through a maze which it would be impossible for him to retrace. These windings no doubt were a safeguard to protect the *cacos* from governmental attack. The line in the darkness scrambled and climbed, circled and turned back on its course, and hit off at acute angles.

Poggioli grew short of breath; his heart thumped; a sweat broke out on him as he struggled to keep up with the steady swinging pace of the black men. Presently the oddness of this encounter forced itself upon him. As he panted along with aching muscles he wondered how Governor Boisrond had ever timed the barouche so that he would fall in exactly with a party of *cacos* or deserters or whatever these men were. This line of march gave a strong color of truth to Mr. Clay's assertion that Boisrond and Jean LaFronde were one and the same person. As the climb grew more onerous, Poggioli thought with rising indignation that perhaps all this was a mere detail in an insurance swindle.

The more he chewed on this thought, the more acrid it became. Clay's whole argument repeated itself in his

thoughts and it all seemed true. He was toiling in the midst
and for the benefit of a complicated fake.

Poggioli stumbled upward, angry and hot. His legs
ached in the calves and above the knees. Grass seed and
the chaff from leaves sifted down the back of his perspiring
neck and set up an intolerable itching, which changed,
when he scratched it, to a burning.

The psychologist was in that state of exquisite irrita-
bility characteristic of a nervous man when from behind
and above the party came the challenge of a voice.

The line halted. When Poggioli looked up he saw the
moth-colored light of dawn filling the tops of the coffee
trees. Then he saw that the party had come to a sheer cliff
some twenty feet high, and on top of this, barely discernible against the fretwork of tree tops and sky, stood a *caco*
guard.

A brief conversation passed between one of the Negroes
in the darkness below and the guard on the cliff; the psychologist caught a single phrase, "voodoo inspector." This
seemed to satisfy the guard, for the men set about climbing
the rock. The first man began mounting the sheer face,
clinging to crevices which he remembered and groped for
in the darkness. Poggioli could make out the bulk of his
form against the faint grayness of the stone. The first
climber then reached down to direct the hands of the next
man in line; then the two forms inched up the precipice.

As this measuring worm of men crept up the stone face,
Poggioli moved slowly up to the take-off, and presently
an invisible man ahead of him clambered upward and became a blur against the upper grayness. When this fellow
found some unseen anchorage he reached down, caught
Poggioli's hand, and placed it in the first crack in the
sheer escarpment.

The white man caught hold and began raking his feet over the lower surface of the cliff trying for some crack, but either there was none or his feet were so insensitive through the leather of his boots that he could not feel it. At any rate, he stood pawing futilely until a Negro behind him braced his foot and gave him a fulcrum. The psychologist went up a step and the man above caterpillared up another half length, then reached down and guided the scientist's hand again.

This time Poggioli found further ascent extremely difficult. When he left the Negro below he was forced to hold up his weight on the very tips of his fingers and boots. He could hardly spare the strength of a hand to explore upward for the next niche. As he tried it his body sank downward, but he caught the next anchorage in a sort of lucky grab. He had no strength at all to reach down and show the lower man the hold he had deserted. He could only center his strength on his clinging fingers. Two more times he made that hazardous upreach and lucky grab, and somehow succeeded in dragging his own immense weight up to a new height. But now, when he was about twelve feet from the ground, his tortured fingers began an irresistible straightening out. He exerted every ounce of force to hold his niche, but he saw that in a minute or two he would drop. The fall would mean a bruise, perhaps a break. The man above was groping down to guide Poggioli higher, but the psychologist did not dare relax a single straining muscle.

"I—can't make it," he gasped in a whisper.

The top man grunted something, shifted himself somehow against the face of the ledge, stretched down like a great monkey, and succeeded in getting his finger tips around Poggioli's wrist. His grip hurt; then he began a careful, powerful upward drawing. At first Poggioli thought he was being helped; then with a little shiver of horror he realized he was being lifted bodily. He knew he must fall. He tried not to let go his anchorage, but was lifted off. His body swung out, dangled against the cliff. He quit breathing with the certainty that the precarious hold of his helper must break under this added strain and they would both dash down the cliff together.

Then, to his amazement and increased suspense, he felt himself rise slowly, very slowly, up the cliff, past the bulk of the black man. He could feel the fellow's hand quivering under the strain; a hundred and seventy-two pounds' dead weight forced upward while the fellow clung spiderwise to the face of the precipice.

Once Poggioli's body bumped against the black man's. His trembling ascent stopped; the man wheezed; Poggioli started upward again, on up. At last the lifter gave a tortured gasp:

"Take him!"

After an interminable period the hand of the *caco* guard on top of the cliff reached down and caught the scientist's fingers. A little later he was swung over the top to an ignominious safety.

Poggioli had never been so ashamed of his physical condition. The thought of what the man below had endured wrung at his pride. He sat shaken on the edge of the cliff, vowing silently that he would take setting-up exercises; he would whip himself into some physical fitness. His hand which had been gripped ached with the renewed flow of blood. He peered down and watched his helper follow up the cliff. He came up, an arm's reach at a time, no niggling, but with the effortless, mechanical certainty of an insect. He was a bulky fellow, and when he looked up to see how to catch the top Poggioli grew almost weak with amazement to see the massive rolling features of Governor Boisrond.

He stared dumbly at the giant, who, however, did not bestow upon the scientist the slightest recognition. Then, as the black Samson gained the top and stood up in the faint light, Poggioli became dubious about the giant's identity. The scientist sat a moment longer, resting, puffing exhaustedly, and watching the fellow. The big man wore the uniform of the *rurales*. He had a rifle. Besides, it was improbable that so old a man as Boisrond would be able to exert so vast a strength as this man had shown. The resemblance might have been a trick of the gray light. Poggioli stared after the fellow.

However, the only man in Haiti who wanted the psychologist to reach the *caco* camp earnestly enough to lift him up a precipice with one hand was Governor Boisrond.

Clay's theory that Boisrond was LaFronde returned to Poggioli's mind. He could not make heads or tails out of any of it. But if this were Boisrond, then Poggioli hoped from the depths of his heart that he would win. The natural hero worship due enormous strength and courage caught up the psychologist and changed him from spectator to rank partisan. He didn't know what Boisrond wanted; he didn't care what Boisrond wanted. His sole desire now was that Boisrond should get it, whatever it might be.

All the men were up now and moving briskly along. Poggioli followed, wetting his dry lips with his tongue.

As the psychologist hurried forward an extraordinary thing occurred. As he passed a certain point in the brush he seemed to step out of the ordinary jungle silence into the rhythm of an enormous singing. It was as amazing as a buffet out of thin air. Yet what he heard was not the opening of a song; it was music in full flight. The rush of its phrasing, the hot tempo of its tom-toms, women's voices skirling up in an obbligato of unutterable melancholy made it impossible that what he heard should be the first crash of an overture.

Yet the possibility of a zone of complete silence contiguous to a sector of tremendous music astounded the psychologist.

The blackmen did not puzzle their heads about the phenomenon. The moment the beat fired their nerves they broke into a run, and a few minutes later the little party stood on the edge of a great natural bowl in the mountains. It was filled with the blue shadows and opalescent lights of early dawn.

Presently Poggioli saw that a fire burned in the center of this natural amphitheater; but its flames mixed with the light of morning until they were almost as transparent as the blaze of an alcohol lamp. As Poggioli stared, in the shadowy scene developed a great number of the figures dancing, flinging up their arms and reeling about the almost invisible fire.

Beyond this center of action, the other side of the great bowl was formed by the sheer stone escarpment of the mountain, and on this Poggioli made out what appeared to be a vast wavering human face. It was glimpsed or completely lost according to the heat waves from the central fire or the winding gossamer of the morning mist.

The whole ensemble looked so shadowy, was such an elusive mixture of gray dawn and delicate firelight, like an opal in a porphyry bowl, that it seemed impossible that this could be the source of such strong and imperious harmonies. But the concentration of the music now explained itself to the scientist. The shape of this great natural sounding chamber focussed the sounds upward so that nothing could be heard three yards beyond the tonal zone. It was a perfect retreat in which the *cacos* could conduct their orgies unheard by the countryside.

One of the Negroes now turned to Poggioli and the men and said hurriedly in Creole: "I'll go tell him you are here," and he set off down the smooth grassy incline at top speed.

While their guide went down to announce their coming, Poggioli began studying Governor Boisrond once more, if the great soldier were indeed the executive. The huge Negro peered at the scene with the narrowed eyes and poised posture of some animal stalking its prey. As Poggioli watched the expression of that massive, rolling face there suddenly dawned on the psychologist his real design in coming to the *caco* camp. He meant to make an abrupt assault on the *caco* leader in the midst of his men. If he could kill the Papa Loi with his bare hands such a *coup d'état* would certainly reëstablish the huge man's leadership over all the deserting *rurales*.

From the moment this intuition flashed on Poggioli his whole attention centered on the great figure. The strange surroundings, the fire and central altar, the huge face outlined and partially carved on the opposite cliff, the sonant turmoil of the *cacos*—all became the mere dramatic accessories of the coming nemesis. It was all like a Greek play leading to a terrific and inevitable dénouement.

The guide came running back. The newcomers started down into the bowl. The *caco* army was disposed in two long lines through which it must march down to the central altar. Poggioli noted vaguely the motley assortment of firearms: ancient flintlocks which had been preserved since the French invasion; cap-and-ball rifles; single shots and

Krags brought in by the deserting *rurales*. Besides these every Negro had a machete swung at his side—a heavy cane knife, which in the hand of a Haitian plantation worker could sever even Boisrond's powerful body at a blow.

At the apex of these two lines flamed the altar. It burned on a dais of carved stone, a sort of devil's shrine for voodoo rites. In the center stood a pot or urn of red clay, and around this leaped the colorless flames. As an uncanny architectural detail, on each corner of the dais lay two skulls, a man's and a woman's. The queer thing was that these relics of mortality did not leap out at the attention, as such things usually do; they were reduced by the grimness of their surroundings to mere decorative details.

As Poggioli approached this altar he scrutinized the two lines of *cacos* for some hint of LaFronde, but could not identify the *caco* chief. He expected to see a man with a knife in his wrist. There was nothing of the sort. With a little tug of dismay he realized the voodoo priest had absented himself. It would be impossible for Boisrond suddenly to destroy the man whose power he meant to seize. The irony of the situation bit at the white man's nerves— that Boisrond should waste his enormous strength in a hopeless battering at these two lines of machetes from the sugar plantations.

The psychologist wondered apprehensively whether the giant would attack. He would be cut down, and their whole group might easily be killed. The skulls on the corners of the dais became rather more than ornaments. The scientist looked at them with a strained expression. As he did so his eyes followed the lines of the altar up to its center, and he suddenly observed something which took his breath —a figure wearing a grotesque African devil's mask stood motionless in the midst of the flames. Poggioli did not know how it got there or when it came.

As he stared at this extraordinary apparition an odd observation was thrust upon him. This sinister figure was just the touch which welded the whole altar and background into a decorative whole. It held such a malign significance that even the skulls became mere bosses, the careless beading of a sculptor about this central figure.

At the sight, the six Negro novices dropped their jaws and stared, ready to collapse at a touch. Boisrond was attentively surveying this figure, which was either in or behind a wall of flame. The ritual chanting of the *cacos* increased in volume with the appearance of their priest. Two of the black guards sprang forward and took the arms of the first novice in line. The fellow went forward on legs that barely supported him.

Poggioli watched the ritual with tense attention, then his heart increased its beat as he saw the devil's mask step through the flames to meet the approaching recruit. He knew this detail would not be varied for any of the other candidates or for Boisrond, because the very essence of a ritual is its inviolability. The man behind the mask must now meet the black Hercules at the altar of the skulls.

The thing grew in Poggioli's brain like the horror of a nightmare. He watched one after the other of the novices go up to the devil doctor. There would be a colloquy. The novice would touch his heart, then kneel, hold up an arm to the priest, who apparently made a slight incision and then placed the lips of the mask to the wound. After each performance there was a fumbling behind the robes of the devil doctor, and once Poggioli saw, but hardly observed, a shred of paper fall from the priest's skirts. The huge Boisrond's slow approach to the place of initiation played on the scientist's nerves. It was like watching a fuse fizzle slowly toward a bomb. Mixed with this were certain apprehensions for his own safety. His brief musing was interrupted by two guards coming for Boisrond.

They were powerful blacks, and as the psychologist watched them he was conscious of a pulse in his neck. The three moved down between the files of *cacos* to the man in the devil's mask. The scientist watched with a strained feeling. Came the stereotyped colloquy. Boisrond knelt and held up his gorillalike arm for the priest's operation. Each instant now Poggioli expected him to make his lunge. But the devil doctor, skirting destruction, went on with his rigmarole of putting the mouth of the mask to the incision.

Now the black arm would crush the voodoo in an ursine grip. But the next moment, to the psychologist's confusion, the huge Negro arose and walked away between his escorts. Still the scientist held his breath. This might be a clever trick to lead off the guards for a sudden charge back, but a little later he was too far away; he was walking off between his escorts to whatsoever place the other recruits had been led.

A chill, weak feeling came over Poggioli; he stared with a slack jaw when he realized that Boisrond had run his gantlet in order that he, Poggioli, might see and explain the rites they had just witnessed.

The impossibility of doing Boisrond any service whatever dismayed the American. There was nothing he could do. He knew the devil doctor standing in the fire was so much pure legerdemain, but Poggioli knew nothing of the mechanics of illusions. He could not explain it to the runaway *rurales*. In the midst of his chagrin two Negroes came for him. He went forward between them nervously, keeping step irresistibly to the immense chanting song. When he came to the mask he raised his voice and said in French:

"I am the psychologist who came out to see your feats and give a scientific explanation of them. I—I will make a report to the American Society for Psychological Research."

As he said it this struck Poggioli as the queerest sentence ever uttered before a devil's altar decorated with human skulls. As he looked at the grotesque mask he hoped in his heart that the man behind it would understand the complete pacifism of his errand. The heat of the flames, which seemed to be fed by some sort of oil in a trench in the stone, made him step back in discomfort and turn his face away.

The grotesque figure before him made a slight gesture and said in a somber tone:

"You may look; there is nothing to explain. All there is you see."

And with that the figure stepped back into the flame and seemed to disappear into the stone pediment which upheld the great red clay urn. When the voodoo doctor withdrew from between Poggioli and the flames the heat was great enough to drive the scientist in discomfort from the dais.

That ended the ceremony. The *cacos* fell out of formation laughing and talking. They called loudly to each other that it, the drama they had just witnessed, was *bon bagaille*, a phrase which the Haitians use in indiscriminate praise. It evidently had satisfied in them a certain appetite for pageantry and dramatic mystery, which in the white race is not so well developed.

The trench of flaming oil gradually burned low, began making yard-long flickers around the stone pediment, and

finally, with a sort of hushed snap, went out. Some slatternly Negro women came up with manioc paste and
poured it on the hot stone to fry cakes. Everywhere was
a buoyant air, a tingling of good spirits as a leftover from
the performance. The black men strolled about and chaffed
the women. The bowl was filled with the loud, oily laughter
of Negroes.

Poggioli was filled with anxiety to do something for
Boisrond. He walked around the altar and stared at it.
But there was really nothing to explain. The mechanism
of the illusion must have been a simple trapdoor, but he
didn't happen to know where it was. Also the phenomenon
of fire-walking lay in that mixed region between hypnosis,
thick skin on the walker's feet, and the use of ointments
which did not conduct heat. There was nothing new to
say.

The scientist walked about the outer edge of the dais,
looking for the trapdoor, but the stones were still too hot
for him to come close. As he scrutinized the surface from
a little distance, he noticed the bit of paper which he now
remembered seeing the Papa Loi drop. He bent away from
the heat of the stone and reached after it. He looked at it
with interest. It proved to be a paper band which had come
from around some vial. It bore the address of a French
drug-manufacturing concern. The incongruity of such a
label in a *caco* camp struck the American. He had suspected the use of drugs more or less all along, but he felt
they should be native drugs, alkaloids brewed out of the
jungle.

The use of French drugs in voodoo rites seemed mal-
practice, somehow. It also suggested that the voodoo priest
had avenues of communication with the outside world and
something of a technical education. He recalled that Bois-

rond had warned him of just these probabilities when he
had first taken the case. Poggioli looked at the band again.
In the dim light it appeared to have nothing on it beyond
the signature of the firm printed in black; the name of the
drug, no doubt, had been erased, thoughtfully, by La-
Fronde.

The little tag cast an interesting and puzzling light over
the devil doctor. The fellow must not have risen up from
the natives; he must have come down from the upper
classes—some Haitian schooled in Paris where all the
wealthier citizens go. At any rate, this stamped the devil
doctor as a pure charlatan who did not even ignorantly
believe in his own mysteries. Poggioli slipped the band in
his vest pocket with a little tang of disgust.

The white man had seen all there was to see. The utter
futility of the whole expedition irritated the American.
Presently, after the human fashion, he began to justify
himself, to shift the blame. He thought acridly that Boisrond should have known better than to launch so quixotic
an adventure. He, Poggioli, could do nothing. To these
Haitian Negroes a purely intellectual explanation of the
caco rites would be the sheerest whistling down the wind.
As Mr. Clay had said, there was neither public nor public
opinion in Haiti. The Haitian mind functioned in a child's
world of illusion where, if a man stepped through a trapdoor, he vanished supernaturally and gained the oblation
due gods and devils. The crassness, the hardihood of the
imposture, bit into Poggioli's patience.

The scientist moved in odd isolation among the four or
five hundred cacos in the great green bowl. Wherever he
went it just happened that the Negroes had all strolled
to another part. The West Indian Negroes, taken as a
whole, have a fixed habit of avoiding white men when they

can. But although the *cacos* avoided Poggioli, he could see they were laughing at him. It was clear all the *cacos* knew his purpose in their camp—to elucidate mysteries, to inspect the devil's works. They had taken him fearfully enough at first, but now he had shrunk to a mere ineffective human being, quite on a par with themselves. He heard a group laugh and ask why he didn't follow the Papa Loi through the fire down into the stone if he were the devil's inspector.

Poggioli's thoughts came back to Boisrond. He wondered if the black giant were safe. He hoped he was at least safe, for the whole expedition had turned out entirely to the advantage of the *caco* chief. No matter what Poggioli told when he returned to Cap Haitien, it would strengthen LaFronde's position. If Poggioli told of the devil doctor's disappearance, the Negroes would get the fact that he had disappeared, but would miss the explanation of how he vanished. If Poggioli said nothing at all, that would be taken as a confession of bewilderment and would swell LaFronde's reputation as a wizard.

No matter what he did, it would make good press-agent material for the *cacos*. Indeed, he should have listened to Clay. The whole matter had turned against him so simply that he was surprised and chagrined he had not foreseen so obvious a termination.

His fiasco oppressed him so greatly that he had little attention for the really extraordinary scene around him. By this time pink sunlight slanted into the great green bowl and illuminated the face carved on the cliff. It was an incomplete carving, but even Poggioli's distracted attention saw that it was formed with that almost inhuman somberness which is characteristic of Egyptian and African sculpture. Already a number of Negroes were climbing the face of the cliff, about to begin work on the great sinister countenance.

The conception of the work was as simple and gigantesque as the African sphinx. The pink light slowly creeping down the western cliff gave it the appearance of rising mysteriously out of blue shadows, washed in sanies, growing taller and taller every moment like those monstrous images one sees in delirium. Its mere size somehow suggested the brevity and tragedy of human life. All enormous statuary connotes the swift coming of death to the mortals who carved it. The certainty that it will stand through ages shrinks the life of man to the fluttering of a midge. And that is why all African works of art tend toward the gigantic. It is an art based upon obliteration; it is an elevation of the somber and mysterious beauty of death.

This great face was filled with the same art motif which had sounded that morning in the frightened tempo of the tom-toms, and the obbligato of the *caco* women lifted in high and unutterable tragedy above the grim, rhythmic basso of the men.

The white man jerked his attention from the face of the great masque and set himself to the imperative need of finding Governor Boisrond again. He wondered apprehensively what had become of the executive. He looked around among the groups of *cacos*, but did not see any member of the party who had escorted him to this extraordinary place. He set out walking about the amphitheater with a notion of inquiring discreetly for his friends.

Somehow, he couldn't get closer to any of the men. When he approached a group it seemed to break up casually, without any reference to him, and the individuals in it set off briskly about their business. After three or four such trials the psychologist discovered that these black folk were avoiding him. He did not know why; perhaps because of his satanic flavor as a voodoo inspector; or it may have been they were acting under orders from Jean LaFronde.

Poggioli's aimless, isolated movements to and fro in the huge *caco* amphitheater, carrying a bag of instruments, at last touched the psychologist himself with its droll irony. It was perhaps the most absurd position in which he had ever found himself.

In the bowl was the greatest variety of black folk: men, women, and children, graybeards and crones. They lived in a row of *yagua* huts which dotted the rim of the huge concavity. The sight of these trivial living quarters compared to the intricate ornateness of the central altar and the cyclopean carving on the face of the cliff showed Poggioli how far away was the spirit of Negro life from the conventional, personal acquisitiveness of the white American and European civilization. To carve a strange vast face on a cliff—and live in a palm-scarf hut!

In his gradually increasing anxiety about the governor Poggioli looked around to see if there were not some person whom he could overtake unobtrusively, and from whom he could glean some information as to Boisrond's whereabouts. He saw a wrinkled old Negress gathering some sticks for her early-morning fire. The American went toward her and overhauled her easily enough, although she did attempt to get away from him with the tremulous, ineffective haste of age. When he caught her up she was breathless and perhaps angry at the chase.

"Granddam," said the white man, walking along at her side, "where in this place do they keep the recruits that have just arrived?"

The old woman looked at Poggioli with half-frightened, half-cunning black eyes.

"M'sieu," she croaked in her blurred Creole, "you came in with them, did you not?"

"I know it," admitted Poggioli in a worried voice, "but I have lost sight of them."

The old creature wrinkled up her face in grotesque interrogation.

"You don't know where they are?"

The stress on the "you" was clearly reminiscent of Poggioli's satanic commission.

"I wish I did, Granddam," replied the psychologist in simple distress. "I had a special friend——"

He broke off, fearful of saying too much.

The old grimalkin seemed to get over her fear of the white man and gave a grimace of mirth.

"If you can't keep track of a friend, m'sieu, how do you hope to trail down a Papa Loi?"

"I am not so much interested in Papa Lois now as I am in my friend."

The old creature relented somewhat at his distress. She peered inquisitively into his face.

"Your friend is a big man?" she divined.

"Yes, Granddam."

"With an ugly face?"

"Yes."

She nodded wisely, still staring into Poggioli's eyes.

"I see he is a great person somewhere, some other place than here in Canaan."

Such a name as "Canaan" for a camp of outlaws sent its flicker of amusement across Poggioli's mind, but the next instant he was uneasy at the old witch's close guesses.

"I am not asking who he is. I am asking where he is, what is happening to him!"

The old hag gave her malicious cackle again as she scrutinized him.

"The devil does very little for you, m'sieu. You must be a stepchild."

"Tell me where is this man?" said Poggioli.

The old creature placed clawlike fingers to her mouth; her ugly face took on a rapt look. After a moment she said:

"I see the big man, m'sieu, sitting in an old chair. The Papa Loi is speaking to him. The big man struggles. His heart rages like a great fire. He can do nothing. Look, he flings the guards about! He is like a great drunk bear! Now, *ehue!* Your huge friend wears flowers of guilt on his head! They bloom like red roses!"

She broke into an eerie cachinnation, turned, and went hurrying away with her bundle of sticks hugged to her skinny breast.

Poggioli sprang after her and caught her roughly by the shoulder.

"But where is he?" he cried. "You didn't tell me where he is."

The old woman squirmed under his clutch and pointed angrily.

"Yonder is one of your friends in that *yagua!*" she squealed wrathfully. "Go and may the devil take you!"

The professor of psychology turned and went legging it up the long slope of the bowl, leaving the only hint of any uncanny psychology he had found since his arrival in Haiti. The old woman's hint that Boisrond was undergoing some sort of violence filled the American with foreboding. As he ran to the *yagua* he thought what he would do. He meant to rush into the hut and attack the devil doctor with his bare hands; but the folly of such a course came to him long before he reached the *yagua*. He would argue the matter, upbraid them, threaten them with a return of the American marines. With this on the tip of his tongue he sprinted up to the entrance and dashed inside.

The place was empty. The psychologist had a momentary impression that the struggle had been real, that it had been spirited away in the twinkling of an eye by the infernal powers of the Papa Loi. Reverberations of the conflict seemed still quivering in the *yagua*.

It was the most fantastic impression to fall over a man in a simple hut in the clear light of dawn. Poggioli stood trembling and staring at a great mahogany four-poster which was the solitary piece of furniture the hut contained. It was the one article which every West Indian Negro must have to start housekeeping—a rich, marvelously carved mahogany four-poster. Then the psychologist saw, sprawled out on this bed, a Negro lying in deep sleep. He was a rather smallish Negro in dirty khaki, and his Krag, taken from the *rurales*, sat in the corner. Poggioli stood looking at this smallish black, and presently recognized him as one of the Negroes who had come with him to Canaan, if that was the name of this place, earlier that morning. Apparently the fellow was sleeping off the weariness of his night's exertions.

Poggioli seized on his erstwhile companion and shook him.

"Boy," he cried, "wake up. Where is Governor Boisrond?" The Negro groaned and opened glazed eyes.

"In Cap Haitien," he mumbled, and closed his eyes again.

"I mean where is the big fellow who came with us this morning?"

"Don't know—he came—behind me."

There seemed to be no arousing the fellow from his lethargy.

"Where is Jean LaFronde, the Papa Loi?"

"In this *yagua*. Asked if I were a true *caco*. Certainly, m'sieu, I am a true *caco*. I cut my wife's throat before I left home."

He drew a deep groaning breath and dropped into his heavy stupor again.

This dulled mention of murder shocked Poggioli, but beyond that it held still more dismaying suggestions. It recalled to the American the drug label he had picked up on the voodoo altar, and it suggested the drug used. Poggioli fumbled in his pocket after the little band, found it, and hurried to the door of the *yagua* for light. He readily found the manufacturer's signature again, then, still searching, he saw the label in pale blue letters which had been rubber-stamped on the band. In his previous search the blue light of morning had disguised the imprint perfectly. But in this increased and ruddier light he read the name easily:

SCOPOTHALAMIN

As he stared a sudden flood of illumination broke over Poggioli. He knew well enough the peculiar psychical action of this newly discovered drug. It destroyed all sense of caution and concealment. The Negro on the bed evidently had been heavily doped with it. It had left him with the whole contents of his memory open to anyone who cared to question him. So this was the stuff the voodoo priest used on recruits to test their fidelity to the *caco* cause. The sharp modernity of the method was what amazed Poggioli. He had not been prepared for the very latest products of a synthetic chemical laboratory in the Haitian brush. No wonder there was an unaccountable gap in the narrative of each prisoner whom he had interviewed in La Ferrière. No wonder LaFronde reached certitude with an uncanny precision. The new drug, "the truth drug."

At that moment Poggioli suddenly realized that somewhere Governor Boisrond was in the hands of his enemies, a victim of this revealing drug.

Poggioli stepped out of the hut with a tightening in his throat. He looked up and down the *yaguas*. They were irregularly spaced around the arc of the bowl in clumps of palm trees with which the great arena was decorated. In some of these huts Poggioli did not doubt the black giant was being probed and probably mutilated, as were the victims in La Ferrière.

A last flash of anger that Boisrond should ever have risked himself in such a place, then Poggioli started at a trot around the whole immense circle of the bowl. As he went he was wretchedly certain that he was taking the longest arc to reach the hut where Boisrond lay. No matter which way he went, it would turn out to be the longer route. He would threaten them with the American marines! He would see to a report in Washington! Such savagery!

This mental upbraiding was broken into by a frantic outburst of barking by some distant dog. The sound came from the direction of the coffee bushes where he and the governor had entered the bowl early that morning. He paused a moment to peer in that direction. The distance was too great to see the dog, but as he stared a queer thing happened. A squad of *cacos* in that sector of the bowl suddenly came flying toward the central altar as if the devil himself were after them. This devil, apparently, was the dog. For such a puny foe to rout a number of men armed with machetes was grotesque. Poggioli stared more curiously when out of the screen of coffee bushes broke the hard, tearing crash of army rifles. At the volley four or five of the flying *cacos* pitched forward, and one who was hit but not killed scrambled along down the slope on all fours.

This amazing and opportune rifle fire cleared the air for Poggioli like a thunder crash. A sudden glorious exhilaration filled him. He turned and went running toward the coffee fringe shouting:

"The *rurales!* The *rurales!*"

At the same moment enormous confusion developed in the *caco* camp. Men came running out of the huts all around the circle with antiquated arms in their hands. Then Poggioli saw a line of khaki-clad *rurales* dash down the rim of the bowl with bayonets shining in the morning light. He saw them kneel and fire into the swarming *cacos*. Came the whine of bullets in the air, every shot seeming to pass within a foot of Poggioli's ears. One slapped a palm some ten yards from him. The American thought quickly what to do. He felt sure he would be hit, no matter which way he ran.

At that instant his mind was switched from his personal peril by a huge black figure lunging out of one of the *yagua* huts just ahead of him and roaring out:

"Charge, my *rurales!* Let them have it!"

Then, even amid the steady crashing of the rifles, Poggioli heard the frantic yipping of a dog. He saw a mongrel hound come dashing around the long arc of palms toward the huge reeling Negro. Even in the excitement of the moment Poggioli saw that the governor's great gargoyle face had scarlet patches for the ears and nose.

The battle between the *rurales* and the *cacos* quickly grew to such confusion that Poggioli caught but flashes of it. He himself was running like a jumping jack toward the *rurale* lines howling, "American! American!" at every leap.

He saw the *rurales* spread out in front of him fanwise and drop on their bellies in the grass, after the tactics of the American marines. Their rifle shots sounded like a steady hammering and looked like a continual spouting of vapor, which puffed up and drifted leisurely across their sector of the bowl. Every bullet droned past Poggioli's ears as he sprinted toward the *rurale* lines in an interminable run and at last got safely behind those deadly vaporing puffs. When he was fifty yards to the rear he turned and watched the conflict.

The *cacos* were in a jumbled mass behind the central altar from which they expected miraculous protection. Their ancient guns belched out a pall of black smoke. Echoes of their rifles stuttered back from the great sinister face on the cliff. In front of Poggioli the marine-trained *rurales* lay spread out, firing into the devil worshipers with a sort of savage efficiency. The tearing sound of the riflery seemed to go on forever. Poggioli's feeling of personal danger vanished completely and the whole scene became a sort of drama. In the scrambling *caco* masses individuals would topple out, crumple up.

In the uproar he could hear fragments of their shouts, oaths, their prayers to Papa Loi. Now and then one of the *rurales* near the white man would collapse and cease firing. Once a *caco* bullet flicked a hole in the white man's coat.

Poggioli jumped aside to let it pass and continued his entranced staring at the fight.

Presently the fire of the *cacos* began to weaken. What was happening in the center of the bowl, who was dead, who alive, Poggioli could not make out. He was lying prone on the ground just behind the regular troops. Now at this slackening of the *caco* fire a heady feeling of triumph seized him. He scrambled to his feet to run forward, when suddenly out of the black gun smoke about the altar charged a long line of Negroes brandishing machetes.

The hammering of the Krags grew heavier. Some of the charging *cacos* dropped out, but the greater part came on. They began shouting and waving their heavy blades. They galloped up the slope at menacing speed. Poggioli could see their contorted faces, bare feet, the swell of up-lifted biceps. They grew swiftly larger, clearer.

In the van of the charging column came the weird figure of the priest in the devil's mask, brandishing a machete and leading his *cacos* into the very muzzles of the guns. A dozen rifles fired at him. The wizard seemed indeed to brush aside the bullets. Even Poggioli felt the glamour of the uncanny about him.

When the macheteers were in the midst of the soldiers the crashing of the rifles abruptly ceased. The *rurales* leaped up with fixed bayonets. A shocking silence swept over the bowl as the plantation Negroes swinging sugar knives clashed with other plantation Negroes wielding Krags. The whole field around Poggioli was filled with swift duels, a thrust, a stroke. Now and then a hurried shot muffled against the very body of a man. This and the hard gasping breaths of the fighting men, the headachy smell of smokeless powder, and the repulsive odor of desperately wounded men filled the air.

In the midst of this struggle the priest in the mask lunged, cut and parried with the address of a finished duellist. He became the axis of the fight. A zone of miraculous safety spread around him. Poggioli saw one of the *rurales* level his Krag straight at the menacing figure; the weapon failed fire or was empty.

The Negro flung down his gun with a despairing shout, turned, and dashed for the coffee thicket. Two or three men followed. The alarm spread. The *rurales* teetered on the edge of a rout. Then an ursine roar from the rear fetched up the fugitives. The next moment the gigantic black form of the governor charged toward the devil doctor.

Boisrond plunged forward, wading shoulder deep among the duellists. Machetes sheared at him; the wavering bayonets solidified around him. The next moment the giant clashed with the grotesque devil's mask.

Poggioli glimpsed the mask make a swift cut with the sugar knife; Boisrond crashed down an immense sweeping two-handed stroke with a clubbed Krag. The mask disappeared. Rose shouts, howls; men crushed together like an enormous steel-tipped football scrimmage. After two or three minutes the murderous equipoise gave way. The combatants flowed rapidly back toward the center of the bowl, the machetes shrieking in front, the Krags on their heels howling and cursing and thrusting.

Then the rifle shots began again. They multiplied as the *rurales* stopped trying to bayonet and fell to loading and firing. Again there was a brief resistance behind the sinister altar in the center of the field; but the *rurales* spread out like workmen and began a converging fire that sent the *cacos* flying aimlessly toward the rim if they were not shot before they reached the brush.

Poggioli watched the clean-up with singing nerves. Every living thing in the bowl was hunted out by the *rurales*. When the massacre swept into the farther sector of the bowl the white man could not make out the details, but an occasional shot, the scream of a woman, the shriek of a child told its terror. Some of the refugees the soldiers picked out of the palms, some behind stones, others in the *yagua* huts. Now and then some wretch leaped out of a covert and became a moving target for the triumphant *rurales*. The finish was carried out with an unmerciful thoroughness characteristic of warfare in the Haitian brush.

When the last shot was fired the soldiers spent about an hour looting the bodies and the huts, but the voodoo altar in the center of the bowl they left untouched, and also the figure of the devil's mask up near the fringe of the coffee bushes. Its carved face was curiously meshed so that it wore a certain sardonic leer as it lay at the farthest point the *cacos* had won during the battle. Around it were ranked windrows of machetes and bodies.

While the *rurales* were gathering their spoils Poggioli walked around to the *yagua* he had entered and found the Negro deserter slumped over the footboard of the mahogany bed. Some *rurale* had seen him when he attempted to get out of the four-poster.

From the door of the *yagua* the psychologist looked across the charnel bowl and saw the great unfinished face on the cliff. It gazed down with its somber, brooding mystery on the dead bodies of these strange black men who had spent their strength in carving it. And it struck Poggioli as he looked at it that the profound reason why these carvers lay scattered before their handiwork was precisely because their passion lay in creating this great gloomy face, and not in producing sugar cane on flat plantations. That was the crime for which the European civilization of the world had no forgiveness. The spirit of these dead Negroes had been far more revolutionary than that of the Russian Reds. For the Reds wanted only to rearrange the distribution of food and clothes, but these black men had transposed the whole ictus of human life. The stress had been shifted from belly to emotions; so their carving had been stopped and their black corpses sown to the rising heat of the sun.

On the march back to Cap Haitien Governor Boisrond walked beside Poggioli, looking scarcely more grotesque now than before he lost his nose and ears. His wounds gave his rumble a certain nasal sound as if from a severe coryza. He carried in his arms the body of his hound, which a stray shot had killed. He was getting it back to Cap Haitien, he said, to bury it.

"I knew if I could ever march into the *caco* camp barefooted," he explained in his ponderous, stopped voice, "my hound would follow me and lead my men to me."

The sun was overhead now, and the dewy jungle was a hot, wet blanket. A chilly shiver went through Poggioli.

"So that's why you came here with me?" he asked dully.

"That is why I cabled you at Curaçao."

Poggioli stumbled on down the choked slopes of the mountain in silence. There were details in the black giant's tortuous plans which the white man did not fathom, but the larger outlines were clear enough.

The giant rumbled on meditatively.

"I knew he could not resist the coup of this"—the governor indicated his nose and ears—"but he did not take into account this." He moved the dead dog which he carried carefully in his arms.

When they reached the American-built highway Poggioli found the governor's brougham awaiting them, all evidently arranged according to the executive's schedule. As the two men drove back to Cap Haitien Poggioli shivered again painfully in the heat.

"Paludisme," rumbled the governor.

"I must see Vauquière," shivered the psychologist.

There was a pause, then Boisrond rumbled: "When you see Madame Vauquière again, M'sieu Poggioli, you must be sure to tell her that her husband died like a hero at the head of his men."

For a moment Poggioli was shocked out of his malaise.

"Vauquière—dead?"

The grotesque held up a warning hand.

"Softer, m'sieu. Nobody knows it but us. Let us spread the report and some of my *rurales* will remember they saw him fighting at the head of our ranks. Then others will recall the same thing, and finally it will become a truth no man can deny, for all my soldiers were afraid to touch the mask of the dead voodoo priest in Canaan."

Three days later Poggioli was at sea on the French steamer *Talleyrand,* and was sitting in a steamer chair musing to himself, with an occasional remark to Osterwasski, who chanced to occupy the adjoining seat. The glimmering mountains of Haiti had sunk into the sea.

The psychologist was chewing somewhat astringently upon his recent adventures in the island. His own rôle in the tragedy was still a little obscure to him. He saw clearly enough that both Vauquière and Boisrond had wanted him to come to Cap Haitien to conduct the investigation. Evidently the physician had hoped to gain wide publicity and many new recruits by Poggioli's visit to the camp. Or he may have hoped that Poggioli's reports would bring about an American influence which would force a change of governors; then he, Vauquière, would probably have stepped into the executive mansion and would instantly have quelled the power of Jean LaFronde.

The psychologist did not doubt now that it was Vauquière himself who had made the mock attack upon him on the terrace of the governor's mansion in an effort to bolster up the fictitious personality of the *caco* chief.

The type of government the retired actor proposed to establish in Cap Haitien was clearly enough a tyranny, under the model of the old Haitian emperor, Henri Christophe, but an artistic tyranny. That was a queer idea in an era of undiluted commercialism.

As Poggioli sat staring out at sea it occurred to him that all great flowerings of art which history records came to bloom under an artistic tyrant—the French Henris, the Italian Medicis, the Greek Pericles, and even the English Elizabeth.

It was an odd fact; he had never thought of it before. Perhaps under a little kindlier star Vauquière might have developed that weird, mysterious beauty that lies in the heart of the Children of the Sun.

Boisrond's rôle was much simpler. He had wanted some reasonable excuse for walking barefooted in Canaan, and to escort Poggioli there was the simplest device. Had he attempted to enter on his own initiative, the *cacos* would immediately have suspected some ruse, and no one would have guided him through the labyrinth of the jungle.

Vauquière had known the governor was coming to his camp. The governor knew that Vauquière knew, but the physician did not think of the dog, and so Canaan fell. That was the final and exquisite note of irony, that the actor's dream and the development of a people should fall through the nose of a cur.

The psychologist turned to his companion and continued his musing aloud:

"The future may bring a day, Osterwasski, when some enormously advanced civilization will welcome any alien race because a different race means a different culture and a different mode of looking at life. That is a precious thing, Osterwasski—I should say the most precious thing, because when a man advances beyond a primitive concern about clothes for his back and food for his belly, the chief occupation and delight of man is the contemplation of life. It embraces religion, philosophy, metaphysics, and every great and good thing. The day may come, Osterwasski, when it is conceivable that all races will cherish and not war against other races for their intellectual and spiritual novelties."

Osterwasski looked around curiously at his companion.

"But that day is remote, Osterwasski, and possibly may never come. It is quite conceivable by the time that far-off era arrives the mind of the whole world will be thoroughly Caucasianized. Then every man will devote every second of every day to the production of food. Nobody will know what to do with it; nobody will ever ask. It will be a tenet universally held that food should be produced, not used, and garments made, not worn."

"What are you talking about?" asked Osterwasski, regarding his companion suspiciously. "You ought to try to sleep all you can. You've been under a strain."

Poggioli hushed.

Somewhat later the ship's printer came on deck with his daily gist of news caught over the radio. The psychologist bought one of the little hand sheets for ten centimes. He glanced through the typewritten digest of the world's doings. In it he found this item:

Owing to recent *caco* outbreaks in the department of Cap Haitien, the Federal authorities in Port-au-Prince have requested the resignation of Governor Boisrond and have appointed in his stead M. Jean Baptiste Lafayette Napoleon LeClerc, formerly assistant collector of customs in the port of Cap Haitien.

The Prints of Hantoun

*In which it appears that the evil that men
do lives after them.*

THE PRINTS OF HANTOUN

IN FORT-DE-FRANCE, Martinique, Professor Henry Poggioli, American psychologist and criminologist, struck up a very pleasant friendship with the Chevalier Gervais Antoinette Beauhart Marion de Creviceau, a gentleman with a fellow interest in the philosophic aspects of crime.

The Chevalier de Creviceau, following the general temperament of the French in Martinique, elaborated innumerable theories about his hobby without putting one to the touchstone of investigation. He had become a theoretical spider, spinning his web not to catch flies, but to indulge a passion for geometry.

So, at nine o'clock in the morning, while Fort-de-France lay under a downpour of sunshine already torrid, these two gentlemen sat at a *déjeuner* at one of the little tables which had been placed on the wide pavement in front of the Hôtel Colonial, discussing the highly theoretical question of how far the architectural surroundings of a people influenced their crimes.

The reason they had picked on this peculiar topic was that the street in which they sat spread before them a glare of multicolors which perhaps could not be duplicated anywhere else in the world. Some of the houses were painted in blazing blue and red bands, like a Brobdingnagian barber sign; the surface of others were enormous zigzags of yellow and vermilion; some were struck off in diagonals of umber and orange. The whole street vibrated with these hot, clashing colors and screwed up the impression of heat to a degree almost unbearable.

Poggioli, with his American flair for simplicity, suggested that this futuristic decoration would tend to produce crimes as bizarre and grotesque as the pied and streaked surroundings in which they were committed. But the Chevalier de Creviceau, with French subtlety, took exactly an opposite view. He held a theory exactly analogous to that of Stanley Hall in *Adolescence*. Just as the vicarious criminal experience obtained during youth by novel-reading tended to produce sober-minded men, so these clashing colors would tend to produce simplicity in the approach to life of all the Martiniquais, whether criminal or normal members of society. He reënforced this opinion with humorous cleverness by declaring that the apocalyptic vision of St. John on Patmos described heaven itself as a highly colored place not so very dissimilar to Fort-de-France.

"Now," pursued the chevalier with inexorable if fantastic logic, "if the seer of Patmos had not had some subconscious inkling of the soothing effects of a jangle of color he would never have made so grave a mistake as to decorate heaven with walls of jasper, pavements of gold, gates of pearl, ruby, topaz, chrysolite, and so forth. *Cá mon ami*," he concluded, "compared to heaven, Fort-de-France is a drab enough place, yet you would never agree that the abode of the blessed is a hotbed of crime. That would be nonsense!"

Professor Poggioli burst out laughing at this typical Martiniquean argument and said he would venture a hundred-franc note against any such bizarre theory.

The chevalier nodded. "Taken, m'sieu, but it will be

difficult to determine such a matter through pure dia-
lectic."

Now the American really had not intended laying a
wager. He had merely followed the habit of his countrymen in appealing to money as a strong expression of
opinion where one of another nationality would have appealed to his sword, or his honor, or his God; but since
the chevalier had taken him literally, he was willing enough
to carry out his wager.

"Suppose we investigate the next six crimes that come
before the police court of Fort-de-France and see whether
they are simple or complex."

The Chevalier de Creviceau was a carefully groomed,
triangular-shaped man, and now he lifted black arched
brows in a yellow triangular face.

"My friend, that will require exertion!"

"Quite so, but we must settle our wager."

"But six, that's too many; one crime is enough, the
first."

Since the wager was trivial, Poggioli laughingly agreed
to allow the very first crime to settle the discussion.

The chevalier, who launched a new theory at every turn
of the conversation, now began discussing the relative
value of theory and practical tests.

"Now it is like this," he asserted. "I do not say there is
nothing to actuality. I admit there is such a thing. It is
just possible that without life we could develop no theories
about it, but I hold with certainty that without theories
life would be impossible; it would disintegrate into a series
of accidents and fortuities. But to get back to our wager,
when shall we begin this curious research?"

Here the chevalier lifted his voice and asked the garçon

to bring him a calendar, evidently to select a day, while Poggioli himself drew out a watch. Whether the investigation should start by the calendar or the chronometer would itself, no doubt, have been a point of long dispute had not at that moment the garçon come threading the tables to the two gentlemen and, with a little courteous salute, said in an undertone, "M'sieu Poggioli, His Honor, M. Percin, prefect of police, desires the favor of a few words over the telephone."

This timely message naturally put an end to the argument. The American hurried inside the hotel to the telephone booth and was gone for some thirty minutes, because conversations in Martinique, whether by wire or face to face, are long-drawn-out affairs. After a while he reappeared in a state of obvious excitement, but at the same time laughing.

"What is it?" cried the chevalier.

When Poggioli reached the table he said in a voice not to be heard by the other diners:

"The Banque Nationale has been robbed!"

De Creviceau stared at this.

"Then why do you smile?"

Poggioli burst out laughing.

"Because M. Percin, the prefect of police, declared he and all his force were thrilled over the robbery and they would pursue with the utmost enthusiasm every clue to bring the robber to justice. They invited me to come down and help them."

The chevalier lifted his arched brows.

"Frankly, I do not see why you smile over that!"

"Well—saying the police were thrilled over the robbery, and would pursue with the utmost enthusiasm——"

"*Cá!* Aren't you also thrilled!" cried the chevalier. "I am!"

"Certainly," agreed Poggioli, sobering, "but it sounds funny for the police department to talk of a robbery as if it were a theatrical performance put on for their benefit."

"My dear man, if there were no crimes there could be no law and no police. Crimes call the law and the police into existence. I should say the greatest force for law and order in Martinique to-day are the criminals. And what is more thrilling to a professional man than an interesting case in his profession? A surgeon thrills over a rose cancer; a beach guard thrills to rescue a beautiful woman drowning in the sea; a policeman thrills to trace down and arrest a bank robber; that is, if they are Frenchmen!"

Poggioli now had stopped laughing completely.

"Well," he said soberly, "I told him I would come down at once and begged permission to bring you with me."

"Charmed! Thrilled!" cried the chevalier, reaching behind his chair to pick up a slender ivory cane made out of a narwhal's tusk.

So saying, the two gentlemen fell in at each other's side and, as the chevalier elected to be pacemaker, they began a leisurely stroll through the streaked and striped streets of Fort-de-France toward the despoiled bank.

The Banque Nationale, when the two investigators eventually reached this edifice, lifted a flaring, checkered façade of ocher and sienna to the barbs of the sun. In front of the building a mob of Martiniquais milled about the entrance, crowded up the steps, and stood jammed against its bronze doors. As the two gentlemen approached they could hear shouts of "Open the bank!" "Let us in!" "When does the bank open?" and a medley of a similar tenor.

The Chevalier de Creviceau paused and twirled his ivory cane.

"The news is out," he commented; "a run on the bank."

"How are we going to get inside?" queried the American, quickening his steps. "We can't push through that mob."

De Creviceau surveyed the brilliant scene through wrinkled eyes.

"There must be some other entrance to the building."

"From the side perhaps?"

"Or the rear."

They went forward, studying the solid row of shops which flanked the edifice on both sides. Presently De Creviceau caught sight of a mere crack between two shops several doors from the mob. The two investigators circled the crowd and trusted themselves to it.

The passage was typical of old West Indian towns, a foot and a half wide, malodorous, roofed over in places, widening here and there, and winding about with the accidents of ownership and erratic building. In one place a kind of den had been curtained off with jute bagging and was occupied by a saggy-breasted yellow woman and three babies of different colors. At another turn a long-headed, sooty-black Negro wearing a tall red fez stood in a niche in the wall and sold rum in glasses made of broken bottles whose edges had been painstakingly smoothed. At a little distance beyond this was a donkey's stall; farther on, a door made of sheet iron, blackened with smoke and with a round hole cut in it. Past the door was a booth where a fat yellow Negro sat surrounded by sacred pictures on cards, crucifixes, wax candles for votive offerings, and rosaries. Beyond this the explorers saw a brilliant vertical

streak where the passage opened into the sunlight again.
The chevalier paused at the reliquary stand and asked
if there were a door to the bank in the alley outside.

The dealer in ecclesiastical properties shook his head
vacantly.

"What bank, m'sieu?"

De Creviceau was irritated.

"Didn't you know there was a bank robbed last night?"

The man crossed himself.

"God's distribution from the rich to the poor, m'sieu."

"A pious man," ejaculated the chevalier, and the two
men went on and looked out the end of the passage. They
saw a street of hovels filled with stark-naked children,
greasy women, and listless men. The houses were of *pise*
or *adobe*. There were shops in this meaner part of the city:
tailors, dealers in firearms, a fish market with an amazing
odor; all indescribably poverty-ridden and squalid.
Scrawled in charcoal at this end of the passage was its
name—"Allée des Chats"—and the hideous thoroughfare
before them was the "Rue des Quatre Vents." The two gentlemen might have been a thousand miles from Banque
Nationale, so puzzlingly are opulence and penury wedged
together in the ancient town of Fort-de-France.

Poggioli turned back into the little alley, hopeless of
finding the criminal in such a milieu. The two men retraced their steps by the reliquary, and as the American
brushed against the iron door he paused and tapped it
experimentally. Then, curious to see where such a door
might lead—into some obscenity or other, no doubt—he
stooped and looked through the hole. After a moment's
focusing of his eyes to a deeper gloom he saw a pair of
legs in dingy blue uniform. He peered in a little farther

and found himself looking up at a Negro guard seated on a stool almost directly above him.

The Negro sensed his presence, jerked himself to attention, looked down at the American's head, and blurted out: "Is you M'sieu Poggioli?"

"Yes," ejaculated the American, as surprised as his *vis-à-vis*. The black man jumped up in great excitement.

"Welcome, m'sieu!" he cried, jerking away his stool to admit the white man through the hole. Then he shouted up the passage or tunnel where he stood:

"Messieurs! Ho, gentlemen! M'sieu Poggioli has arrived!"

Then he turned to assist the psychologist through the hole.

To meet such a reception committee in such a place amazed the psychologist. At the Negro's uproar two men entered the passage from some door farther on and came hurrying down before Poggioli could fairly scramble out of the preposterous hole which had admitted him. In fact, they helped him to his feet. The American arose flushed and rumpled to see two gentlemen, evidently French from their carefully tailored clothes and trimly cut hair; however, a certain slight crinkling of their hair suggested an infusion of African blood in their veins.

"M'sieu Poggioli!" cried one of these men, seizing the American by the hand and shaking it with the nervous quickness of the Latin, "this is a propitious omen." He turned to his companion. "It simply means, M'sieu le Président, that the thieves are captured and your money returned!" Then he remembered his duties and made a bow.

"M'sieu Poggioli, allow me to present the president of Banque Nationale, M'sieu Pinville, and I am M. Percin, the prefect of police. I had heard you were in the city and, when this matter came up, I determined to avail myself of your brilliant talent as a criminologist."

The American shook hands.

"I had no idea this passage would lead to——"

Mr. Percin stuck up a gay forefinger and tipped his head to one side with a bright smile.

"My idea entirely, m'sieu. The question was: How would we ever get you into the bank? M. Pinville was afraid to open the front door for fear all Fort-de-France would rush in and perhaps break up the place if they did not get their money immediately. Now unfortunately their money is gone. M'sieu Pinville was distracted. 'Percin!' he cried, 'we are lost with rescue in sight! There is no way to admit the great American criminologist to Banque Nationale!' 'Why could he not come in the way the thief entered?' I demanded. 'Impossible to ask such a thing of a gentleman!' cried Pinville. 'Then don't ask it,' I cried, 'and if M'sieu l'Americain is the sleuth I think him he will presently appear at the hole under the wall!' Pinville was doubtful, but I placed Joub on guard with instructions to apologize to you the moment you showed your head. So here you are! *Voilà!*"

The prefect slapped fist in palm. "A magnificent beginning!"

They were starting up the mean passage when Poggioli cried: "One moment, gentlemen; my friend, the Chevalier de Creviceau, is waiting outside."

"He is welcome!" cried M. Percin. "You spoke to me of him over the telephone."

"Yes, he came with me to settle a little wager."

"Joub, invite the gentleman in."

The Negro guard thrust his head in the hole and called for the chevalier to enter. Came a wait, then the chevalier's yellow triangle of a head entered the aperture, but his broad straight shoulders could not enter it at all. He pushed and twisted. The three gentlemen inside almost dislocated his arms, but his big shoulders were incompressible. At last he grunted:

"When I knock—three times with my cane—on the front door—open and let me in."

M. Pinville flew up at once.

"*Non*, m'sieu, it is impossible! The bank will be looted!"

In the midst of this excited refusal the chevalier gave a great bang on the sheet-iron door with the head of his cane.

"When I rap three times like that on the front door of the bank, open and let me in," he repeated; "no one will enter with me." His yellow head was instantly withdrawn.

The three men and the Negro guard remained for a moment staring at the empty hole.

"*Parbleu!* A hell of a fellow!" ejaculated M. Pinville.

"I believe it will be safe to open and admit him," said the prefect. "I feel sure he will enter alone."

Then they turned up the passage for the interior of the bank.

The men presently pushed up through a trapdoor into a small cloakroom of the Banque Nationale.

"This building was once a roulette establishment," explained M. Percin as the men helped each other out, "and you know in occupations of that character, m'sieus, a private exit or two is very necessary."

"They are no disadvantage to a bank either," seconded M. Pinville in a depressed tone, "except when they are criminally used as this one was."

The group walked on into the accounting room of the bank, which appeared normal except for a hole cut in the big steel door of the vault. The sheet steel had been ripped from around the combination, leaving exposed the shining inner bolts like the viscera of some animal as seen through a tear in its stomach.

"Who found this first?" asked Poggioli, surveying the scene.

"Joub there, who comes in early every morning to dust."

"Had anything been touched or moved?" inquired the American of the Negro.

Joub shook his head with the rapid shake of a Negro portentously serious.

"*Non*, m'sieu. When I saw this I called M. Pinville on the 'phone and he came down."

The American looked at the layout more attentively. The vault door was a huge affair, imposing but quite out of date, whose steel sheets a modern burglar with an oxy-acetylene torch could strip with the facility of a child peeling an onion. The safe inside the vault was of the same construction and had been treated in the same manner.

The floors of both the vault and the office were free from any litter of castaway books or papers, but in a wastebasket was a single folded newspaper. The psychologist picked this up, unfolded it, and displayed burnt-looking dust and a number of burnt match ends and cigarette stubs. He stood looking at the contents a moment and presently observed that the burglar, whoever he was, had a very interesting psychology indeed.

M. Pinville, whose money was gone, made a little annoyed gesture at so abstract a subject, but the prefect inquired with interest:

"What do you make of him?"

"First, I should say this burglar was a very fastidious amateur——"

The prefect threw up his hands.

"*Parbleu,* m'sieu!" he cried. "Amateur! Certainly he is a professional! Why that circle of steel is cut out of the vault door with the precision of a compass."

"Yes, but look at the time he spent on the job," retorted Poggioli, motioning toward the cigarette stubs.

"Time—how do you deduce a time factor in——"

"By the number of cigarettes the gentleman used while burning a hole in the vault door."

The prefect looked at the stubs a little vacuously.

"Weren't they left by the paying teller from yesterday?"

"No. All the other wastebaskets are empty; I fancy Joub disposed of them yesterday evening."

"I did, m'sieu," nodded the Negro.

"But why should a thief waste time disposing of his stubs in a wastebasket?"

"Because he is an aristocrat and a highly fastidious and finical man. Also I can say that he is a perfectly phlegmatic person. For instance, when a man burning a hole through a vault door takes time to spread a paper to catch the particles of burned steel, spends an extra forty minutes to make his circle perfectly round, when he pinches out his cigarette stubs, I call him highly phlegmatic and highly finical. In fact, his only sign of nerves was that he grew so absorbed in his labors that he allowed his cigarette to die between his lips. You see here are more than a dozen like that. He forgot to draw. Now, since keeping a cigarette alive is pure automatism, we may conclude that his nerves were a little ruffled, although I suspect he would be the first to deny it. In person the burglar is very carefully attired, since he was so neat in his robbery. He is very probably a man of wealth, since he was so wasteful of these very fine imported cigarettes. He is very probably a man of luxury who has recently lost his money, since this certainly was his first effort to rob a bank."

Here the prefect interrupted to ask explosively why the psychologist thought it was a first effort since he was so eminently successful.

"From the length of time it required for him to cut the door. Here are twenty-one cigarettes, nineteen of which have been given a puff or two and then allowed to die. It requires about three minutes for a cigarette to expire. There are sixty minutes accounted for. We can easily add three more minutes to each stub to allow for the time the burglar worked on while holding the dead tobacco between his lips. There is another hour. Now, for any man to work two hours at this job shows he was not only an amateur, but a beginner. He should have done it in thirty minutes."

"But why did he turn out such a perfect piece of work?"

"Because he is the sort of man who performs every task with a very deliberate perfection. He must be, in fact, a *capre*, that is, of mixed French and Negro blood. He has inherited the perfect finish of the French with the patient slowness of the Negro."

M. Pinville shrugged hopelessly.

"That is about as definite, M'sieu Poggioli, as to say a certain frog you were seeking in a marsh had web feet— everything in Martinique is some sort of mixture of French and Negro, except my family, and one or two others."

The prefect made a little bow at his inclusion in the banker's list, while Poggioli said:

"At least, M. Pinville, if my deductions are correct the burglar was no poor man. Frankly, I was very discouraged when I saw the Rue des Quatre Vents. If it had been someone out of that scum I should have been hopeless. I don't know the psychology of the miserable. I am an American."

"How shall we proceed now?" inquired the prefect briskly.

"I think we should make a list of the employees of this bank."

At this suggestion President Pinville was startled.

"My own employees?"

"The character of the robbery suggests it. Was the secret passage which leads from the bank to the alley known to all your men?"

"I can't say, m'sieu." Pinville looked worried. "It was no secret, but I don't suppose it was mentioned once in ten years. I knew the passage was there, just as I know there is an old water spigot in the corner of my private office which was used for something when this building was run as a lottery and a gambling house, but I never have any reason to think of or mention the matter."

"It won't be amiss," suggested M. Percin, "to take a list of the bank employees and have my city detectives investigate the personal habits of each one."

The president went to his desk and began making out a list of his clerks, pausing now and then to bite his pen over a street address which he could not instantly recall.

As he did this Poggioli continued moving about the office, scrutinizing the safe, its exposed bolts; and finally he stooped and picked up from the floor a small brown button. He interrupted the men at the desk to exclaim:

"By the way, gentlemen, it is hardly worth while to make out a list of the bank clerks."

M. Percin turned.

"Why do you say that? You have described the psychology of a finical bank clerk exactly."

"On account of this button," said the American, holding up the tiny object. "It is a glove button. The thief evidently burst it off his glove in some manipulation of his tools. This shows that he was not only a fastidious man but an extremely scientific one. You see he was clever enough to wear gloves throughout his work to avoid leaving finger prints on the steel."

M. Percin made a sharp blow in the air.

"*Donc!* How unfortunate! M'sieu, I have made a specialty of finger prints. I have thousands of finger prints. Every person who passes through the courts of Fort-de-France, I have his finger-print record. Now for this burglar to avoid leaving any prints! That is too bad!"

The prefect twisted his hands together and displayed other signs of agitation at this downfall of his hobby when the three men were startled by three booming taps on the front door.

"*Voilà!* The chevalier!" cried M. Percin. "I had forgot him!"

And the trio rushed to the entrance of the bank.

At the door President Pinville stood for a fluttering moment of indecision, when the three great knocks boomed again. Then he unlocked the door, meaning to open it a little way, but instantly both shutters were flung wide open by the chevalier outside and in marched two villainous Negroes and a slatternly woman, all convoyed by the chevalier himself. The mob had been cleared from the steps and now stood at a respectful distance watching this performance in silence.

M. Pinville hastily reclosed the doors. The men in the bank looked at the newcomers in astonishment. At last M. Percin queried:

"Are these preferred creditors, m'sieu?"

"Riffraff I found in the alley," explained the chevalier. "I thought we would need their testimony to see what sort of man broke into the bank last night. I wanted to decide a little wager I made with M'sieu Poggioli."

Here De Creviceau made a courteous gesture toward the psychologist, inviting him to interrogate the witnesses.

M. Percin immediately made a note of the names and occupations of these troglodytes out of the runway of "Cats' Alley." The woman was Sylvia Gerrerd, by profession a woman of the streets. The sooty rum seller was Bimbo Allemaro, a Negro of the French Congo who had immigrated to Martinique; while the mulatto owner of the reliquary was Henry LeTour, a grandson, he assured M. Percin, of Archbishop LeTour, spiritual father of the Cathedral of Fort-de-France.

"How came a man of your lineage selling sacred pictures in the Allée des Chats?" inquired Percin.

"Ah, Your Excellency," cried the mulatto, "I am very well placed indeed. When a man passes through the hands of Mme. Gerrerd, M'sieu Allemaro, and M'sieu Jevrat he finds himself in need of spiritual comfort, so I sell him a candle to burn to the saints. The archbishop, my grandfather, and I are, you might say, collaborators."

"This Jevrat," inquired Poggioli at once, "who is he? I didn't see him as I came through the alley."

"No, he is never in during the day. He goes out sharpening knives and mending tins all day long—at least so he says."

"And what does he do at night?"

The archbishop's grandson hesitated.

"M'sieu, I do not want to cast any unjust suspicions on a good man; a spiritual minister attached even remotely to the cloth must guard his tongue."

"Come, come," reproved M. Percin, "you are no priest, M. LeTour; the law does not hold inviolate confessions made to you. What does M. Jevrat do at night?"

LeTour was a little frightened at this tone.

"I think—to be plain, Your Excellency, my impression was a—well, I was careful not to change any piece of money he offered me."

"A coiner!" ejaculated the prefect.

LeTour shrugged and spread his hands.

"That was merely my impression, Your Excellency; his forge was going all night long, and then in the day he would be out—mending tins and sharpening knives, so he said, but I fancied he was changing his money for something better."

At this M. Percin was seriously angered.

"M. LeTour, why did you not report such a serious offense? This is no peccadillo, debasing the coinage!"

"Your Excellency," replied LeTour with a certain spirit, "I attempt to look at this matter from the standpoint of the Church. The world is unequally divided between the rich and the poor. The rich have mints, the poor have coiners. The only way the poor can obtain a ten-louis piece, for example, is to make it themselves. The fact that they cannot afford to make their ten-louis pieces out of gold is their misfortune, they are poor." Here the man shrugged again. "But they should be allowed to do the best they can. I would not have reported this M. Jevrat under any circumstances. I attempt to look at this matter from the standpoint of our holy Church."

M. LeTour was so obviously summoning his spiritual fortitude to play the rôle of martyr that the prefect gave up his heckling.

"Where did this M. Jevrat have his forge, m'sieu?"

"At an old iron door in the side of the alley. He cut a hole in it for his smoke to escape."

The four men were alert at once.

"Describe this Jevrat!" cried Poggioli.

The mulatto looked at the psychologist in surprise.

"He was a hunchback, m'sieu; a smallish man, always very neat in his clothes——"

The prefect waggled a confirming finger at this word "neat."

"The same man, M'sieu Poggioli!"

"Sharp-faced," went on the owner of the reliquary. "He wore a gray English suit, tailored to fit his hump, and a hat made of the same cloth, a gray tie——"

"Quite a toff," suggested the prefect.

The man shrugged. "He could very well be—in his trade."

"And you have no idea where he stayed during the day?"

"No-o, m'sieu," pondered LeTour thoughtfully.

"Never an inkling of his daily associations outside of Cats' Alley?"

"I had an idea, m'sieu, that he took his meals in some rather fine café."

"What gave you that impression?"

"A very trifling thing, m'sieu; you will think slightly of it perhaps."

"Tell me and I will decide."

"The songs he hummed when he worked."

The four gentlemen were indeed surprised at this quirk, and Poggioli took up the interrogatory. He asked how Jevrat's songs suggested a fine café.

"Because he never hummed or whistled the same tune twice, m'sieu, and then they were always what they call classical music. Now an ordinary laborer hums only two or three such songs at most, so I decided he remembered the last tunes he heard and that he dined at some stylish café here in the city which had an orchestra."

"A shrewd observation to make!" exclaimed the prefect admiringly.

LeTour shrugged modestly.

"I even went a little further than that, Your Excellency."

"Go on. What else did you observe?"

"A few days ago, three days to be exact, M. Jevrat came to his forge in exceptionally gay spirits. A smile wrinkled his sharp face all night long, but strange to say, that evening he was humming the 'Stabat Mater' and a 'Te Deum.' I called to him:

" 'M'sieu Jevrat, you have attended a funeral to-day.'

" 'That is true,' he admitted. 'How did you guess it, mon père?' The whole of Cats' Alley calls me 'mon père' because of my occupation.

" 'I guessed it,' said I, liking to be as mysterious to him as he was to me. 'Also, I can tell you, M. Jevrat, this person whom you buried to-day was a wealthy kinsman of yours and has left you a fortune.'

"He looked me straight in the eyes and said: 'Père LeTour, you are a wonderful man.'

" 'That,' said I, declining a compliment as becomes a son of the cloth, 'is as it may be, but if I were you I would give up my coining now that I have come into a fortune and I would be a gentleman all night long as well as all day long."

"He stared at me harder than ever and said, 'Your advice is excellent—have you a son?'

" 'None that I know of,' said I.

" 'Then if you wish to leave a noble line to honor your grandfather, the archbishop, I would suggest that you cease commenting on my activities, Père LeTour.' "

The man shrugged.

"He did not frighten me, but I am a man of peace by profession, Your Excellency. That is why I have never mentioned the fellow's occupation to a human soul."

"I see your viewpoint," nodded the prefect. He turned to Poggioli. "M'sieu, here is another clue tossed up. If we get a list of the deaths of the last week, select the rich ones and investigate their legatees, we may find a humpbacked man who wears a gray suit."

The psychologist stood thinking over this curious story; finally he said:

"By the way, M. LeTour, do you happen to have inherited a musical ear through your illustrious grandfather?"

LeTour spread his hands deprecatingly.

"So-so."

"Are you at all familiar with the tunes M. Jevrat hummed on the different nights, and if possible could you recall them in the order they came?"

"M'sieu," said the dealer in ecclesiastical properties, "I make no boast and exhibit no pride because that would be out of place in a descendant of the cloth, but the Archbishop of Fort-de-France is my grandfather."

"Then you would oblige me greatly by making a list of

the different tunes this Jevrat hummed while he was at work counterfeiting money."

"That will require some concentration."

"We will furnish you a desk, pen, and paper; you may ponder as long as you will while we proceed with our investigation of the bank vault."

At this all three of the other gentlemen burst out.

"Really, M. Poggioli—" from M. Pinville—"music—how do you hope to link up the tunes this man was humming with the return of my money?"

Chevalier de Creviceau protested: "M'sieu, I object. You are making an unnecessary mystery of this; you are giving it an air of bewilderment, merely to suggest the crime was complex and win your wager."

The prefect interpolated: "M. Poggioli, I agree that the sort of music a bank robber sings suggests the sort of fellow he is, but really, to write out his programs—that is carrying the matter beyond the practical; that is sheer Anglo-Saxon mysticism."

"Humor my whim, gentlemen," cajoled Poggioli in good spirits. "Remember I am a psychologist as well as criminologist. It will be instructive to learn exactly what arias stick in a criminal's brain on the eve of a great coup. We were arguing, Chevalier, the influence of architecture on crime. Who has investigated the influence of music on crime? It is quite possible that some tunes incite robbery, some murder, others assault. If we could learn this we might formulate laws forbidding certain airs and thus protect the morals of the people."

"Spoken like an American!" cried the prefect, laughing. "And if you organize propaganda for that idea in the United States, God help the Metropolitan Opera Company of New York!"

All the gentlemen laughed at this thrust except M. Pinville, who had lost his money. Poggioli declared he was through with the witnesses just as soon as the archbishop's nephew made out the list.

"I would like to suggest something to simplify this crime," said the chevalier, "since my friend, the psychologist, who has a wager up on the result, has done so much to complicate it."

"Certainly, that's your privilege," declared the prefect.

"I think you gentlemen will agree that M'sieu Poggioli has been trying to give this affair just as mysterious a twist as he possibly could."

"I agree with you heartily," cried M. Pinville, who was evidently getting out of patience.

"I think the prefect should allow me to enter the vault and see if I cannot make something very simple and straightforward out of the crime."

"My dear friend, you are more than welcome!" cried the prefect.

"Gentlemen," protested Poggioli, vaguely offended at this speech, "I assure you I am much more interested in catching the robber than I am in proving any theory or winning any wager."

"Spoken like a gentleman!" cried the prefect. "Chevalier, you are welcome to look into the gutted vault."

"May I inquire," asked the chevalier politely, "if you gentlemen have developed the bright knob to the combination with a view to finding out what were the last finger prints impressed upon it."

"The combination knob is torn away," said the prefect.

"Blown out?" queried the chevalier.

"Cut out," said the prefect. "Just step in and observe for yourself."

As the group walked to the bank vault again, Poggioli put in with a faint note of triumph in his tones:

"Your simple criminal, Chevalier, was at least too clever to leave finger traces; he used gloves as all up-to-date crooks do nowadays."

"How do you know that?" asked De Creviceau in surprise.

"I found a glove button on the floor which he burst off in using his tools."

The chevalier looked thoughtfully at Poggioli:

"That is very slight proof, m'sieu."

"It doesn't require *much* proof to prove anything, Chevalier. It requires only positive proof; and that is positive that the burglar wore gloves."

The triangular gentleman shrugged, twitched his ivory cane, and by that time the men were at the vault door again. De Creviceau looked at the exposed bolts in the great steel shutter with his hands and cane held conspicuously together behind his back. After peering for about a minute he said:

"I think I can refute Professor Poggioli's theory without the aid of any developing mixture to bring out the finger prints."

"How?" asked the prefect.

"The bolts have been oiled some time ago. A very faint viscid film of oil is over them. I believe I can actually see with my unaided eyes the prints of two or three fingers."

"Is it possible?" cried the prefect, striding to the chevalier's side. "If that is true, then I have the culprit if he has ever been before a court in Fort-de-France."

"There it is. Look carefully on that bolt."

The prefect looked; in fact all the men were staring into

the open mechanism of the vault. Sure enough, on the palish yellow film could be seen the faint impressions of human fingers.

The chevalier chuckled briefly.

"M'sieu Poggioli, doesn't that allay at least three fourths of your aura of mystery about this crime?"

"Allay it!" cried the psychologist, staring at the bolts, then at the men. "Why, it deepens it a hundred, a thousandfold, Chevalier, can't you see that?"

"I do not," retorted the chevalier.

"How is it possible?" cried the prefect.

"Because," explained the psychologist crisply, as if he were demonstrating a theorem to his class back in the Ohio State University, "you observe, gentlemen, here we have two flatly contradictory pieces of evidence. A glove button on the floor; finger prints on the bolts. The robber wore gloves—yet he left finger prints. How is it possible that he did both? There is the hiatus you must bridge!"

"But perhaps," cried the chevalier, "this robber had worn holes through the fingers of his gloves!"

"Impossible. He was a fastidious man; also his liberty depended on the integrity of his gloves."

"Perhaps that was a button from the glove of one of my clerks," suggested Pinville.

"Joub has swept out the bank since yesterday afternoon. Besides, a bank clerk never wears gloves at work."

"Perhaps the robber pulled off his gloves after he got to work"—from M. Percin.

"As likely a soldier pull off his gas mask in a gas attack."

"Well what do *you* make of it?" cried the chevalier.

"I don't know what theory to advance. I will have to develop some hypothesis which will embrace these two paradoxical discoveries."

The chevalier began laughing.

"I see what you make of it."

"What?"

"A deeper mystery than ever, and—a win of your wager?"

"Precisely my reaction," declared Poggioli with pedagogic curtness.

The prefect interrupted good-humoredly: "You will excuse me, M'sieu Poggioli, if I go ahead and use these finger prints precisely as if there were no mystery attached to them?"

"Oh, certainly," assured Poggioli, now a little ashamed of his heat after the suavity of M. Percin. "That is what I want you to do, m'sieu."

Thereupon the prefect called for a wrench, which Joub produced, and set about removing the bolts without smudging the faint traces which could be seen upon them. At the same time LeTour arose from the desk which had been assigned him and handed Poggioli a list of about twelve musical numbers. Poggioli thanked the archbishops grandson.

The prefect said: "Well, we will see which develops criminal first, m'sieu; your program of music or these finger prints."

Fifteen minutes later Poggioli, the prefect, and the chevalier had removed the telltale bolts from the safe and were on their way with them to M. Percin's residence where the officer kept his private collection of finger prints of the criminals of Martinique.

As the trio skimmed through the street Poggioli sank back in the cushions of his taxi, staring at the harlequin houses and musing on the contradictory proposition that the burglar of Banque Nationale both did and did not wear gloves.

Such a thesis, of course, was a blank impossibility; the psychologist's reflections broke against it futilely. His brooding was presently diverted by a lively and typically French discussion which had sprung up between his two companions.

"As a matter of fact," the chevalier was saying in his detached tones, "the law does not forbid bank robbery, or indeed any sort of crime, M'sieu Percin."

"The statutes then are very misleading, Chevalier," smiled the prefect in friendly satire.

"They suffer from lack of precision in expression, as do most human utterances," said the chevalier. "It seems fairly clear to me when the law says a man shall go to prison for twenty years if he robs a bank."

"But does he?"

"Certainly, if he is caught!" cried the prefect.

"Ah, there you are! If he is caught. Observe the conditional clause; even so stupid an aggregation as a body of lawmakers must have borne that in mind."

"Naturally," shrugged the prefect.

"But don't you see that changes the whole face of the proposition? Now analyze what is the whole complete idea behind a bank robbery. It comprehends not only the cracking of a safe and the appropriation of funds, but also the use of those funds for the robber's enjoyment, and the robber's ultimate escape from retribution. That is the whole outline of action in the robber's mind, is it not?"

"Why certainly, but——"

"And anything less is really an incomplete robbery?"

"Possibly, but——"

"So you see at once, all the law really forbids are incomplete robberies. A genuinely successful robbery lies quite outside the law. It is impossible to forbid a man anything when there is no power to enforce the prohibition. Therefore we may say the law is directed at bunglers, nincompoops, pretenders to the purple. When you come to refine it down to its last and subtlest social analysis, m'sieu, the function of the law is not to thwart or discourage criminals at all, but to perfect and refine them. The constabulary of a country is really a university, paradoxically supported by the crowd-mind for the perfection of a few individualists. It is the ultimate triumph of the aristocracy over the demos."

Poggioli glanced at the man who was airing such peculiar sentiments. The chevalier's yellow face held the utmost seriousness; in fact, there was almost a fanatical air about the fellow.

The prefect, who was also staring, now burst into a great laugh.

"*Sacrebleu*, what a wag! M'sieu Poggioli, did you ever hear such a man?"

The chevalier hesitated a moment and then joined the prefect in his mirth.

The taxi driver drew up before a curb and the men got out in front of the prefect's residence. They entered a gate and M. Percin led the way around by the side of his house through a yard decorated with tropical trees. They entered a wing of the house and Poggioli found himself in a single long room completely filled with cabinets for filing cards.

"No," cried the prefect, holding the steel bolt carefully by the ends, "all that is necessary is to place this steel in a good light and then run through my finger-print collection and find prints to match these on the bolt."

Poggioli looked at the cabinets in despair.

"Run through this whole collection?"

"Oh, no, I am French; this is all arranged with the greatest care and science. I will soon sift this print down to a single file, and I'll finish in an hour or two."

Here he placed his bolt on a wooden rack in a window, picked up a large magnifying glass, and began examining it.

The Chevalier de Creviceau stood by, greatly interested in this phase of criminal research; but Poggioli did not want to waste his time in mere watching. He told the two men he would go back to town and occupy himself with the musical end of the clue, and they could communicate with him if they discovered anything.

M. Percin nodded abstractedly.

"As you will, *mon ami*, and good luck."

The psychologist retraced his steps through the tropical lawn and found the taxi still waiting at the gate; for where American taxis have to be told to wait, Martinique must be told to go. For once, Poggioli was grateful for this somewhat expensive custom, climbed into the car and signaled the driver to be off.

"Where to?" asked the fellow.

Poggioli pondered.

"I don't know exactly—what cabarets have the best music in the city, m'sieu?"

"The Chat Noir," nodded the chauffeur at once.

"Then to the Chat Noir."

As the fellow leaped out to crank his antiquated machine Poggioli bethought himself.

"By the way, what sort of music do they have at the Chat Noir?"

"American jazz," cried the taxi driver enthusiastically. "Magnificent music!"

Poggioli shook his head.

"I perceive, m'sieu, your grandfather was not an archbishop."

The driver stared at his fare astonished.

"Nobody knows, m'sieu—my grandmother is dead."

"I feel that he was not an archbishop," repeated Poggioli. "Mention some hotel in town where the music is solemn, at least serious."

The motor now rattled away as the driver scratched his head.

"I can take you to the Petit Palais, m'sieu, but you are an American tourist, and I advise you frankly, as man to man, that you can get drunker in less time at the Chat Noir than you can at the Petit Palais."

"Everything has its advantages," acknowledged Poggioli, "but let us get to the Petit Palais as quickly as possible."

And he settled back in his cab to decide on some method to pursue in this nebulous clue of M. Jevrat's music.

As Poggioli reëntered the rainbow business section of Fort-de-France he drew out the paper M. LeTour had given him and was disheartened to see, not the titles of M. Jevrat's whistlings and hummings, but the actual musical themes themselves crudely jotted down on the paper. Each day was jotted down on the calendar with a musical theme after it. It was a kind of musical diary; or, to be more exact, a musical noctuary kept on the bank robber by the archbishop's grandson.

The idea of attempting to trace a mysterious crime

through this striped and dappled city by the aid of crudely scrawled musical scores struck Poggioli with its *bizarrerie*. Where under heaven, except among the French, would a man find himself resorting to such grotesque expedients?

At the Petit Palais Poggioli asked the manager where he could find the musician who put on the dinner programs for his café. The manager, a genial little man, almost a full-blooded Frenchman, gave the psychologist a list of seven names: two singers, a harp, violin, and flute trio, and two orchestra conductors. One of the singers was a Mlle. Héloïse Becquard, 14 Rue Chantilly.

The psychologist reasoned that any man whose nerves were constantly on the alert, as a criminal's would be, and who possessed a passion for music, would most likely be moved by so sensuous a delight as a woman singer. This bit of reasoning gave Poggioli a peculiar thrill of certainty, so he got back to his cab with gusto and called out:

"Fourteen, Rue Chantilly, and move along lively, *s'il vous plaît*."

He hurtled off again and fifteen minutes later halted before a château done in pink stucco, and on the lawn in front of it stood a plaster figure of a girl with a guitar— painted in colors which the artisan mistakenly believed to be natural.

A ring at the bell brought out a coal-black maid who ushered the American into a music room which was in extraordinary disarray. Poggioli stood in the midst of this chaos when Mlle. Becquard entered in a rose morning gown, still tucking in a wisp of her jet-black shining hair. She was the sort of young woman who "carried well" across the footlights; in private she was pretty enough, but wore too aggressive an air to promote comfort in others. Poggioli presented his card.

"I have come, mademoiselle, to ask you about your singing."

"I don't sing jazz," stipulated this dinner *diva* at once.

"So I was informed—that's why I came here."

Mademoiselle Becquard warmed to her caller at once.

"M'sieu, it is a pleasure to hear you say that. The bourgeoisie here in our island—what musical taste! No soul, no escaping the flesh into the universe of pure music." Mademoiselle laid a small hand on her full bosom, which mounded under the rose gown, and then added casually, still holding her pose, "I am usually paid two hundred francs a night."

"I am not an impresario," corrected Poggioli. "I have ventured to come here, mademoiselle, to ask you about a certain program you have already given."

Here Mademoiselle became a little more attentive to Poggioli himself, looking at him with a certain appraising light in her black eyes.

"Have you heard me sing, m'sieu?" She lifted her carefully plucked black brows with a touch of commercialized coquetry.

"To what dining places could I go to hear you sing regularly, mademoiselle? A man of taste likes to avoid the clap-trap," he added diplomatically.

This did pique the woman's interest; usually men heard her sing and then begged to see her at home. This fellow saw her at home and begged to know where she sang.

"Gentlemen like you are the hope of Martinique, m'sieu," she declared in a moved tone, "but don't let me keep you standing. Let's sit here on this sofa." She preceded him to a wide brocaded seat at a French window and sank on it, surrounding him with an aura of heavy perfume.

"Let me see. I sing at the Chatillon, the Empire, the Italienne, the Republique—also I sing to my friends here at home."

Poggioli drew out his list of themes and spread the paper on his knees.

"You are charming. And now I have rather an odd question to ask. Does it happen that recently you have sung any of these airs at the places you mention?"

The singer looked at the crude scores in some surprise.

"Who copied these, m'sieu?"

"An archbishop's grandson."

"An archbishop's——"

Mlle. Becquard burst out laughing.

"You're a wag," she reproved gayly, hitting his arm. "Well, he did it badly enough. Let me see, what is this first one. . . . *Tra la la.*" She lifted her full bosom slightly to go over the score *sotto voce.*

"*Cá,* that isn't a song at all, m'sieu. It's the prelude to *Le Jongleur de Notre Dame.*"

"That's what I wanted you to do," said Poggioli. "Pick out in this list any song you have sung within the last two weeks."

"Why is this, m'sieu?" asked the singer curiously. "Frankly I don't see where this leads to."

Poggioli burst into a laugh.

"Mademoiselle, pick out the songs you sang and tell me where you sang them—it will settle a wager."

"A wager!"

"*Oui,* mademoiselle."

The woman studied him a moment and then shrugged.

"I don't mind obliging you, but you are not doing this on a wager."

She started humming down the list, and presently:

"I sang this at the Empire; this was at the Italienne; and this—oh, this, it is a song I sang at Hôtel Colonial night before last by special request."

"Who requested it?"

"I don't recall—he wrote me a note."

"Have you the note?" asked the psychologist with a faint thrill of excitement.

"*Oui*, m'sieu, here it is."

Mlle. Becquard thrust an impulsive hand into her bosom and fished for a moment. She drew out a pink envelope on which was written in a strong, odd handwriting, "To the Prima Donna."

Poggioli reached for the envelope, but the Becquard withheld it.

"M'sieu, you didn't write this note?"

"No."

"Then you must really tell me why you want it. You might do my unknown admirer some injury with it."

Poggioli was now trembling to see the note.

"Is there a name signed to it?"

"Certainly, m'sieu."

"Then tell me who it is."

"*Non, non*, m'sieu," she denied him with French rapidity. "Not until you tell me truly what you want with it."

"Listen," cried Poggioli, deciding to risk the truth with her. "The Banque Nationale has been robbed——"

"*Oui*," nodded the woman, opening her eyes, "my maid told me that."

"I have this curious clue to the robber's identity—the music he loves."

"Ah, the robber was musical—how romantic, m'sieu!"

"Yes, but the point is that on the very night of the robbery he came home singing the song you sang at the Hôtel Colonial, so it is barely possible he is the man who sent you this note. That is why I want to see his name."

For answer the girl swung up and away from the sofa and in the same instant tore the note in two.

"I betray a man who risks his life singing my song, m'sieu! Nevaire! He has a soul! I wish I could see him! Oh, how often I have wished I could see such a man!"

Poggioli sprang after the woman, who was jerking the note to pieces with fingers trained to piano rapidity.

"You imbecile, you are aiding and abetting a criminal!" cried the American.

"I am aiding a fellow lover of the beautiful!" screamed the singer, more than willing to make a scene of it. "I am aiding a soldier of fortune! How I wish he had come to me himself! How I could have loved such a man!"

"You are insane!" cried Poggioli. "I'll take you before the prefect and make you tell his name!"

"I don't know it!"

"He'll make you tell!"

"But I don't!" she screamed. "I get dozens of such requests; I don't memorize them!"

"Well, confound your antisocial reactions!" cried the psychologist, trembling from frustration.

For answer the woman flung the note at him as a shower of confetti and made a dramatic gesture, showing Poggioli out of the room.

The American went out, got back to his waiting cab, and snapped out at his chauffeur:

"To the Colonial, quick!"

And he rode back to town with nerves on edge at the thought of the narrow margin by which he had missed getting the name of the robber pointblank.

Before the glowing, checkered façade of the Hôtel Colonial Poggioli got out, paid off his driver, and went inside. His plan now was to interview the garçons of the establishment and see if one of them could remember taking a note to Mlle. Becquard on the preceding night. He went up to the clerk's desk, which was deserted as usual. He glanced about the vacant place and was about to ring when he observed a note lying on the counter directed to the clerk. A certain peculiar backhand slant to the writing on the note caught his attention. He glanced around the empty lobby with a twinge of academic guilt, then picked up the note and read it. It was a simple request for a porter to be sent to room thirty-six. It was unsigned, but it was in the same handwriting which he had seen on the note in Mlle. Becquard's music room.

Poggioli studied the queer handwriting a moment longer, then his heart began beating rapidly and he started upstairs to room thirty-six.

On the second floor he lost himself. In Martinique the rooms on the different floors are not numbered by the hundreds. The whole of a hotel is a higgledy-piggledy assemblage of rooms, numbered in the order in which they were built, no matter where that happened to be. The result was that if a man found thirty-five in one end of the house that was no hint that thirty-six was in the neighborhood. Amid his perplexities Poggioli at last found a maid who directed him amid a labyrinth of halls and finally showed him thirty-six.

Poggioli tipped her, bowed and thanked her away, then tapped on the door. Nobody answered. He tried the bolt, but it was locked. He placed shoulder to the flimsy shutter and after a few silent rams it came open.

The moment Poggioli stepped into the room he became aware of a faint, peculiar odor of decay. The windows were thrown open, and even the tenant's trunks were open and his clothing scattered about the bed and chairs as if to present everything to the air. This last gave Poggioli the impression that the occupant meant to leave the hotel soon. The note to the clerk was evidently a request for a man to move his luggage. The clothes and underwear in the room showed their owner to be a man of fastidious taste. The puzzling feature was the smell. Such an odor in the room of a Beau Brummel scotched the American. He looked for its origin. His nose led him to a little round table in the corner of the room. This table appeared perfectly clean; on it lay a bachelor's sewing outfit, a diminutive pair of tailor's shears, and a bottle of yellow liquid. A label stated its contents as tannic acid.

The whole outfit was a riddle. A man who affected silken haberdashery would hardly repair his own clothing, nor would he have any use for a pint of tannic acid. Such an acid did not go to the making of explosives, so would hardly be helpful in vault-cracking.

The criminologist stood with the bottle in his hand, absorbed in the riddle it posed, when he was painfully startled by a voice in the room ejaculating:

"Thank God, I've found you at last!"

The American whirled and saw the Chevalier de Creviceau standing in the doorway. The black eyes in the yellow triangular head started at him. The newcomer went on hurriedly:

"A maid said I would find you in room thirty-six—is this your room?"

"No, it isn't, De Creviceau," replied Poggioli in a swift undertone. "I have every reason to believe that it belongs to the man who robbed the Banque Nationale!"

The chevalier glanced around the room curiously.

"That's fantastic. The prefect has just located the criminal's finger prints definitely. I wonder if you've found the same man."

"He has!"

"Yes, he told me to hurry and find you. He wants to consult with you."

"I think we'd better wait for the return of the occupant of this room."

The Chevalier de Creviceau stared at Poggioli and then burst out laughing.

"I think your end of the clue is incorrect, m'sieu."

"Why?"

"Because the occupant has returned."

"He has!" cried the American, at sea.

"Yes, he is with you now; this is my room."

A rather keen embarrassment swept over Poggioli.

"Why did you ask me if it were my room?" he ejaculated, flushing.

The Chevalier de Creviceau shrugged and spread a palm.

"That was more polite than to say, 'M'sieu Poggioli, what are you doing in my room?' It gave you a chance to explain without embarrassment. And you must excuse the condition of my apartment," went on the chevalier smoothly. "I was trying a little chemical experiment and got a nasty odor in my rooms. I spread my clothes out to air and left a note for a *garçon* to come and repack them,

but he never has done it—but tell me how in the name of
Beelzebub did your investigations ever lead you to my
apartment?"

Poggioli told of his encounter with Mlle. Becquard, the
note he had glimpsed, which she had torn up.

The chevalier broke into laughter.

"Splendid! Magnificent! But it is a pity she did not
show you the note at once; you would have seen my name
on it and saved yourself all this trouble."

"Isn't it odd," cried Poggioli, "that the little humpbacked robber should have whistled the very tune you requested on the very night you requested it."

"Dare say he heard Mlle. Becquard sing it," returned
the chevalier lightly.

"You see, m'sieu, the prefect and I happen to know
who the actual criminal is. We have his finger prints and
his whole criminal history."

"Who is he?" cried Poggioli.

"A certain M. Hantoun; one of the most picturesque of
men. He mulcted the Transatlantique Steamship Company out of three million francs during the World War."

"How was that?" queried the psychologist, interested.

"He was a rum shipper. The French government made
a law forcing the steamship company to transport freight
from Martinique to France at a certain low rate. The
Transatlantique refused to carry cargo at the governmental figure, so Hantoun went to the steamship officials
and arranged to pay them a higher figure than the statute
provided, so he shipped his rum across while the spirits
of the other distillers lay idle on the dock. When Hantoun
had shipped all his rum he went to Paris, filed suit against
the steamship company, and collected his excess freight."

"Why, that's extraordinary!" exclaimed Poggioli.

"I don't know. Any clever man might have thought of that."

"I don't mean that. The queer thing is that such a financier should stoop to bank robbery."

De Creviceau hesitated a moment.

"I understand he lost his money, but, m'sieu, I do not quite see why you should say 'stoop' to bank robbery."

"Because it is lowering oneself," replied Poggioli tartly.

"I can't see that. A bank robbery does not imply a breach of faith, and M. Hantoun's transaction does. When this rum seller accepted a freight rate it was a tacit pledge of good faith between the two parties; but M. Hantoun made no such pledge to the Banque Nationale. Those gentlemen were on their guard. The mere fact that they kept their money in ponderous vaults was a mute recognition of the ancient guild of safe breakers. It seems to me, m'sieu, that you should say M. Hantoun has risen from the treachery of crooked financial deals to the higher plane of self-respecting safe-blowing. You should commend him for his moral reformation."

The American did not follow this absurd sophistry; he merely heard the chevalier talking while his own mind was reviewing the different bits of evidence of the case.

"By the way," he ejaculated, "that bears out perfectly my theory that the man who committed the robbery had once been a wealthy man."

"I must congratulate you there," acknowledged the chevalier. "That was a clever deduction. However, I think you will have to forego your contention that the crime is mysterious."

"No crime is myterious, Chevalier, once you understand it."

"Well, of course that's true; let us say complicated.

This crime is not complicated, and it seems to me I have fairly won our wager."

Poggioli laughed.

"You have itching fingers, m'sieu. Let us wait for the dénouement, the prefect's arrest."

"Certainly, certainly," agreed the chevalier with a courteous gesture, and the two men hurried out of the hotel to the chevalier's cab. They leaped inside and set out at once for police headquarters. As they spun through the rainbow streets they passed the statue of the Empress Josephine. At sight of this charming marble the chevalier observed:

"Extraordinary women, these Martiniquaises, had you observed, M. Poggioli?"

The psychologist nodded absently.

"And by the way, that singer, Mlle. Becquard—what was her address?"

"Fourteen, Rue Chantilly."

"And she said she wished she could see the gallant who wrote her that note?" asked the chevalier, smiling.

"Something to that effect."

The chevalier shrugged and laughed aloud.

"I regret to seem romantic, m'sieu. I understand it is very bad form in America to exhibit the slightest interest in the opposite sex openly; but in all my life, m'sieu, I never recall any woman, ma'mselle or madame, desiring my company but what I made every effort to gratify her. Do you happen to know the point on our route nearest number 14, Rue Chantilly?"

Poggioli looked up to see if his companion were in earnest. Apparently he was.

"You are not going to see Mlle. Becquard now!"

"After she braved the law in my defense? Certainly!"

Poggioli was amazed.

"But this Hantoun," he cried. "Let's see how it turns out!"

The chevalier shrugged.

"The real kernel of the problem has been solved, *mon ami*. The actual arrest of M. Hantoun is mere detail work which we may leave to M. Percin. There can be no intellectual interest attached to the arrest of a safe-cracker. I really think you owe me the hundred francs now, but I'm willing to wait. Come, what do you say, suppose we both call on Mlle. Becquard?"

"Impossible!" cried the American.

"We could twit her with this mystery. I can prove to her I wrote the note and then she would never know what to make of you."

"Why, a moment ago," cried Poggioli, vaguely outraged, "you were hot for both of us to rush off to the police station."

The chevalier shrugged.

"That was before I considered the ma'mselle. Any man of taste, m'sieu, will fling away a ticket to melodrama to enjoy grand opera."

Poggioli was let down to have this much of his adventure fizzle out into a mere intrigue.

"I suppose this is as close to Rue Chantilly as we come," he said flatly, and signaled the car to stop.

Poggioli opened the door of the cab in a disapproving silence and the chevalier climbed out. The triangular man bowed the psychologist a graceful farewell.

"Here is luck in your arrest of M. Hantoun," he remarked gayly, "but I hope you will think that he lifted his plane of endeavor when he took to bank robbery."

And he moved off on the pavement, flipping his cane in

the gay fashion of a man setting forth to see a pretty, and somewhat equivocal, woman.

When Poggioli reached the police station a Negro policeman ushered him at once to the office of M. Percin. The prefect arose with a brisk gesture.

"I'm glad you have come at last," he cried with relief in his tones. "Did M. de Creviceau bring you?"

"He started with me; he didn't come all the way."

"Why?"

"He said the thrill of the hunt was over; the rest would be routine."

M. Percin frowned thoughtfully.

"*Cá*, perhaps it will; but I would not have sent for you if I had been entirely satisfied with the correspondence between the two sets of prints." He indicated the steel bar he had removed from the door of the bank vault and a card which came from his files. "If they had corresponded perfectly I should have proceeded with the routine, as M. de Creviceau calls it."

"What's the difficulty?" inquired the criminologist, going to the table.

"The two prints coincide perfectly in design, but not in detail of line," explained the prefect with a puzzled expression.

Poggioli had to look at the impressions through a magnifying glass to see precisely what M. Percin meant. After a brief study he saw that, while the whorls and curves on the card and bar were replicas, the lines on the bar were not clear and smooth, but were crinkled and broken in places.

"Do you consider it possible," queried the prefect, "that there are two persons on earth, the only difference between whose finger prints is, you might say, integrity of lines?"

"You are an expert in finger prints, m'sieu, I am not."

"I believe it impossible, and yet I shouldn't want to make a false arrest of M. Hantoun. He is a wily fox; it would cost the government dearly. Have you heard what he did to the Transatlantique Company?"

"Yes. He seems to be the sort of man to handle with care."

"He is. But I am surprised that he is implicated in that robbery. Usually a man who specializes in what you might call legal robbery seldom changes to illegal robbery."

"The two branches of the industry do require a different psychology," agreed Poggioli.

As he was saying this, one of those perfectly unaccountable explanations popped into his head. He remembered the glove button he had found on the bank floor.

"I've got it," he cried; "he was wearing a wet glove!"

"What do you mean?" ejaculated the prefect.

"That M. Hantoun soaked his hands in water to shrivel them and change his finger prints; then he wore damp gloves to the vault to keep his fingers withered. That's why he broke off a glove button. The glove was wet and difficult to unbutton."

"I see," cried the prefect, illuminated. "He hoped to leave false prints by this method."

"Certainly. You see, prints that did not correspond would be better than no prints at all; false prints would be a positive proof of his innocence."

"*C'est vrai!*" cried the prefect. "M'sieu Poggioli, I salute you. Your great reputation does not belie you. Now I feel justified in starting at once to make the arrest. Will you come with me?"

"Where do we go?"

"Out to M. Hantoun's country place near Petite Lachaise. He has quite an establishment out there, although
I hear his funds were running short, prior to this last
coup, of course."

The prefect pressed a buzzer and when an officer appeared said: "Have the patrol wagon follow my motor in
the direction of Petite Lachaise."

The officer saluted and retired. M. Percin slipped a re-
volver in his pocket, and after a moment's hesitation
handed Poggioli one. A little later they hurried into the
prefect's motor and glided away through the streaked and
banded city. As they sped along a whimsy occurred to
Poggioli, that these crinkled finger prints made the robbery sufficiently complicated to win his wager from De
Creviceau.

The establishment of M. Hantoun in the northern fau-
bourg of Fort-de-France was an Italian villa of white
stone overlooking the indigo sweep of the bay. Palm trees
in front of the villa spaced its broad white wings with
French precision.

The notion that a bank robber, an ordinary safe blower,
dwelt in such finished loveliness was almost incredible to
Poggioli. Although he was a psychologist, he never could
get over that naïve idea that beauty and morals are somehow connected; although the reverse of the theory is daily
demonstrated in the lives of the artists who create beauty
and the rich who possess it.

The two men stopped the motor some distance down the
boulevard and approached the entrance of the estate at a
stroll.

"Are we going to walk straight from the gate to the
house?" queried Poggioli.

"How else could we get there?" smiled the prefect.

"I thought M. Hantoun might recognize you and attempt to escape," murmured Poggioli, concealing his true uneasiness.

"No, he's not very likely to do *that*." The prefect's stress on "that" suggested more hazardous complications.

The situation was now thoroughly distasteful to Poggioli. He wished warmly that he had adhered to the purely intellectual side of this adventure. If M. Hantoun meant to resist, if there was to be shooting—such a dénouement would be intolerably crude and childish after the severe logic which had worked up this situation.

The prefect opened the gate and the two gentlemen started across the lawn on a path of white sea gravel.

As Poggioli approached it in the intense sunshine the villa seemed preternaturally quiet. As Poggioli stared at it he had a feeling that somebody was peering at them from behind the green jalousies of the French windows. Someone could easily be hidden thus, nursing a loaded gun, watching them.

A strange feeling came to Poggioli that he was walking out of the aura of law and order into a sort of palpable anarchy. As he drew closer to the deathlike villa a curious titillation set up along the psychologist's backbone, in his fingers, on his scalp. As he drew still closer he momentarily expected the clap of a gun and the numbing impact of a bullet somewhere in his body. At every step toward the lifeless mansion this probability grew more and more imminent. Poggioli wet his dry lips and fingered the flat lump of the automatic in his pocket. He had never shot one and he scarcely knew which end of the thing to hold. He had never before realized in his own person how utterly dependent are the majority of human beings upon the force of the law. He decided that when he placed his foot on the first marble step he would be shot dead in his tracks—instantly killed.

He drew near these fatal steps; he swallowed dryly; he placed a foot on the first step.

In the ring of an old-fashioned lion's-head door pull on the villa door was tied a bow of crape. At this universal token of mortality the two men stopped stock still. It was one of the most shocking, one of the most unexpected things—a bow of crape.

"Somebody is dead," murmured the American in shaken tones.

"Suicide, possibly," mumbled the prefect. He put out a hand and pulled the bronze ring. A bell sounded somewhere far in the interior of the dead villa. The men stood in silence. At last the prefect said:

"Shall we force a window?"

Poggioli demurred. He was on the edge of his nerves. The crape had a peculiarly distressing influence upon him.

At last M. Percin was making preparations to break into a window when a glissade of footsteps sounded in the hallway; a little later the door opened and a Negro servant with a melancholy face stood before them.

"Where is your master, M. Hantoun?" asked the detective.

"M'sieu," said the Negro, "my master is dead."

"M. Hantoun dead!"

"*Oui*, m'sieu."

"When did this happen?"

"Three days ago, m'sieu."

The two men stood before the great still house. Poggioli's brain groped among mountains of impossibilities.

"When was he interred!" interrogated the prefect sharply.

"Day before yesterday, m'sieu."

"Where?"

"In Petite Lachaise."

"Did you personally see him laid in his coffin and buried in Petite Lachaise?"

"Oh, certainly, certainly, m'sieu," snuffled the old Negro, and he wiped the tears from his eyes with the back of his rusty wrist.

The two men pondered another moment. M. Hantoun really was dead; or at least this servant thought so.

"Do you object to us entering the villa, m'sieu?" inquired the prefect.

The caretaker made way mournfully.

"You are the prefect of police, m'sieu; I suppose you have come to see about M. Hantoun's debts and invoice the furnishings—it is all very soon after my master's burial."

Not without a certain sense of indecency, the two men entered the villa. Its darkened hallway still hung heavy with the smell of funeral flowers, as the great wreaths had not yet been removed. In a reception room on the right hand tall wax tapers about half consumed still burned with motionless yellow flames beneath a crucifix on a wall. In the corner of the apartment stood a great black curtained catafalque where the dead man had lain in state.

The Negro stood with bent head, silently exhibiting this magnificence.

"Will you look through the other rooms, m'sieu?"

"No—where is the telephone?"

The servant slowly led the way to an alcove in the hall and withdrew a little way.

The prefect seated himself on the little telephone seat and put the receiver to his ear.

"The thing to do, evidently," he said, turning his head to Poggioli, "is to probe into the burial of M. Hantoun?" he questioned in a low voice.

"That's all there is to do."

"A substitution of bodies, don't you suppose?"

"It could hardly be anything else."

But even as he agreed to this *outré* theory, a shivery prescience of still more uncanny complications swept over him. He stood and heard M. Percin order a police squad to report at Petite Lachaise with picks and shovels.

A little later the two investigators returned to their motor and drove around to the cemetery themselves.

The sexton, an old mulatto, immediately directed them to the grave of M. Hantoun. But as he pointed it out Poggioli observed a slight but significant detail of the newly made grave. He indicated it to M. Percin. One of the wilted wreaths lay to one side of the grave and was almost completely covered with dirt.

The prefect looked at it and nodded.

"I see, the grave has been opened since the funeral."

"That's correct. It was at night; the ghoul dropped this wreath and lost it in the excavated earth."

"Then what do you think really happened?" inquired the prefect.

Poggioli spread his hands hopelessly.

"The only thing that comes to my mind is hypnotism, burial, resurrection as practised by the fakirs of India."

"You mean Hantoun was an adept?" gasped M. Percin, "that he was buried *before* the robbery, was dug up, then committed it and escaped?"

"That's too fantastic to be credible, but that is all that occurs to me at this moment."

The prefect clutched at the side of his trim head in a sort of paroxysm of cogitation.

"That would account for the shriveled fingers——"

"But not for M. Jevrat in Cats' Alley; nor M. Jevrat humming the Te Deums. A hypnotized man could not possibly hear his own funeral dirge."

Here these futile speculations were interrupted by the police squad arriving with picks and shovels. M. Percin set them to work exhuming the body.

"I say the coffin will be empty," said M. Percin.

"I say it will contain a substituted body," said the psychologist. "M. Hantoun has never been interred."

The squad dug rapidly and presently exposed a metal coffin. They brushed the dirt carefully away from the top of the container and unscrewed the plate that fitted above the face. When it was laid back both men peered inside. There was a face under the glass. The prefect scrutinized the sunken features a moment, then shook his head.

"It is M. Hantoun himself. His grave clothes are awry, as if he had struggled."

Poggioli got down into the grave beside the prefect. A sudden wild explanation seized on him, springing from some obscure recess of his mind.

"M'sieu," he shivered, "open the glass, draw out his arm, and look at his hand."

M. Percin wrought at the task like a navvy. The hand he finally drew into sight was raw and grewsome—it had been skinned.

Poggioli flung himself upward out of the grave.

"To the Hôtel Colonial! Quick!" he cried. "Seize De Creviceau!"

"How? Why?" cried the prefect, charging after the American.

"He has made a glove out of M. Hantoun's skin!"

"*Sacrebleu!* How simple!" gasped the prefect.

As they flung themselves in the motor and dashed back to town the American clattered over the evidence:

De Creviceau had simply waited in Cats' Alley for some man to be buried. It was pure accident that he had selected a man whose finger prints were in M. Percin's files. De Creviceau had pointed out the prints himself. The stench in his rooms; his note to the singer . . .

Twenty minutes later they whirled up to the flaring façade of the Hôtel Colonial and the clerk came to Poggioli with a letter left for him by the Chevalier de Creviceau.

Before the fellow could deliver it both prefect and psychologist cried out:

"Where is the chevalier!"

"He left with his baggage for the docks two hours ago, m'sieus."

The men dashed to the docks. There they found a waterman who had rowed the chevalier to the *Tiflis*, which had weighed anchor some hour ago.

They rushed to the radio station and got into communication with the *Tiflis* and asked the arrest of the passenger De Creviceau.

As the operator flashed the message Poggioli turned suddenly to the prefect.

"Have you a Mercator's projection of this harbor, M. Percin?"

"Certainly. What do you want with it?"

"The chevalier will not be on the *Tiflis*."

"But, m'sieu, how, why?"

"Why, he would expect us to radio; that's simple. He

has probably arranged for a fish boat to pick him up somewhere."

"But that is fantastic."

"It's natural. Get the projection, plot the course and speed of the *Tiflis*, then plot the positions of a jack boat sailing at right angles from the course of the steamer. You know the rate of the *Tiflis*, also the probable speed of a jack boat in this wind."

"But how do you know he will sail at right angles, m'sieu?" puzzled the prefect.

"That's the psychology of flight. It would apparently be placing the greatest distance between himself and the track of the steamer."

"I see," agreed the Martiniquais as he made a rapid gesture for the clerk to spread out the chart. "But we'll need two police launches, m'sieu, to search fish boats to the windward and the lee of the *Tiflis*."

"To the lee," snapped Poggioli, "he would sail faster in that direction."

"That's fortunate," ejaculated M. Percin. "We have only one boat."

Thirty minutes later, during which time the crew at sea had opportunity to search their ship, the message came back that neither De Creviceau nor his bags were aboard. The captain tagged an official opinion that his passenger had leaped overboard and committed suicide.

Poggioli and M. Percin set out for the harbor. As they went the American recalled the envelope which the clerk at the Colonial had given him. He opened it. It contained a hundred-franc note which later was identified as once belonging to the Banque Nationale. Along with it was this note:

You win.—De Creviceau.

Cricket

*In which the Anglo Saxon runs true to
form in sport and crime.*

CRICKET

UNFORTUNATELY, Professor Henry Poggioli,
American psychologist and unprofessional investigator of
crimes, did not observe the precise minute or from exactly
what direction the gentleman with the drooping blond
mustache came out on the piazza of Bay Mansion Hotel
in Bridgetown, Barbados. Either of these data would have
been of incalculable assistance later to Mr. Poggioli in
his investigation of the mysterious murder or suicide of
Oswald Hemmingway. Because if the gentleman came out
of the hotel itself, that meant one thing; if he had hurried from the cricket ground along Beckles Road and
had entered Bay Mansion ground by the postern gate, that
meant quite another. But when or whence he came lay
completely outside the American's mental record—unless,
indeed, one included his subconscious, which is supposed
to keep a sleepless tab on every nervous impulse of the
whole sensorium; but that, of course, lay quite outside the
practical politics of Poggioli's usable, everyday experience.

As a matter of fact, the psychologist sat brooding over
the depressing, highly colored tragedy which he had
witnessed in Haiti, and in which he had taken a minor
but painful rôle.

He was aroused from this melancholy reverie by a peculiarly ingratiating odor. His thoughts slowly returned
to the present, bringing an impression that some woman
had come out on the veranda possessed of some new and
delicate incense which she was burning, probably for the

midges. He looked up and saw the gentleman with the blond mustache leaning over, elbows on knees, nursing a cigar in his forefingers while he upheld his chin with his thumbs. The fellow stared fixedly through the grove of mango trees which shaded the hotel grounds, evidently facing a keen self-reproach on some count or other.

At that moment Poggioli's thoughts were diverted by the crowd from the cricket game beginning to flow back down Beckles Road into Bay Street. Some lined themselves up in the shade of the mangoes to await the mule tramcar which serves Bridgetown; others with inveterate English pedestrianism started walking on down town through the glaring white dust of the thoroughfare. Over the crowd hung a tense, shocked atmosphere which held quite different spiritual overtones from the usual English reserve after a cricket game. Just then three cricketeers in the uniform of the Wanderers' Club came trotting with grim faces down Beckles Road to the corner of Bay Street. They stopped, stared down the brilliant thoroughfare, and such was the silence that Poggioli heard one of them say to his companions:

"Yonder come the bobbies now."

A second player answered:

"Do you think Cap McCabe did it?"

"Makes no difference whether he did or not, we can't have a story like this coming out about our club."

Poggioli turned to his companion on the porch because he had an impression that the fellow had just come from the game and knew all about what the players were discussing.

"What's happened at the match?" he asked sharply.

The man with the blond mustache turned and apparently observed Poggioli for the first time.

"Seems to have been an accident of some kind."

The fellow's pronunciation was not the broad, gargling Barbadian, but was crisper; English, undoubtedly, possibly a native of Kent.

"Weren't you there?"

The gentleman pulled at his mustache, which was yellow in the center from tobacco smoke.

"No, I wasn't there."

The American was vaguely surprised at the answer.

"I had an impression you were."

"No."

Here a police detachment came hurrying up Bay Street and around the corner. At the same time two or three of the guests of the hotel entered the postern gate off Beckles Road. They got to the piazza at a rather brisker pace than the climate commended. As they passed Poggioli he asked the group in general what had occurred at the cricket game. A younger man paused just before entering the hotel door.

"Chap named Hemmingway bumped off at the bath house."

"Murdered?" asked the American sharply.

"Don't know whether he did it himself or somebody did it for him. I'm cutting away because I don't like to be around when the police begin taking names—dragging you to court. Besides, I don't know a thing about it. If I did it would be different." And the youngish gentleman passed inside, leaving Poggioli and his companion to assimilate this startling information.

This new tragedy coming on top of the American's somber reflections gave the psychologist a thrill of dismay. He got up from his seat nervously, and in default of any other listener addressed the blond gentleman.

"I'd give a month's salary not to have been on this island when this occurred."

The man with the mustache came out of his meditation to look curiously at Poggioli.

"How can it affect a completely detached American like you?"

"Somehow or other I'll be dragged into this investigation."

"Why?"

"Because I am a psychologist. People seem to think I can unravel crimes."

"Can you?"

"Why no—that is, no more than any other layman with a somewhat analytical mind."

The gentleman with the blond mustache pondered a moment, then asked with that sharp tilt with which the English twirl the end of their questions:

"May I inquire if your name happens to be Poggioli?"

"Yes, I'm he. I don't believe I recall——"

"No, you don't. Cheswick is my name. I saw a notice of your arrival in the Bridgetown Times day before yesterday. They tooted you up pretty stiff—human sleuth, a kind of Conan Doyle hero."

The gentleman's pale, inscrutable blue eyes rested on Poggioli with some curiosity and perhaps some amusement.

"Yes, I saw that. The captain of the ship gave the reporter all that stuff," explained Poggioli defensively.

"Perhaps you gave some of it to the captain?" Another sharp upward twirl.

Poggioli thought he caught in this a certain flavor of impudence.

"I was not talking for publication."

A pause. The blond gentleman removed his cigar, saw it was out, and as he made preparations to relight it, continued:

"Don't you like to—er—exert your talents?"

"Well—no, I don't," admitted Poggioli.

"You don't enjoy—what is it—analysis?"

"I like theoretic analysis," delimited the American. "I enjoy an abstract problem. If someone would bring me all the data and say, 'Here it is, what happened?' I'd like such a problem. But when human lives depend upon your efforts—very often brilliant men, your friends—and then see them——"

"Hanged?" inquired the gentleman in an odd tone.

"No, trapped and murdered," stated Poggioli hotly, thinking of his Haitian adventure. "I tell you, the detection of crime is a damnable occupation. A man who follows it will become a monster. I, for one, will never again engage in the sport or trade of man-hunting. That's why I say I wish I had never come to this island."

"You feel keenly on the point," observed the blond gentleman philosophically. "Well, eschew this vile trade, Mr. Poggioli, shake its dust from your skirts. Certainly you are under no moral or legal obligation to turn into—what did the paper call you?—a human sleuth?"

"That's exactly what I am going to do."

At this moment the crowd in Bay Street was somewhat disturbed by a ragged woman pushing her way toward the hotel gate; a little later she hurried up the graveled path under the mangoes. She was half sobbing as she came and was one of the most wretched-looking creatures Poggioli had ever seen. She was thin, her clothes were filthy and hung upon her in rags, her hair was disheveled and dirty. She came unsteadily up the path as if struck by the tropic sun. As she approached the piazza she looked miserably at the two men on the veranda.

"Masters," she said in a shaken whine, "may I be so bold as to ask if either of you kind gentlemen could tell me where I can find Mr. Poggioli?"

Cheswick made a gesture with his cigar.

"That's Mr. Poggioli."

"Master," wailed the woman, turning to the American, "I was advised to come to you. They said if ever a gentleman could work a poor boy out of a bad case it would be you. I haven't any money, Master, but I'll give you an order for my wages at the sugar mills."

"Madam," interposed Poggioli, rather at sea amid these wailing complaints, "may I ask who you are?"

"I'm the widow McGabe."

"What do you want, Mrs. McGabe?"

"I want you to loose my son, Cap, from the bobbies. You know he didn't kill young Oswald Hemmingway, my master. Why would he? Certainly it is reported he treated my daughter illy, but is that enough for my boy to murder him? He was always a gentle lad for all his strength and activity. I told him when he got on the team with the gentlemen, 'Son,' says I, 'this will bring ye bad luck, a boy the likes of you playing cricket with the gentlemen.' But he says, 'They pay me, I'm a professional.' But I says, 'It's not according to nature, the son of a red leg on a team with the heir of Sir Alexander Hemmingway. Some bad luck——' "

Here the old hag's interminable weeping monologue was interrupted by three Negro policemen wearing the queer girlish sailor hats and white blouses of the Barbadian police, who came out of Beckles Road with a wiry youth among them.

Mrs. McGabe burst into passionate, almost grotesque grief.

"There he goes, my poor boy Cap on his way to the gallows for defending the honor of his sister, though he didn't do it a-tall. More likely he killed himself, as some say. But, Master, if you'll look into it—just step and see who it was, if you please, and tell the bobbies who to arrest. They read about you in the *Times* and sent me to you——"

The woman had turned and was staring after the black policemen as they moved down the dusty road with the cricket player in their midst. When they passed out of sight Mrs. McGabe slumped down on the hotel step in a sort of syncope of grief.

Mr. Cheswick continued sitting impassively stroking his blond down-curved mustache with the yellow stains in the center. In an interval in the woman's noises he glanced at the American and said with a certain faint satire, or perhaps a faint brutality, in his voice:

"Mr. Poggioli, your premonition was justified. Publicity did it. Unless a modern Sherlock Holmes wants to go on with his—what do you call it?—monstrous trade of man-hunting, he really oughtn't to advertise himself in the papers."

Poggioli disregarded Mr. Cheswick's observation and began a sort of explanatory argument with the old woman to the effect that he could be of no assistance to her son.

"I'm not a lawyer, Mrs. McGabe. If your son really committed this rash act——"

"But is it reasonable, Master, that poor Cap would strike down a gentleman who played cricket with him?"

"You suggested it yourself."

"That was by way of telling you what I heard him say!"

"What you need is a good lawyer——"

Mr. Cheswick interrupted to growl at the woman:
"Be off with you! Go to Holt and Logan, solicitors, on
Cheapside. They'll take the order for your wages."

The hag looked helplessly at Cheswick, then back at
Poggioli, then took herself off with the air of one who has
suffered unending misfortune and poverty.

Her manner somehow touched Poggioli; perhaps Cheswick's harshness had something to do with it. At any rate,
he hesitated, then followed Mrs. McGabe out into the road.
Not until she turned to latch the gate did she see him.
Then she gasped out:

"Oh, Master, will you help me?"

"I'll go down and listen to the preliminary examination," said Poggioli, moved again in spite of himself. "I'm
afraid I can't be of much service to you."

"Thank you, Master. When you look at my poor boy
you'll see he didn't do it. You can tell the judges who did."

The two fell in with the crowd which flowed down Bay
Street in the wake of the black policemen and their prisoner, the hag looking at Poggioli with a beatific expression through her tears, as if a saint had come down to help
her in her trouble.

The walk was disagreeable enough. Hot white dust was
over their shoes and swirled in the air with the tramp of
the cricket crowd. The high walls beside the road cut off
the trade wind which swayed the treetops overhead. The
whole thoroughfare was a long breathless solarium.

As the two hurried along, gradually gaining on the main
body of pedestrians, Poggioli mopped his face, rather
vexed at himself for being led by sympathy into this investigation. The affair promised no complication whatever.
An ordinary criminal had committed an ordinary crime.

There was nothing in it calling for those delicate and subtle inductions which entertained and moved Poggioli. In the midst of these reflections the hag at his side gasped:

"Yonder they are, Master, starting across the bridge!"

The American looked where the harbor of Bridgetown narrows into an inner harbor called the Carenage. Across this a long pontoon bridge baked in the sunshine. The Carenage was a forest of masts, jammed with schooners and small freighters loading molasses, sugar, and cotton. The vessels were so thick a man could have walked from one shore to the other by stepping from deck to deck.

As Poggioli watched the Negro policemen take their prisoner across the bridge, he grew more and more averse to becoming mixed up in the vulgarity of the case. He walked a little more slowly, casting about in his mind for some words with which to end, politely, his relations with this woman. At that moment Mrs. McGabe suddenly stared and gasped:

"La, there he goes!"

Poggioli looked around just in time to see the cricket player jerk loose from the Negroes, seize the handrail of the bridge, and make a headlong dive over it.

All three policemen grabbed at him, but he tore out of their hands and fell, apparently, onto the deck of a nearby vessel in the crowded harbor. However, since the police remained staring emptily downward, he must have fallen between decks into the murky water of the Carenage. A shout of excitement went up from the crowd. Everybody rushed to the rail to stare. A shock went through Poggioli. He turned to the woman.

"My God, he's drowned himself!"

Mrs. McGabe's face brightened with a crude joy.

"Drowned hisse'f!" she exulted. "He's got away!"

"Escaped!"

"Sure he has, Master. A lad's gone for good when he gets under the boats in the Carenage!"

Poggioli looked blankly at this novel asylum for escaped prisoners.

"When can he get out?"

"Oh, the bobbies will keep him hiding in the water for two or three days, maybe a week. But one of these dark nights he'll slip out. I thank you very much, Master, for what you've done. You've a kind heart, but I won't need you no more unless the bobbies ketch him ag'in."

She bobbed a queer, awkward curtsy, then deserted Poggioli and the next instant ran to the rail herself, shouting:

"Keep hid, Cap! There's a bobby on the fourth scow from the bank. Cut away, laddie!"

The tragedy of the murder was lost in this queer, rather farcical escape. Everybody was laughing now. Poggioli himself was relieved at his sudden deliverance from a stupid undertaking.

Then the fact that he had dreaded this very simple problem struck the psychologist as an odd reaction. As he stood peering into the Carenage he began an introspective analysis to know exactly why he had been so averse to aiding a poor wretch of a woman whose son was in jeopardy. Presently he discovered the reason. The problem held no possibility of a *tour de force* of induction. The Bridgetown paper had acclaimed him as a wizard, but chance had flung him a dull, commonplace crime which no amount of talent could twist into something dramatic and startling. That was what had repelled him. He had wanted to perform in a theatrical rôle before Bridgetown.

What had delayed his steps at Mrs. McGabe's side was his vanity.

When Poggioli realized this he was amazed and disgusted with himself.

"What a cad I am!" he thought.

But back of his self-contempt persisted this feeling of relief that he had not been forced to appear before the Barbadian public with a dull performance.

In the midst of this curious and unflattering analysis a somewhat sardonic voice called out: "There he is, Sir Alexander. That's Mr. Poggioli, the American gentleman who has attracted such favorable comment in the papers."

Poggioli turned and saw, what was very uncommon in Bridgetown, a big English automobile which had whispered up behind him. It was a brougham. On the driver's seat sat a Negro chauffeur in livery. The front seat was unoccupied; in the rear seat sat Mr. Cheswick and a thin, elderly man with iron-gray hair and the finely graven face of an aristocrat. This gentleman now wore the pale, strained look which accompanies a sharp and sudden grief. Mr. Cheswick stepped out of the car.

"Mr. Poggioli," he began ceremoniously, "may I introduce Sir Alexander Hemmingway?" Whether Cheswick reversed the natural order of the introduction out of confusion or ignorance or sarcasm, Poggioli could not be sure. "Sir Alexander drove to the hotel inquiring for you. I told him you had just walked down Bay Street, and he brought me along to point out such a celebrity."

Such ill-timed sarcasm before the grief-stricken father irritated Poggioli. He offered his hand to the peer.

"I will be too happy to serve you in any way I can, Sir Alexander," he said.

"And I'm glad to find you, Mr. Poggioli," replied the

baronet in a moved tone. "You have landed in Bridgetown at a most opportune moment for us. I think you were sent here providentially to assist me and—er—my business associates in this hour of necessity."

"Your business associates?" repeated the psychologist curiously.

"Yes, my associates." Here Sir Alexander turned to Cheswick with an "I thank you very much, my man," at the same time drawing Poggioli into the rear seat with him.

Cheswick stood back and growled out something as the motor murmured forward across the bridge into Trafalgar Square.

"I assume," began the baronet, looking at Poggioli with his grief-drawn face, "that you are a man of discretion, Mr. Poggioli."

"Any confidences you care to make will naturally be guarded, Sir Alexander."

"Thank you. Then I will tell you pointblank that I and the directors of the Imperial Bank of Barbados desire you to prove that this young fellow, Cap McGabe, is the—" his thin face became more bloodless—"the murderer of my son, Oswald Hemmingway."

"That will require no effort, Sir Alexander. The fellow has practically confessed his crime. He's out there in the Carenage now somewhere under the vessels."

The baronet looked back at the waterfront, startled.

"He is!"

"Yes. I saw him break away from the police and leap over the handrail."

A look of extraordinary relief came into the banker's face.

"That—that's helpful. That's very good!"

Poggioli could see no cause for gratitude in this and sat looking at the gentleman curiously.

After a moment the baronet continued: "That will change somewhat the task we would like for you to perform, Mr. Poggioli."

"Naturally, you would like to have me assist in his recapture."

"No-o," said the baronet slowly, "we would now like for you to assist this McGabe in escaping from the Carenage and leaving Barbados permanently."

"You want me to help him escape!" echoed Poggioli in a lowered but amazed voice.

"Yes, we want him out of the island."

Poggioli could not believe he had heard correctly.

"You want me to assist the murderer of your son in evading the police and flying from justice!"

The baronet shook his head.

"McGabe is not the murderer of my son."

"Then who is?"

"I think I have only too good reasons to believe that he died of his own hand, Mr. Poggioli."

The American stared at his companion.

"Didn't you just ask me to assist in proving that McGabe had assassinated your son?"

"That was before I knew he had escaped. His flight is an admission of guilt. Now I ask you to help him get away so he may never come to trial."

Poggioli was on the verge of crying, "But I don't understand," when a certain ray of comprehension filtered into the enigma. The baronet's son was a suicide. Sir Alexander did not want the details of his death made public in a criminal trial.

The banker, who was watching the American's face, sighed heavily.

"I see you suspect the truth."

"Something about the bank?" insinuated Poggioli in a low voice.

"You have peculation in your mind," prompted the baronet.

"I can only surmise something of the sort."

"Well, we are not certain yet. We have already found out he has been plunging heavily on the New York Stock Exchange. My clerk, Hodges, got it from a friend of his at the cable office. He telephoned me at the Wanderers. He heard of Oswald's death sooner than I did. The manager telephoned to the bank at once, and then Hodges asked for me."

"Do you know how much he lost?"

"No, we are on our way now to the cable office for a record of his transactions."

"You think he used the bank's money in his speculations?"

Sir Alexander made a heavy gesture.

"My son had no private fortune of his own."

The car murmured on through Trafalgar Square with its monument to Nelson, its cab stands, its venders squatting around the boles of enormous tropical trees. It pursued its way up Broad Street, where the smartest shops in Bridgetown possess dingy windows crisscrossed with iron bars so that they display nothing whatever. As Poggioli stared at these dull, respectable shops a thought struck him.

"Sir Alexander, doesn't it strike you as incongruous for your son to commit suicide just after winning a cricket game? It is very unnatural that he should have picked a

moment filled with the elation of victory for such an act."
The baronet made a hopeless gesture.

"I had thought of that. I am sure he delayed this mad-
ness merely to assist his teammates in the hardest contest
of the season. When it was over and won, then—" Sir
Alexander made another movement of his hand—"to have
done less would not have been cricket."

On the way to the cable office the brougham stopped at
the Imperial Bank and picked up Hodges. As the fellow
came out into the street and entered the car the baronet
inquired anxiously:

"Have you found out anything so far, Hodges?"

The clerk hesitated.

"Nothing definite, sir."

The baronet shook his head.

"That tells me you are on the track of a shortage—it
will be definite soon enough."

"We can only hope it won't, Sir Alexander," said the
clerk in a low voice.

The banker did not press his man any further, but
leaned back against the cushions and closed his eyes as if
in pain. Hodges was a sandy-colored man, with the reddish
eyes of his type. He stared woodenly ahead of him out of
respect for the baronet, and tried to touch Poggioli, by
whom he sat, as slightly as possible. The American himself began planning some method to get Cap McGabe out
of the island. The ethics of shouldering a murder off on
an innocent man crossed his mind. He leaned and murmured this observation to Hodges. The clerk looked
around with a certain surprise in his pinkish eyes.

"It would be best for him to go, sir," whispered Hodges.
"He'd have to stand his trial, which would be expensive.
Then we don't know Mr. Oswald killed hisself. Cap might

have done it, after all. And we can't have anything out that would shake confidence in the bank, sir. Somebody's got to bear it."

This reply, with its implications spreading in every direction from sheer equivocation to the basic concern for the general practical welfare of Bridgetown, Hodges whispered off without a pause for reflection. The patness of it amazed the psychologist. It was less a studied reply than a racial reflex. It struck Poggioli as the most English attitude imaginable. He had a feeling that any Englishman would have said the same thing, phrased according to the culture of the speaker. Through Hodges, the British Empire had whispered the answer in Poggioli's ear.

The brougham drew up silently before the cable office, and the three men passed the heavy stone building. Hodges knew the clerk in the office, a Mr. Dwight, and explained the situation in a few words. Dwight, a dark little man with perhaps a Welsh strain in him, went quickly to the files, thumbed through the recent dispatches with clerkly fingers, and presently brought out the orders which Oswald Hemmingway had cabled to the brokerage firm of Johnson & Company in New York. He spread the file on a desk before Hodges and Poggioli.

The American glanced briefly at the yellow sheets, which told the story of Oswald Hemmingway's downfall with telegraphic brevity. It was a series of orders to buy and sell different stocks. Hodges had brought some ledger paper and began making a digest of his friend's operations.

Sir Alexander, who found this systematic accounting of his dead son's misfeasance too painful to endure, now said in a strained voice:

"I'll go back. Show me later what you find, Hodges."
Poggioli noticed the baronet's white face.
"Shall I bring you a glass of water?" he asked in alarm.
"No, I'm very well, thank you." And he walked un-
steadily back to his motor.

The psychologist sat down again and returned his
thoughts to the cablegrams. Again he realized that he had
before him an inadequate problem for the proper exertion
of his talents. This was an ordinary case of embezzlement
for the ancient reason. He began questioning Hodges in
a low tone, not because he expected any development, but
out of intellectual habit, as a hunter walks through a field
kicking at coverts which he knows are empty.

"Did you know Mr. Hemmingway dabbled in stocks?"
"No, sir, I didn't know that he *dabbled* in stock."
Hodges' stress on the word invited further questioning.
"You knew he was inclined that way?"
"Well," said Hodges, staying his pen from an entry,
"all us young fellows in the street, sir, follow the stock
reports. We say to each other at the club, 'Reading jumped
five points,' or in a big flurry, such as we've just had,
'Amalgamated hopped thirty-nine in two hours,' and none
of us can help thinking, 'Five thousand pounds in this or
that would have made us rich men.' It's a queer thing, sir,
to see fortunes, motor cars, villas, wives, and even private
yachts swing so easy back and forth in the stock reports,
when a lucky shot of say five thousand pounds would bring
'em down; and us penned up there in the hot office handling
fifty times that amount every day and getting twenty bob
a week for it." Hodges blinked his pinkish eyes as if troubled by some passing mote, then resumed his steady regard
of the American. "Of course, we wouldn't like you to mention such things outside. We bank employees aren't sup-

posed to think of such things, sir. We can't have anything like that going on in our heads, sir, even if it does."

"Why, no, certainly not," agreed Poggioli gravely.

At this point Dwight, the cable operator, who had been casting glances at the two men, now came around the counter to their table in the solicitous fashion of an underling whose curiosity is aroused.

"If there is anything further I can do for you gentlemen . . ." he suggested in a lowered tone one uses in the presence of a tragedy.

"Thanks," mumbled Hodges, without looking up.

"Quite a shock, Mr. Poggioli," pursued the cable dispatcher in vague sympathy. Then he added, "I haven't been introduced to you, Mr. Poggioli, but I knew it was you. I knew Sir Alexander would have the finest talent he could get on a mystery like this."

"I am afraid the mystery is not very deep," said the psychologist.

"Well—it does look simple," agreed the clerk, falling instantly in line with expert opinion. Then after a moment he added diffidently, "Still, it has its points."

"What are those?" inquired Poggioli, more out of courtesy than anything else.

"We-ell——" Mr. Dwight scratched his sleek black head in an effort to crystallize his general feeling for the mystery he thought should lie behind such a tragedy. "Mr. Oswald never did come here to the office to sign his own cablegrams; he always telephoned 'em in."

Poggioli nodded slightly.

"That was against our rules really," frowned Mr. Dwight. "You aren't supposed to telephone your messages, you're supposed to bring 'em in yourself and sign 'em yourself."

"Why did you permit Hemmingway to break the rules?"

"We were good friends. Then I knew it wouldn't do for a bank cashier to be seen too often around the cable office. A man in his position has got to keep up appearances. It's a duty he owes his bank."

Poggioli nodded.

"And then he paid me in an odd way," pursued Mr. Dwight hopefully.

"How? Send you a check?"

"Oh, no, sir," cried Mr. Dwight. "He wouldn't have checks coming to the bank from the cable company. That would have led to questions at once. No, he just mailed me a five-pound note, and 'phoned me what was coming. 'Let me know when it's used up, Dwight,' he said, 'and another's coming.' But he never did use his first remittance quite up. I've got it in my desk in an envelope. Show it to you."

Mr. Dwight hurried around his counter, moved by that human eagerness to exhibit any relic of a tragedy and thus help reconstruct its impression. In half a minute he was back with the envelope, which he handed to Poggioli.

The psychologist opened it and took out the five-pound note. He glanced at the pure white paper and flourishing black script. It was quite new. Apparently, it had never been folded except to place it in its present envelope. The only stain on it was a bluish smudge in the corner. It really corroborated the theory that Oswald had sent the money to the telegrapher, if so simple an act needed corroboration.

"Came straight out of the bank," observed the psychologist.

"What I don't understand," mused Dwight, scratching his head diffidently with the tip of one finger, "is how this spot came there." He pointed at it. "I—er—wondered what *you* would make of that?"

His faintly embarrassed stress on the "you" bespoke a layman presuming to make suggestions to a great criminal expert. Poggioli understood well enough the workings of the telegrapher's mind. Dwight expected every stain and streak to be filled with an intricate meaning, which Poggioli's subtlety would make clear. This was the clerk's reaction from reading the elaborately constructed fiction of the modern detective stories. The psychologist suppressed a smile.

"I dare-say some fellow with dirty fingers owned this bill."

Dwight was crestfallen.

"Yes, sir, but—er——" Then he continued with British persistence in his fanciful idea. "But you see, sir, that's its first folding. It was folded by Mr. Oswald, himself, a bank cashier. Now did you ever in your life know a bank cashier to have dirty fingers, sir? No, you never did. They don't have 'em, sir."

"That's a fact," agreed Poggioli good-humoredly.

He was amused at the little telegrapher standing there so avid for a mystery to develop in his office. Fate had given him a glimpse of a great criminal expert, and Dwight wanted him to unravel then and there, for his amazement, out of a single stain on a bank note, one of those complicated woofs of crime which had so often beguiled his leisure through the pages of his favorite shilling shocker. He began again still more timidly:

"I have a magnifying glass, Mr. Poggioli——" when Hodges interrupted to say:

"Most extraordinary series of investments I ever heard of, Mr. Poggioli."

Mr. Dwight gave up his thrill and went slowly back around his counter to his work.

The American looked from the note to the sheet of figures Hodges had collated.

"What's odd about it?"

"Oswald Hemmingway had the most amazing run of bad luck you can imagine. If it had been reversed he would have been a millionaire to-day."

Poggioli leaned over the paper. Hodges continued:

"The poor boy made every buy exactly at the peak of prices, and every sell in the center of the trough. Now look at this. Compare the hourly prices on the stock-exchange list with his cablegrams. Here, at one o'clock, Oswald sold International Oil at forty-seven; two hours later it was fifty-five, and an hour later fifty-six, when he bought. He lost eleven points. Or take his deal in D. & Q., Ltd. He bought at nine o'clock at seventy-two. The hourly quotations read, 72-71-72-70-68-65, when he sold. The poor chap played a bull market right in the middle of a bear raid."

"Do all his buys and sells meet with the same sort of disaster?" asked Poggioli curiously.

"Every single one; he didn't make a penny in all his operations."

"How many sells and buys did he make?"

"Eighteen in three days."

"In a perfectly erratic market?"

"Yes, sir, the flurry in New York stocks during the last two weeks; nobody really had it in hand, sir."

The American pondered and fished for his cigarette case, an action habitual with him when he started thinking.

"Hodges, that's an extraordinary sequence."

"That's what I was saying, sir."

"It is not only extraordinary, but I should say for sheer undirected fortuity it is impossible—that is, practically impossible."

"I don't see why you say it is impossible, sir; he did it, here it is."

"Mathematically impossible, I mean. It is just as unlikely to bet eighteen times and lose every time as it would be to bet eighteen times and win every time. That is the equivalent in roulette of red coming up eighteen times in succession."

"You can see for yourself," began Hodges, tapping his sheet.

"I said *if* it were undirected. The probabilities of such a series of losses may be obtained roughly by multiplying two by itself for eighteen times. The chances are one in two hundred and sixty-two thousand that such a thing would not occur—if it were undirected."

Even Hodges began to grasp the implication by this time. He looked at the American.

"Blime me, but you are not saying Mr. Oswald meant to lose, are you?"

Poggioli made no reply, but leaned over the table, studying the sheet.

"How much were his losses?"

"I figure up only five hundred pounds," puzzled Hodges, "but I suppose I must be wrong. That's too small an amount for Oswald Hemmingway to do a thing like that over."

"You mean approximately five hundred pounds?"

"No, I mean five hundred pounds precisely, to a penny."

Poggioli shook his head and made that gentle clicking sound with his tongue against his upper teeth which signifies pity, or gentle shame, or sympathy; indeed, an oddly varied gamut of gentle emotions.

"I can hardly believe Oswald would do such a thing over a five-hundred-pound loss," repeated Hodges blankly.

"Odd, odd," agreed Poggioli, then he added briskly: "Well, that's the information we came after. We might as well return to the bank."

"Right you are, sir."

Hodges folded his papers and stored them carefully in his pocket.

As they walked out Mr. Dwight followed them to the door. Even if his splotch on the bank note had been neglected, this last conversation about the probability of losses held a certain flavor of mystery. It would have been more to the point if Poggioli had used his magnifying glass on the note and had said, "The murderer of Oswald Hemmingway is a tall dark man with a clubfoot who has seen service in the Punjab," but what he had heard was something. Just then it occurred to Mr. Dwight that the Colonial banks of Barbados never imported English bank notes. They use a West Indian currency struck especially for them. He went flying after Poggioli with this information.

The psychologist received this somewhat absently.

"But they do use regular English currency, do they not?"

"Yes, but they don't import it, and this note was new, absolutely new except for the stain."

"Exactly."

"So it couldn't possibly have come out of the bank, sir."

"You are right."

"So there must be a very great mystery here after all, sir!" ejaculated Mr. Dwight excitedly.

Poggioli moved away, nodding his head at the clerk, but to be perfectly truthful he was occupied neither with this clue of the unusual currency nor his clue of mathematical probabilities. Both of these facts were stored away in appropriate mental niches to be used later. Just at this moment he was moved by a sort of dawning elation that there was something in the covert after all. He was going to have his game, an aristocratic melodrama of mental brilliance to spread before the Barbadian public. The psychologist walked along the hot, respectable street of Bridgetown with a light, gay feeling; and this gayety, he realized, was based on his vanity. He smiled at himself and murmured audibly:

"What a cad I am!"

"Pardon?" ejaculated Hodges, looking around at him interrogatively.

"I said," repeated Poggioli, still smiling, "there is no such thing as art for art's sake; that saying is a sham and a humbug; art is for approbation's sake, to show people how wonderful we are."

Mr. Hodges closed one pinkish eye insinuatingly.

"Right you are, sir. It's not every clerk could have done as I did, sir—tipped off a great detective with a clue—eh?"

Hodges' thoughts evidently were running along the same lines as Poggioli's, only with more *naïveté*.

Had the Imperial Bank of Barbados been located in London or in New York, its furnishings would have been described by the simple word "marble," but in the dusty, sunstruck port of Bridgetown the only adjective which could properly qualify the imperial grandeur is the polysyllable "marmoreal." For the force of adjectives, like gravitation, the speed of light, and the beauty of women, is relative.

The marmoreal interior of the Bank of Barbados, when Poggioli entered it, was in a state of extreme disturbance. This, too, was relative. In New York any patron would have said the bank was functioning with oily precision. The queues of depositors and withdrawers were approaching their respective windows. A floorman piloted the uninitiated to the windows tagged with their initials. But, for example, the teller in window K-L, instead of being posted exactly in the center of his cage, had dislodged himself through some emotional stress, and now stood some six inches to one side and twelve inches to the rear, so that he could peer back into the marmoreal interior of the bank for any new symptoms of the investigation going on therein. The floor man himself, in stout, respectable uniform, so far forgot himself as to glance backward, or to peer around his convoys in an effort to see who was entering the door. Now that would have been efficiency in New York, but in ultra-English Bridgetown it was chaos. In short, the morale of the Imperial Bank of Bridgetown was shot to pieces.

When Poggioli entered the floor man actually deserted a client and hurried to the psychologist.

"They're waiting for you in the director's room, sir," he whispered huskily. "Mr. Hodges will show you in. You're to come at once, sir."

The fellow somehow gave Poggioli the impression that he had once been a cabman but had had reverses.

A few moments later Hodges bowed Poggioli into a room, entered himself, placed his sheets of paper on a table before the baronet, and retired.

Sir Alexander arose and formally drew up a seat for his

guest, then picked up his clerk's report with unsteady fingers. After a single glance he lowered the sheet with a long expiration and a shake of his head.

"This settles the matter, Mr. Poggioli. The clerks have found a shortage in my son's accounts—five hundred pounds. His losses set out in this sheet balance exactly with the shortage."

"That's an extremely small sum to produce so violent a reaction in a young man of your son's position, Sir Alexander."

"I had thought of that. It was not the amount, Mr. Poggioli. He knew my strong sentiment against stock gambling. His remorse had much to do with it."

"But wasn't it several days between his losses and his death?"

"Four days."

"Remorse is a cynical emotion, Sir Alexander. Within four days a normal man of your son's age would have dropped his self-destructive impulse."

"He was a young man of great determination."

"Nevertheless, depression and recuperation lie back of determination and control it."

"I can't see where your speculations are leading, Mr. Poggioli. My son—is dead."

The American, who was more nearly thinking aloud at this point than conducting a conversation, turned to the practical end of the problem.

"The shortage you speak of—was it difficult to trace?"

"No, very simple."

"Your son had made no elaborate effort to cover it up?"

"None at all. He had simply made out his ticket for cash withdrawn."

"For five hundred pounds?"

"Yes."

"What was the date of the ticket?"

The banker replaced his glasses on his high, thin nose, picked up his memorandum.

"April the eleventh."

"And the stock transactions took place on April thirteenth, fourteenth, and fifteenth?"

"Yes, he evidently withdrew the money with the intention of speculating."

"Doesn't it strike you as extraordinary that he should foretell to a penny the amount he would lose in his gambling?"

The baronet removed his glasses and drew a dry hand across his eyes.

"He evidently deposited with his broker in New York and drew against it until it was gone."

"That's impossible," pointed out the American, "because money in bulk cannot reach America in four days from Barbados, and it has not been cabled to New York."

Sir Alexander, his wits dulled by grief, was still evidently unaware of whither the psychologist's argument tended.

"Did your son have a financial rating in Dun or Bradstreet?"

"Yes."

"Then the natural course for him to have pursued would have been to gamble first and draw on the bank for his losses afterward. To my mind it's against all law of behavior for a man to draw out five hundred pounds and then apparently speculate with the greatest care to lose precisely that amount."

The banker looked his astonishment.

"Mr. Poggioli, I am accepting you as an expert in your profession. But frankly, I do not understand why you suggest my son intended to lose five hundred pounds."

"I do not believe your son did it."

"I gathered that much. But why do you think anyone speculated carefully to lose five hundred pounds?"

"Because the reports there before you show that unless these losses were intentional three almost impossible coincidences occurred simultaneously: the first is that a stock gambler should lose on every speculation for eighteen times in succession; the second is that these losses should total up precisely with an amount of money already predetermined; the third is that, after these two impossible events had coincided, your son's emotional recuperative cycle should not have functioned within the space of four days. When three improbabilities pile up on each other like that, Sir Alexander, I decline to believe any of them."

"Then what do you believe?" cried the baronet, his voice edged with excitement.

"I think the person who manipulated these carefully planned losses had some powerful motive for losing. It looks as if it were arranged purely to give the color of suicide to your son's death."

"Then you think he was murdered after all?" asked the peer in a low tone, his face growing even paler than it was.

"This theory is further upheld by the fact that the trading orders were not placed in the cable office by your son in person. They were telephoned in against the rules of the company."

The banker stared at the psychologist.

"Then who did it?" he gasped.

"I can't say."

At this moment came a tap on the door and Hodges entered.

"Some gentlemen of the cricket club to see you, sir."

"Let them come in, Hodges. Will you wait here, Mr. Poggioli, and see what these gentlemen have to say?"

The psychologist made a gesture of assent, and a moment later four men entered the door.

As they came forward Poggioli was surprised to see Mr. Cheswick among them. Cheswick performed the introductions. The other three men were Messrs. Jones, Wilberforce, and Santee. They were of different types, but all three had the sunburnt, outdoor quality of cricket players. When the baronet asked what he could do for them the youth named Jones made a little bow and began what was evidently a prepared address.

"Sir Alexander, we are a committee from the Wanderers Cricket Club, to which your son Oswald belonged. We have come to see you, sir, on a mission of a very intimate nature. We have come to make a request of you, which will call upon you for a—we can only say, sir—a very great generosity, a far more than usual generosity."

The baronet looked at the four men lined stiffly before him.

"May I hear the nature of your request, gentlemen?"

"We would like if possible, sir, to keep the name of the Wanderers Club out of the tragedy which has just occurred, Sir Alexander." Here Jones caught his breath, apparently at his own effrontery, then hurried on. "The Wanderers Club is a very old institution, sir. Our charter dates back to 1712 when the Prince of Wales visited our island on the frigate *Indomitable*. His Highness was gracious enough to make us an address at the founding of our club."

"Yes," said the baronet in a bleak voice, "I am acquainted with those facts."

"Since that time," went on Mr. Jones, "no legal action has ever originated in the Wanderers Club. No doubt within the space of two hundred years there have been provocations, Sir Alexander, but up until now everything has been arranged without publicity. We have always been a club of gentlemen, sir, devoted to the sport of cricket."

Mr. Jones ceased speaking. The baronet drew a deep sigh and for several moments sat looking at the men before him.

"What course of action have you to suggest, gentlemen?" he asked at length.

"We await your decision entirely, Sir Alexander. The whole resources of the club, both physical and moral, are at your disposal."

"I don't doubt your good will, but I can't see any possible use I can make of your offer."

Mr. Jones took a step nearer and lowered his voice.

"We had thought of two possible courses of action, Sir Alexander."

"Mention them."

The cricket player glanced significantly at Poggioli.

"He is my confidential adviser in this matter," said the baronet.

"Very well, sir. Our first hope is that you will permit us simply to expel the criminal from Barbados and never permit him to return."

"Could the club do that?"

"We will take it upon ourselves, sir."

The baronet pondered a moment.

"And the other alternative?"

Jones hesitated again.

"Two of our members meant to accompany the miscreant from Barbados and see to it that he is settled away from here. At a pinch, sir—" here the speaker's voice went lower still—"at a pinch, he would never arrive at his destination—another case of suicide."

Sir Alexander made a gesture of repulsion.

"That is unthinkable."

"We felt so, too," echoed Jones in relief.

"However, I would like to know that the assassin of my son is no longer in Barbados."

"That is very, very generous, sir," thanked Jones, evidently moved, and the other three echoed. "Very generous. We will answer for his permanent removal from the island."

"I—I think if—if Oswald were alive——" The baronet ceased speaking to control the emotion which threatened his composure.

The four Wanderers nodded slightly to signify that they too believed the dead youth, if he were alive, would approve this course.

The baronet regained his self-possession and suggested in a gray voice:

"You will have to spirit him out from under the surveillance of the police."

"That will be done, sir."

"I would suggest that you work with Mr. Poggioli, here. He represents my interest in the matter."

"We will be proud to coöperate with such a distinguished criminologist," assured Jones.

"Then I will leave the details of the matter in your hands." The baronet leaned back in his chair with a deep sigh, perhaps from the strain such a concession made upon his charity.

As Poggioli followed the men out he glanced back at

his employer with a feeling that here, indeed, was a gentleman of peculiar worth and dignity.

The committee and Poggioli retired to one of the waiting rooms in the bank to work out the details of their plan
to banish Oswald Hemmingway's assassin. As they seated
themselves around a small table Poggioli turned curiously
to Cheswick.

"I didn't know you were a member of the Wanderers."

"I am not," explained Mr. Cheswick at once. "I was at
the club talking this matter over with Mr. Jones. He was
regretting the unfortunate publicity of the matter, the
first in the history of the club, and I suggested some ar-
rangement like this might be made with Sir Alexander;
he's a very fine gentleman."

"You suggested it!"

Poggioli was faintly surprised at the idea's originating
outside the club members.

"Yes. I had heard of some such arrangements being made
in other places. I even suggested that I might escort the
criminal to some designated port, as I am leaving this
island in a few days. However," he added, glancing around
the group, "I would not be responsible for his remaining
there."

Here Jones, Wilberforce, and Santee agreed at once
that this would be beyond his rôle.

"Then the only thing left for us to do," proceeded Mr.
Cheswick, stroking his yellow mustache, "is to arrange
the details of McGabe's deportation."

This was the first time McGabe's name had been mentioned openly at the meeting.

"What sort of fellow is this McGabe?" queried the
psychologist.

"He is what is called here in Barbados a 'red leg,' " replied Jones. "The 'red legs' are descendants of white criminals who were banished from England to Barbados back in the Seventeenth Century. They were sold as slaves to the gentlemen colonists of the island. They were called red legs because their owners clothed them in kilts and their legs sunburned."

Poggioli nodded slowly.

"I see. Criminality is inherited in the McGabe family. The grandfather was banished to Barbados, the grandson is banished from Barbados."

There was a moment's silence at this stark unrolling of destiny.

"It's enough to make a man sorry for the rotter!" ejaculated Santee.

The American sat meditating if it were possible for Cap McGabe to have sent the fraudulent cable orders.

"Is this young fellow well educated?" he inquired.

"I doubt if he knows his three R's," said Santee. "He is in our club as a professional."

"I see. He is one of those shrewd, untutored fellows."

Santee looked at Jones.

"He never impressed me that way, did he you, Jones?"

"Not at all," agreed Jones. "He was just a wiry lad with a batting eye. Why did you think he might be clever, Mr. Poggioli?"

"Perhaps Mr. Poggioli has already discovered something we don't know?" suggested Cheswick, looking keenly at the psychologist.

"Oh, no," hastened Poggioli. "I am simply groping after McGabe's character. His escape from the police in the Carenage struck me as a *tour de force*."

"It was not original," smiled Jones. "That has been done several times."

"It seems to me," interposed Cheswick, "that we are more interested in the question: Will McGabe resist our effort to deport him? However, I am not criticizing any question asked by an expert."

"He probably wouldn't resist if he were approached right," said Jones.

"If it is a matter of diplomacy, you would be a good man to approach him," suggested Poggioli.

"I don't want to go by myself," retreated Jones at once.

"Cheswick and Wilberforce could go along, since they are to accompany him from the island," planned Santee.

"How are you going to arrange about his passport?" inquired Cheswick.

"How are you going to find him at all?" added Santee.

"And him under the surveillance of the police," concluded Wilberforce.

Poggioli saw that the committee expected him, as an expert, to answer these questions.

"I hope some of these details will work themselves out as we get into the problem," answered the psychologist.

"One thing sure," interposed Jones, "all of us men can't go down to the harbor and interview McGabe. That would be too conspicuous. I think Mr. Poggioli is the man."

"Hear! Hear!" agreed Mr. Santee, nodding his head decisively.

"Certainly," agreed Cheswick, with a slight drawl and a pull at his yellow mustache. "There is no use in us laymen intruding on the almost uncanny powers of a master mind—did you gentlemen read the notice with which the *Times* honored Mr. Poggioli?"

"That very fact," agreed Jones simply, "will give him

the entrée with the harbor police. He can go anywhere without suspicion."

"That's a fact," seconded Wilberforce. "Just let Mr. Poggioli see McGabe and make arrangements for the three of us to leave Barbados together."

"Gentlemen," demurred the psychologist with a grave smile, "this matter of evading the police and the passport regulations—I don't want to incriminate myself even for so worthy an object as protecting the name of an old cricket club."

"We don't want you actually to do anything at all," assured Cheswick at once. "You are the master mind, the consulting hijacker or scofflaw, to use an Americanism. There is no penalty attached to thinking up evasions of the law, Mr. Poggioli, provided you don't do it yourself; otherwise every lawyer would be clapped into Bridewell at once."

Upon the formulation of these plans Mr. Santee glanced at his watch and observed that practice would begin in thirty minutes. Thereupon the meeting adjourned. The men passed out of the bank into the street. The psychologist went one direction, Mr. Cheswick another, while the three cricketeers hailed a cab and drove off to their club to resume practice at the ancient and honorable game of cricket.

Poggioli for his part moved slowly down the hot, dusty street, past the solid, respectable shops, his mind full of the loose ends of his problem. The salient misfit in the situation seemed to be Cap McGabe. If Cap were the ignorant, loutish fellow the Wanderers described, his was not the brain back of the false stock orders. The stock losses themselves puzzled Poggioli. Why should exactly five hundred pounds enter into the criminal combination? Oswald Hemmingway had checked this amount from the bank. Why had he withdrawn it, and what had he done with it? Poggioli fished patiently for an answer to these questions. He moved on down Broad Street toward Trafalgar Square, and perhaps meant to go on to the Carenage where Cap McGabe was in watery hiding, but at the end of two blocks he did a slow about-face and started back to the bank. He had no conscious reason for doing this. He was moved by some inner impulse which did not even trouble to explain itself to his conscious mind. The vulgar would have put it that Poggioli "had a hunch," that there was something more to be discovered at the bank. To be more exact, the hunch had Poggioli. He moved slowly back up through the hotly illuminated dullness of Bridgetown, gazing steadfastly at certain mental objects: the five hundred pounds withdrawn from the bank, the speculative losses—which balanced the five hundred. It occurred to Poggioli that five hundred pounds was a sum large enough to tempt an ordinary man to almost any crime, whereas to a baronet's son it would be mere spending money. Oswald Hemmingway might well have wagered that whole amount on one cricket game and thought little of it. Abruptly, this last reflection stood out in Poggioli's mind in rubric. It startled him. And the next moment the explanation of the whole riddle flashed upon him, bringing a feeling of immense relief. It was as simple as lending an umbrella on a rainy day. Oswald Hemmingway had meant to gamble on the cricket match. He had withdrawn the money from the bank some days before so as to avoid the suspicion of his father, who opposed gambling. Then some person discovered he had this money, and knew that he would carry it on his person to the game. The unknown then had worked out elaborate stock losses tallying to a penny with the amount Oswald had withdrawn, and so suggested suicide. After the game was over, and before Hemmingway had paid his debts, this unknown person had stabbed the youth in the bath house, rifled his clothes in the confusion caused by the murder, and had escaped. There was more than a touch of the improbable in this theory, but when a man has only one horse he cannot choose his steed.

The moment this solution popped into Poggioli's mind he automatically rejected Cap McGabe as the possible murderer. He believed such complications were beyond the brain of a red leg. Then, sliding from one theme into another without any obvious connection, Poggioli found himself trying to recall when it was, and from exactly what direction, Mr. Cheswick had entered the piazza of Bay Mansion Hotel. Had he come out of the hotel itself, or entered through the side gate from Beckles Road? The American had no clear-cut reason to suspect Mr. Cheswick, but the fellow seemed to have the brains and a cold, sardonic temperament which might work up such a complex crime. If he could only remember whether Cheswick came out of the hotel or through the postern gate. . . .

The American began trying to review just what were his impressions as he sat on the hotel porch in the opening movement of this tragedy. He recollected that he had been thinking of Haiti, and had smelled a peculiar fragrance. . . .

At this point Poggioli really seemed to catch again that odd aroma and glanced up. He was not surprised to see Mr. Cheswick himself standing not far from him, looking at him with a faint, equivocal smile on his ruddy face and with a cigar stuck in the yellowed part of his blond, down-curved mustache.

"So you didn't go to the docks after all," observed Cheswick, removing his cigar, looking at the end, and beginning an automatic fumbling for his match box to relight it.

"No, I was mulling over the details of our problem, so I thought I would take a turn back and have all my questions at my tongue's end to ask McGabe when I saw him." Poggioli really thought that was why he had come back. It sounded reasonable, and two thirds of the time a man has to guess at his own motives as if he were an arrant stranger to himself.

"Now that's a coincidence," mumbled Mr. Cheswick, relighting his cigar and talking around it in a muffled tone. "For I, too, was walking along chewing on this proposition when it suddenly popped into my head that you knew something else about McGabe—or about Hemmingway— or something."

Mr. Cheswick removed his cigar, now fully lighted, and waved it vaguely.

"Knew something about what?"

"Those questions you were asking in the bank about McGabe— Was he educated? Was he a cunning fellow? It just struck me you must have something back of that."

"Why, no-o." Poggioli shook his head slowly.

"Come, now, why should you ask if McCabe was cunning if you didn't have some sort of evidence to make you think he was cunning?"

Mr. Cheswick stuck his tobacco into his mouth again; its perfumed smoke drifted up and caused him to close one pale eye so that he now stood with one eye closed and the other stretched wide in a sort of grotesque interrogation.

"Come," he pursued, "confess; you threw the other boys

off the track easy enough because they were thinking about cricket, but not me. I was thinking the same thing you were. What new thing have you found out?"

Poggioli began laughing.

"You take a deep interest in this case to be a rank outsider, Mr. Cheswick."

The blond gentleman's highly colored face went a shade pinker.

"I don't see I'm such an outsider. I have a moral reason for wanting to know any—er—new information."

The droll way men invent reasons for their actions reimpressed itself upon Poggioli for the hundredth time. He laughed with more amusement than ever.

"What is your moral reason, Mr. Cheswick?"

"Why, damn it, if I am to escort McGabe out of this country I ought to know the full case against him. I am, you might say, his executioner."

Poggioli laughed more heartily than ever.

"Nobody is sure you are going to escort him out of the country."

"Certainly I have to find him first."

Poggioli stopped laughing but continued with an amused smile on his face:

"I am sorry I haven't anything new against him. You are like all the rest of the fellows, seem to think I'm a magician. If I inquire if a man is tall, short, dull, or keen, you think that is the clue to the maze. It's all because of that confounded article in the *Times*. They tooted me up as a sleight-of-hand performer who can run his hand into an empty bag"—here Poggioli made a reaching gesture—"and pull out a murderer!"

Here Poggioli caught Cheswick's lapel and mimicked holding him up to an audience.

Mr. Cheswick's cigar tumbled out of his mouth. He stared for a moment at the American with wide pale eyes, then burst into great laughter.

"I'll be swizzled if you aren't more of a card than I thought. Why—do you know, for the moment I fancied——"

Mr. Cheswick did not have opportunity to say what for the moment he fancied; he stopped laughing with disconcerting abruptness and looked soberly toward the bank.

Poggioli glanced around and saw Sir Alexander and Hodges standing on the top of the bank steps. Hodges was pointing and said, "Yonder he is, sir."

The next moment the banker beckoned the psychologist. Both the American and Cheswick went up. Sir Alexander addressed them in agitated tones.

"Gentlemen, we have found the five hundred. The bank has lost nothing, nothing at all!"

The American stared as his theory of the crime fell abruptly to pieces.

"Found the five hundred!" he repeated blankly.

The baronet clenched his fists with almost an hysterical gesture.

"Oh, my God, yes! The uncertainty, the suspense, the tragic mystery that surrounds my poor dead boy!"

Mr. Cheswick was getting out another cigar.

"I think the best thing we can do," he said with his eyes on his case, "is to go in and have a look at the five hundred they found."

When the men entered the bank they found the paying teller had discovered the missing money, a package of Bank of England notes stuck away in a corner inside the vault. Outside the package in Oswald Hemmingway's handwriting was the sentence:

Do not place in circulation, O. H.

The baronet stood wiping his eyes, looking at the notes spread out on the table.

"This clears Oswald of any action unbecoming to a banker and a gentleman."

"I wish he had made a notation why the notes should not be returned to circulation," said the paying teller.

Poggioli bent over the bills, scrutinizing them.

"They are not counterfeited or raised?"

"Hodges is investigating that point now," said the banker.

Mr. Cheswick stood twisting his yellowed mustache.

"It is possible, Sir Alexander, that these notes are entirely disconnected with your son's tragedy."

The baronet shook his head.

"I can't think that. Yet what connection can there be between a sum of money retired from circulation and Oswald's death?"

Cheswick, who stood staring at the money, asked suddenly: "Sir Alexander, will you sell me one of these notes?"

"Why?"

"I want to take it to the wharf, try to find Cap McGabe and confront him with it."

"You can take as many as you like without purchase."

"No," demurred Cheswick, drawing out a wallet of colonial currency, "to exchange money is no loss to either of us; then if I should happen not to return it you would be whole."

The banker made an assenting gesture.

Mr. Cheswick riffled over the notes.

"I'll take this one. It has a spot on it so I won't get it mixed up with the other money in my purse."

Poggioli glanced at the note in question and saw a bluish smudge near its center. Apart from this smudge the paper appeared perfectly new, without even a crease to mark its crispness.

As Mr. Cheswick took the note Poggioli stared at it with a feeling of retarded recognition. The blond gentleman stowed it away and bowed himself out of the bank, saying he would go and find McGabe. Not till he was gone did the American recall the bank note at the cable office marked with a similar smudge. A nervous spasm caught his throat. He made a movement to rush out of the bank and catch Cheswick up, but a second impulse held him back to the table, where he made a hurried examination of the rest of the notes. Certainty seized the American that somehow the bluish spot formed a clue to the mystery and Cheswick knew it. Then, for a moment, Poggioli was astonished that Cheswick wanted a clue. While these thoughts chased through his head he was turning the reverse sides of the notes with nervous rapidity. By good luck he found another faint bluish smudge on an edge. His relief at this find answered his question. The smudge was a clue. Cheswick had purchased the note to obliterate his own tracks. The American picked out the other stained note with a feeling of narrow escape.

"I'll take this one, Sir Alexander," and he reached in his pocket to pay for it.

The baronet made a gesture.

"No, take it along."

Poggioli murmured his thanks and hurried to the full

light of a window to examine the note to which Mr. Dwight, hours earlier, had directed his attention.

As he did so Hodges came into the room with a circular letter he had found in the files.

"This is what we were after, Sir Alexander," he said in an excited voice. "I've found the numbers of the notes."

"What has happened to them?"

"They were stolen from the Bank of England on the third of January. We received this lookout circular about two months ago. Its corner was crimped down, sir, as you see."

The baronet took the sheet, which rattled in his hand.

"Oswald did that, to refer to it quickly."

"Undoubtedly, sir."

"My unfortunate son!"

"But why didn't he report the stolen money at once?" cried Hodges. "Why did he simply retire it?"

Poggioli interrupted their speculations.

"Mr. Hodges," he requested, "have you a magnifying glass?"

The clerk brought one and the American bent down to a careful scrutiny of the stain.

It seemed a pity that Mr. Dwight of the cable office could not have seen him at the moment.

The stain itself, however, was not very dramatic. It was simply dirt, a touch of clay. Poggioli assembled two or three particles on the white paper and ran the back of his thumb nail over them; they made a soft streak—a stain of blue clay.

This was as informing as would have been a sparrow track, a rain drop, or the leaf of any tree. He could turn anywhere in wood or field, in mine or on mountain top and find clay.

Poggioli straightened up in keen frustration. His clue pointed in any direction he cared to look; an obsequious clue!

The American had no clear-cut idea of what he had expected to find. A finger print, perhaps; one of Mr. Cheswick's own finger prints possibly. It suddenly occurred to Poggioli that the other note did have on it one of Mr. Cheswick's finger prints, and the fellow had leaped to rescue this betraying sign.

Ideas now rushed rapidly in on the American.

"Hodges," he called, "was that five hundred pounds all that was stolen from the Bank of England, according to your circular?"

"Bless you, no!" cried the clerk. "Here's the list, sir. It tots up fifty thousand pounds."

"A quarter of a million dollars! Now there, gentlemen, at last, is a sufficient incentive for murder!"

"What do you mean?" cried the baronet.

"I mean, the man who murdered your son has a fortune of fifty thousand pounds in stolen bank notes hidden somewhere. He is traveling through the remote provinces trying to sell these bulletined notes by the little so nothing will be suspected. Oswald cashed a few, discovered the notes were stolen, and the thief murdered him before he revealed his discovery."

A pallor spread over the baronet's thin face. "Certainly, how simple it is! Who do you suppose did it? Not—McGabe."

"I'm going down to the dock this moment and work out the details with Cheswick."

"But wait! Wait!" cried the banker. "Mr. Cheswick is a—er——"

"Yes, sir, what is it?"

The banker's eyes were wide. He looked into Poggioli's face and stammered.

"Perhaps you have a better grasp of the situation than I."

The American left the bank and went legging it down through the hot street on the lookout for Mr. Cheswick. He hurried to Trafalgar Square and stared up and down the waterside out over the forest of masts in the Carenage. He strained his attention over the myriad figures that swarmed the waterside. The place worked like a formicary. The hopelessness of finding any particular man in the crowded sun-shot jam forced itself upon the American. Also it told him how safe was Cap McGabe in his water-logged retreat.

As Poggioli moved up and down the hot wharf, squinting his eyes and rather hopeless of finding anyone he knew, he heard his name shouted in the din. He looked around and saw Wilberforce and Mr. Santee hurrying to him through the crowd. When they drew near, Santee called:

"We've been looking everywhere for you; thought you were down here hours ago!"

"I'm looking for Cheswick," in a tone which invited their coöperation.

"He's not here!" cried Wilberforce.

"Where is he?"

"We met him in a motor going out Bay Street as we came in from the club. He said he was going out to look at Codrington College."

"Look at what?" echoed Poggioli in amazement.

"Codrington College," repeated Mr. Santee. "He said he wanted to see it before he left Barbados. You know it's one of our show places: the oldest university in the West

Indies. It was founded in 1710; two years older than our cricket club."

Poggioli was struck dumb. For a bank robber and a murderer in the midst of an effort to escape suddenly to turn tourist and motor off to admire the ivied walls of an old college—that was too much for the American. He stood blinking his eyes.

"Did he say when he was coming back?"

"Said he would meet us here about four; for us to go right ahead and make arrangements with McGabe."

Both Wilberforce and Santee seemed to think this the most natural thing in the world for Cheswick to do. Poggioli had a sinking sensation that he had seen his last of Mr. Cheswick. He suspected that the fellow had sensed the suspicion in which he was held; as no doubt he had. The American brought his harassed thoughts back to the subject in hand.

"How have you fellows got on with your search for Cap McGabe?"

"We've got feelers out for him."

"How?"

"A Captain Dorgan on a schooner out there," Santee nodded toward the Carenage, "saw Cap, and chucked him a bite to eat. Said if he saw him again he would appoint an hour for us to meet him."

"And then what'll we tell him?"

"We'll tell him there's a slaver called the *Hercules* lying just outside the harbor. She's sailing for Santo Domingo up our east coast to-night. I thought we could run McGabe onto the schooner as a nigger laborer."

"How'll you do that?"

Mr. Santee grinned and drew out of his pocket a box of shoe polish.

"Black him up. If the harbor police see us taking him out they'll think he's a nigger. I've arranged with a waterman to take us out at four-thirty."

"If you can meet McGabe."

"Certainly."

By this time Poggioli had fallen in with his two acquaintances and the three walked down to the wharf, got aboard a schooner, crossed her deck to another, and so from one boat to another picked their way to Captain Dorgan's vessel out in the Carenage. In the unobstructed sunshine tar boiled out of the seams of the decks; an odor of bilge water, of sugar, of oakum, and the sea saturated the hot air. Noises of clicking capstans, creaking sails, chanting sailors, and shouting Negroes assailed their ears.

As they clambered from vessel to vessel Mr. Santee explained what a slave ship was: a schooner which transported Negro labor from one island in the West Indies to another without the formality of passports; for indeed such wholesale shipping of labor was against the British laws.

"It seems," observed Poggioli, fishing out his handkerchief to mop his face, "that we are continually running afoul of the law at every turn."

Mr. Santee glanced his surprise.

"Certainly, these matters have to be arranged. Barbados is one of the most densely populated spots on earth. We have thousands and thousands of Negro laborers who have got to be jobbed around or they'll starve. There isn't work enough here. The British labor laws are merely a theory that follows actual practice more or less closely. Just here it is a little wide. Parliament may eventually revise the statutes to make them fit."

This English notion of arranging law to fit conduct

surprised Poggioli, who was accustomed to the American idea of arranging human life to fit some theory. It struck him that both systems were rather like shoes: an old pair of shoes and a new pair of shoes. His reflections were cut short by Mr. Santee's calling out:

"Cap'n Dorgan on deck!"

The three men had come to a schooner, the *Laughing Lass* of Halifax, Nova Scotia. As Santee shouted, a short, stocky, sandy-haired sailor turned out of a hammock which was swung under a canvas stretched over the after deck of the vessel. This fellow stood rubbing his eyes and blinking as he watched the three men climb over his rail and come aboard.

"Here he is!" called Santee with the exuberance of one exhibiting a curiosity.

"Don't say so!" ejaculated the captain, stretching his eyes to waken himself, then lifting a hand in salute to Poggioli.

"They tell me, sir, you're a great detective. I dare say you're something fancy with a pistol, or throwing a knife, sir."

The college professor hardly knew how to answer such a burst of admiration. Evidently Captain Dorgan had drawn his conception of a detective from the "Old Sleuth" series.

"Did you ever see McGabe again?" queried Poggioli.

"Yes, I told him to be here at four."

"Did he say he would?"

"Said he'd listen for the ship's bells, sir."

"None of the police have been nosing around your boat?" inquired Wilberforce.

"A nigger dressed up like a girl came aboard. When I

saw he was a man I told him I'd pipe him if I needed him."

Everybody laughed. Santee glanced at his watch.

"Well, all we've got to do is to wait here and see if he shows up."

He glanced at his companions, who agreed wordlessly that that was all there was to do. The three men moved automatically back to the shade of the canvas. Here they seated themselves on a coil of rope, a cask, and Captain Dorgan found Poggioli a canvas-covered folding stool, then he sat down in his hammock.

The American began trying to fathom Cheswick's last move. Thinking was difficult with the other men talking and the sun beating the canvas overhead until it felt like a stove radiating heat. Reflections from the water fell on the under side of the canvas and drew upon it wavering designs of light. The light circled or marched in rows or fell into tremulous confusion. Drops of sweat trickling down inside of Poggioli's clothes felt like crawling insects. The heat pressed down on the American's skull like the thumb of a giant. Poggioli blinked the sting of perspiration out of his eyes and thought doggedly of Codrington College; Cheswick's visit to Codrington College. Presently an explanation filtered into his heat-drugged brain. Cheswick had made that as an excuse to go and bring the rest of his stolen bank notes aboard the schooner preparatory to leaving the country.

The American shook the stuffiness out of his head and planned what to do. He must get in touch with some of the harbor police and seize Cheswick when he reappeared with the notes. That would be a sharp, sensational end to the man hunt. The melodrama appealed to Poggioli even under a Barbadian sun.

Captain Dorgan arose from his hammock and said he

would go below for the makings of a gin swizzle. At that
moment from over the harbor came a myriad of little ringing double taps of the bells of many vessels. A little later
the reflections on the under side of the canvas awning fell
into a wild flurry; with it came a soft splashing below.
Instead of going down into his cabin, Dorgan turned to
the rail with the low observation:

"There's McGabe."

Wilberforce strode to the rail and stood. in the white
flame of the sun.

"That you, Cap?" he called down softly.

"Yes, sir."

"Cap, we've seen the old man; we've got you off."

"Have you, sir?"

"Provided you are willing to clear out of Barbados."

"Wha-at?"

"Leave the island."

Came a silence broken by a faint plashing, then a
dubious:

"Where to, sir?"

"We've got a passage for you on a slave ship going to
Santo."

"With niggers?" sharply.

"That's the only way you can get away and the police
not see you."

The man in the water evidently chewed on this. The en-
mity between the red legs and the Negroes had begun
when both were slaves in the Barbadian sugar fields, and
time had only strengthened the rancor between them.

"I wouldn't want to go with the niggers, sir—after
being a gentleman in a gentleman's cricket club."

Poggioli stepped to the rail. He looked down but could

see nothing, as the fugitive kept himself covered by the schooner's overhang.

"It will be a lot better than soaking here in the Carenage, Cap; you'll be with a schooner for three or four days, then you'll be turned loose in Santo a free man."

The top of a head and two eyes floated cautiously out in the oily water and looked up the side of the *Laughing Lass.*

"Who are you?" asked Cap suspiciously.

"The man your mother employed to look after your case. That was the best I could do: make those arrangements with Sir Alexander."

The eyes stared up strickenly at Poggioli.

"I didn't kill Mr. Oswald. I'll swear I didn't."

Poggioli made a gesture.

"I've thought that over. This is the easiest way out for you."

Mr. Santee took up the conversation.

"Cap, here's a box of shoe polish. Catch it and black your face. If the police see you they'll think you're a nigger."

The red leg was humiliated; after a lifelong feud with the Negroes to become one of them!

"You can wash off on the schooner. She's standing outside the harbor now. We'll have a waterman pick you up in a dory in about half an hour. You swim to the stern of that steamer that lies right across the Carenage from the customhouse; we'll come by and pick you up. Black your face."

Santee dropped the blacking. The water-soaked figure caught the polish and the next moment, with a faint swirl, vanished from sight. The lights under the canvas leaped to and fro in silent fury.

Poggioli straightened up with a sun-ache in his temples. He must go at once and get the police. He was framing an excuse to get away from his companions when he looked through the glare of sunshine and saw Mr. Cheswick making his way toward them. He climbed from vessel to vessel, evidently in high good humor. He mopped his face and waved his handkerchief at the men.

Then Poggioli was dismayed to see that Cheswick had no baggage.

Santee answered his friend's gayety with a responsive wave.

"Everything's all arranged," he called.

Cheswick stroked his mustache with his handkerchief.

"Fine! Topping!"

The three men were deserting the *Laughing Lass* without ceremony, hurrying to meet Cheswick.

"How'd you like Codrington?" cried Santee.

"Very, very much!" pæaned Cheswick.

"Ever been there before?" asked Wilberforce.

"First visit."

A certain impishness entered Poggioli's aching head.

"Which did you consider the most beautiful building, Mr. Cheswick?"

Cheswick hesitated.

"The library."

"What point did you admire especially?"

The blond gentleman scratched his head.

"Well, I especially admired—er—the memorial window to Sir Philip Easton, and then over in the chapel I thought the old mahogany stalls very, very lovely."

Poggioli glanced at Santee and Wilberforce to see if Mr. Cheswick was describing actualities. They were nodding their heads. He was.

Mr. Cheswick actually had made a pilgrimage to Codrington. The man's conduct subscribed to no rationale whatsoever.

Santee came back to the business in hand.

"We have arranged for you and Wilberforce to go to Santo Domingo with McGabe on a slaver. She sails at four-thirty." He glanced at his watch. "And we've only twenty minutes to go."

"Righto!" cried Cheswick in a great mood. "Let's get to the pier!"

The four men hurried across the boats, jumped ashore, and.started.almost at a trot for the dory pier.

It suddenly struck Poggioli that these men were going to slip right out of his hands, and there was no way to stop them. As they approached the pier half a dozen black boatmen came running, shouting the names of their dories:

"The *Majestic*, masters!" "The *Titanic!*" "*Princess Mary* will set you over, gentlemen!"

One fat doryman laughed and shouted in the grotesque gargling English peculiar to the West Indian:

"Dem gen'lemen done ingage de *Mauretania* half hour ago!"

The *Mauretania* was a brightly painted dory with white canvas upholstering on the seats. Poggioli's heart sank as he.saw his companions hurry down the steps of the pier to the dory. Everything seemed quite lost. Just then Mr. Cheswick hesitated.

"By the way, does it happen that this nigger ship is going to sail around the coast to Bathsheba?"

Santee said she was.

"Fine!" cried the blond gentleman. "I have a little baggage I really ought to get aboard with me. If you will in-

dulge me by letting me take the train to Bathsheba I'll
get aboard to-morrow morning when the schooner reaches
that port."

"Certainly," cried Wilberforce. "I'll be on the lookout."

"Righto!" cried Cheswick.

Santee, Poggioli, and Cheswick stood on the pier and
waved Wilberforce off. The trio watched the dory pull
away and stop under the stern of the freighter that lay
just across from the customhouse. There something was
pulled into the *Mauretania*. It might have been a sack. It
lay flat down in the bottom of the dory under the beating
sun. It was such a trifling detail in the torrid animation
of the harbor that nobody could have observed it except
the three men on the pier.

That night Poggioli went around to the police station
on Coleridge Street and asked for a plain-clothes man to
stand watch on Bathsheba wharf on the following day. At
first the police sergeant demanded brusquely enough the
reason for such an unusual request, but when he discovered that he was addressing Mr. Poggioli he became at
once respectful, not to say obsequious.

"Yes, sir, I've heard of you; read about you in the
Times. I'd take it as a great privilege to coöperate with
such a distinguished criminologist. There will not only be
a man down there, Mr. Poggioli, I'll be there myself. All
you'll have to do, sir, is simply give me the tip who you
want pinched, sir, and I'll pinch 'em. You needn't be
known in it at all."

This appealed to Poggioli as being the ideal procedure
for a criminal investigator: the planning brain while other
men applied the physical force. Poggioli had the Latin
aristocrat's dislike for all violent physical contacts, which

has sublimated even their personal encounters to the finical but deadly aloofness of duelling.

The plan put him in high spirits and sent him walking briskly through the night to his hotel. Once or twice a wonderment came to him as to what could have prompted Mr. Cheswick to make his excursion to Codrington College. Could the thief have buried his bank notes in the campus of that ancient institution? Such a disposal would possess unexpectedness. On the other hand, Mr. Cheswick might have visited the old seat of learning out of a traveler's curiosity. His visit to Codrington probably could not be linked with the stolen bank notes.

When Poggioli reached Bay Mansion Hotel he found the guests sitting on the dimly illuminated piazza talking of the tragedy. The psychologist saw Mr. Cheswick and threaded the groups to ask him when the early morning train started for Bathsheba. Then he went on up to his bedroom. It struck Poggioli as rather a salty thing that he should be asking Cheswick about the train schedule which would land the fellow, if everything went right, on the gallows.

Next morning the professor awoke with a certain feeling of imminent adventure which he seldom before had experienced. Borne on the wings of this stimulation, he hurried through his bath, then down to the breakfast room, where a lazy black boy spread before him a sweet lemon, coffee, rolls, and fried flying fish. At this hour the breakfast room was deserted and the psychologist asked the boy if Mr. Cheswick had come down. He had not. Poggioli looked at his watch, then sent the boy up to wake him—he hesitated in his thoughts between "friend," "traveling companion," and "victim."

The boy went up and in a few minutes came back down with the news that Mr. Cheswick was not in his room, that he must have gone to the beach for an early dip.

It was getting near train time. The American deserted the remnants of his breakfast and hurried down to the beach to look for his—he decided on the term "man." Then he recalled that police officers, detectives, sheriffs, and so forth always used the word "man." Looking for their "man"; catching their "man"; hanging their "man" —a loathsome euphemism by which they disguised their treacherous trade!

On the beach only a fat old man and two Barbadian women were bathing. Just as he saw there was no Mr. Cheswick visible, he heard the distant rattle of a tram on Bay Street. He turned and went springing back to the thoroughfare, which he reached in time to swing aboard and ride downtown.

At any other time than this he would have enjoyed the slow village-like progression of the mule car, the jingling bells, the lush trees leaning their green branches over the walls, the upright palms, the bland light of early morning in which lingered the perfume of a tropical night as delicately sweet as the memory of a tryst with a woman. Ordinarily he would have been charmed.

This morning all the poetry was lost in a growing uneasiness in regard to Mr. Cheswick. Poggioli looked over the crowded tram, full of Negroes going to work, seeking his "man's" face. Cheswick was not on the car.

The mules jingled along. The black passengers laughed and talked noisily after the manner of their kind. The ride was interminable. Poggioli could not decide whether to go on and catch the train for Bathsheba or to drop off downtown and institute a search for Cheswick here in Bridgetown. The obstacle was, if he found Cheswick without the notes, he would have no proof of his guilt. He decided he would go on and risk Cheswick's being on the train.

Just before the tram passed over the bridge at the Carenage Poggioli dropped off the running board and ran across Fairchild Street to the station. A small army of Negroes were being sucked into the depot for the morning train. The American darted in among them, got to the ticket window, bought a first-class ticket, and hurried out to the train, where he got a seat by a window to scrutinize the crowd as it climbed aboard up and down the line of cars.

The train itself was a very tiny affair, but slightly larger than the toy railroads children ride at street fairs in America. Ahead, the engine was whistling like a peanut roaster. The little coaches filled rapidly. Evidently the little thing meant to be off in a pair of minutes.

As Mr. Cheswick continued not to appear, uneasiness wound up in Poggioli more and more, like the spring of an alarm clock. He was on the point of jumping off when the little train made a lunge, the cars moved, then went clicking off up the little two-foot track at quite a brisk gait.

As soon as the train was out of town the dusty white Barbadian landscape began a slow turntable effect outside the car window. Everything was white: the fences dividing the dusty white fields of sugar cane; the stone cottages, bungalows, and Negro huts; old-fashioned windmills which flapped their white sails on the horizon like great lazy birds too languid to fly. Now and then the train passed a park of great mahogany trees, their profound green filmed with white dust. Poggioli would glimpse, seated back in the grove, the white walls or roof of a venerable old English manor, the eminently respectable country seat of some ultra-English Barbadian aristocrat, like Sir Alexander Hemmingway. An amazing folk, the English; nobody quite like them in the world. Poggioli wondered, where was Cheswick?

The continual white glare pained the American's eyes and he turned back inside the coach to avoid it. Then he observed to his seat-mate in a vaguely complaining voice: "They build absolutely everything on this island of white stone."

This seat-mate, now that Poggioli looked at him, was an old gentleman with white whiskers, russet face, tempery nose, and high-cut nostrils. He regarded Poggioli, evidently astonished and incensed at being addressed in a public conveyance.

"Certainly," he replied stiffly, "this island is formed of white coral rock. We are hardly wealthy enough to import colored stone to build ornamental fences around our sugar fields for the delectation of American tourists."

This typically British reply, with its quietly acid way of telling the other fellow to go to the devil, shut up Poggioli for a few minutes.

A little later, with American persistency, he made another effort to engage the old war horse. He said something about the shocking murder that had been committed on the cricket grounds. The old gentleman observed that all murders were shocking in Barbados. He didn't know how they were regarded in America. After that Poggioli remained silent.

The little train rattled on amid the hot blanched scenery.

It stopped at half a dozen stations; folk got on and off; everywhere Poggioli strained his attention over these movements of the crowds, hoping Cheswick had gone ahead to take the train at some station beyond Bridgetown, but he saw nothing of him. In about an hour and a half the train ran into Bathsheba. There Poggioli and his gruff seatmate both got out. The old gentleman set off at a stout walk for his home, where no doubt he was a loving husband and a tender father. The English are a wonderful people.

The American himself, unfortunately, had no such decision of purpose. He stood for a moment on the asphalt driveway outside the railway station, orienting himself in this new town. It was a characteristic English watering place. Big rooming houses lined the boulevard, and still higher up on an acclivity stood a fashionable hotel with an English ensign floating from a tall flagpole. Down below, on the right-hand side looking northward, lay the harbor with a few old piers thrust out into the liquid turquoise of the ocean. Northward beyond the piers curved the long pure-white arc of the beach, spotted here and there with the reds and greens of parasols and bathing suits.

It seemed to Poggioli that this brilliantly white beach was a very focusing of the whole blanched island of Barbados. It shrilled at the psychologist that Barbados was white. It italicized the fact so persistently that a certain curious notion filtered into Poggioli's head that this fanfare of white was not purely objective, that it held some private and particular meaning for him and for him alone.

He moved along slowly, staring at it, pondering the color, wondering what conceivable connection this whiteness had with Oswald Hemmingway's murder. The association seemed, as the saying goes, right on the tip of his tongue, but eventually it eluded him. He had the miserable

feeling that something in his head softly closed. Whatever
was on the threshold of recognition sank into the limbo
of the unconscious. The beach became simply an ordinary
stretch of white coral sand, and a queer depression of
spirit settled over Poggioli.

He moved on somberly down the wharf for the simple
part he was about to play. He would await the arrival of
the *Hercules*. Then, when Cheswick attempted to board her
with a bag, he would have him arrested. If, on the other
hand, Cheswick did not come, then Wilberforce and Mc-
Gabe would sail on to Santo. The unfortunate red leg
would be rusticated through no crime of his own, while the
real thief and murderer would escape. English justice
would make a characteristic bungle, but over the whole
affair would hang a certain drab veil of respectability.

Poggioli spat and went down a flight of ancient wooden
steps full of landings and turns that led from the level of
the driveway down between two tall rooming houses, over
one back yard, around another, and so to the level of the
beach and piers.

On the sand were a number of little fishing boats, left
careened by the outgoing tide. A browned fisherman sat
under the shade of a boat repairing his net with the endless patience of his tribe. Poggioli approached this fellow
and asked when the *Hercules* was expected in. The fisherman paused in the midst of a small but intricate knot.

"The *Hercules*, sir? P'raps you mean the *Albatross?*"

"No, the *Hercules;* she's due from Bridgetown to-day
sometime," repeated the American uneasily.

The old fellow shook his head.

"You must mean the *Albatross*, sir; she runs from here
to Bridgetown every other day."

"The *Hercules*," explained Poggioli, "is a slaver. She's bound to Santo with a cargo of Negroes."

The seamed face became full of comprehension.

"I see, she's in no reg'lar trade. Then she won't come in the harbor here, naturally, sir. You know it's against the law, exporting labor wholesale. We couldn't have her coming right into port taking on niggers. That wouldn't be right, sir. No, I say let everything be done decent and respectable——"

"But how the hell does she get her passengers?" cried Poggioli, thoroughly impatient at this rambling homily.

"Why, she picks 'em up along the coast, sir."

"No especial place?"

"None in partic'lar, sir. The niggers go out to her in jack boats in a decent underhand sort of way."

"Where is she now?"

"I fancy she's just over the horizon there, tacking up and down the coast till she gets her men, sir."

"And where can I see the small boats coming in and going out?" asked the American anxiously.

"Not here in Bathsheba, naturally. We couldn't have nothing like that right under our eyes, sir. But if you'd tramp up and down the coast, say five or six miles, sir, you might happen to see a jack boat going out loaded with niggers, or coming in empty. If you did it would probably be bound for the *Hercules*, or just getting back from her."

Mr. Poggioli, who had been stooping involuntarily to peer into his informant's face, now straightened and stared up and down the white strand with a lost feeling. Cheswick might be anywhere. The psychologist was seized with an irrational notion that at this moment Cheswick was somewhere along the coast, escaping to the *Hercules* with his loot. But the sheer whiteness seemed to weave a maze in which no fugitive could ever be found. Then a certain tenuous suggestion from the color itself filtered once more into the American's mind. He framed a question to the fisherman.

"By the way, friend, in all this white scenery do you happen to know whether there is any clay near here?"

The old fellow removed his pipe and fell into thought. With an ordinary laborer's disconnectedness, it did not strike him as odd for a man to inquire about slave ships one moment and clay the next.

"Clay, sir? You've come to a bad island for clay. Precious little here. Now if you'd care for sandstone, sir——"

"No, it's clay—blue clay."

The old man thought again.

"Blue clay, blue clay—since you mention it, I do bear in mind a little outcrop of blue clay down at the crab coves, sir. You might get enough to daub a cooking place with, but if you want it to make brick——"

A little thrill of exultation shot through Poggioli.

"Where are the crab coves?" he snapped.

The old man pointed down toward the south.

"About two miles down the beach. You'll know 'em by the thicket of sea grape growing around 'em."

This last sentence was wasted as Poggioli already had turned and was dashing down the white sand at a pace which he could not possibly hold for two miles. Whatever the old fisherman thought of a tourist who began talking of slavers and started on a dead run at the mention of blue clay, Poggioli never found out.

The psychologist was thinking how simple was the clue of the blue stains, now that the solution had struck him. Cheswick had hidden his notes in the crab caverns, buried no doubt in the clay. In getting the five hundred pounds

out he had stained a note or two. It was this simple reasoning that had been stirring in his mind back on the driveway. Now it flooded him with a great elation. Presently
his failing legs in the hot morning sunshine slowed him
down, much to his impatience. The run became a trot, then
a hurried walk down the linen whiteness of the sand.

He wanted to run again. It seemed to Poggioli that each
instant was allowing Cheswick to escape. It was an absurd
feeling, but as Poggioli hurried down the sinuous, bicolored
stretch of white beach and blue sea it seemed that Cheswick
was escaping over and over again. So long as Poggioli
could see nothing except the dazzling empty perspective
of white and blue Cheswick continued his momentary
escapes. Then far out across the water the American caught
the flicker of a small boat's sail. That stabilized his fancy
and pegged Cheswick to an exact position. The boat was
something to race against. Poggioli had either a good deal
of time to spare, or he was already too late. He stopped his
leaden trot and stared at the distant fleck of canvas. It
was either coming or going, he couldn't tell which. At every
beat of his heart the sail vibrated up and down. He mopped
his face, blinked the sweat from his stinging eyes, and
peered with face screwed up against the glare. If the small
boat was outbound, then he must turn and hurry back
to Bathsheba, notify the police sergeant, and get a revenue
launch to the *Hercules*. If the boat was inbound, he would
get down to the beach, hide in the sea grapes, and verify
his own deductions.

The American eventually decided the boat was coming
in. He started down the beach where he could see the gray-
green sea grapes painted on the lower slopes of the cliffs.
As he hurried forward he began to be anxious lest some-

one on the boat should see his dark form against this white background. Certainly unaided eyes could not pick him up at this distance, but seafaring men usually have binoculars. No doubt those faraway boatmen were scanning the coast for Cheswick, or at least for bearings to locate the crab coves. The sea-grape thicket was about a quarter of a mile distant, and he made a last run for it.

This last dash Poggioli made on sheer doggedness. The boat was coming in rapidly. Poggioli flung all his strength into getting across that last stretch of white sand. He finished with a drumming heart and flung himself prone on the ground in the edge of the thicket. He gasped for breath through a dry mouth. His legs felt paralyzed. Face and clothes were drenched with sweat. He swallowed slime. He lay with his head limp in the crook of his elbow and the sunlight pulsed red through his closed eyelids. But he was happy. He had worked the whole thing out so cleverly; a series of bungles, it is true, but after all, all reasoning is a series of trials and errors. There is no compulsive logic holding any two human propositions together. The feel of logic is merely our reaction to sequences. Berkeley was right and Kant wrong. Great reasoners are simply lucky guessers—or inspired gropers. He himself had groped in this tangle from one hypothesis to another, and now here he was with verity arrived at—which was, concretely, a quarter of a million dollars in bank notes. It was one of the happiest moments of Poggioli's life.

He opened his eyes, shook his head, then lifted himself cautiously to get the exact position of the boat. As he did so a voice in the thicket snarled:

"Poggioli, do you want your damned empty head blown off?"

The psychologist was struck to stone in a half-risen posture. Then he peered slowly around and presently made out the shape of Mr. Cheswick among the bushes some twenty or thirty feet distant. The thing he could see most clearly was the glint of a drawn pistol; the murderer's clothes were of the same dull gray as the grape branches.

"No-o, I don't," stuttered Poggioli in a whisper, realizing for the first time that he was pursuing a bank robber, a murderer, and a desperate man.

"Then lie back down. One dead man's enough on a job like this."

So the fellow had a conscience. Poggioli subsided again on his belly, deeply grateful for that fact. He supposed he would not be killed.

He lifted his head slowly and peered at Cheswick among the cross-hatching of the sea-grape stems. It seemed to him that he was seeing the man for the first time; a naked foe of all men. Even in the midst of his danger a kind of understanding of such a gusty, wanton, salty existence crept into Poggioli's chameleon mind. The imbecility of his own approach amazed him, but in the same breath explained itself to him in the highly complimentary terms a man's own mind always explains itself. It was simply because he was a sublimated intellect, and pure intelligence has never yet felt fear or taken a precaution. Only the animal emotions in a man make him defensive and crafty. Pure cognition never has a queasy moment; it knows everything and avoids nothing. There idiot and sage meet— Archimedes slaughtered in Syracuse while drawing circles in the sand.

Even while this analysis ran through his mind, the psychologist was speculating on what Cheswick would do with

him: take him aboard the *Hercules?* bind him and leave him
in the cavern until the schooner was clear of the island?
or possibly, after all, kill him?

In the midst of this grisly speculation the keel of a boat
grated on the sand below. Poggioli remained motionless,
staring with his whole sensorium alert. Now he could hear
someone from the boat pushing his way up among the
small growths.

Even in his own jeopardy this little circumstance hit
him as odd. It was, in fact, faintly contradictory to his own
dilemma. It was not correct psychology for a boatman to
leave his boat and grope among bushes for his passenger.
An intimation that he had made some strange and funda-
mental error began to move in Poggioli. He lifted his head
and stared through the bushes with wide, speculative eyes.

The man from the boat pushed on through the sea grapes
and apparently disappeared in the earth. He passed abruptly out of sight and hearing. For some ten minutes
came a silence. Then as a curious and amazing hypothesis
began to dawn on the American came a renewed rustle in
the bushes. The next instant Mr. Cheswick launched out
of his hiding. Came an explosion of blows, curses, snarls.
Poggioli leaped to his feet to see two men fighting among
the bushes. As he jumped up they went down, rolling and
crashing under the gray cover. Poggioli hurried toward
them and out of the uproar he heard Mr. Cheswick pant:

"Grab his gun, quick, Poggioli! He'll kill himself—
or me!"

For the fraction of an instant the American hesitated,
the Latin in him loathing the physical contact; next moment he plunged under the foliage and his head and shoulder came squarely upon Wilberforce and Cheswick grap-
pling on the ground. Cheswick was straining Wilberforce's

arm up from his pocket. The psychologist gripped this upstretched arm, whipped around and caught it in the crotch of his leg with a scissors hold. This left Cheswick a free hand. He jerked handcuffs from his pocket and snapped one on Wilberforce's left, then he maneuvered the other loop up to the hand Poggioli held, and the man was manacled. Cheswick then ran a deft hand over the outside of Wilberforce's clothes, located a pistol and removed it. He got up, walked a few steps back in the bushes, and picked up a tin container full of bank notes.

"Now," he puffed, and with the same breath gave a short laugh, "you can let him up, Poggioli."

The American professor got up off the prisoner, filled with a just indignation.

"Why in the hell didn't you——"

Cheswick's mustache gave a downward quirk.

"I didn't like what you said on the hotel porch—a detective's occupation being the most damnable in the world; and then, if I had confided in you you might have published it in the *Times*."

Poggioli was angrier than ever. He brushed the white sand from his clothes, then he did the same for Wilberforce, who couldn't assist himself. On Wilberforce's garments were two or three smudges of blue clay.

Mr. Cheswick sent the Negroes in the longboat back to the *Hercules*, then the three men began a stolid, silent tramp back to Bathsheba to make the afternoon train to Bridgetown. Mr. Cheswick wore a fixed, detestable grin under his yellowed mustache.

On the following day an article appeared in the Bridgetown *Times* as a follow-up of the Hemmingway tragedy. It bore a ten-point caption which extended across two columns, which is the equivalent in Bridgetown to full-page streamers in New York. The headlines ran:

MASTER MIND
UNRAVELS MYSTERY

Deducing His Whole Clue From Stain on Bank Note American Sherlock Holmes Brings Murderer to Gallows

---

Professor Henry Poggioli, the celebrated American criminologist, who is spending a few days in Barbados, once more exhibited his uncanny powers of deduction in bringing to justice one of the cleverest rogues and the most bloodthirsty murderer our island empire has ever known. The story of the arrest of one Charles Wilberforce reads more like a romance from the pen of A. Conan Doyle than a recountal of sober fact.

After the tragic death of Oswald Hemmingway circumstances suggested that young Hemmingway had committed suicide after some heavy losses in stock speculation. Mr. Poggioli went to the cable office and was shown simply a five-pound note with a clay stain on it, and by a series of the most ingenious inductions announced not only that Mr. Hemmingway was murdered, but gave a complete description and the whereabouts of the murderer.

In an interview to-day Mr. Dwight, an employee of the cable company, made the following statement:

"He glanced at the stained notes and immediately remarked, 'This stain was not made by Oswald Hemmingway because all bank cashiers have clean hands.' He then took the reports prepared by Mr. Hodges, and proved mathematically that the person speculating in the name of Oswald Hemmingway had intended to lose five hundred pounds, no more and no less. This established the fact that some interested person was attempting to cast a shadow of suicide over young Hemmingway's death."

In an interview Mr. Hodges of the Imperial Bank then took up the narrative so replete with intellectual marvels. Said Hodges:

"Professor Poggioli then told me that we would probably discover the amount of these speculative losses tucked away in some

corner of our bank in either counterfeit bank notes or stolen
currency. When I asked his reasons, he explained:

" 'Because some man has tried to swindle young Oswald, who
found him out after Oswald had advanced the fellow five hundred
pounds in West Indian money in exchange for the vitiated currency.'

"I asked him who had done this.

"He said:

" 'Without doubt some member of the cricket team to which
Oswald belonged. The culprit evidently begged young Hemmingway to postpone any legal action about the bogus money until
after a certain important game of cricket which was about to be
played. Through patriotism to his club, Oswald agreed to this.
Then the criminal set about laying a basis of suicide with forged
cablegrams upon which to murder his teammate with impunity.
The fact that Oswald was slain in the bath house immediately
after the game bore out this deduction.' "

The police sergeant, Mr. O'Brien, was interviewed and furnished the next link in the processes of this master mind. Said
O'Brien:

"The question then was, which player had killed Oswald Hemmingway? We suspected a young man who lived here in Bridgetown, but this wizard of crime said, 'No, we will allow the criminal to declare himself.'

" 'How will you accomplish that?' I asked.

" 'By pretending this member under suspicion is about to be
deported, and requesting some other member of the club to accompany him from the island.'

"This was done, and Wilberforce fell into the trap instantly.
The police were then about to seize the criminal when the great
savant interposed:

" 'Wait,' he said, 'this fellow could hardly have stolen only
five hundred pounds; this is too small an amount to justify a murder. The residue is somewhere on the island.'

" 'Where is it?' I inquired.

"For answer Professor Poggioli returned to the same bank
note. 'This is a white coral island,' he said, 'and it is not likely
that blue clay can be found in many parts of it. Send this note
with the clay on it to the professor of geology at Codrington

College and he will inform you where such outcrops can be found.'

"This was done; a certain Scotland Yard man who had been on the trail of the missing bank notes for a number of months being the one actually to take the bank note to Professor Getty, instructor in geology in Codrington. Professor Getty located three outcrops of such clays in the island of Barbados; two were inland and one was in the Cavern of the Crabs near Bathsheba."

Here the Scotland Yard man, whose name is withheld by request, gave to the representative of the *Times* the following interview:

"Professor Henry Poggioli is the most remarkable investigator of crimes it has ever been my fortune to meet. We have nothing like him in Scotland Yard. When he first glimpsed me on the piazza of the Bay Mansion Hotel he observed that I was a detective by a false blond mustache I was wearing, and he immediately told me that he had a very low opinion of the ordinary detective, such as I regret to say I am. When he sent me with a stained bank note to Professor Getty and I learned that the money which I had been vainly trying to recover for the Bank of England for three months was buried in the Cavern of the Crabs I said at once, 'I'll go dig it up.'

"Professor Poggioli stopped me. 'No,' he objected, 'you would have a herculean task to move all the clay in those caverns. Make the brain do the work of your hands.'

" 'How?' I inquired.

" 'Let Wilberforce dig it up for you. Go and conceal yourself at the mouth of the cavern and allow Wilberforce to come and dig it up. As he comes out, leap on him and arrest him with the money in his possession.'

"This was done with the happy result of Wilberforce's capture and incarceration in Bridgetown jail."

Captain Dorgan of the *Laughing Lass,* a Nova Scotian schooner now lying in the Carenage, assured the reporter that he had never seen a pistol shot of such expertness as Professor Poggioli. He said the American gave an amazing demonstration in the harbor and he understood that Poggioli once had been a cowboy and had fought Indians, or redskins, in the American West, near Sioux City, a village belonging to the fierce Iowa tribe.

Sir Alexander Hemmingway of Norman Hall, St. Michael Parish, the bereaved father of the murdered youth, was interviewed. He said:

"Amazing, subtle, a superman. I am thankful a divine providence directed his footsteps here to clear my son's memory."

Professor Poggioli read the above account thoughtfully several times. At the end of the third perusal he remembered all the above events happening practically as they were printed by the enterprising reporter of the *Times*.

When Poggioli had first returned from Bathsheba to Bay Mansion Hotel he was in a very depressed state; and was fully resolved to leave Barbados on the next steamer south. However, after reading this report, which he conceded as practically correct from start to finish, he purchased a number of copies of the paper to send home to friends, and decided to remain a few weeks longer in the pleasant, sunny island of Barbados.

A Passage to Benares

*In which the professor should not have
investigated a certain Hindu custom.*

A PASSAGE TO BENARES

In PORT OF SPAIN, Trinidad, at half-past five in the morning, Mr. Henry Poggioli, the American psychologist, stirred uneasily, became conscious of a splitting headache, opened his eyes in bewilderment, and then slowly reconstructed his surroundings. He recognized the dome of the Hindu temple seen dimly above him; the jute rug on which he lay; the blur of the image of Krishna sitting cross-legged on the altar. The American had a dim impression that the figure had not sat thus on the altar all night long—a dream, no doubt; he had a faint memory of lurid nightmares. The psychologist allowed the thought to lose itself as he got up slowly from the sleeping rug which the cicerone had spread for him the preceding evening.

In the circular temple everything was still in deep shadow, but the gray light of dawn filled the arched entrance. The white man moved carefully to the door so as not to jar his aching head. A little distance from him he saw another sleeper, a coolie beggar stretched out on a rug, and he thought he saw still another farther away. As he passed out of the entrance the cool freshness of the tropical morning caressed his face like the cool fingers of a woman. Kiskadee birds were calling from palms and saman trees, and there was a wide sound of dripping dew. Not far from the temple a coolie woman stood on a seesaw with a great stone attached to the other end of the plank, and by stepping to and fro she swung the stone up and down and pounded some rice in a mortar.

Poggioli stood looking at her a moment, then felt in his pocket for the key to his friend Lowe's garden gate. He found it and moved off up Tragarette Road to where the squalid East Indian village gave way to the high garden walls and ornamental shrubbery of the English suburb of Port of Spain. He walked on more briskly as the fresh air eased his head, and presently he stopped and unlocked a gate in one of the bordering walls. He began to smile as he let himself in; his good humor increased as he walked across a green lawn to a stone cottage which had a lower window still standing open. This was his own room. He reached up to the sill and drew himself inside, which gave his head one last pang. He shook this away, however, and began undressing for his morning shower.

Mr. Poggioli was rather pleased with his exploit, although he had not forwarded the experiment which had induced him to sleep in the temple. It had come about in this way: On the foregoing evening the American and his host in Port of Spain, a Mr. Lowe, a bank clerk, had watched a Hindu wedding procession enter the same temple in which Poggioli had just spent the night. They had watched the dark-skinned white-robed musicians smiting their drums and skirling their pipes with bouffant cheeks. Behind them marched a procession of coolies. The bride was a little cream-colored girl who wore a breastplate of linked gold coins over her childish bosom, while anklets and bracelets almost covered her arms and legs. The groom, a tall, dark coolie, was the only man in the procession who wore European clothes, and he, oddly enough, was attired in a full evening dress suit. At the incongruous sight Poggioli burst out laughing, but Lowe touched his arm and said in an undertone:

"Don't take offense, old man, but if you didn't laugh it might help me somewhat."

Poggioli straightened his face.

"Certainly, but how's that?"

"The groom, Boodman Lal, owns one of the best curio shops in town and carries an account at my bank. That fifth man in the procession, the skeleton wearing the yellow *kapra*, is old Hira Dass. He is worth something near a million in pounds sterling."

The psychologist became sober enough, out of his American respect for money.

"Hira Dass," went on Lowe, "built this temple and rest house. He gives rice and tea to any traveler who comes in for the night. It's an Indian custom to help mendicant pilgrims to the different shrines. A rich Indian will build a temple and a rest house just as your American millionaires erect libraries."

The American nodded again, watching now the old man with the length of yellow silk wrapped around him. And just at this point Poggioli received the very queer impression which led to his night's adventure.

When the wedding procession entered the temple the harsh music stopped abruptly. Then, as the line of robed coolies disappeared into the dark interior the psychologist had a strange feeling that the procession had been swallowed up and had ceased to exist. The bizarre red-and-gold building stood in the glare of sunshine, a solid reality, while its devotees had been dissipated into nothingness.

So peculiar, so startling was the impression, that Poggioli blinked and wondered how he ever came by it. The temple had somehow suggested the Hindu theory of Nirvana. Was it possible that the Hindu architect had caught some association of ideas between the doctrine of obliteration and these curves and planes and colors glowing before him? Had he done it by contrast or simile? The fact that Poggioli was a psychologist made the problem all the more intriguing to him—the psychologic influence of architecture. There must be some rationale behind it. An idea how he might pursue this problem came into his head. He turned to his friend and exclaimed:

"Lowe, how about staying all night in old Hira Dass's temple?"

"Doing what?" with a stare of amazement.

"Staying a night in the temple. I had an impression just then, a——"

"Why, my dear fellow!" ejaculate Lowe, "no white man ever stayed all night in a coolie temple. It simply isn't done!"

The American argued his case a moment:

"You and I had a wonderful night aboard the *Trevemore* when we became acquainted."

"That was a matter of necessity," said the bank clerk. "There were no first-class cabin accommodations left on the *Trevemore*, so we had to make the voyage on deck."

Here the psychologist gave up his bid for companionship. Late that night he slipped out of Lowe's cottage, walked back to the grotesque temple, was given a cup of tea, a plate of rice, and a sleeping rug. The only further impression the investigator obtained was a series of fantastic and highly colored dreams, of which he could not recall a detail. Then he waked with a miserable headache and came home.

Mr. Poggioli finished his dressing and in a few minutes the breakfast bell rang. He went to the dining room to find the bank clerk unfolding the damp pages of the

Port of Spain *Inquirer*. This was a typical English sheet using small, solidly set columns without flaming headlines. Poggioli glanced at it and wondered mildly if nothing worth featuring ever happened in Trinidad.

Ram Jon, Lowe's Hindu servant, slipped in and out of the breakfast room with peeled oranges, tea, toast, and a custard fruit flanked by a half lemon to squeeze over it.

"Pound sterling advanced a point," droned Lowe from his paper.

"It'll reach par," said the American, smiling faintly and wondering what Lowe would say if he knew of his escapade.

"Our new governor general will arrive in Trinidad on the twelfth."

"Surely that deserved a headline," said the psychologist.

"Don't try to debauch me· with your American yellow journalism," smiled the bank clerk.

"Go your· own way if you prefer doing research work every morning for breakfast."

The bank clerk laughed again at this, continued his perusal, then. said:

"Hello, another coolie kills his wife. Tell me, Poggioli, as a psychologist, why do coolies kill their wives?"

"For various reasons, I fancy, or perhaps this one didn't kill her at all. Surely now and.then some other·person——"

"Positively no! It's always the husband, and instead of having various reasons, they have none at all. They say their heads are hot, and so to cool their own they cut off their wives'!"

The psychologist was amused in a dull sort of way.

"Lowe, you Englishmen are a nation. with fixed ideas.

You genuinely believe that every coolie woman who is murdered is killed by her husband without any motive whatever."

"Sure, that's right," nodded Lowe, looking up from his paper.

"That simply shows me you English have no actual sympathy with your subordinate races. And that may be the reason your empire is great. Your aloofness, your unsympathy—by becoming automatic you become absolutely dependable. The idea, that every coolie woman is murdered by her husband without a motive!"

"That's correct," repeated Lowe with English imperturbability.

The conversation was interrupted by a ring at the garden-gate bell. A few moments later the two men saw through the shadow Ram Jon slithering across the grass with his greasy black hair shining in the morning sunlight. Lowe watched his servant with distaste.

"Something about these Hindus I don't like," he observed.

Poggioli smiled.

"Another evidence of your racial unsympathy."

"Now look here," defended Lowe, "nobody could like them. The way they walk makes me think of snakes gliding about on their tails."

Poggioli sat smiling and watched Ram Jon unlock the wall door, open it a few inches, parley a moment, and receive a letter. Then he came back with his limber, gliding gait.

Lowe received the note through the open window, broke the envelope, and fished out two notes instead of one. The clerk looked at the inclosures and began to read with a growing bewilderment in his face.

"What is it?" asked Poggioli at last.

"This is from Hira Dass to Jeffries, the vice-president of our bank. He says his nephew Boodman Lal has been arrested and he wants Jeffries to help get him out."

"What's he arrested for?"

"Er—for murdering his wife," said Lowe with a long face.

Poggioli stared.

"Wasn't he the man we saw in the procession yesterday?"

"Damn it, yes!" cried Lowe in sudden disturbance, "and he's a sensible fellow, too, one of our best patrons." He sat staring at the American over the letter, and then suddenly recalling a point, drove it home English fashion.

"That proves my contention, Poggioli—a groom of only six or eight hours' standing killing his wife. They simply commit uxoricide without any reason at all, the damned irrational rotters!"

"What's the other letter?" probed the American, leaning across the table.

"It's from Jeffries. He says he wants me to take this case and get the best talent in Trinidad to clear Mr. Hira Dass's house and consult with him." The clerk replaced the letters in the envelope. "Say, you've had some experience in this sort of thing. Won't you come with me?"

"Glad to."

The two men arose promptly from the table, got their hats, and went out into Tragarette Road once more. As they stood in the increasing heat waiting for a car, it occurred to Poggioli that the details of the murder ought to be in the morning's paper. He took the *Inquirer* from his friend and began a search through its closely printed columns. Presently he found a paragraph without any heading at all:

Boodman Lal, nephew of Mr. Hira Dass, was arrested early this morning at his home in Peru, the East Indian suburb, for the alleged murder of his wife, whom he married yesterday at the Hindu temple in Peru. The body was found at six o'clock this morning in the temple. The attendant gave the alarm. Mrs. Boodman Lal's head was severed completely from her body and she lay in front of the Buddhist altar in her bridal dress. All of her jewelry was gone. Five coolie beggars who were asleep in the temple when the body was discovered were arrested. They claimed to know nothing of the crime, but a search of their persons revealed that each beggar had a piece of the young bride's jewelry and a coin from her necklace.

Mr. Boodman Lal and his wife were seen to enter the temple at about eleven o'clock last night for the Krishnian rite of purification. Mr. Boodman, who is a prominent curio dealer in this city, declines to say anything further than that he thought his wife had gone back to her mother's home for the night after her prayers in the temple. The young bride, formerly a Miss Maila Ran, was thirteen years old. Mr. Boodman is the nephew of Mr. Hira Dass, one of the wealthiest men in Trinidad.

The paragraph following this contained a notice of a tea given at Queen's Park Hotel by Lady Henley-Hoads, and the names of her guests.

The psychologist spent a painful moment pondering the kind of editor who would run a millionaire murder mystery, without any caption whatever, in between a legal notice and a society note. Then he turned his attention to the grewsome and mysterious details the paragraph contained.

"Lowe, what do you make out of those beggars, each with a coin and a piece of jewelry?"

"Simple enough. The rotters laid in wait in the temple

till the husband went out and left his wife, then they murdered her and divided the spoil."

"But that child had enough bangles to give a dozen to each man."

"Ye-es, that's a fact," admitted Lowe.

"And why should they continue sleeping in the temple?"

"Why shouldn't they? They knew they would be suspected, and they couldn't get off the island without capture, so they thought they might as well lie back down and go to sleep."

Here the street car approached and Mr. Poggioli nodded, apparently in agreement.

"Yes, I am satisfied that is how it occurred."

"You mean the beggars killed her?"

"No, I fancy the actual murderer took the girl's jewelry and went about the temple thrusting a bangle and a coin in the pockets of each of the sleeping beggars to lay a false scent."

"Aw, come now!" cried the bank clerk, "that's laying it on a bit too thick, Poggioli!"

"My dear fellow, that's the only possible explanation for the coins in the beggars' pockets."

By this time the men were on the tramcar and were clattering off down Tragarette Road. As they dashed along toward the Hindu village Poggioli remembered suddenly that he had walked this same distance the preceding night and had slept in this same temple. A certain sharp impulse caused the American to run a hand swiftly into his own pockets. In one side he felt the keys of his trunk and of Lowe's cottage; in the other he touched several coins and a round hard ring. With a little thrill he drew these to the edge of his pocket and took a covert glance at them. One showed the curve of a gold bangle; the other the face of an old English gold coin which evidently had been soldered to something.

With a little sinking sensation Poggioli eased them back into his pocket and stared ahead at the coolie village which they were approaching. He moistened his lips and thought what he would better do. The only notion that came into his head was to pack his trunk and take passage on the first steamer out of Trinidad, no matter to what port it was bound.

In his flurry of uneasiness the psychologist was tempted to drop the gold pieces then and there, but as the street car rattled into Peru he reflected that no other person in Trinidad knew that he had these things, except indeed the person who slipped them into his pocket, but that person was not likely to mention the matter. Then, too, it was such an odd occurrence, so piquing to his analytic instinct, that he decided he would go on with the inquiry.

Two minutes later Lowe rang down the motorman and the two companions got off in the Hindu settlement. By this time the street was full of coolies, greasy men and women gliding about with bundles on their heads or coiled down in the sunshine in pairs where they took turns in examining each other's head for vermin. Lowe glanced about, oriented himself, then started walking briskly past the temple, when Poggioli stopped him and asked him where he was going.

"To report to old Hira Dass, according to my instructions from Jeffries," said the Englishman.

"Suppose we stop in the temple a moment. We ought not to go to the old fellow without at least a working knowledge of the scene of the murder."

The clerk slowed up uncertainly, but at that moment

they glanced through the temple door and saw five coolies sitting inside. A policeman at the entrance was evidently guarding these men as prisoners. Lowe approached the guard, made his mission known, and a little later he and his guest were admitted into the temple.

The coolie prisoners were as repulsive as are all of their kind. Four were as thin as cadavers, the fifth one greasily fat. All five wore cheesecloth around their bodies, which left them as exposed as if they had worn nothing at all. One of the emaciated men held his mouth open all the time with an expression of suffering caused by a chronic lack of food. The five squatted on their rugs and looked at the white men with their beadlike eyes. The fat one said in a low tone to his companions:

"The sahib."

This whispered ejaculation disquieted Poggioli somewhat, and he reflected again that it would have been discretion to withdraw from the murder of little Maila Ran as quietly as possible. Still he could explain his presence in the temple simply enough. And besides, the veiled face of the mystery seduced him. He stood studying the five beggars: the greasy one, the lean ones, the one with the suffering face.

"Boys," he said to the group, for all coolies are boys, "did any of you hear any noises in this temple last night?"

"Much sleep, sahib, no noise. Police-y-man punch us 'wake this morning make sit still here."

"What's your name?" asked the American of the loquacious fat mendicant.

"Chuder Chand, sahib."

"When did you go to sleep last night?"

"When I ate rice and tea, sahib."

"Do you remember seeing Boodman Lal and his wife enter this building last night?"

Here their evidence became divided. The fat man remembered; two of the cadavers remembered only the wife, one only Boodman Lal, and one nothing at all.

Poggioli confined himself to the fat man.

"Did you see them go out?"

All five shook their heads.

"You were all asleep then?"

A general nodding.

"Did you have any impressions during your sleep, any disturbance, any half rousing, any noises?"

The horror-struck man said in a ghastly tone:

"I dream bad dream, sahib. When police-y-man punch me awake this morning I think my dream is come to me."

"And me, sahib."

"Me, sahib."

"Me."

"Did you all have bad dreams?"

A general nodding.

"What did you dream, Chuder Chand?" inquired the psychologist with a certain growth of interest.

"Dream me a big fat pig, but still I starved, sahib."

"And you?" at a lean man.

"That I be mashed under a great bowl of rice, sahib, but hungry."

"And you?" asked Poggioli of the horror-struck coolie.

The coolie wet his dry lips and whispered in his ghastly tones:

"Sahib, I dreamed I was Siva, and I held the world in my hands and bit it and it tasted bitter, like the rind of a mammy apple. And I said to Vishnu, 'Let me be a dog in the streets, rather than taste the bitterness of this world,' and then the policeman punched me, sahib, and asked if I had murdered Maila Ran."

The psychologist stood staring at the sunken temples and withered chaps of the beggar, amazed at the enormous vision of godhood which had visited the old mendicant's head. No doubt this grandiloquent dream was a sort of compensation for the starved and wretched existence the beggar led.

Here the bank clerk intervened to say that they would better go on around to old Hira Dass's house according to instructions.

Poggioli turned and followed his friend out of the temple.

"Lowe, I think we can now entirely discard the theory that the beggars murdered the girl."

"On what grounds?" asked the clerk in surprise. "They told you nothing but their dreams."

"That is the reason. All five had wild, fantastic dreams. That suggests they were given some sort of opiate in their rice or tea last night. It is very improbable that five ignorant coolies would have wit enough to concoct such a piece of evidence as that."

"That's a fact," admitted the Englishman, a trifle surprised, "but I don't believe a Trinidad court would admit such evidence."

"We are not looking for legal evidence; we are after some indication of the real criminal."

By this time the two men were walking down a hot, malodorous alley which emptied into the square a little east of the temple. Lowe jerked a bell-pull in a high adobe wall, and Poggioli was surprised that this could be the home of a millionaire Hindu. Presently the shutter opened and

Mr. Hira Dass himself stood in the opening. The old Hindu was still draped in yellow silk which revealed his emaciated form almost as completely as if he had been naked. But his face was alert with hooked nose and brilliant black eyes, and his wrinkles did not so much suggest great age as they did shrewdness and acumen.

The old coolie immediately led his callers into an open court surrounded by marble columns with a fountain in its center and white doves fluttering up to the frieze or floating back down again.

The Hindu began talking immediately of the murder and his anxiety to clear his unhappy nephew. The old man's English was very good, no doubt owing to the business association of his latter years.

"A most mysterious murder," he deplored, shaking his head, "and the life of my poor nephew will depend upon your exertions, gentlemen. What do you think of those beggars that were found in the temple with the bangles and coins?"

Mr. Hira Dass seated his guests on a white marble bench, and now walked nervously in front of them, like some fantastic old scarecrow draped in yellow silk.

"I am afraid my judgment of the beggars will disappoint you, Mr. Hira Dass," answered Poggioli. "My theory is they are innocent of the crime."

"Why do you say that?" queried Hira Dass, looking sharply at the American.

The psychologist explained his deduction from their dreams.

"You are not English, sir," exclaimed the old man. "No Englishman would have thought of that."

"No, I'm half Italian and half American."

The old Indian nodded.

"Your Latin blood has subtlety, Mr. Poggioli, but you base your proof on the mechanical cause of the dreams, not upon the dreams themselves."

The psychologist looked at the old man's cunning face and gnomelike figure and smiled.

"I could hardly use the dreams themselves, although they were fantastic enough."

"Oh, you did inquire into the actual dreams?"

"Yes, by the way of professional interest."

"What is your profession? Aren't you a detective?"

"No, I'm a psychologist."

Old Hira Dass paused in his rickety walking up and down the marble pavement to stare at the American and then burst into the most wrinkled cachinnation Poggioli had ever seen.

"A psychologist, and inquired into a suspected criminal's dreams out of mere curiosity!" the old gnome cackled again, then became serious. He held up a thin finger at the American. "I must not laugh. Your oversoul, your *atman*, is at least groping after knowledge as the blind-worm gropes. But enough of that, Mr. Poggioli. Our problem is to find the criminal who committed this crime and restore my nephew Boodman Lal to liberty. You can imagine what a blow this is to me. I arranged this marriage for my nephew."

The American looked at the old man with new ground for deduction.

"You did—arranged a marriage for a nephew who is in the thirties?"

"Yes, I wanted him to avoid the pitfalls into which I fell," replied old Hira Dass seriously. "He was unmarried, and had already begun to add dollars to dollars. I did the same thing, Mr. Poggioli, and now look at me—an empty old man in a foreign land. What good is this marble court where men of my own kind cannot come and sit with me, and when I have no grandchildren to feed the doves? No, I have piled up dollars and pounds. I have eaten the world, Mr. Poggioli, and found it bitter; now here I am, an outcast."

There was a passion in this outburst which moved the American, and at the same time the old Hindu's phraseology was sharply reminiscent of the dreams told him by the beggars in the temple. The psychologist noted the point hurriedly and curiously in the flow of the conversation, and at the same moment some other part of his brain was inquiring tritely:

"Then why don't you go back to India, Mr. Hira Dass?"

"With this worn-out body," the old Hindu made a contemptuous gesture toward himself, "and with this face, wrinkled with pence! Why, Mr. Poggioli, my mind is half English. If I should return to Benares I would walk about thinking what the temples cost, what was the value of the stones set in the eyes of Krishna's image. That is why we Hindus lose our caste if we travel abroad and settle in a foreign land, because we do indeed lose caste. We become neither Hindus nor English. Our minds are divided, so if I would ever be one with my own people again, Mr. Poggioli, I must leave this Western mind and body here in Trinidad."

Old Hira Dass's speech brought to the American that fleeting credulity in transmigration of the soul which an ardent believer always inspires. The old Hindu made the theory of palingenesis appear almost matter-of-fact. A man died here and reappeared as a babe in India. There was nothing so unbelievable in that. A man's basic energy, which has loved, hated, aspired, and grieved here, must go somewhere, while matter itself was a mere dance of atoms. Which was the most permanent, Hira Dass's passion or his marble court? Both were mere forms of force. The psychologist drew himself out of his reverie.

"That is very interesting, or I should say moving, Hira Dass. You have strange griefs. But we were discussing your nephew, Boodman Lal. I think I have a theory which may liberate him."

"And what is that?"

"As I have explained to you, I believe the beggars in the temple were given a sleeping potion. I suspect the temple attendant doped the rice and later murdered your nephew's wife."

The millionaire became thoughtful.

"That is good Gooka. I employ him. He is a miserably poor man, Mr. Poggioli, so I cannot believe he committed this murder."

"Pardon me, but I don't follow your reasoning. If he is poor he would have a strong motive for the robbery."

"That's true, but a very poor man would never have dropped the ten pieces of gold into the pockets of the beggars to lay a false scent. The man who did this deed must have been a well-to-do person accustomed to using money to forward his purposes. Therefore, in searching for the criminal I would look for a moneyed man."

"But, Mr. Hira Dass," protested the psychologist, "that swings suspicion back to your nephew."

"My nephew!" cried the old man, growing excited again. "What motive would my nephew have to slay his bride of a few hours!"

"But what motive," retorted Poggioli with academic

curtness, "would a well-to-do man have to murder a child? And what chance would he have to place an opiate in the rice?"

The old Hindu lifted a finger and came closer.

"I'll tell you my suspicions," he said in a lowered voice, "and you can work out the details."

"Yes, what are they?" asked Poggioli, becoming attentive again.

"I went down to the temple this morning to have the body of my poor murdered niece brought here to my villa for burial. I talked to the five beggars and they told me that there was a sixth sleeper in the temple last night." The old coolie shook his finger, lifted his eyebrows, and assumed a very gnomish appearance indeed.

A certain trickle of dismay went through the American. He tried to keep from moistening his lips and perhaps did, but all he could think to do was to lift his eyebrows and say:

"Was there, indeed?"

"Yes—and a white man!"

Lowe, the bank clerk, who had been sitting silent through all this, interrupted.

"Surely not, Mr. Hira Dass, not a white man!"

"All five of the coolies and my man Gooka told me it was true," reiterated the old man, "and I have always found Gooka a truthful man. And besides, such a man would fill the rôle of assailant exactly. He would be well-to-do, accustomed to using money to forward his purposes."

The psychologist made a sort of mental lunge to refute this rapid array of evidence old Hira Dass was piling up against him.

"But, Mr. Hira Dass, decapitation is not an American mode of murder!"

"American!"

"I—I was speaking generally," stammered the psychologist, "I mean a white man's method of murder."

"That is indicative in itself," returned the Hindu promptly. "I meant to call your attention to that point. It shows the white man was a highly educated man, who had studied the mental habit of other peoples than his own, so he was enabled to give the crime an extraordinary resemblance to a Hindu crime. I would suggest, gentlemen, that you begin your search for an intellectual white man."

"What motive could such a man have?" cried the American.

"Robbery, possibly, or if he were a very intellectual man indeed he might have murdered the poor child by way of experiment. I read not long ago in an American paper of two youths who committed such a crime."

"A murder for experiment!" cried Lowe, aghast.

"Yes, to record the psychological reaction."

Poggioli suddenly got to his feet.

"I can't agree with such a theory as that, Mr. Hira Dass," he said in a shaken voice.

"No, it's too far-fetched," declared the clerk at once.

"However, it is worth while investigating," persisted the Hindu.

"Yes, yes," agreed the American, evidently about to depart, "but I shall begin my investigations, gentlemen, with the man Gooka."

"As you will," agreed Hira Dass, "and in your investigations, gentlemen, hire any assistants you need, draw on me for any amount. I want my nephew exonerated, and above all things I want the real criminal apprehended and brought to the gallows."

Lowe nodded.

"We'll do our best, sir," he answered in his thorough-going English manner.

The old man followed his guests to the gate and bowed them out into the malodorous alleyway again.

As the two friends set off through the hot sunshine once more the bank clerk laughed.

"A white man in that temple! That sounds like pure fiction to me to shield Boodman Lal. You know these coolies hang together like thieves."

He walked on a little way pondering, then added, "Jolly good thing we didn't decide to sleep in the temple last night, isn't it, Poggioli?"

A sickish feeling went over the American. For a moment he was tempted to tell his host frankly what he had done and ask his advice in the matter, but finally he said:

"In my opinion the actual criminal is Boodman Lal."

Lowe glanced around sidewise at his guest and nodded faintly.

"Same here. I thought it ever since I first saw the account in the *Inquirer*. Somehow these coolies will chop their wives to pieces for no reason at all."

"I know a very good reason in this instance," retorted the American warmly, taking out his uneasiness in this manner. "It's these damned child marriages! When a man marries some child he doesn't care a tuppence for—— What do you know about Boodman Lal, anyway?"

"All there is to know. He was born here and has always been a figure here in Port of Spain because of his rich uncle."

"Lived here all his life?"

"Except when he was in Oxford for six years."

"Oh, he's an Oxford man!"

"Yes."

"There you are, there's the trouble."

"What do you mean?"

"No doubt he fell in love with some English girl. But when his wealthy uncle, Hira Dass, chose a Hindu child for his wife, Boodman could not refuse the marriage. No man is going to quarrel with a million-pound legacy, but he chose this ghastly method of getting rid of the child."

"I venture you are right," declared the bank clerk. "I felt sure Boodman Lal had killed the girl."

"Likely as not he was engaged to some English girl and was waiting for his uncle's death to make him wealthy."

"Quite possible, in fact probable."

Here a cab came angling across the square toward the two men as they stood in front of the grotesque temple. The Negro driver waved his whip interrogatively. The clerk beckoned him in. The cab drew up at the curb. Lowe climbed in but Poggioli remained on the pavement.

"Aren't you coming?"

"You know, Lowe," said Poggioli seriously, "I don't feel that I can conscientiously continue this investigation, trying to clear a person whom I have every reason to believe guilty."

The bank clerk was disturbed.

"But, man, don't leave me like this! At least come on to the police headquarters and explain your theory about the temple keeper, Gooka, and the rice. That seems to hang together pretty well. It is possible Boodman Lal didn't do this thing after all. We owe it to him to do all we can."

As Poggioli still hung back on the curb, Lowe asked: "What do you want to do?"

"Well, I—er—thought I would go back to the cottage and pack my things."

The bank clerk was amazed.

"Pack your things—your boat doesn't sail until Friday!"

"Yes, I know, but there is a daily service to Curaçao. It struck me to go——"

"Aw, come!" cried Lowe in hospitable astonishment, "you can't run off like that, just when I've stirred up an interesting murder mystery for you to unravel. You ought to appreciate my efforts as a host more than that."

"Well, I do," hesitated Poggioli seriously. At that moment his excess of caution took one of those odd, instantaneous shifts that come so unaccountably to men, and he thought to himself, "Well, damn it, this is an interesting situation. It's a shame to leave it, and nothing will happen to me."

So he swung into the cab with decision and ordered briskly: "All right, to the police station, Sambo!"

"Sounds more like it," declared the clerk, as the cab horses set out at a brisk trot through the sunshine.

Mr. Lowe, the bank clerk, was not without a certain flair for making the most of a house guest, and when he reached the police station he introduced his companion to the chief of police as "Mr. Poggioli a professor in an American university and a research student in criminal psychology."

The chief of police, a Mr. Vickers, was a short, thick man with a tropic-browned face and eyes habitually squinted against the sun. He seemed not greatly impressed with the titles Lowe gave his friend but merely remarked that if Mr. Poggioli was hunting crimes, Trinidad was a good place to find them.

The bank clerk proceeded with a certain importance in his manner.

"I have asked his counsel in the Boodman Lal murder

case. He has developed a theory, Mr. Vickers, as to who is the actual murderer of Mrs. Boodman Lal."

"So have I," replied Vickers with a dry smile.

"Of course you think Boodman Lal did it," said Lowe in a more commonplace manner.

Vickers did not answer this but continued looking at the two taller men in a listening attitude which caused Lowe to go on.

"Now in this matter, Mr. Vickers, I want to be perfectly frank with you. I'll admit we are in this case in the employ of Mr. Hira Dass, and are making an effort to clear Boodman Lal. We felt confident you would use the well-known skill of the police department of Port of Spain to work out a theory to clear Boodman Lal just as readily as you would to convict him."

"Our department usually devotes its time to conviction and not to clearing criminals."

"Yes, I know that, but if our theory will point out the actual murderer——"

"What is your theory?" inquired Vickers without enthusiasm.

The bank clerk began explaining the dream of the five beggars and the probability that they had been given sleeping potions.

The short man smiled faintly.

"So Mr. Poggioli's theory is based on the dreams of these men?"

Poggioli had a pedagogue's brevity of temper when his theories were questioned.

"It would be a remarkable coincidence, Mr. Vickers, if five men had lurid dreams simultaneously without some physical cause. It suggests strongly that their tea or rice was doped."

As Vickers continued looking at Poggioli the American continued with less acerbity:

"I should say that Gooka, the temple keeper, either doped the rice himself or he knows who did it."

"Possibly he does."

"My idea is that you send a man for the ricepot and teapot, have their contents analyzed, find out what soporific was used, then have your men search the sales records of the drug stores in the city to see who has lately bought such a drug."

Mr. Vickers grunted a noncommittal uh-huh, and then began in the livelier tones of a man who meets a stranger socially:

"How do you like Trinidad, Mr. Poggioli?"

"Remarkably luxuriant country—oranges and grapefruit growing wild."

"You've just arrived?"

"Yes."

"In what university do you teach?"

"Ohio State."

Mr. Vickers's eyes took on a humorous twinkle.

"A chair of criminal psychology in an ordinary state university—is that the result of your American prohibition laws, Professor?"

Poggioli smiled at this thrust.

"Mr. Lowe misstated my work a little. I am not a professor, I am simply a docent. And I have not specialized on criminal psychology. I quiz on general psychology."

"You are not teaching now?"

"No; this is my sabbatical year."

Mr. Vickers glanced up and down the American.

"You look young to have taught in a university six years."

There was something not altogether agreeable in this observation, but the officer rectified it a moment later by saying, "But you Americans start young—land of specialists. Now you, Mr. Poggioli—I suppose you are wrapped up heart and soul in your psychology?"

"I am," agreed the American positively.

"Do anything in the world to advance yourself in the science?"

"I rather think so," asserted Poggioli, with his enthusiasm mounting in his voice.

"Especially keen on original research work——"

Lowe interrupted, laughing.

"That's what he is, Chief. Do you know what he asked me to do yesterday afternoon?"

"No, what?"

The American turned abruptly on his friend.

"Now, Lowe, don't let's burden Mr. Vickers with household anecdotes."

"But I am really curious," declared the police chief. "Just what did Professor Poggioli ask you to do yesterday afternoon, Mr. Lowe?"

The bank clerk looked from one to the other, hardly knowing whether to go on or not. Mr. Vickers was smiling; Poggioli was very serious as he prohibited anecdotes about himself. The bank clerk thought: "This is real modesty." He said aloud: "It was just a little psychological experiment he wanted to do."

"Did he do it?" smiled the chief.

"Oh, no, I wouldn't hear to it."

"As unconventional as that!" cried Mr. Vickers, lifting sandy brows.

"It was really nothing," said Lowe, looking at his guest's rigid face and then at the police captain.

Suddenly Mr. Vickers dropped his quizzical attitude.
"I think I could guess your anecdote if I tried, Lowe.
About a half hour ago I received a telephone message from
my man stationed at the Hindu temple to keep a lookout
for you and Mr. Poggioli."

The American felt a tautening of his muscles at this
frontal attack. He had suspected something of the sort
from the policeman's manner. The bank clerk stared at
the officer in amazement.

"What was your bobby telephoning about us for?"

"Because one of the coolies under arrest told him that
Mr. Poggioli slept in the temple last night."

"My word, that's not true!" cried the bank clerk. "That
is exactly what he did not do. He suggested it to me but I
said No. You remember, Poggioli——"

Mr. Lowe turned for corroboration, but the look on his
friend's face amazed him.

"You didn't do it, did you, Poggioli?" he gasped.

"You see he did," said Vickers dryly.

"But, Poggioli—in God's name——"

The American braced himself for an attempt to explain.
He lifted his hand with a certain pedagogic mannerism.

"Gentlemen, I—I had a perfectly valid, an important
reason for sleeping in the temple last night."

"I told you," nodded Vickers.

"In coolie town, in a coolie temple!" ejaculated Lowe.

"Gentlemen, I—can only ask your—your sympathetic
attention to what I am about to say."

"Go on," said Vickers.

"You remember, Lowe, you and I were down there
watching a wedding procession. Well, just as the music
stopped and the line of coolies entered the building, suddenly it seemed to me as if—as if—they had——" Pog-

gioli swallowed at nothing and then added the odd word,
"vanished."

Vickers looked at him.

"Naturally, they had gone into the building."

"I don't mean that. I'm afraid you won't understand
what I do mean—that the whole procession had ceased to
exist, melted into nothingness."

Even Mr. Vickers blinked. Then he drew out a memorandum book and stolidly made a note.

"Is that all?"

"No, then I began speculating on what had given me
such a strange impression. You see that is really the idea
on which the Hindus base their notion of heaven—oblivion,
nothingness."

"Yes, I've heard that before."

"Well, our medieval Gothic architecture was a conception of our Western heaven; and I thought perhaps the
Indian architecture had somehow caught the motif of the
Indian religion; you know, suggested Nirvana. That was
what amazed and intrigued me. That was why I wanted
to sleep in the place. I wanted to see if I could further my
shred of impression. Does this make any sense to you,
Mr. Vickers?"

"I dare say it will, sir, to the criminal judge," opined
the police chief cheerfully.

The psychologist felt a sinking of heart.

Mr. Vickers proceeded in the same matter-of-fact tone:
"But no matter why you went in, what you did afterward
is what counts. Here in Trinidad nobody is allowed to go
around chopping off heads to see how it feels."

Poggioli looked at the officer with a ghastly sensation
in his midriff.

"You don't think I did such a horrible thing as an experiment?"

Mr. Vickers drew out the makings of a cigarette.

"You Americans, especially you intellectual Americans, do some pretty stiff things, Mr. Poggioli. I was reading about two young intellectuals——"

"Good Lord!" quivered the psychologist with this particular reference beginning to grate on his nerves.

"These fellows I read about also tried to turn an honest penny by their murder—I don't suppose you happened to notice yesterday that the little girl, Maila Ran, was almost covered over with gold bangles and coins?"

"Of course I noticed it!" cried the psychologist, growing white, "but I had nothing whatever to do with the child. Your insinuations are brutal and repulsive. I did sleep in the temple——"

"By the way," interrupted Vickers suddenly, "you say you slept on a rug just as the other coolies did?"

"Yes, I did."

"You didn't wake up either?"

"No."

"Then did the murderer of the child happen to put a coin and a bangle in your pockets, just as he did the other sleepers in the temple?"

"That's exactly what he did!" cried Poggioli, with the first ray of hope breaking upon him. "When I found them in my pocket on the tram this morning I came pretty near throwing them away, but fortunately I didn't. Here they are."

And gladly enough now he drew the trinkets out and showed them to the chief of police.

Mr. Vickers looked at the gold pieces, then at the psychologist.

"You don't happen to have any more, do you?"

The American said No, but it was with a certain thrill of anxiety that he began turning out his other pockets. If the mysterious criminal had placed more than two gold pieces in his pockets he would be in a very difficult position. However, the remainder of his belongings were quite legitimate.

"Well, that's something," admitted Vickers slowly. "Of course, you might have expected just such a questioning as this and provided yourself with these two pieces of gold, but I doubt it. Somehow, I don't believe you are a bright enough man to think of such a thing." He paused, pondering, and finally said, "I suppose you have no objection to my sending a man to search your baggage in Mr. Lowe's cottage?"

"Instead of objecting, I invite it, I request it."

Mr. Vickers nodded agreeably.

"Who can I telegraph to in America to learn something about your standing as a university man?"

"Dean Ingram, Ohio State, Columbus, Ohio, U. S. A."

Vickers made this note, then turned to Lowe.

"I suppose you've known Mr. Poggioli for a long time, Mr. Lowe?"

"Why n-no, I haven't," admitted the clerk.

"Where did you meet him?"

"Sailing from Barbuda to Antigua. On the *Trevemore*."

"Did he seem to have respectable American friends aboard?"

Lowe hesitated and flushed faintly.

"I—can hardly say."

"Why?"

"If I tell you Mr. Poggioli's mode of travel I am afraid you would hold it to his disadvantage."

"How did he travel?" queried the officer in surprise.

"The fact is he traveled as a deck passenger."

"You mean he had no cabin, shipped along on deck with the Negroes!"

"I did it myself!" cried Lowe, growing ruddy. "We couldn't get a cabin—they were all occupied."

The American reflected rapidly, and realized that Vickers could easily find out the real state of things from the ship's agents up the islands.

"Chief," said the psychologist with a tongue that felt thick, "I boarded the *Trevemore* at St. Kitts. There were cabins available. I chose deck passage deliberately. I wanted to study the natives."

"Then you are broke, just as I thought," ejaculated Mr. Vickers, "and I'll bet pounds to pence we'll find the jewelry around your place somewhere."

The chief hailed a passing cab, called a plain-clothes man, put the three in the vehicle and started them briskly back up Prince Edward's Street, toward Tragarette Road, and thence to Lowe's cottage beyond the Indian village and its ill-starred temple.

The three men and the Negro driver trotted back up Tragarette, each lost in his own thoughts. The plain-clothes man rode on the front seat with the cabman, but occasionally he glanced back to look at his prisoner. Lowe evidently was reflecting how this contretemps would affect his social and business standing in the city. The Negro also kept peering back under the hood of his cab, and finally he ejaculated:

"Killum jess to see 'um die. I declah, dese 'Mericans——" and he shook his kinky head.

A hot resentment rose up in the psychologist at this continued recurrence of that detestable crime. He realized with deep resentment that the crimes of particular Americans were held tentatively against all American citizens, while their great national charities and humanities were forgotten with the breath that told them. In the midst of these angry thoughts the cab drew up before the clerk's garden gate.

All got out. Lowe let them in with a key and then the three walked in a kind of grave haste across the lawn. The door was opened by Ram Jon, who took their hats and then followed them into the room Lowe had set apart for his guest.

This room, like all Trinidad chambers, was furnished in the sparest and coolest manner possible; a table, three chairs, a bed with sheets, and Poggioli's trunk. It was so open to inspection nothing could have been concealed in it. The plain-clothes man opened the table drawer.

"Would you mind opening your trunk, Mr. Poggioli?"

The American got out his keys, knelt and undid the hasp of his wardrobe trunk, then swung the two halves apart. One side held containers, the other suits. Poggioli opened the drawers casually; collar and handkerchief box at the top, hat box, shirt box. As he did this came a faint clinking sound. The detective stepped forward and lifted out the shirts. Beneath them lay a mass of coins and bangles flung into the tray helter-skelter.

The American stared with an open mouth, unable to say a word.

The plain-clothes man snapped with a certain indignant admiration in his voice: "Your nerve almost got you by!"

The thing seemed unreal to the American. He had the same uncanny feeling that he had experienced when the procession entered the temple. Materiality seemed to have slipped a cog. A wild thought came to him that somehow the Hindus had dematerialized the gold and caused it to reappear in his trunk. Then there came a terrifying fancy that he had committed the crime in his sleep. This last clung to his mind. After all, he had murdered the little girl bride, Maila Ran!

The plain-clothes man spoke to Lowe:

"Have your man bring me a sack to take this stuff back to headquarters."

Ram Jon slithered from the room and presently returned with a sack. The inspector took his handkerchief, lifted the pieces out with it, one by one, and placed them in the sack.

"Lowe," said Poggioli pitifully, "you don't believe I did this, do you?"

The bank clerk wiped his face with his handkerchief.

"In your trunk, Poggioli——"

"If I did it I was sleepwalking!" cried the unhappy man. "My God, to think it is possible—but right here in my own trunk——" he stood staring at the bag, at the shirt box.

The plain-clothes man said dryly: "We might as well start back, I suppose. This is all."

Lowe suddenly cast in his lot with his guest.

"I'll go back with you, Poggioli. I'll see you through this pinch. Somehow I can't, I won't believe you did it!"

"Thanks! Thanks!"

The bank clerk masked his emotion under a certain grim facetiousness.

"You know, Poggioli, you set out to clear Boodman Lal —it looks as if you've done it."

"No, he didn't," denied the plain-clothes man. "Bood-

man Lal was out of jail at least an hour before you fellows
drove up a while ago."

"Out—had you turned him out?"

"Yes."

"How was that?"

"Because he didn't go to the temple at all last night
with his wife. He went down to Queen's Park Hotel and
played billiards till one o'clock. He called up some friends
and proved that easily enough."

Lowe stared at his friend, aghast.

"My word, Poggioli, that leaves nobody but—you."

The psychologist lost all semblance of resistance.

"I don't know anything about it. If I did it I was asleep.
That's all I can say. The coolies——" He had a dim notion
of accusing them again, but he recalled that he had proved
to himself clearly and logically that they were innocent.
"I don't know anything about it," he repeated helplessly.

Half an hour later the three men were at police headquarters once more, and the plain-clothes man and the
turnkey, a humble, gray sort of man, took the American
back to a cell. The turnkey unlocked one in a long row of
cells and swung it open for Poggioli.

The bank clerk gave him what encouragement he could.

"Don't be too downhearted. I'll do everything I can.
Somehow I believe you are innocent. I'll hire your lawyers,
cable your friends——"

Poggioli was repeating a stunned "Thanks! Thanks!"
as the cell door shut between them. The bolt clashed home
and was locked. And the men were tramping down the iron
corridor. Poggioli was alone.

There was a chair and a bunk in the cell. The psychologist looked at these with an irrational feeling that he

would not stay in the prison long enough to warrant his sitting down. Presently he did sit down on the bunk.

He sat perfectly still and tried to assemble his thoughts against the mountain of adverse evidence which suddenly had been piled against him. His sleep in the temple, the murder, the coins in his shirt box—after all he must have committed the crime in his sleep.

As he sat with his head in his hands pondering this theory, it grew more and more incredible. To commit the murder in his sleep, to put the coins in the pockets of the beggars in a clever effort to divert suspicion, to bring the gold to Lowe's cottage, and then to go back and lie down on the mat, all while he was asleep—that was impossible. He could not believe any human being could perform so fantastic, so complicated a feat.

On the other hand, no other criminal would place the whole booty in Poggioli's trunk and so lose it. That too was irrational. He was forced back to his dream theory.

When he accepted this hypothesis he wondered just what he had dreamed. If he had really murdered the girl in a nightmare, then the murder was stamped somewhere in his subconscious, divided from his day memories by the nebulous associations of sleep. He wondered if he could reproduce them.

To recall a lost dream is perhaps one of the nicest tasks that ever a human brain was driven to. Poggioli, being a psychologist, had had a certain amount of experience with such attempts. Now he lay down on his bunk and began the effort in a mechanical way.

He recalled as vividly as possible his covert exit from Lowe's cottage, his walk down Tragarette Road between perfumed gardens, the lights of Peru, and finally his entrance into the temple. He imaged again the temple attendant, Gooka, looking curiously at him, but giving him tea and rice and pointing out his rug. Poggioli remembered that he lay down on the rug on his back with his hands under his head exactly as he was now lying on his cell bunk. For a while he had stared at the illuminated image of Krishna, then at the dark spring of the dome over his head.

And as he lay there, gazing thus, his thoughts had begun to waver, to lose beat with his senses, to make misinterpretations. He had thought that the Krishna moved slightly, then settled back and became a statue again—here some tenuous connection in his thoughts snapped, and he lost his whole picture in the hard bars of his cell again.

Poggioli lay relaxed a while, then began once more. He reached the point where the Krishna moved, seemed about to speak, and then—there he was back in his cell.

It was nerve-racking, tantalizing, this fishing for the gossamers of a dream which continually broke; this pursuing the grotesqueries of a nightmare and trying to connect it with his solid everyday life of thought and action. What had he dreamed? What had he done in his dream?

Minutes dragged out as Poggioli pursued the vanished visions of his head. Yes, it had seemed to him that the image of the Buddha moved, that it had even risen from its attitude of meditation, and suddenly, with a little thrill, Poggioli remembered that the dome of the Hindu temple was opened and this left him staring upward into a vast abyss. It seemed to the psychologist that he stared upward, and the Krishna stared upward, both gazing into an unending space, and presently he realized that he and the great upward-staring Krishna were one; that they had always been one; and that their oneness filled all space with enormous, with infinite power. But this oneness which was

Poggioli was alone in an endless, featureless space. No other thing existed, because nothing had ever been created; there was only a creator. All the creatures and matter which had ever been or ever would be were wrapped up in him, Poggioli, or Buddha. And then Poggioli saw that space and time had ceased to be, for space and time are the offspring of division. And at last Krishna or Poggioli was losing all entity or being in this tranced immobility.

And Poggioli began struggling desperately against nothingness. He writhed at his deadened muscles, he willed in torture to retain some vestige of being, and at last after what seemed millenniums of effort he formed the thought:

"I would rather lose my oneness with Krishna and become the vilest and poorest of creatures—to mate, fight, love, lust, kill, and be killed than to be lost in this terrible trance of the universal!"

And when he had formed this tortured thought Poggioli remembered that he had awakened and it was five o'clock in the morning. He had arisen with a throbbing headache and had gone home.

That was his dream.

The American arose from his bunk filled with the deepest satisfaction from his accomplishment. Then he recalled with surprise that all five of the coolies had much the same dream; grandiloquence and power accompanied by great unhappiness.

"That was an odd thing," thought the psychologist, "six men dreaming the same dream in different terms. There must have been some physical cause for such a phenomenon."

Then he remembered that he had heard the same story from another source. Old Hira Dass in his marble court had expressed the same sentiment, complaining of the emptiness of his riches and power. However—and this was crucial—Hira Dass's grief was not a mere passing nightmare, it was his settled condition.

With this a queer idea popped into Poggioli's mind. Could not these six dreams have been a transference of an idea? While he and the coolies lay sleeping with passive minds, suppose old Hira Dass had entered the temple with his great unhappiness in his mind, and suppose he had committed some terrible deed which wrought his emotions to a monsoon of passion. Would not his horrid thoughts have registered themselves in different forms on the minds of the sleeping men!

Here Poggioli's ideas danced about like the molecules of a crystal in solution, each one rushing of its own accord to take its appointed place in a complicated crystalline design. And so a complete understanding of the murder of little Maila Ran rushed in upon him.

Poggioli leaped to his feet and halloed his triumph.

"Here, Vickers! Lowe! Turnkey! I have it! I've solved it! Turn me out! I know who killed the girl!"

After he had shouted for several minutes Poggioli saw the form of a man coming up the dark aisle with a lamp. He was surprised at the lamp but passed over it.

"Turnkey!" he cried, "I know who murdered the child —old Hira Dass! Now listen——" He was about to relate his dream, but realized that would avail nothing in an English court, so he leaped to the physical end of the crime, matter with which the English juggle so expertly. His thoughts danced into shape.

"Listen, turnkey, go tell Vickers to take that gold and develop all the finger prints on it—he'll find Hira Dass's prints! Also, tell him to follow out that opiate clue I gave him—he'll find Hira Dass's servant bought the opiate. Also, Hira Dass sent a man to put the gold in my trunk. See if you can't find brass or steel filings in my room where the scoundrel sat and filed a new key. Also, give Ram Jon the third degree; he knows who brought the gold."

The one with the lamp made a gesture.

"They've done all that, sir, long ago."

"They did!"

"Certainly, sir, and old Hira Dass confessed everything, though why a rich old man like him should have murdered a pretty child is more than I can see. These Hindus are unaccountable, sir, even the millionaires."

Poggioli passed over so simple a query.

"But why did the old devil pick on me for a scapegoat?" he cried, puzzled.

"Oh, he explained that to the police, sir. He said he picked on a white man so the police would make a thorough investigation and be sure to catch him. In fact, he said, sir, that he had willed that you should come and sleep in the temple that night."

Poggioli stared with a little prickling sensation at this touch of the occult world.

"What I can't see, sir," went on the man with the lamp, "was why the old coolie wanted to be caught and hanged— why didn't he commit suicide?"

"Because then his soul would have returned in the form of some beast. He wanted to be slain. He expects to be reborn instantly in Benares with little Maila Ran. He hopes to be a great man with wife and children."

"Nutty idea!" cried the fellow.

But the psychologist sat staring at the lamp with a queer feeling that possibly such a fantastic idea might be true after all. For what goes with this passionate, uneasy force in man when he dies? May not the dead struggle to reanimate themselves as he had done in his dream? Perhaps the numberless dead still will to live and be divided; and perhaps living things are a result of the struggles of the dead, and not the dead of the living.

His thoughts suddenly shifted back to the present.

"Turnkey," he snapped with academic sharpness, "why didn't you come and tell me of old Hira Dass's confession the moment it occurred? What did you mean, keeping me locked up here when you knew I was an innocent man?"

"Because I couldn't," said the form with the lamp sorrowfully, "Old Hira Dass didn't confess until a month and ten days after you were hanged, sir."

And the lamp went out.

THE END

A CATALOGUE OF
SELECTED DOVER BOOKS
IN ALL FIELDS OF INTEREST

A CATALOGUE OF SELECTED DOVER
BOOKS IN ALL FIELDS OF INTEREST

RACKHAM'S COLOR ILLUSTRATIONS FOR WAGNER'S RING. Rackham's finest mature work—all 64 full-color watercolors in a faithful and lush interpretation of the *Ring*. Full-sized plates on coated stock of the paintings used by opera companies for authentic staging of Wagner. Captions aid in following complete Ring cycle. Introduction. 64 illustrations plus vignettes. 72pp. 8⅝ x 11¼. 23779-6 Pa. $6.00

CONTEMPORARY POLISH POSTERS IN FULL COLOR, edited by Joseph Czestochowski. 46 full-color examples of brilliant school of Polish graphic design, selected from world's first museum (near Warsaw) dedicated to poster art. Posters on circuses, films, plays, concerts all show cosmopolitan influences, free imagination. Introduction. 48pp. 9⅜ x 12¼. 23780-X Pa. $6.00

GRAPHIC WORKS OF EDVARD MUNCH, Edvard Munch. 90 haunting, evocative prints by first major Expressionist artist and one of the greatest graphic artists of his time: *The Scream, Anxiety, Death Chamber, The Kiss, Madonna,* etc. Introduction by Alfred Werner. 90pp. 9 x 12. 23765-6 Pa. $5.00

THE GOLDEN AGE OF THE POSTER, Hayward and Blanche Cirker. 70 extraordinary posters in full colors, from Maitres de l'Affiche, Mucha, Lautrec, Bradley, Cheret, Beardsley, many others. Total of 78pp. 9⅜ x 12¼. 22753-7 Pa. $5.95

THE NOTEBOOKS OF LEONARDO DA VINCI, edited by J. P. Richter. Extracts from manuscripts reveal great genius; on painting, sculpture, anatomy, sciences, geography, etc. Both Italian and English. 186 ms. pages reproduced, plus 500 additional drawings, including studies for *Last Supper,* Sforza monument, etc. 860pp. 7⅞ x 10¾. (Available in U.S. only) 22572-0, 22573-9 Pa., Two-vol. set $15.90

THE CODEX NUTTALL, as first edited by Zelia Nuttall. Only inexpensive edition, in full color, of a pre-Columbian Mexican (Mixtec) book. 88 color plates show kings, gods, heroes, temples, sacrifices. New explanatory, historical introduction by Arthur G. Miller. 96pp. 11⅜ x 8½. (Available in U.S. only) 23168-2 Pa. $7.95

UNE SEMAINE DE BONTÉ, A SURREALISTIC NOVEL IN COLLAGE, Max Ernst. Masterpiece created out of 19th-century periodical illustrations, explores worlds of terror and surprise. Some consider this Ernst's greatest work. 208pp. 8⅛ x 11. 23252-2 Pa. $6.00

DRAWINGS OF WILLIAM BLAKE, William Blake. 92 plates from Book of Job, *Divine Comedy, Paradise Lost,* visionary heads, mythological figures, Laocoon, etc. Selection, introduction, commentary by Sir Geoffrey Keynes. 178pp. 8⅛ x 11. 22303-5 Pa. $4.00

ENGRAVINGS OF HOGARTH, William Hogarth. 101 of Hogarth's greatest works: *Rake's Progress, Harlot's Progress, Illustrations for Hudibras, Before and After, Beer Street and Gin Lane,* many more. Full commentary. 256pp. 11 x 13¾. 22479-1 Pa. $12.95

DAUMIER: 120 GREAT LITHOGRAPHS, Honore Daumier. Wide-ranging collection of lithographs by the greatest caricaturist of the 19th century. Concentrates on eternally popular series on lawyers, on married life, on liberated women, etc. Selection, introduction, and notes on plates by Charles F. Ramus. Total of 158pp. 9⅜ x 12¼. 23512-2 Pa. $6.00

DRAWINGS OF MUCHA, Alphonse Maria Mucha. Work reveals draftsman of highest caliber: studies for famous posters and paintings, renderings for book illustrations and ads, etc. 70 works, 9 in color; including 6 items not drawings. Introduction. List of illustrations. 72pp. 9⅜ x 12¼. (Available in U.S. only) 23672-2 Pa. $4.00

GIOVANNI BATTISTA PIRANESI: DRAWINGS IN THE PIERPONT MORGAN LIBRARY, Giovanni Battista Piranesi. For first time ever all of Morgan Library's collection, world's largest. 167 illustrations of rare Piranesi drawings—archeological, architectural, decorative and visionary. Essay, detailed list of drawings, chronology, captions. Edited by Felice Stampfle. 144pp. 9⅜ x 12¼. 23714-1 Pa. $7.50

NEW YORK ETCHINGS (1905-1949), John Sloan. All of important American artist's N.Y. life etchings. 67 works include some of his best art; also lively historical record—Greenwich Village, tenement scenes. Edited by Sloan's widow. Introduction and captions. 79pp. 8⅜ x 11¼. 23651-X Pa. $4.00

CHINESE PAINTING AND CALLIGRAPHY: A PICTORIAL SURVEY, Wan-go Weng. 69 fine examples from John M. Crawford's matchless private collection: landscapes, birds, flowers, human figures, etc., plus calligraphy. Every basic form included: hanging scrolls, handscrolls, album leaves, fans, etc. 109 illustrations. Introduction. Captions. 192pp. 8⅞ x 11¾. 23707-9 Pa. $7.95

DRAWINGS OF REMBRANDT, edited by Seymour Slive. Updated Lippmann, Hofstede de Groot edition, with definitive scholarly apparatus. All portraits, biblical sketches, landscapes, nudes, Oriental figures, classical studies, together with selection of work by followers. 550 illustrations. Total of 630pp. 9⅛ x 12¼. 21485-0, 21486-9 Pa., Two-vol. set $15.00

THE DISASTERS OF WAR, Francisco Goya. 83 etchings record horrors of Napoleonic wars in Spain and war in general. Reprint of 1st edition, plus 3 additional plates. Introduction by Philip Hofer. 97pp. 9⅜ x 8¼. 21872-4 Pa. $4.00

THE EARLY WORK OF AUBREY BEARDSLEY, Aubrey Beardsley. 157 plates, 2 in color: *Manon Lescaut, Madame Bovary, Morte Darthur, Salome,* other. Introduction by H. Marillier. 182pp. 8⅛ x 11. 21816-3 Pa. $4.50

THE LATER WORK OF AUBREY BEARDSLEY, Aubrey Beardsley. Exotic masterpieces of full maturity: *Venus and Tannhauser, Lysistrata, Rape of the Lock, Volpone,* Savoy material, etc. 174 plates, 2 in color. 186pp. 8⅛ x 11. 21817-1 Pa. $5.95

THOMAS NAST'S CHRISTMAS DRAWINGS, Thomas Nast. Almost all Christmas drawings by creator of image of Santa Claus as we know it, and one of America's foremost illustrators and political cartoonists. 66 illustrations. 3 illustrations in color on covers. 96pp. 8⅜ x 11¼. 23660-9 Pa. $3.50

THE DORÉ ILLUSTRATIONS FOR DANTE'S DIVINE COMEDY, Gustave Doré. All 135 plates from Inferno, Purgatory, Paradise; fantastic tortures, infernal landscapes, celestial wonders. Each plate with appropriate (translated) verses. 141pp. 9 x 12. 23231-X Pa. $4.50

DORÉ'S ILLUSTRATIONS FOR RABELAIS, Gustave Doré. 252 striking illustrations of *Gargantua and Pantagruel* books by foremost 19th-century illustrator. Including 60 plates, 192 delightful smaller illustrations. 153pp. 9 x 12. 23656-0 Pa. $5.00

LONDON: A PILGRIMAGE, Gustave Doré, Blanchard Jerrold. Squalor, riches, misery, beauty of mid-Victorian metropolis; 55 wonderful plates, 125 other illustrations, full social, cultural text by Jerrold. 191pp. of text. 9⅜ x 12¼. 22306-X Pa. $7.00

THE RIME OF THE ANCIENT MARINER, Gustave Doré, S. T. Coleridge. Dore's finest work, 34 plates capture moods, subtleties of poem. Full text. Introduction by Millicent Rose. 77pp. 9¼ x 12. 22305-1 Pa. $3.50

THE DORE BIBLE ILLUSTRATIONS, Gustave Doré. All wonderful, detailed plates: Adam and Eve, Flood, Babylon, Life of Jesus, etc. Brief King James text with each plate. Introduction by Millicent Rose. 241 plates. 241pp. 9 x 12. 23004-X Pa. $6.00

THE COMPLETE ENGRAVINGS, ETCHINGS AND DRYPOINTS OF ALBRECHT DURER. "Knight, Death and Devil"; "Melencolia," and more—all Dürer's known works in all three media, including 6 works formerly attributed to him. 120 plates. 235pp. 8⅜ x 11¼. 22851-7 Pa. $6.50

MECHANICK EXERCISES ON THE WHOLE ART OF PRINTING, Joseph Moxon. First complete book (1683-4) ever written about typography, a compendium of everything known about printing at the latter part of 17th century. Reprint of 2nd (1962) Oxford Univ. Press edition. 74 illustrations. Total of 550pp. 6⅛ x 9¼. 23617-X Pa. $7.95

THE COMPLETE WOODCUTS OF ALBRECHT DURER, edited by Dr. W. Kurth. 346 in all: "Old Testament," "St. Jerome," "Passion," "Life of Virgin," Apocalypse," many others. Introduction by Campbell Dodgson. 285pp. 8½ x 12¼. 21097-9 Pa. $7.50

DRAWINGS OF ALBRECHT DURER, edited by Heinrich Wolfflin. 81 plates show development from youth to full style. Many favorites; many new. Introduction by Alfred Werner. 96pp. 8⅛ x 11. 22352-3 Pa. $5.00

THE HUMAN FIGURE, Albrecht Dürer. Experiments in various techniques—stereometric, progressive proportional, and others. Also life studies that rank among finest ever done. Complete reprinting of Dresden Sketchbook. 170 plates. 355pp. 8⅜ x 11¼. 21042-1 Pa. $7.95

OF THE JUST SHAPING OF LETTERS, Albrecht Dürer. Renaissance artist explains design of Roman majuscules by geometry, also Gothic lower and capitals. Grolier Club edition. 43pp. 7⅞ x 10¾ 21306-4 Pa. $3.00

TEN BOOKS ON ARCHITECTURE, Vitruvius. The most important book ever written on architecture. Early Roman aesthetics, technology, classical orders, site selection, all other aspects. Stands behind everything since. Morgan translation. 331pp. 5⅜ x 8½. 20645-9 Pa. $4.50

THE FOUR BOOKS OF ARCHITECTURE, Andrea Palladio. 16th-century classic responsible for Palladian movement and style. Covers classical architectural remains, Renaissance revivals, classical orders, etc. 1738 Ware English edition. Introduction by A. Placzek. 216 plates. 110pp. of text. 9½ x 12¾. 21308-0 Pa. $10.00

HORIZONS, Norman Bel Geddes. Great industrialist stage designer, "father of streamlining," on application of aesthetics to transportation, amusement, architecture, etc. 1932 prophetic account; function, theory, specific projects. 222 illustrations. 312pp. 7⅞ x 10¾. 23514-9 Pa. $6.95

FRANK LLOYD WRIGHT'S FALLINGWATER, Donald Hoffmann. Full, illustrated story of conception and building of Wright's masterwork at Bear Run, Pa. 100 photographs of site, construction, and details of completed structure. 112pp. 9¼ x 10. 23671-4 Pa. $5.50

THE ELEMENTS OF DRAWING, John Ruskin. Timeless classic by great Viltorian; starts with basic ideas, works through more difficult. Many practical exercises. 48 illustrations. Introduction by Lawrence Campbell. 228pp. 5⅜ x 8½. 22730-8 Pa. $3.75

GIST OF ART, John Sloan. Greatest modern American teacher, Art Students League, offers innumerable hints, instructions, guided comments to help you in painting. Not a formal course. 46 illustrations. Introduction by Helen Sloan. 200pp. 5⅜ x 8½. 23435-5 Pa. $4.00

THE ANATOMY OF THE HORSE, George Stubbs. Often considered the great masterpiece of animal anatomy. Full reproduction of 1766 edition, plus prospectus; original text and modernized text. 36 plates. Introduction by Eleanor Garvey. 121pp. 11 x 14¾. 23402-9 Pa. $6.00

BRIDGMAN'S LIFE DRAWING, George B. Bridgman. More than 500 illustrative drawings and text teach you to abstract the body into its major masses, use light and shade, proportion; as well as specific areas of anatomy, of which Bridgman is master. 192pp. 6½ x 9¼. (Available in U.S. only) 22710-3 Pa. $3.50

ART NOUVEAU DESIGNS IN COLOR, Alphonse Mucha, Maurice Verneuil, Georges Auriol. Full-color reproduction of Combinaisons orne-mentales (c. 1900) by Art Nouveau masters. Floral, animal, geometric, interlacings, swashes—borders, frames, spots—all incredibly beautiful. 60 plates, hundreds of designs. 9⅜ x 8-1/16. 22885-1 Pa. $4.00

FULL-COLOR FLORAL DESIGNS IN THE ART NOUVEAU STYLE, E. A. Seguy. 166 motifs, on 40 plates, from Les fleurs et leurs applications decoratives (1902): borders, circular designs, repeats, allovers, "spots." All in authentic Art Nouveau colors. 48pp. 9⅜ x 12¼. 23439-8 Pa. $5.00

A DIDEROT PICTORIAL ENCYCLOPEDIA OF TRADES AND IN-DUSTRY, edited by Charles C. Gillispie. 485 most interesting plates from the great French Encyclopedia of the 18th century show hundreds of working figures, artifacts, process, land and cityscapes; glassmaking, paper-making, metal extraction, construction, weaving, making furniture, clothing, wigs, dozens of other activities. Plates fully explained. 920pp. 9 x 12. 22284-5, 22285-3 Clothbd., Two-vol. set $40.00

HANDBOOK OF EARLY ADVERTISING ART, Clarence P. Hornung. Largest collection of copyright-free early and antique advertising art ever compiled. Over 6,000 illustrations, from Franklin's time to the 1890's for special effects, novelty. Valuable source, almost inexhaustible.
Pictorial Volume. Agriculture, the zodiac, animals, autos, birds, Christmas, fire engines, flowers, trees, musical instruments, ships, games and sports, much more. Arranged by subject matter and use. 237 plates. 288pp. 9 x 12. 20122-8 Clothbd. $14.50

Typographical Volume. Roman and Gothic faces ranging from 10 point to 300 point, "Barnum," German and Old English faces, script, logotypes, scrolls and flourishes, 1115 ornamental initials, 67 complete alphabets, more. 310 plates. 320pp. 9 x 12. 20123-6 Clothbd. $15.00

CALLIGRAPHY (CALLIGRAPHIA LATINA), J. G. Schwandner. High point of 18th-century ornamental calligraphy. Very ornate initials, scrolls, borders, cherubs, birds, lettered examples. 172pp. 9 x 13. 20475-8 Pa. $7.00

ART FORMS IN NATURE, Ernst Haeckel. Multitude of strangely beautiful natural forms: Radiolaria, Foraminifera, jellyfishes, fungi, turtles, bats, etc. All 100 plates of the 19th-century evolutionist's *Kunstformen der Natur* (1904). 100pp. 9⅜ x 12¼. 22987-4 Pa. $5.00

CHILDREN: A PICTORIAL ARCHIVE FROM NINETEENTH-CENTURY SOURCES, edited by Carol Belanger Grafton. 242 rare, copyright-free wood engravings for artists and designers. Widest such selection available. All illustrations in line. 119pp. 8⅜ x 11¼. 23694-3 Pa. $4.00

WOMEN: A PICTORIAL ARCHIVE FROM NINETEENTH-CENTURY SOURCES, edited by Jim Harter. 391 copyright-free wood engravings for artists and designers selected from rare periodicals. Most extensive such collection available. All illustrations in line. 128pp. 9 x 12. 23703-6 Pa. $4.50

ARABIC ART IN COLOR, Prisse d'Avennes. From the greatest ornamentalists of all time—50 plates in color, rarely seen outside the Near East, rich in suggestion and stimulus. Includes 4 plates on covers. 46pp. 9⅜ x 12¼. 23658-7 Pa. $6.00

AUTHENTIC ALGERIAN CARPET DESIGNS AND MOTIFS, edited by June Beveridge. Algerian carpets are world famous. Dozens of geometrical motifs are charted on grids, color-coded, for weavers, needleworkers, craftsmen, designers. 53 illustrations plus 4 in color. 48pp. 8¼ x 11. (Available in U.S. only) 23650-1 Pa. $1.75

DICTIONARY OF AMERICAN PORTRAITS, edited by Hayward and Blanche Cirker. 4000 important Americans, earliest times to 1905, mostly in clear line. Politicians, writers, soldiers, scientists, inventors, industrialists, Indians, Blacks, women, outlaws, etc. Identificatory information. 756pp. 9¼ x 12¾. 21823-6 Clothbd. $40.00

HOW THE OTHER HALF LIVES, Jacob A. Riis. Journalistic record of filth, degradation, upward drive in New York immigrant slums, shops, around 1900. New edition includes 100 original Riis photos, monuments of early photography. 233pp. 10 x 7⅞. 22012-5 Pa. $7.00

NEW YORK IN THE THIRTIES, Berenice Abbott. Noted photographer's fascinating study of city shows new buildings that have become famous and old sights that have disappeared forever. Insightful commentary. 97 photographs. 97pp. 11⅜ x 10. 22967-X Pa. $5.00

MEN AT WORK, Lewis W. Hine. Famous photographic studies of construction workers, railroad men, factory workers and coal miners. New supplement of 18 photos on Empire State building construction. New introduction by Jonathan L. Doherty. Total of 69 photos. 63pp. 8 x 10¾. 23475-4 Pa. $3.00

THE DEPRESSION YEARS AS PHOTOGRAPHED BY ARTHUR ROTH-STEIN, Arthur Rothstein. First collection devoted entirely to the work of outstanding 1930s photographer: famous dust storm photo, ragged children, unemployed, etc. 120 photographs. Captions. 119pp. 9¼ x 10¾.
23590-4 Pa. $5.00

CAMERA WORK: A PICTORIAL GUIDE, Alfred Stieglitz. All 559 illustrations and plates from the most important periodical in the history of art photography, Camera Work (1903-17). Presented four to a page, reduced in size but still clear, in strict chronological order, with complete captions. Three indexes. Glossary. Bibliography. 176pp. 8⅜ x 11¼.
23591-2 Pa. $6.95

ALVIN LANGDON COBURN, PHOTOGRAPHER, Alvin L. Coburn. Revealing autobiography by one of greatest photographers of 20th century gives insider's version of Photo-Secession, plus comments on his own work. 77 photographs by Coburn. Edited by Helmut and Alison Gernsheim. 160pp. 8⅛ x 11.
23685-4 Pa. $6.00

NEW YORK IN THE FORTIES, Andreas Feininger. 162 brilliant photographs by the well-known photographer, formerly with Life magazine, show commuters, shoppers, Times Square at night, Harlem nightclub, Lower East Side, etc. Introduction and full captions by John von Hartz. 181pp. 9¼ x 10¾.
23585-8 Pa. $6.95

GREAT NEWS PHOTOS AND THE STORIES BEHIND THEM, John Faber. Dramatic volume of 140 great news photos, 1855 through 1976, and revealing stories behind them, with both historical and technical information. Hindenburg disaster, shooting of Oswald, nomination of Jimmy Carter, etc. 160pp. 8¼ x 11.
23667-6 Pa. $5.00

THE ART OF THE CINEMATOGRAPHER, Leonard Maltin. Survey of American cinematography history and anecdotal interviews with 5 masters— Arthur Miller, Hal Mohr, Hal Rosson, Lucien Ballard, and Conrad Hall. Very large selection of behind-the-scenes production photos. 105 photographs. Filmographies. Index. Originally Behind the Camera. 144pp. 8¼ x 11.
23686-2 Pa. $5.00

DESIGNS FOR THE THREE-CORNERED HAT (LE TRICORNE), Pablo Picasso. 32 fabulously rare drawings—including 31 color illustrations of costumes and accessories—for 1919 production of famous ballet. Edited by Parmenia Migel, who has written new introduction. 48pp. 9⅜ x 12¼. (Available in U.S. only)
23709-5 Pa. $5.00

NOTES OF A FILM DIRECTOR, Sergei Eisenstein. Greatest Russian filmmaker explains montage, making of Alexander Nevsky, aesthetics; comments on self, associates, great rivals (Chaplin), similar material. 78 illustrations. 240pp. 5⅜ x 8½.
22392-2 Pa. $4.50

HOLLYWOOD GLAMOUR PORTRAITS, edited by John Kobal. 145 photos capture the stars from 1926-49, the high point in portrait photography. Gable, Harlow, Bogart, Bacall, Hedy Lamarr, Marlene Dietrich, Robert Montgomery, Marlon Brando, Veronica Lake; 94 stars in all. Full background on photographers, technical aspects, much more. Total of 160pp. 8⅜ x 11¼. 23352-9 Pa. $6.00

THE NEW YORK STAGE: FAMOUS PRODUCTIONS IN PHOTOGRAPHS, edited by Stanley Appelbaum. 148 photographs from Museum of City of New York show 142 plays, 1883-1939. Peter Pan, The Front Page, Dead End, Our Town, O'Neill, hundreds of actors and actresses, etc. Full indexes. 154pp. 9½ x 10. 23241-7 Pa. $6.00

DIALOGUES CONCERNING TWO NEW SCIENCES, Galileo Galilei. Encompassing 30 years of experiment and thought, these dialogues deal with geometric demonstrations of fracture of solid bodies, cohesion, leverage, speed of light and sound, pendulums, falling bodies, accelerated motion, etc. 300pp. 5⅜ x 8½. 60099-8 Pa. $4.00

THE GREAT OPERA STARS IN HISTORIC PHOTOGRAPHS, edited by James Camner. 343 portraits from the 1850s to the 1940s: Tamburini, Mario, Caliapin, Jeritza, Melchior, Melba, Patti, Pinza, Schipa, Caruso, Farrar, Steber, Gobbi, and many more—270 performers in all. Index. 199pp. 8⅜ x 11¼. 23575-0 Pa. $7.50

J. S. BACH, Albert Schweitzer. Great full-length study of Bach, life, background to music, music, by foremost modern scholar. Ernest Newman translation. 650 musical examples. Total of 928pp. 5⅜ x 8½. (Available in U.S. only) 21631-4, 21632-2 Pa., Two-vol. set $11.00

COMPLETE PIANO SONATAS, Ludwig van Beethoven. All sonatas in the fine Schenker edition, with fingering, analytical material. One of best modern editions. Total of 615pp. 9 x 12. (Available in U.S. only) 23134-8, 23135-6 Pa., Two-vol. set $15.50

KEYBOARD MUSIC, J. S. Bach. Bach-Gesellschaft edition. For harpsichord, piano, other keyboard instruments. English Suites, French Suites, Six Partitas, Goldberg Variations, Two-Part Inventions, Three-Part Sinfonias. 312pp. 8⅛ x 11. (Available in U.S. only) 22360-4 Pa. $6.95

FOUR SYMPHONIES IN FULL SCORE, Franz Schubert. Schubert's four most popular symphonies: No. 4 in C Minor ("Tragic"); No. 5 in B-flat Major; No. 8 in B Minor ("Unfinished"); No. 9 in C Major ("Great"). Breitkopf & Hartel edition. Study score. 261pp. 9⅜ x 12¼. 23681-1 Pa. $6.50

THE AUTHENTIC GILBERT & SULLIVAN SONGBOOK, W. S. Gilbert, A. S. Sullivan. Largest selection available; 92 songs, uncut, original keys, in piano rendering approved by Sullivan. Favorites and lesser-known fine numbers. Edited with plot synopses by James Spero. 3 illustrations. 399pp. 9 x 12. 23482-7 Pa. $9.95

PRINCIPLES OF ORCHESTRATION, Nikolay Rimsky-Korsakov. Great classical orchestrator provides fundamentals of tonal resonance, progression of parts, voice and orchestra, tutti effects, much else in major document. 330pp. of musical excerpts. 489pp. 6½ x 9¼.   21266-1 Pa. $7.50

TRISTAN UND ISOLDE, Richard Wagner. Full orchestral score with complete instrumentation. Do not confuse with piano reduction. Commentary by Felix Mottl, great Wagnerian conductor and scholar. Study score. 655pp. 8⅛ x 11.   22915-7 Pa. $13.95

REQUIEM IN FULL SCORE, Giuseppe Verdi. Immensely popular with choral groups and music lovers. Republication of edition published by C. F. Peters, Leipzig, n. d. German frontmaker in English translation. Glossary. Text in Latin. Study score. 204pp. 9⅜ x 12¼.
23682-X Pa. $6.00

COMPLETE CHAMBER MUSIC FOR STRINGS, Felix Mendelssohn. All of Mendelssohn's chamber music: Octet, 2 Quintets, 6 Quartets, and Four Pieces for String Quartet. (Nothing with piano is included). Complete works edition (1874-7). Study score. 283 pp. 9⅜ x 12¼.
23679-X Pa. $7.50

POPULAR SONGS OF NINETEENTH-CENTURY AMERICA, edited by Richard Jackson. 64 most important songs: "Old Oaken Bucket," "Arkansas Traveler," "Yellow Rose of Texas," etc. Authentic original sheet music, full introduction and commentaries. 290pp. 9 x 12.   23270-0 Pa. $7.95

COLLECTED PIANO WORKS, Scott Joplin. Edited by Vera Brodsky Lawrence. Practically all of Joplin's piano works—rags, two-steps, marches, waltzes, etc., 51 works in all. Extensive introduction by Rudi Blesh. Total of 345pp. 9 x 12.   23106-2 Pa. $14.95

BASIC PRINCIPLES OF CLASSICAL BALLET, Agrippina Vaganova. Great Russian theoretician, teacher explains methods for teaching classical ballet; incorporates best from French, Italian, Russian schools. 118 illustrations. 175pp. 5⅜ x 8½.   22036-2 Pa. $2.50

CHINESE CHARACTERS, L. Wieger. Rich analysis of 2300 characters according to traditional systems into primitives. Historical-semantic analysis to phonetics (Classical Mandarin) and radicals. 820pp. 6⅛ x 9¼.
21321-8 Pa. $10.00

EGYPTIAN LANGUAGE: EASY LESSONS IN EGYPTIAN HIERO-GLYPHICS, E. A. Wallis Budge. Foremost Egyptologist offers Egyptian grammar, explanation of hieroglyphics, many reading texts, dictionary of symbols. 246pp. 5 x 7½. (Available in U.S. only)
21394-3 Clothbd. $7.50

AN ETYMOLOGICAL DICTIONARY OF MODERN ENGLISH, Ernest Weekley. Richest, fullest work, by foremost British lexicographer. Detailed word histories. Inexhaustible. Do not confuse this with Concise Etymological Dictionary, which is abridged. Total of 856pp. 6½ x 9¼.
21873-2, 21874-0 Pa., Two-vol. set $12.00

CATALOGUE OF DOVER BOOKS

A MAYA GRAMMAR, Alfred M. Tozzer. Practical, useful English-language grammar by the Harvard anthropologist who was one of the three greatest American scholars in the area of Maya culture. Phonetics, grammatical processes, syntax, more. 301pp. 5⅜ x 8½.　　23465-7 Pa. $4.00

THE JOURNAL OF HENRY D. THOREAU, edited by Bradford Torrey, F. H. Allen. Complete reprinting of 14 volumes, 1837-61, over two million words; the sourcebooks for *Walden*, etc. Definitive. All original sketches, plus 75 photographs. Introduction by Walter Harding. Total of 1804pp. 8½ x 12¼.　　20312-3, 20313-1 Clothbd., Two-vol. set $70.00

CLASSIC GHOST STORIES, Charles Dickens and others. 18 wonderful stories you've wanted to reread: "The Monkey's Paw," "The House and the Brain," "The Upper Berth," "The Signalman," "Dracula's Guest," "The Tapestried Chamber," etc. Dickens, Scott, Mary Shelley, Stoker, etc. 330pp. 5⅜ x 8½.　　20735-8 Pa. $4.50

SEVEN SCIENCE FICTION NOVELS, H. G. Wells. Full novels. *First Men in the Moon, Island of Dr. Moreau, War of the Worlds, Food of the Gods, Invisible Man, Time Machine, In the Days of the Comet.* A basic science-fiction library. 1015pp. 5⅜ x 8½. (Available in U.S. only)
20264-X Clothbd. $8.95

ARMADALE, Wilkie Collins. Third great mystery novel by the author of *The Woman in White* and *The Moonstone.* Ingeniously plotted narrative shows an exceptional command of character, incident and mood. Original magazine version with 40 illustrations. 597pp. 5⅜ x 8½.
23429-0 Pa. $6.00

MASTERS OF MYSTERY, H. Douglas Thomson. The first book in English (1931) devoted to history and aesthetics of detective story. Poe, Doyle, LeFanu, Dickens, many others, up to 1930. New introduction and notes by E. F. Bleiler. 288pp. 5⅜ x 8½. (Available in U.S. only)
23606-4 Pa. $4.00

FLATLAND, E. A. Abbott. Science-fiction classic explores life of 2-D being in 3-D world. Read also as introduction to thought about hyperspace. Introduction by Banesh Hoffmann. 16 illustrations. 103pp. 5⅜ x 8½.
20001-9 Pa. $2.00

THREE SUPERNATURAL NOVELS OF THE VICTORIAN PERIOD, edited, with an introduction, by E. F. Bleiler. Reprinted complete and unabridged, three great classics of the supernatural: *The Haunted Hotel* by Wilkie Collins, *The Haunted House at Latchford* by Mrs. J. H. Riddell, and *The Lost Stradivarious* by J. Meade Falkner. 325pp. 5⅜ x 8½.
22571-2 Pa. $4.00

AYESHA: THE RETURN OF "SHE," H. Rider Haggard. Virtuoso sequel featuring the great mythic creation, Ayesha, in an adventure that is fully as good as the first book, *She.* Original magazine version, with 47 original illustrations by Maurice Greiffenhagen. 189pp. 6½ x 9¼.
23649-8 Pa. $3.50

UNCLE SILAS, J. Sheridan LeFanu. Victorian Gothic mystery novel, considered by many best of period, even better than Collins or Dickens. Wonderful psychological terror. Introduction by Frederick Shroyer. 436pp. 5⅜ x 8½.   21715-9 Pa. $6.00

JURGEN, James Branch Cabell. The great erotic fantasy of the 1920's that delighted thousands, shocked thousands more. Full final text, Lane edition with 13 plates by Frank Pape. 346pp. 5⅜ x 8½.
23507-6 Pa. $4.50

THE CLAVERINGS, Anthony Trollope. Major novel, chronicling aspects of British Victorian society, personalities. Reprint of Cornhill serialization, 16 plates by M. Edwards; first reprint of full text. Introduction by Norman Donaldson. 412pp. 5⅜ x 8½.   23464-9 Pa. $5.00

KEPT IN THE DARK, Anthony Trollope. Unusual short novel about Victorian morality and abnormal psychology by the great English author. Probably the first American publication. Frontispiece by Sir John Millais. 92pp. 6½ x 9¼.   23609-9 Pa. $2.50

RALPH THE HEIR, Anthony Trollope. Forgotten tale of illegitimacy, inheritance. Master novel of Trollope's later years. Victorian country estates, clubs, Parliament, fox hunting, world of fully realized characters. Reprint of 1871 edition. 12 illustrations by F. A. Faser. 434pp. of text. 5⅜ x 8½.   23642-0 Pa. $5.00

YEKL and THE IMPORTED BRIDEGROOM AND OTHER STORIES OF THE NEW YORK GHETTO, Abraham Cahan. Film *Hester Street* based on *Yekl* (1896). Novel, other stories among first about Jewish immigrants of N.Y.'s East Side. Highly praised by W. D. Howells—Cahan "a new star of realism." New introduction by Bernard G. Richards. 240pp. 5⅜ x 8½.   22427-9 Pa. $3.50

THE HIGH PLACE, James Branch Cabell. Great fantasy writer's enchanting comedy of disenchantment set in 18th-century France. Considered by some critics to be even better than his famous *Jurgen*. 10 illustrations and numerous vignettes by noted fantasy artist Frank C. Pape. 320pp. 5⅜ x 8½.   23670-6 Pa. $4.00

ALICE'S ADVENTURES UNDER GROUND, Lewis Carroll. Facsimile of ms. Carroll gave Alice Liddell in 1864. Different in many ways from final Alice. Handlettered, illustrated by Carroll. Introduction by Martin Gardner. 128pp. 5⅜ x 8½.   21482-6 Pa. $2.50

FAVORITE ANDREW LANG FAIRY TALE BOOKS IN MANY COLORS, Andrew Lang. The four Lang favorites in a boxed set—the complete *Red, Green, Yellow* and *Blue* Fairy Books. 164 stories; 439 illustrations by Lancelot Speed, Henry Ford and G. P. Jacomb Hood. Total of about 1500pp. 5⅜ x 8½.   23407-X Boxed set, Pa. $15.95

CATALOGUE OF DOVER BOOKS

HOUSEHOLD STORIES BY THE BROTHERS GRIMM. All the great Grimm stories: "Rumpelstiltskin," "Snow White," "Hansel and Gretel," etc., with 114 illustrations by Walter Crane. 269pp. 5⅜ x 8½.
21080-4 Pa. $3.50

SLEEPING BEAUTY, illustrated by Arthur Rackham. Perhaps the fullest, most delightful version ever, told by C. S. Evans. Rackham's best work. 49 illustrations. 110pp. 7⅞ x 10¾. 22756-1 Pa. $2.50

AMERICAN FAIRY TALES, L. Frank Baum. Young cowboy lassoes Father Time; dummy in Mr. Floman's department store window comes to life; and 10 other fairy tales. 41 illustrations by N. P. Hall, Harry Kennedy, Ike Morgan, and Ralph Gardner. 209pp. 5⅜ x 8½. 23643-9 Pa. $3.00

THE WONDERFUL WIZARD OF OZ, L. Frank Baum. Facsimile in full color of America's finest children's classic. Introduction by Martin Gardner. 143 illustrations by W. W. Denslow. 267pp. 5⅜ x 8½.
20691-2 Pa. $3.50

THE TALE OF PETER RABBIT, Beatrix Potter. The inimitable Peter's terrifying adventure in Mr. McGregor's garden, with all 27 wonderful, full-color Potter illustrations. 55pp. 4¼ x 5½. (Available in U.S. only)
22827-4 Pa. $1.25

THE STORY OF KING ARTHUR AND HIS KNIGHTS, Howard Pyle. Finest children's version of life of King Arthur. 48 illustrations by Pyle. 131pp. 6⅛ x 9¼. 21445-1 Pa. $4.95

CARUSO'S CARICATURES, Enrico Caruso. Great tenor's remarkable caricatures of self, fellow musicians, composers, others. Toscanini, Puccini, Farrar, etc. Impish, cutting, insightful. 473 illustrations. Preface by M. Sisca. 217pp. 8⅜ x 11¼. 23528-9 Pa. $6.95

PERSONAL NARRATIVE OF A PILGRIMAGE TO ALMADINAH AND MECCAH, Richard Burton. Great travel classic by remarkably colorful personality. Burton, disguised as a Moroccan, visited sacred shrines of Islam, narrowly escaping death. Wonderful observations of Islamic life, customs, personalities. 47 illustrations. Total of 959pp. 5⅜ x 8½.
21217-3, 21218-1 Pa., Two-vol. set $12.00

INCIDENTS OF TRAVEL IN YUCATAN, John L. Stephens. Classic (1843) exploration of jungles of Yucatan, looking for evidences of Maya civilization. Travel adventures, Mexican and Indian culture, etc. Total of 669pp. 5⅜ x 8½. 20926-1, 20927-X Pa., Two-vol. set $7.90

AMERICAN LITERARY AUTOGRAPHS FROM WASHINGTON IRVING TO HENRY JAMES, Herbert Cahoon, et al. Letters, poems, manuscripts of Hawthorne, Thoreau, Twain, Alcott, Whitman, 67 other prominent American authors. Reproductions, full transcripts and commentary. Plus checklist of all American Literary Autographs in The Pierpont Morgan Library. Printed on exceptionally high-quality paper. 136 illustrations. 212pp. 9⅛ x 12¼. 23548-3 Pa. $12.50

AN AUTOBIOGRAPHY, Margaret Sanger. Exciting personal account of hard-fought battle for woman's right to birth control, against prejudice, church, law. Foremost feminist document. 504pp. 5⅜ x 8½.

20470-7 Pa. $5.50

MY BONDAGE AND MY FREEDOM, Frederick Douglass. Born as a slave, Douglass became outspoken force in antislavery movement. The best of Douglass's autobiographies. Graphic description of slave life. Introduction by P. Foner. 464pp. 5⅜ x 8½. 22457-0 Pa. $5.50

LIVING MY LIFE, Emma Goldman. Candid, no holds barred account by foremost American anarchist: her own life, anarchist movement, famous contemporaries, ideas and their impact. Struggles and confrontations in America, plus deportation to U.S.S.R. Shocking inside account of persecution of anarchists under Lenin. 13 plates. Total of 944pp. 5⅜ x 8½.

22543-7, 22544-5 Pa., Two-vol. set $12.00

LETTERS AND NOTES ON THE MANNERS, CUSTOMS AND CONDITIONS OF THE NORTH AMERICAN INDIANS, George Catlin. Classic account of life among Plains Indians: ceremonies, hunt, warfare, etc. Dover edition reproduces for first time all original paintings. 312 plates. 572pp. of text. 6⅛ x 9¼. 22118-0, 22119-9 Pa.. Two-vol. set $12.00

THE MAYA AND THEIR NEIGHBORS, edited by Clarence L. Hay, others. Synoptic view of Maya civilization in broadest sense, together with Northern, Southern neighbors. Integrates much background, valuable detail not elsewhere. Prepared by greatest scholars: Kroeber, Morley, Thompson, Spinden, Vaillant, many others. Sometimes called Tozzer Memorial Volume. 60 illustrations, linguistic map. 634pp. 5⅜ x 8½.

23510-6 Pa. $10.00

HANDBOOK OF THE INDIANS OF CALIFORNIA, A. L. Kroeber. Foremost American anthropologist offers complete ethnographic study of each group. Monumental classic. 459 illustrations, maps. 995pp. 5⅜ x 8½.

23368-5 Pa. $13.00

SHAKTI AND SHAKTA, Arthur Avalon. First book to give clear, cohesive analysis of Shakta doctrine, Shakta ritual and Kundalini Shakti (yoga). Important work by one of world's foremost students of Shaktic and Tantric thought. 732pp. 5⅜ x 8½. (Available in U.S. only)

23645-5 Pa. $7.95

AN INTRODUCTION TO THE STUDY OF THE MAYA HIEROGLYPHS, Syvanus Griswold Morley. Classic study by one of the truly great figures in hieroglyph research. Still the best introduction for the student for reading Maya hieroglyphs. New introduction by J. Eric S. Thompson. 117 illustrations. 284pp. 5⅜ x 8½. 23108-9 Pa. $4.00

A STUDY OF MAYA ART, Herbert J. Spinden. Landmark classic interprets Maya symbolism, estimates styles, covers ceramics, architecture, murals, stone carvings as artforms. Still a basic book in area. New introduction by J. Eric Thompson. Over 750 illustrations. 341pp. 8⅜ x 11¼.

21235-1 Pa. $6.95

GEOMETRY, RELATIVITY AND THE FOURTH DIMENSION, Rudolf Rucker. Exposition of fourth dimension, means of visualization, concepts of relativity as Flatland characters continue adventures. Popular, easily followed yet accurate, profound. 141 illustrations. 133pp. 5⅜ x 8½.
23400-2 Pa. $2.75

THE ORIGIN OF LIFE, A. I. Oparin. Modern classic in biochemistry, the first rigorous examination of possible evolution of life from nitrocarbon compounds. Non-technical, easily followed. Total of 295pp. 5⅜ x 8½.
60213-3 Pa. $4.00

PLANETS, STARS AND GALAXIES, A. E. Fanning. Comprehensive introductory survey: the sun, solar system, stars, galaxies, universe, cosmology; quasars, radio stars, etc. 24pp. of photographs. 189pp. 5⅜ x 8½. (Available in U.S. only)
21680-2 Pa. $3.75

THE THIRTEEN BOOKS OF EUCLID'S ELEMENTS, translated with introduction and commentary by Sir Thomas L. Heath. Definitive edition. Textual and linguistic notes, mathematical analysis, 2500 years of critical commentary. Do not confuse with abridged school editions. Total of 1414pp. 5⅜ x 8½.
60088-2, 60089-0, 60090-4 Pa., Three-vol. set $18.50